Women's Circus: Leaping off the Edge

WOMEN'S CIRCUS

LEAPING OFF THE EDGE

FOOTSCRAY COMMUNITY
ARTS CENTRE
MAKING ART IN THE WEST

SPINIFEX

Spinifex Press Pty Ltd
504 Queensberry Street
North Melbourne, Vic. 3051
Australia
spinifex@publishaust.net.au
Homepage: http://www. publishaust.net.au/~spinifex

First published by Spinifex Press, 1997

Edited by Ev Beissbarth and Jo Turner,
Typeset in Janson and Gill Sans by Claire Warren
Scans by Libby Fullard
Cover design by Lin Tobias
Inside cover photograph: Flagfall, Vivienne Méhes
Made and printed in Australia by Australian Print Group.

National Library of Australia
Cataloguing-in-Publication data:

Women's Circus: Leaping off the edge.
ISBN 1 875559 55 8.
1. Circus performers – Victoria – Biography. 2. Circus – Victoria – History.
3. Women entertainers – Victoria – Biography.

79.30922945

Circus skills described in the book can be dangerous and should only
be conducted by someone who has trained and developed skills.

The publication of this book is supported by the Victorian Government
through Arts Victoria – Department of Premier and Cabinet.

Contents

III
THE WOMEN'S CIRCUS AT WORK

IV
IN THE SPOTLIGHT

V

EVALUATION

Acknowledgements

Thanks to all the women who contributed to this book and who are generously donating royalties to the Women's Circus; to the editors of the book, Adrienne Liebmann, Deb Lewis, Jean Taylor, Jen Jordan (deceased), Louise Radcliffe-Smith and Patricia Sykes who donated their time and energy as well as their writings. Additional thanks are due to Adrienne who co-ordinated the project with true Virgoan enthusiasm.

Thanks also to the Footscray Community Arts Centre for supporting and auspicing the circus, and to the many sponsors of the circus, who are: Australia Council for the Arts, Arts Victoria, VicHealth, The Stegley Foundation, Reichstein Foundation, Myer Foundation, Victorian Women's Trust, Aussie Jigsaw Mats, Australian Drug Foundation and the City of Maribyrnong. Without the support of these organisations there would not have been a circus story to write.

This book is also an acknowledgment of the three women who made the Women's Circus happen: Donna Jackson, director (1991–1996) whose vision and drive got the circus off the ground and made it such an artistic success; Sally Forth, trainer (1991–1993) whose holistic approach to training inspired and toughened all who trained under her; and Elizabeth Walsh, director of the Footscray Community Arts Centre (1991–1994) whose administrative and managerial flair helped make the circus a viable project.

We are grateful to the following for permission to reproduce copyright material: Pamela Bone for the extract from her article on the Beijing Declaration, Fourth UN Conference on Women, originally published in the *Age*, 20 September, 1995, and Helen Thomson for her article, "Circus of Joy and Politics" originally published in the *Age*, 27 November, 1995.

Special thanks to Spinifex Press, especially Susan Hawthorne, Jo Turner and Libby Fullard. Thanks to Claire Warren for her inspired typesetting and to Ev Beissbarth for her careful editing.

We acknowledge and thank all authors; some of the material contained in this book has been extracted from the circus journal and various issues of the *Women's Circus Newsletter*. Thanks also to graphic artist, Nicole Hunter and photographers, Vivienne Méhes and Naomi Herzog for allowing their work to appear in this book. Viv's work was assisted by a grant from Arts Victoria.

Every effort has been made to contact the copyright holders. The publisher would be happy to hear from any copyright holders not acknowledged or acknowledged incorrectly.

This book is dedicated to all the women
who have helped create the Women's Circus.

Mission Statement

The Women's Circus provides opportunities for women from all backgrounds to acquire physical, technical and musical skills while working in a safe, non-competitive and supportive environment. It presents feminism to the wider community through dynamic, high-quality circus/physical theatre, performances and workshops.

Preface

Weaving the Tapestry

Jen Jordan

The Women's Circus is an extraordinary, successful and innovative community arts project. The critical and box office success of circus performances over the past five years is remarkable in itself.

However, the Women's Circus means far more than that to the hundreds of women whose lives, hopes and dreams have woven its rich tapestry. Women from many different walks of life have shared their experiences, wisdom and energy to create a unique organisation.

Their voices illuminate the development of strong, complex networks of social relationships within a very diverse group. Their commitment to the feminist philosophy and practice of the circus has broken down barriers of ability, age, class, ethnicity, sexual orientation and other differences.

The Women's Circus represents a renewal of face-to-face community in a society increasingly suffering from atomisation and alienation. It challenges dominant forms of oppression, denial and prejudice within the broader culture and society by validating the experiences of groups of women who traditionally have been silenced and marginalised.

To be part of the Women's Circus is to be passionate about it. This vital, growing, changing community of women has enriched their own and many others' lives. This book celebrates their hopes, courage, strength and creativity, as well as their disappointments, frustrations and conflicts. Extracts from our journal reflect the process, the pain, the effort and joy that has gone into the making of the Women's Circus.

Writing the Story of the Women's Circus

Adrienne Liebmann

We have written our story because we don't want the Women's Circus to become a fantasy in the future. We want living and written proof of our existence. We want herstory told as well as history.

One of the Women's Circus' most important herstorical records is its journal. Begun in 1991, the Journal provides vital documentation of the experiences, emotions and voices of the women in the circus. In many ways, this book is an extension of the Journal and will enable the message underpinning the feminist philosophy of the Women's Circus to reach an audience beyond our warehouse space.

In 1993 I decided to photocopy the Journal because I was concerned that it might be lost or damaged. I did not want our written experiences to be mislaid, forgotten or trivialised. If we lost our Journal, part of us would also be lost. Historically, few women's experiences and stories have been documented, and many that have been recorded are lost. As I had been collating and documenting other material for the circus, director Donna Jackson approached me with the idea of organising a crew who would be interested in sifting through our vast collection of material and collating it into a book.

A group of women expressed interest in working on the book – Patricia (Trish) Sykes, Deb Lewis, Louise Radcliffe-Smith (Rad), Jean Taylor, Jen Jordan and Karen Martin.

Only Trish was able to attend the very first meeting. I was anxious and I remember Donna telling me not to worry, just keep moving forward. The meeting proved to be surprisingly productive and we realised our first task was not to approach publishers, but to inform the women of the circus about the forthcoming book and to obtain feedback from them to clarify what they wanted the book to say. Questionnaires were handed out and from the responses it was evident women wanted the book to reflect our diversity, our personal stories and our sense of community, as well as the herstory of the Women's Circus.

At the next meeting we invited the director, Donna Jackson, and the original Women's Circus trainer, Sally Forth, to brainstorm themes that could be used as chapter headings. We made a list of "F" words – feminism, flight, fisicality (physicality), fantasy, future, fun, and so on. With these words in mind, book crew members each took a theme to explore, using our archival material as reference.

Slowly it dawned upon us that what seemed like a straightforward task was turning into something quite complex and lengthy. Our path seemed confusing and rocky, the process unmanageable. At this point, Sarah Endacott of Sybylla Feminist Press gave us some very good advice: "Treat it as an adventure, paddle the boat, even if you can't see the shore. Just keep paddling and rowing."

Around this time Donna Jackson mentioned three words: purpose, process and perception. We realised we needed to be clearer about our aims and objectives for writing the book. We knew it was urgent that we preserve our stories because to lose them would be to regress terribly. And we wanted to tell people there was another way to do things, that the Women's Circus could serve as a model for other organisations. We felt that if we lost our herstory again, it would take generations to recoup that loss.

We realised we wanted to write this book because we hoped the stories it told of women's strengths, struggles and achievements could provide inspiration to readers. We felt the Women's Circus was a forum for highlighting controversial issues in our society that needed to be exposed or addressed in a way that empowered people to act. It is what we are saying between the double balances and the juggling that is important. Until recently, women's stories have remained on the periphery of mainstream literature or have been written by men. We hoped that by writing our own story we could help to transform and redefine the cultural myths that deeply influence our psyches and shape our society. We wanted to show that women everywhere are making political and social changes. The Women's Circus had chosen to do this through feminist community theatre. Recognising where we had come from and where we were going to, we kept paddling towards the shore.

As we progressed through 1994 and into 1995, it became obvious we could organise the book to reflect the Women's Circus process and annual structure. In part 1, we take our readers into the herstory and feminist philosophies of the circus as if they were present at an Information Day. Then, in the second section, we move on to describe all the women who make up the character of the circus, giving special reference to priority groups – survivors of sexual/physical abuse, immigrant women and women over forty years of age.

Part 3 details our training program, including the health aspect to training of the mind, body and soul. We then introduce some of the trainers, trainees and associated programs.

In the fourth section, we invite readers to follow our preparation for, and participation in, the annual end-of-year performance season, from the initial research through rehearsals and finally on to the stage.

Finally, at the end of the book as at the end of the circus year, we celebrate, evaluate, plan and say goodbye. Like the book, the circus year has a beginning, middle and an end, the difference being that at the end of the circus year the cycle begins again. As it does so, the Women's Circus continues to evolve.

When women's contributions began arriving, we slotted these in, and then approached individual circus women to write specific pieces for the book. Finally we sought extra material from our archival collection. Titles for chapters came to mind. At last the book began to take on a body and a structure. By now the shore was closer and we were rowing solidly.

The women whose names were listed earlier were instrumental in getting this book off the ground. Having farewelled Karen Martin (who pulled out in 1994 because of other commitments), the rest of us continued to work tirelessly to realise our dream of seeing the story of the Women's Circus in print. When the going got tough, we had computer working bees around the kitchen table, and champagne and soup to sustain us.

Towards the end of 1995, when most of the book was written, we tackled the difficult issue of editing. We wanted women's voices to retain their own integrity and we questioned and clarified how much reworking should be done on women's pieces. Agreement was reached by consulting each woman.

Sadly, Jen Jordan, a member of the Women's Circus book crew and a founding member of the circus, died just weeks before the final manuscript was sent to the publisher. Jen finished rewriting "The Journey Towards Healing" only ten days before her death. Her work stands as a testimony to the strength of her convictions and the struggle of her life.

Finally, it must be said that if it were not for the work, commitment, enthusiasm and generosity of all the contributors, illustrators and photographers this book would have remained a dream only. The writings include a diverse range of material – academic, personal, comical, reflective, instructional and herstorical – and reflect the multifaceted community of women who are the Women's Circus.

May the picture the women of the circus have painted in these pages inspire you. Come and share the journey!

Women's Circus Aims and Objectives

- To reaffirm women's control over their bodies.

- To build self-esteem through physical and performance work.

- To allow women to set their own personal goals for development.

- To create a safe, non-competitive environment for women to work in.

- To enable women of different ages, abilities, shapes and sizes to come together to create a theatre event which is of a very high standard.

- To communicate feminist ideas in an entertaining and challenging fashion.

- To establish a women's circus/theatre company which will be on-going at the Footscray Community Arts Centre.

I
The Beginning

What a beautiful thing
we are growing:
a circus of women.

Anonymous

Fine balance: Ruth Bauer, 1991

Being "The Other"

Donna Jackson

I come from a family in which my father drove a truck and my mother did piece work for the local cardigan factory – not a circus-type family! The closest we got to circus was the little carnival that camped a mile from our house at the Mordialloc Beach. We were not allowed to hang around the carnival without our parents. There was some unspecified danger at the carnival which my mother could never articulate, and that made it all the more attractive. I gathered the idea, that the people at the carnival were "the other", outcasts from suburban normality and therefore not to be trusted.

Donna Jackson

I was sent to ballet and youth theatre classes from an early age. I was the biggest, naughtiest ballerina Miss Irvine ever had at her school. "I think she would be better suited to gymnastics. She's a very strong little girl," Miss Irvine informed my mother. So I was sent to gym.

After I left Teacher's College, my first place of work was a refuge for women escaping domestic violence. The feminist processes of the refuge and the very strong and stroppy women who worked there made a huge impression on me. Many of the processes now used by the Women's Circus are a reflection of that experience.

During this time, a group of women's refuge workers got together and decided to make a theatre show for schools on the issue of domestic violence. Our show, No Myth, was directed by Meme McDonald, and I lobbied my way into being her assistant director on the project. She has since continued to train me in community theatre.

After this initial community theatre show, I worked on many projects as a freelance director, performer, fire technician or administrator. Much of my early work was funded by the women's community. Projects I wanted to start couldn't get funding from traditional sources so we ran women's dances and concerts to get the money. I grew up in the "poor" theatre tradition of "borrow it! make it! steal it! – or do without it!"

I wanted to start a women's circus after I heard of another women's circus which happened around 1979–80. I met Ollie

Black, who had been in it, and looked through her photos and press clippings. My first thought was, "Why aren't they around now so I can join?"

There were also other reasons. I had a number of friends who were survivors of sexual abuse and wanted to support them in some practical way. I was tired of demonstrations and campaigns and wanted to find another way of working for social change that included my theatre skills. I wanted to work somewhere where I was employed making theatre that was socially and theatrically relevant and to see if it was possible to have good political processes with great theatrical product as the outcome.

I have a belief in the ideals of socialism and wanted to create a women's theatre company which could experiment with ways of very different individuals working together for a common goal that didn't mean we had to have lots of meetings! It was important to develop a place where we could work on my/our strengths and to present women as strong and in control rather than always working in the defensive. I wanted a place where I could grow, have fun, be challenged, and learn with a whole range of women who had different belief systems to my own and be able to sell ideas of feminism to as wide an audience as possible without compromising our beliefs. I wanted all these things and I got them.

As the Women's Circus developed, it began to challenge audience expectations by combining theatre and circus skills to develop an original style which was absurdist and surreal. (Imagine sixty women in white bathing caps with white faces walking in slow motion towards the audience.)

The rationale behind the circus is to create an environment where women can come together to train in a non-competitive, supportive, safe environment. The circus gives women a vehicle for expressing political views and beliefs to an audience made up from the general public. At a time when the media uses terms such as "post-feminism", I think it is important to have a feminist circus which can be seen as the positive face of the Women's Movement while not compromising itself politically.

We have succeeded so far in these ideals because women weren't afraid to walk down to the carnival at night to that place our mothers told us not to go. The place of "the other". We weren't afraid because there were a lot of us. So now I spend most of my time at the carnival at the edge of the water with the

Think, debate, decide, act.

– Donna Jackson

shy girls, the tattooed ladies, the bearded women, the gruff technicians and the mad musicians. Arriving at this place is not the solution to my life. Through discussion and debate the circus is constantly changing. This suits me fine.

In the Women's Circus, we use the old-style format of having a quasi family group – older, middle-aged and younger women – all working together. Traditional circuses such as Ashton's impress me with their range of ages, shapes and sizes, performing an array of skills. At the Women's Circus we want to challenge our audiences and ourselves to move away from the stereotypical body images associated with ageing women. We incorporate New Circus into our style by not using animals.

The first women invited to join the circus were survivors of sexual abuse. Membership was then offered to women generally, with an overwhelming response from women of many different backgrounds. The circus gives us a chance to explore the strength, endurance and skill our bodies can attain. The workshops are a place where we can reaffirm control over our bodies, and performances communicate our vision and ideas to a broad cross-section of society.

Women are encouraged to set their own personal goals in the workshops. They may want to do a triple back-flip. They may simply want, by the end of the year, to stand on stage and sing in a group. My role and the role of the trainers is to facilitate workshops so women can achieve their goals.

The Women's Circus started as a small project and has grown beyond all expectations. I am growing up theatrically with the circus. The circus is not something I do *for* the women in the circus but something I do *with* the group. I train physically. We try to develop our skills, and ourselves, by doing circus and working together. The circus has many women who contribute to it with skills in printing, design, writing, building, facilitating, rigging and lobbying. It's often frightening to be in the middle and see the many projects this amorphous group can churn out.

The reason the circus is successful is that a diverse group of women have come together to realise shared ideas. For me, it has become a place where I can enjoy being "the other" my family warned me about. I have gone to join the carnival at the water's edge.

Nicole Hunter

Donna doing "the line"

An Herstorical Perspective

Jean Taylor

Vivienne Méhes

Plate spinning: Founding member Jean Taylor practises one of her favourite skills

One of the political aspects of the Women's Circus is the fact that it's part of a feminist continuum of women's circus theatricals in Melbourne.

"In 1979, the Real Mighty Bonza Whacko Women's Circus leapt through flaming hoops, trod domestic tight ropes and trained bags of reluctant washing to do tricks," wrote Robin Laurie for the first issue of the *Women's Circus Newsletter* in April 1991. "Over the next few months they metamorphosed into the Wimmin's Circus and toured Sydney, Adelaide, Perth and places in between, leaving behind kitchens and lounge rooms full of orange and plate jugglers and unashamed muscles flexing."

During training and setting up, the original Wimmin's Circus was supported initially by women from Circus Oz. The concept was also an extension of their experiences as performers in the Women's Theatre Group and the Australian Performing Group at the Pram Factory throughout the 1970s. As Ollie Black wrote in the *Newsletter* in April 1991 "Rehearsals and administration were made that much more possible and practical having the Pram Factory as a base (invaluable) and being able to use the Circus Oz gym."

Reading these accounts is a reminder of how similar the Women's Circus is today. "It was a time to experiment and a time to learn, a time to share, to meet new people and to break down barriers. Our muscles grew with our enthusiasm," Ursula Harrison wrote about her involvement with the Wimmin's Circus in the *Newsletter* in June 1991, "It was exciting working with a large group of women. There was lots of energy, laughter and support."

Ollie Black went on to report, "The original Wimmin's Circus was a group of witty and wonderful women who basically wanted to have a fun time presenting physically inspiring feminist theatre. The versatile acrobatic tumblings and powerful balance routines with all the members including myself created stunning visual puns on standard images of women. We all did everything. Absolutely everything, as well as juggling child care, law degrees, secretarial work, artistic careers and lovers. It was an incredible feat to stay sane let alone last for two years – all with no funding."

The Women's Circus then is a continuation of this tradition of combining circus skills with theatre to make a political statement about women's energy and commitment in creatively empowering and physically challenging ways.

Or, as Donna Jackson put it in the *Newsletter* in October 1991, "I think what's good about the circus is it's different for each woman. Some women are here for political reasons to make a political statement. Some women are just here to learn physical skills. So I think that at different times we do address different things, but overall it is political, it is theatrical, it is circus and it is women working together in a feminist way. With this show we are not trying to hit people over the head with the message. We are bringing in humour and charm. We show women enduring things and also challenging things."

Taking Over the Butter House *

Patricia Sykes

It wouldn't melt in their mouths
the yellow fat that fed
an earlier industry
not these women
who are out to feed
more than their own kind
it's the whole city and far
beyond the straggle suburbs they want

and why they rig trapezes and ropes
in the old butter factory
why they fall and bruise
and try again   why each
year the numbers grow
and the cartwheels reach
faster and farther   why
they learn to talk with drums

* Footscray Community Arts Centre, the home of the Women's Circus, was formerly a butter factory.

why they perform in trees
and upon the water

and more and more
the people come they come
to see what they produce
these labourers these ordinary
workers these women
who've taken up balls
and clubs and balances
to feed themselves and the hungry
who queue at the factory doors
for more than the usual a la carte
or the quick takeaway

How The Circus Works

Patricia Sykes & Adrienne Liebmann

The Women's Circus is an evolving, living entity, as it changes so too does its structure. The circus began as a project of the Footscray Community Arts Centre (FCAC), a multi-cultural arts organisation based in Melbourne's western suburbs. The circus is supported administratively by FCAC and is currently accountable to the centre's board through the circus director. Trainers, special projects and major performances are funded by sponsorship from philanthropic, corporate and government bodies. Equipment is either donated or bought from the proceeds of major performances.

From time to time the Women's Circus also calls on a body of women outside the circus, named as "Big Sisters", these women offer advice, support, forward planning, ideas and information. Between them the Big Sisters have experience in such areas as law, funding, circus, publicity, theatre and politics.

There are between seventy and 120 women involved in the physical, technical, musical or administrative areas of the circus at any one time. This massive and expanding infrastructure is run by no more than three paid workers and relies heavily on voluntary labour from members. The circus training space is a disused factory adjacent to Footscray Community Arts Centre. It is leased from the City of Maribyrnong, a local government body. The lease is in the process of being converted to a long-term arrangement at a peppercorn (nominal) rent by the City of Maribyrnong as part of its contribution to the refurbishment of the centre. The space is also used by other community groups connected with FCAC.

The circus operates at full swing from March to December. In March, existing performers and musicians sign up for the year's training workshops. If there are any vacancies after this point, places are offered to women on the waiting list.

There is a scaled-down summer training period from December to March for those physical performers who wish to further develop and extend their skills. The cost of circus workshops reflects women's ability to pay. There are different costs for workers and unemployed, and a labour exchange system for those of limited means. labour exchange women swap one hour's work for two hours of training.

Women interested in the technical side of the circus (lights, rigging, sound) usually begin meeting in the middle of the year when planning for the year's major performance begins. Women sometimes choose to move between performance, music, and technical work. A few have managed to combine being part of the performing/music or performing/technical crews in the one year, and several now have experience in all three areas.

Each year's calendar is presented by the circus director on sign-up day in March. This covers workshop times, trainers, special projects and minor and major performances. The circus receives many requests to perform and run workshops through-out the year and these are accepted or rejected according to the circus' schedule and priorities.

The circus operates as non-hierarchically as possible. Initially, FCAC employed a single theatre worker, Donna Jackson, to facilitate the Women's Circus project. Gradually some areas of the circus were given over to smaller crews who took on tasks independently. A woman nominated herself as "Top Dog" to lead or co-ordinate each crew. She was then responsible for making sure the task was completed within the agreed framework and on time. Only large policy issues were discussed by the group as a whole.

Amanda Neville

As the circus grew and more demands were placed on the administration and the director in particular, this loose structure became unwieldy. So, in 1995, the circus was restructured to allow members to be more involved in decision making (see diagram). Most policy issues are discussed by an advisory group of twelve to fifteen members comprised of representatives from each area of circus life (child care, newsletter, training, administration, music, technical and workshop representatives, etc). The director takes advice from this group as well as the body of the circus and the board of FCAC.

General discussion and planning days are held throughout the year. A final evaluation is held in December after the conclusion of the major performance season. Ideas and issues arising from the evaluation form part of the next year's planning, and are discussed and debated at advisory group meetings and by "think tank" groups which continue throughout the year.

As with any dynamic body, the circus is constantly changing. The stories, poems graphics, essays and information gathered together in this book will give you a richer idea not only of how the circus works but how it has affected and been affected by the women who keep it alive and growing.

STRUCTURE OF THE WOMEN'S CIRCUS

GR Group Representative
A Whole Circus
B Specialist Groups
C Policy Making
D Administration

'D' Group: Administration

This group, which is made up of the workshop co-ordinator, the administrator and the director, meets on a weekly basis. It is responsible for the day-to-day running of workshops, submissions for funding, performances, memberships and planning. It is also financially responsible to the membership and the Board of Footscray Community Arts Centre.

One Woman's Journey

Adrienne Liebmann

When a woman wishes to join the circus, her name is placed on a waiting list. An Information Day is held in March and if she is still interested she comes along. She will be given a brief herstory of the circus, its aims and objectives and told about the policy for selection.

Once a woman has been invited to join she is encouraged to attend the new women's workshops, but if this is not convenient she attends a day/night that suits her. Some women join the Music Group as well as, or instead of, physical training (see the diagram overleaf).

At these initial workshops she will gradually learn about the various other aspects of the circus as noted in this diagram, including insurance, safety, job description, labour exchange, the structure, sisters and supporters network, any special projects, fund-raising and the journal.

The physical and music workshops are taken by specialist trainers. The training year for new women usually begins with a block of general skills training, followed by another block where women concentrate on two specialist skills. This leads into six weeks of research for the final show, then six weeks rehearsal and the big performance as the finale. This is shown in the diagram overleaf.

The offshoots of the training sessions during the year include independent gigs and small circus gigs, both paid and unpaid. There are also specialist workshops for those interested in directing, clowning, dance, technical work, aerials, acrobatics and so on, and these vary each year.

Finally we have the big performance where we're divided into crews such as first aid, media and publicity, child care, security. Of course, on the last night, we bump out and then celebrate. A week later there's Evaluation Day and Saturday morning training workshops are offered over the summer break. And so the circle keeps on turning with Information Day in February for members and in March for new members. The training workshops start again in March or April and the monthly Advisory Group meetings begin in February.

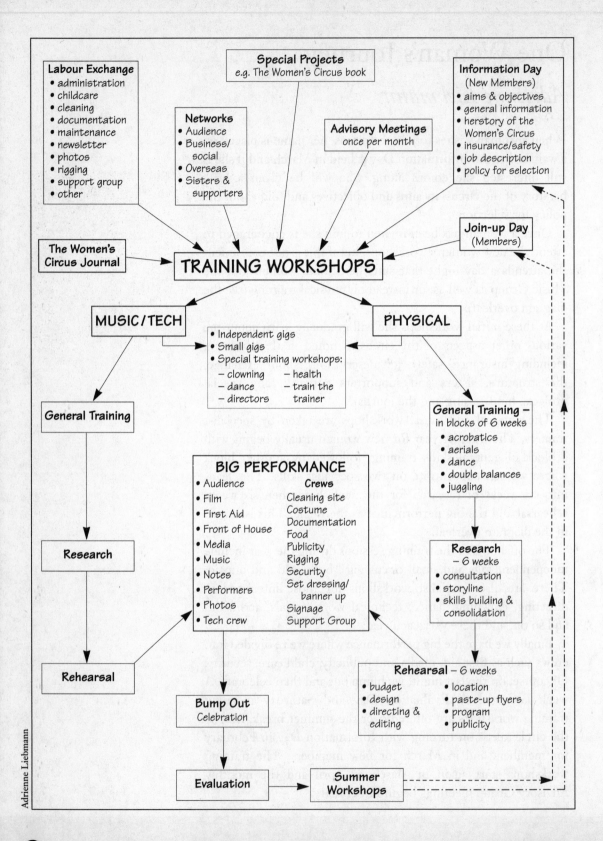

Labour Exchange
- administration
- childcare
- cleaning
- documentation
- maintenance
- newsletter
- photos
- rigging
- support group
- other

Special Projects
e.g. The Women's Circus book

Information Day
(New Members)
- aims & objectives
- general information
- herstory of the Women's Circus
- insurance/safety
- job description
- policy for selection

Networks
- Audience
- Business/social
- Overseas
- Sisters & supporters

Advisory Meetings
once per month

The Women's Circus Journal

TRAINING WORKSHOPS

Join-up Day
(Members)

MUSIC/TECH

PHYSICAL

- Independent gigs
- Small gigs
- Special training workshops:
  - clowning   - health
  - dance   - train the
  - directors   trainer

General Training

General Training –
in blocks of 6 weeks
- acrobatics
- aerials
- dance
- double balances
- juggling

BIG PERFORMANCE

• Audience	**Crews**
• Film	Cleaning site
• First Aid	Costume
• Front of House	Documentation
• Media	Food
• Music	Publicity
• Notes	Rigging
• Performers	Security
• Photos	Set dressing/ banner up
• Tech crew	Signage
	Support Group

Research

Research
– 6 weeks
- consultation
- storyline
- skills building & consolidation

Rehearsal

Rehearsal – 6 weeks
- budget
- design
- directing & editing
- location
- paste-up flyers
- program
- publicity

Bump Out
Celebration

Evaluation

Summer Workshops

Adrienne Liebmann

Why the Women's Circus is Feminist Theatre

Jules De Cinque

The name attracted me immediately: "Women's Circus". It was direct and concise. The name told me everything I needed to know. It clearly wasn't just a gender thing. To proclaim so clearly that this is a women's circus signified more than a group of female performers. The name said that these women were feminists. If they were not feminists, they would have chosen a more subtle name, a name less honest, probably more decorative, a name that tried to make the fact that they were an all-women performance troupe more palatable to the paying audience. And then I could conclude

Gypsy rebel: Jules De Cinque plays a Romanian gypsy in Leaping the Wire, 1995

Naomi Herzog

that if these women were feminists then their way of *working* – the processes they used to create theatre – would be non-traditional, and that feminist principles would underpin the organisation of the circus. In short, the name "Women's Circus" promised a unique experience in feminist theatre.

Then I went to a performance. I was charmed by the spectacle and excited by the power and strength that emanated from the performers. I wanted desperately to be part of it and, what's more, I felt that I could be part of it. This is not a typical response to a theatrical event. Usually I enjoy, I marvel, I empathise, and then return to my life seemingly unchanged. For example, I can say that "West Side Story" had absolutely no impact on my life whatsoever. But after seeing the Women's Circus, I thought to myself: "Yes, I can *do* that, I *can* do that."

I know that I am not the only woman who has witnessed a Women's Circus performance and rushed to join the waiting list of circus aspirants. It happens after each season of performance, testimony to the impact the circus has on the community. There is a powerful message being sent that women can do anything, that women are strong, capable and creative. And the circus is such a *large* group, with over seventy names appearing on the program. This certainly debunks those ugly myths that women don't like each other, can't work together and are over-emotional and bitchy, that women need men around to maintain a peaceful equilibrium and contribute the voice of reason. In fact, I would say that it is these things which so greatly impress women in the audience, rather than just the show itself. Women recognise that the performance is only part of the experience.

In some ways, I think the performance is really just an excuse for the process. Feminist theatre is more than theatre about women. It is a political venture with radical objectives. The process of creation challenges traditional methods of work and the Women's Circus certainly operates in a way that values all contributions at any stage of the process.

The performance season is not the pinnacle of the group's achievements, nor are the performers the precious agents of the circus' success. What has occurred during the months leading up to the performance and what is going on behind the scenes is just as important as what is happening on stage. The aims of the circus reflect this holistic notion, with the creation of theatre only one among others concerned with empowering women and communicating feminist ideas.

The working processes of the Women's Circus reflect feminist principles and I believe access to be of critical importance. There are no auditions for the circus, no pre-requisites, performance experience is not a requirement. So already the competitiveness that is a feature of so many other performing companies is circumvented. Once a member, access is maintained through practical means such as the provision of child care and a labour exchange system for low-income earners. But principally, access is supported by the ethos of the circus which recognises this is not a professional company consisting of well-paid, full-time members. It is always a consideration that we all have lives outside the circus for which we are responsible.

Establishing a non-competitive environment has also meant that there is no "star" in the Women's Circus. But removing the hierarchy of performers is also about deconstructing the signs of our society's dominant culture. Traditional theatre groups will parade their shining stars because the media loves a "rags to riches" story. The success of the individual "proves" that the system works. However, the cost of such success is never counted.

There are other signs that the Women's Circus deliberately avoids or reworks inherited culture. For example, traditional theatre will invariably reaffirm the goodness and rightness of the state/world through their art, which is certainly not our perception of the world in which we live. Material wealth is not on display during a Women's Circus performance. It is not evident in the costumes or set design. I have always wondered why theatre companies feel compelled to pour money into spectacular sets, costumes and lighting effects. Is it more about gaining a competitive edge over other theatre groups than about art? Do technological wonders demonstrate that the system has merit and can provide lively entertainment to deserving and successful workers? (Because, of course, the more elaborate the show, the more expensive the ticket prices, thereby placing patronage out of reach of those workers who are struggling with the system.)

Another fundamental principle practised by the Women's Circus is self-determination. This is a key feature in the philosophy of the circus. The notion of women, or even feminists, being an homogenous group is quite deliberately discarded and, instead, individuality is given value. This means that a woman is recognised as having individual needs, values and abilities and the inalienable right to make decisions about her activities.

This is evident in the training workshops. Women are not encouraged to become obsessive about their bodies. It is not the idea to turn our bodies into finely tuned instruments ready for someone else (the director) to manipulate or choreograph, as it is in traditional dance companies, for example. Each woman is given the opportunity to work to her limits at her own pace. The trainers are expected to consider this concept and accept that they are not training a *corps de ballet*. There is no standard level to be attained. In fact, it can be said that the show is produced by the director working with the range of skills and abilities of the performers, rather than the performers working to the expectations of the director. In this way, each performer retains her sense of self and can make decisions about what she is prepared to do with her body. In other words, she maintains control over her body; one of the aims of the circus.

Theatre is essentially about the relationship between the audience and the performer. The audience has particular significance for feminist theatre, for two reasons. Firstly, feminist theatre attempts to convey a political message. It challenges the order of the dominant culture and confronts the audience with a different perspective. Interestingly, the performers have probably experienced a similar raising of awareness during the process of creating the show. The Women's Circus encourages women to be involved in the research and construction of the narrative and to provide feedback about the sensitivity, or otherwise, of the material being used. The performers may discover that they have gained knowledge and altered their perceptions as they have become more involved in the political ideas being presented.

The second and crucial consideration for the Women's Circus is the way women are represented in theatre. Traditional theatre has assumed that the universal spectator is male, middle-class, white and heterosexual. Generally women's bodies are sexualised to conform to the desires of the men in the audience. The Women's Circus challenges these traditional notions of beauty and sexuality by considering the audience not to be a universal spectator but instead many spectators with a range of life experiences. A Women's Circus show can be very confronting for the male, middle-class, white, heterosexual spectator accustomed to having his values affirmed. A male relative of mine was clearly uncomfortable after watching a performance. The show did not make an issue of sexuality, but the fact that the women were doing these things together without the assistance, support or leadership of men indicated to him that, while they may not all have been lesbians, they certainly weren't behaving like "ladies".

Feminist theatre aims to investigate women's place within the patriarchy and focus specifically on the theatrical signs that represent women. The Women's Circus not only rejects the traditional theatrical signs for women but endeavours to create its own. The bathing caps which cover our hair and the black-on-white make-up on our faces ensure that our bodies are seen as doing the work and are not being objectified. The caps and make-up have also become part of the visual language of the circus, easily recognisable to the community. This is certainly one of the more challenging aspects of the circus. Audiences are accustomed to the traditional theatrical signs in order to make sense of the narrative. The Women's Circus strives to create a new theatrical language and introduce representations of women that are honest, dignified and more realistic.

As a member of the Women's Circus I have access to knowledge about the operation of all parts of the organisation. In the lead-up to a performance season I can be actively involved in whatever facet of the show I choose. The lighting, costumes,

I am stronger today. This is good. I feel like I am relaxing more into this new group. I watched women's faces today doing the killer sit-ups and everyone's expression is so gutsy; determined to grow and change. Me also. It feels like we are improving at our chosen skills and the reality of circus is forming and fattening. The theme of our show still wavers intangibly for me, but snatches of its connection to my journey come through. I have thought of eighty women singing with their souls as my first glimpse.

– Anonymous

security, child care and set do not magically appear. We are all part of the team that creates them. In this way, I am not just a performer, an isolated part of someone else's show, waiting to be manipulated and possibly exploited, by the director/manager/choreographer. For me, this is the essence of the Women's Circus.

But the ideas and ideals don't stop here. The circus is also about empowerment, learning, giving and receiving support, having courage, being creative, extending yourself in the circus and beyond. It is deeply satisfying for me because of the feminist principles that lie at the heart of the circus and because the Women's Circus demonstrates there is a different way of doing things successfully.

Is The Women's Circus A Feminist Enterprise?

Alison Richards

Is the Women's Circus feminist? The very need to pose the question says something about the state of feminism in the 1990s. For those involved in the circus since its first season in 1991, the question answers itself. Of course the circus is feminist; it's about women empowering themselves physically, mentally and socially. It provides a supportive atmosphere in which individual women can set their own goals, while knowing they can share with other women who will welcome their success. The shows deal with physical and social oppression, but also celebrate the power of women's traditions, strengths and knowledge. They create a culture in which both the women involved, and the people who come to see the theatre performances, can participate in a practical demonstration of what women can achieve. The circus is about having fun and being serious at the same time, exploring and presenting issues through physical theatre in a creative way. On the night, it's about delivering a bloody good show!

However, it's precisely the easy association of "woman" with "feminist" that contemporary feminist theoretical debates call into question. The unstable alliances of third-wave feminism reveal fissures within the Women's Movement, which at times threaten to turn the enthusiasms of the 1970s into full-blown splits. Where once consciousness raising promised impending liberation, and sisterhood looked set to rule the world, a look at the worldwide Women's Movement as we near the end of the twentieth century sees the west divided between the mutual suspicions of electoral feminism, radical and essentialist feminisms, and the brave remnants of socialist or materialist feminisms. It is a foolish person who now would assert that the simple fact of having women in power will indicate, let alone guarantee, positive social change – the prime ministership of Britain's Maggie Thatcher has well and truly deflated that particular utopian dream.

The action seems to have crossed over into identity politics – gay and lesbian coalitions, and issue-based alliances. Within the subcultures of what was once Women's Liberation, sexual orientation has become a sign around which ways of living have emerged. These define the sense of self and command a more immediate loyalty than the equalitarian campaigns of second-wave feminism. As recent writings by women such as Anne Summers demonstrate, the women who moved into mainstream political and bureaucratic careers in the wake of the battles for equal pay, child care and so on now feel themselves isolated; they look behind and see very few younger women coming after them.

At the same time, the relative success of intellectual feminists in establishing a base camp in the Academy in the form of departments or streams of women's and gender studies has meant the flowering of an area of scholarship with its own massive body of literature. Feminist scholarship has addressed the patriarchal bias of social institutions, and pointed out the ideological construction of supposedly universal codes such as "science" and "history".

Feminist scholars have also spent a great deal of their time analysing the whole notion of what it means to be a woman, and/or a feminist. Under the influence of (male) European theorists such as Lacan, Derrida and Foucault, difference has replaced equality as a watchword. Theorists such as Judith Butler put forward the notion that the term "woman" is an "unstable signifier" – hence, feminism faces a political problem when it assumes a common identity for "women". For Moira Gatens, to insist on sexual difference as *the* immutable and fundamental difference is to take for granted the use of patriarchal categories at odds with the feminist project. For feminists such as these, the statements of feminism rest uneasily on the ground of womanhood – language, gender and the bodies which articulate and are articulated by them must be equally subject to analysis and deconstruction.

Unfortunately, apart from the stream of women's novels flowing from the feminist publishing houses, the literature of feminist scholarship remains inaccessible and largely irrelevant to women not trained in the specialist discourses of the contemporary academy. Meanwhile, in the rest of the west, the appeal of cultural and essentialist feminisms remains strong, particularly in their performative dimensions through ritual, goddess symbolism and, in some lesbian subcultures, the theatricalised display of S&M. Third world activists regard the whole debate as a pastime for the white and the privileged. Forget both universal claims and analytical distinctions, they cry. Acknowledge the realities of economic, social and religious oppression but above all else stop speaking for us – acknowledge our experiences and embark with us on the practical work which lifts the dead weight of oppression only slowly and inch by inch.

So, back to the circus. On one level, the goals and practices of the Footscray Community Arts Centre's Women's Circus appear to hark back to the second wave. Not only is the welcome to women inclusive, but the promise is of a women's community, a supportive culture within which each participant can grow in spirit through physical achievement. Every member of the circus is encouraged to find their own level and set their own goals. While excellence is acknowledged and increase in skill level is sought after, newcomers are advised not to compare themselves negatively with experienced group members, but to work at their own pace to the best of what they can discover their abilities to be.

The philosophy of the circus is oriented to the tensions of the present, rather than being driven by nostalgia for the past. It has been formed out of a commitment to action. The associations and images of circus employed are eclectic; likewise, the feminist influences. Circus director Donna Jackson acknowledges the direct inspiration of Melbourne's women's theatre and circus groups of the 1970s. Her language is of "women". However, both the goals and working methods of the circus

Nicole Hunter

reveal a consciously pragmatic feminism, engaged with the differences that must be expected in a group of women coming together from a range of backgrounds, with a range of experiences, loyalties and expectations.

The circus' stated aims include a specific reference to "communicating feminist views in an entertaining and challenging manner". The job description circulated to all prospective members further includes a definition of what working in a feminist way might entail: "to recognise all women are different – support, encourage other women". It is that link between the recognition of difference and the imperative of support that distinguishes the feminism articulated within and by the circus from the uneasy relations between the fragments of feminism elsewhere.

Like the link "women – feminism", "difference – support", the organisation of the circus reveals a conjunction of ambiguities held together by an ethic, a pragmatic set of priorities, and a charismatic leader. Each year's circus season is the result of a full year's workshop programme, with new participants having to learn the ropes from the ground up. Learning and polishing performance skills is the clear and primary focus; as the season approaches, the task of making a high-quality performance takes precedence over other concerns (given always the basic ethic of choice, responsibility and support). Although the circus encourages open discussion through information days and co-operative work teams, it is not a collective. Donna, as director, makes the final decisions, and formal authority is delegated through a network of paid and unpaid representative (Top Dog) positions related to training and production tasks. The circus itself remains in an ambiguous yet supportive relationship with its sponsoring body, the Footscray Community Arts Centre. The circus is officially an activity of the Centre, which has created the position of Women's Circus co-ordinator for Donna, and continues to maintain overall financial responsibility for the circus' functionally and artistically independent activities.

The circus' internal dynamics also acknowledge, while attempting to negotiate, the potential tensions of power, identity and issue politics. The circus was founded with the aim of providing a supportive environment for survivors of incest and other forms of violence to join with other women, practising and performing their reclamation of their bodies and themselves.

Lesbian visibility is a concern for many circus women, as are issues of women's health and women's knowledges as well as access to traditionally "male" skills such as sound, lighting and motor mechanics. The last five years have seen the growth of a "Women's Circus culture", in which members increasingly interact within a network of lifestyles and politics, sharing houses, emotional lives and work lives – as the opportunity to earn income from skills learned within the circus increases.

This culture, of course, has the potential to give birth to factions and cliques, ingroups and outgroups. From the outset, there has been an effort to address these tensions within a characteristically pragmatic ethic. Groups of women are encouraged to coalesce around particular skills or tasks; the "musos", the "aerials", the "techies" and "front of house", for example, each have their own group identity and loyalties within the circus as a whole. Women joining the circus are not asked to identify their sexuality, politics or past experiences. Should they choose to do so, it is expected that tolerance and respect will be extended to them. Relationships between circus women are openly accepted – however, the fluctuations of sexual and emotional attachment are expected to be held within a "professional" ethic. The famous "no flirting" rule applies during all formal sessions, as does the expectation that conflict resolution guidelines will be followed when needed. However, it is the overall focus on the task – the job at hand, which is always fundamentally physical and action-oriented – that, while eliding potential tensions, provides a secure framework for the release of energy. The first item on the job description is "to have fun", and that is an imperative which is taken extremely seriously.

The circus' negotiation of feminist ambiguities extends to its performance style and presentational codes. The basic business of the circus in performance is the display of the athletic female body. Each season's show has a theme, and a basic narrative; "stories" about women and institutions, women and work, women and sport, women and death. The circus both uses and subverts the traditions of popular entertainment. Synchronised gymnastic routines and massed fire juggling, tumbling, trapeze work and so on are combined with vaudeville skills in the service of images that are decidedly non-traditional.

The overall impression is of high theatricality, but the female bodies that produce it are far from passive objects of desire or envy. They are, however, almost universally *disguised*. Costume and black-on-white make-up (a circus signature, along with the white bathing caps the women wear) contribute to an impression of anonymity. Closer inspection reveals however that each is an individual variation, as women create their own whimsical, brash or punk interpretation of the general theme. These minutiae of difference contribute to a kaleidoscopic effect which further refracts these particular bodies into thousands more. We are in the realm of the mythopoetic here. Much of the power of the circus' performances lies in the ability of the women to conjure, rather than simply to represent, visions of imagined experience; the nightmares and dreams of a female universe.

While Donna is the image director, the energy with which the women inhabit the goddesses, monsters and innocents of the stage space both demonstrates and reinforces their creative participation in the making of the performance, at the same time facilitating and transforming their individual voices into a collective statement. The now traditional moment at the end of the show, when a line of fifty or so women strip off their caps and hold them aloft, shaking their hair free, is also replete with ambiguities. As the movement ripples down the line, it both diminishes the performers, returning them to the everyday, and enlarges their individual exultation, allowing them to be recognised as "themselves". It also reintroduces that potent sign of femininity, a woman's hair, into an exchange where until now the "stories about women/feminism" have been conducted at a level of theatricality where gender, oppression, body shape and gravity are all, most satisfyingly, held in suspension.

The irony of course is that while the feminist academy continues to draw invidious comparisons between "women's" and "feminist" practices and hence between "women's" and "feminist" theatre, the 500 or so women who have by now had contact with the circus have almost without exception expressed unbridled enthusiasm, and in many cases describe the sort of life-changing experiences – feelings of confidence and physical capacity, gratitude for and confidence in the support of other women, and faith in the strength of a feminist community – that once were daily occurrences, but have been almost forgotten in the midst of feminisms occupied by particular rather than general passions.

How much, then, can the practices of this circus be treated as making a contribution to feminism? I would argue that the opinions expressed by circus participants are worth listening to. As Lizbeth Goodman points out in reference to the variety of positions articulated by practitioners of feminist theatre in the northern hemisphere, it is inappropriate to engage in too narrow a set of definitions when making links between theory and theatre practice. I would certainly want to argue that a woman is a feminist if she says she is – the project is far too complex for anyone mindful of the instability of the category "woman" to be sure of her ground in ruling on the category "feminist". More importantly however, the circus' success demonstrates the imaginative and emotive power of performance – which is after all both symbolic and practical action – to explore and articulate those very large issues of culture and identity in body, space and time which language cannot easily reach and may in fact inhibit.

The question of individual participants' "brand loyalty" to particular kinds of feminism is largely beside the point. So is the question of the ultimate political effectiveness of attitudes or positions articulated through the circus' performances, and so is the question of whether the circus is more to be criticised for its romantic 1970s inclusiveness, or lauded for its happening to stand as a post-representational performance text for current academics interested in the transformability and differences of bodies and selves.

Much more to the point is that the circus has been established and maintained through the enthusiasm of large numbers of women for these and other explorations which they mutually find to be challenging, enlightening and empowering, *and which they are moved to share in a public way* outside the niche audiences which each feminist subculture provides. Theatre activity, while it can inform political action, is not a substitute for it. However, in an era when fragmentation is the overriding political problem for feminism and other movements for social change, the imaginative power and practical example of performance projects like the circus stand in a creative relation to that much-needed public space. In other words, play (imagining feminism, rehearsing and renegotiating feminism), discourse (analysing feminism, arguing feminism, reformulating feminism) and political action (articulating feminism, fighting for feminism) are interdependent activities deserving equal respect – however different they continue to be.

The Women's Circus and Other Religions

Maralann Damiano

Maralann Damiano

November 1992. An old warehouse in Footscray. I watch enthralled as women of all ages and all shapes build pyramids, tumble, play with fire, juggle, ride bikes and roller skates, swing on trapeze and ropes and all the time giving out such energy and enthusiasm. As I left the first Women's Circus performance I had seen, I turned to my partner and said "I want to do that". Within days my name was on the waiting list – I had a foot in the door.

January 1993. A phone call from Donna. She was contacting women on the waiting list to see if they could help with the tech crew for the Williamstown Summer Festival performances. I jumped at the opportunity – my foot was a little further in the door. It was a great experience, working under Sally's watchful eye, helping to put up the many ropes and trapeze in the trees in the Botanical Gardens.

April 1993. I attended the information session for women on the waiting list. I look around the circle, wondering who will get in and who will miss out. I am over forty, which will be an advantage.[1] A few days later I get a letter telling me that I'm in. I wait with excitement and apprehension for the first training session.

My first year in the circus was somewhat mixed. I loved the training, the security of working only with women, and the fact that there was something that I was doing just for me. Yet at times I felt isolated. It seemed that everyone knew each other (though this was not the case) and that everyone seemed to pick up skills much more quickly than I did. But by the time I started my second year, I began to feel more comfortable in the group.

Perhaps because in that first year I was rather solitary, I did a lot of observing and reflecting on how the circus operated, and came to see that the circus provided an alternative model for the workings of any organisation, because it is non-hierarchical. I began to reflect on how this could be applied to the organisation that I work in: the Anglican Church.

The church, of course, is one of the most patriarchal and hierarchical organisations in existence – such a contrast to the

---

1. Women over forty are a priority group on the Circus waiting list.

Naomi Herzog

circus. It seems to me that the circus is able to make much better use of individual talents than the church is, and I believe this is to do with its structure. In the circus, each one of us is encouraged to try new things, but no one is forced to do anything they feel uncomfortable about. We can all find something we can do (ropes, balances, juggling, stilts, clowning) and develop and enjoy this skill. No matter who we are, what age, shape, size, what level of ability, what background, there is a role for each of us in the circus. As we build up to a performance, we all take on other tasks – publicity, rigging, security. By the time of the show, there is a strong sense of ownership and of community. And all of this happens under the direction of one person, Donna (directing is another skill) but in a way that allows each of us to have a say at all stages.

How different things are within the church (and most other organisations). The leaders – bishops and priests – do not necessarily listen to the needs of the rest of the people, and ideas and decisions are imposed from above. Many people, especially women, are not encouraged to develop their talents within the church community, while others are forced to perform tasks for which they might not have the skills. For example, priests are expected to preach sermons even though it might not be their skill. There is often a lack of acceptance of those who are different in ethnicity, sexuality or socio-economic status from the white, middle-class, Anglo-Saxon majority.

You might wonder then, why someone who loves the circus so much can still be part of such a patriarchal structure. First, it provides me with the job that I love – working with the children and families in the high-rise flats in North Melbourne. Second, it gives me the chance to perform in a different way from the physical type of Women's Circus performance. On Sundays, I am at the front of the church in North Melbourne helping to lead the community in worship. It is performance with words rather than body. Third, this small community, even though it is still part of a very large church structure, tries to operate in non-hierarchical ways, and has a strong commitment to social justice. It has given me a sense of belonging to a community which complements the circus community. At the end of 1993, nearly all the people in my church came to watch the show – this was an important affirmation by them of the importance of circus in my life.

I believe that an organisation like the church has much to

learn from the Women's Circus. It is only by "leaping off the edge" and taking a few risks and allowing each individual the freedom to develop their unique talents that change will happen.

The Phenomenon of the Women's Circus

Karen Martin

The Women's Circus. Yes, a circus made up of women. So what? What is it about the circus that people get so excited, so passionate about? We are an event, a happening. We are herstory in the making. But why is the circus considered such a phenomenon?

To date we have existed for six years, growing, changing, taking risks. Our endeavours are supported by a large network of sisters and supporters. We have a large training membership (performers, musicians, technicians) as well as a long list of women eager to join and be involved in this spectacle. So what makes the Women's Circus what it is? I have thought long and hard. And I present to you my reflections. They are simply my opinions, so they may not be the next woman's, and that's okay for in a circus of so many women we do not aim for a collective unity of thought, relegated to the lowest common denominator, but encourage and support individual expression.

There are many aspects to the Women's Circus that together make it a special place to be. It is comprised of a group of wonderful women; supportive, encouraging, fun, inspiring. Yet this alone does not offer any explanation for the unique nature of the Women's Circus. We are working our bodies physically and politically to affirm control of our (in some circumstances) previously abused bodies. Yet aerobics and other sports can also offer physical development. Is it because the circus is gender specific that our feminist ideologies can be encouraged and nurtured with like-minded women? Yet again, there are many organisations involving only women so this factor alone does not account for that "something" that makes the Women's

Circus unique. For we are unique. We are a working model of feminist philosophy that not only develops the individual's physical (and some argue spiritual) being but also displays this growth in an artistic medium that draws capacity crowds of over 4000 a season. We are not paid professionals within this context; we pay to train. Nor are we an elitist group. Every year there is an intake of new women. We are a community arts project. We are women from all walks of life, women you know; sisters, daughters, mothers, lovers, friends.

Drumming up business: Karen Martin helps draw a crowd for the 1995 Beijing tour

To explore the phenomenon of the circus I believe we need to look back to the three major protagonists in the circus' inception and development. Donna Jackson, a woman possessed of energy and inspiration, who created this circus with dreams, a directness that pulls no punches and a belief in women's achievements. She has developed a process that complements her innovative and creative artistic talents and produced a product that intermingles trust and self-expression with great theatre. But the circus is more than just a reflection of Donna's vision.

Her choice of trainer was a vital factor and could not be made lightly. This was a decision that was made with an uncanny sense of future implications, one that has greatly influenced the very core and heart of the circus. Her decision was imperative to the specific growth and evolution of the circus. Sally Forth trained the women of the circus for the initial three years. From her methodology, a safe and non-competitive environment was established. Sally taught us to focus inwardly; on our breath, on our strength and weakness, on our challenges, our aims, our achievements. We were not merely training our muscles, our bodies, but something larger, almost soul-like.

I remember my first workshop. One woman – wearing Doc Martens – showed me how to walk across the tightrope. My initial response was "Why should I bother learning, I could never be as good as her. And even if I reached her standard she would always be better than me. I could never be the best!" Fortunately I did persist and six weeks later, instilled with an unspoken understanding of Sally's (and circus) philosophy, I managed to slowly and shakily make my way across the tightrope. From that point I embraced training with the circus adage: practice, practice, practice! I did not need to demoralise myself with a competitive overview. I learnt to set realistic challenges, sometimes achieving them, sometimes not. It was the process that imparted the knowledge and the skill, any skill, could be acquired with commitment and practice.

Sally's approach was holistic. We embraced the knowledge of working our bodies physically with how we treated ourselves – starting with what we ate. Total control over our own bodies was not simply a case of perfecting a particular exercise. Sally imparted knowledge through health workshops that introduced concepts of healthy eating and preparation of food.

Our training, while done in groups of about twenty, was always individual. Sally would note down our aims, watch our work and feed back individual programmes and exercises to assist us in attaining our dreams. She encouraged our diversity and individuality, fostering an inward journey while encouraging outward expression. When I think back to my initiation into the circus, the training – a blend of Oki-do yoga, corrective exercise, Iyengar yoga, ballet, European and Chinese circus skills with a good mix of Sally's own creativity, sensitivity and intuition – I feel privileged and very lucky. I have been exposed to and experienced an energy and wisdom that has manifested major positive effects in my life.

There is another woman whose contribution to the Women's Circus has also enabled us to be where we are today. She was not involved in the training process but in getting us known. Her skills in publicity fuelled by her belief in the project enabled more people to gain access to the Women's Circus and made us known to the funding bodies who witnessed the impact we had and consequently support us.

It was a lucky coincidence that Elizabeth Walsh took up the position of director of the Footscray Community Arts Centre during the first year of the Women's Circus. Liz had previously worked with the youth circus group, the Flying Fruit Fly Circus, among other things, and one can safely assume she had a streak of circus blood in her veins. Her absolute belief in the project transformed it from a small community arts project into something larger than life. With her expertise and panache, Liz got the first large-scale Women's Circus performance well into the limelight. And the media loved it! From an anticipated 120-

a-night audience, we were sold out at 400 strong. Through Liz's amazing accomplishment in getting the circus known, the pressure was on Donna to come up with "the goods" without losing the process and integrity of the circus. Our hard work and belief in ourselves, encouraged and nurtured by Sally, and our respect and trust in Donna culminated in a debut that was raw, honest and gutsy. We were proud, we were strong, our process reflected in a product that was publicly acclaimed.

The combined force and dynamics of these three women – their strengths, weaknesses, integrity and generosity of spirit – has given birth to the phenomenon which we call the Women's Circus. Their focus and direction, as well as the energy and support from the other women of the circus, has taught and inspired me to be true to my own creative potential, as a performer and as a woman. With this sense of being and strength I am able to give back to the circus. My energy, combined with the energy of every other woman touched by this event, transforms the circus from an empty warehouse into a dynamic living expression. The Women's Circus has soul, breath, passion and desire. It is not merely muscle and bone to be flexed and strengthened. It is alive. It continues to need nurturing, but with continual reflection on our aims, objectives and philosophy, a continual belief in ourselves and our own journeys, and a continual intake of new women with new dreams and fresh energy, it is (and we are) continually nourished and enriched. Ultimately it is the balance between process and product, a balance established by Donna and Sally, that makes the Women's Circus the phenomenon that it is.

From the Journal

I've joined the Women's Circus. The theme of our November (1991) performance will be "power". At one of the workshops we were making human pyramids. Three women formed the base of the pyramid and three others had to climb onto their shoulders and then stand and join hands. Many other women's hands were there in case our inexperienced, wobbly limbs caused us to fall. I was one of the women who climbed up. I wanted to weep when I made it to the ground again. It was terrifying, but why?

I realised how full of fear I am. I learnt about the limited trust I had in myself. I was dependent on these women's solid support and their many hands. I gave in to my dependence.

As I was climbing I was at first thinking only of myself, of doing it well. As others climbed to where I already was, I was fearful they would upset my tenuous hold. I didn't think to help them, that they might feel like me. I even had the urge to push them away.

I learnt that we had to watch each other's eyes closely, that we had to be conscious of our dependence on each other. That we were a formation of intricate links, minds and bodies. That we had to work together for each other and for ourselves. I learnt that I was very brave.

If we cannot realise our dependence and our strength, care for each other and climb together, then what? This is our power base. Or is this only our reality because men have valued us according to the care we give them and we could probably use some? Is our morality perhaps not morality in a different voice but morality in a higher register?

(Anon)

II
The Women

I used to feel different in the worst of ways, now I feel different in the best of ways.

— Linda Wilson

Three ring circus: A photo shoot with (left to right)
Judy Crowe, Jan Crowe and Kerry Ann Murphy in 1991

Chance

Jude Johns

Beginning to make choices, beginning to make changes,
beginning to take risks and step over the edge.
Beginning to balance.
To fly high, swing on ropes, to extend my body to move in
    ways it never has before.
Beginning to find new ways to explore.
Exploring aspects of mind, body, emotions.
Beginning to discipline.
Beginning to not give up so easily as to find the nights
    seemingly endless.
Beginning to pick flowers and smell scents strange and
    wonderful.
To sense the slightest change in season and detect hints of
    spring flowers and rain.
Beginning to notice the world in a way I've never seen
    before.
Beginning to live life breaking the shackles of fear.
Beginning to trust.
Beginning new ideas.

Meet the Women

Louise Radcliffe-Smith

The Women's Circus would not exist without the women who built it. These women are as diverse as society itself: radical lesbian feminists, mothers, workers, unwaged, young, old, immigrant, Aboriginal, survivors of sexual abuse, disabled, political, playful, big and small. In any circus year, participants range in ages from twelve through to fifty-five, although, as a rule, school-age girls are not encouraged to join.

The Women's Circus is not so much a machine with component parts as an ever-expanding network of women who come, go, work, play, create, discuss and grow. The circus is not perfect.

Louise Radcliffe-Smith (Rad)

There are quibbles and quarrels and occasionally competition. The strength of the organisation, however, lies in its ability and desire to look back and evaluate honestly, to build on what works while acknowledging and trying to overcome what doesn't.

Women join the circus for an enormous variety of reasons. For some women the circus is a means of putting feminist beliefs into action; for others it is a way of making friends, building business networks, overcoming body memories or getting fit. Though the circus espouses no single feminist view, circus members are united by a belief that "the strength is in the doing". We do what we do to the best of our ability and we encourage others to do the same.

One of the most heartwarming aspects of the circus is the support it receives from the general community. In addition to the members who train as performers, technicians, musicians or administrators, the circus also has access to a body of about 500 sisters and supporters (supporters are men) who choose to pay $25 or $35 to become honorary members. Sisters and supporters receive a T-shirt and other circus paraphernalia, and a yearly subscription to the circus newsletter. The circus also has access to an amorphous group known as the Big Sisters, a body of about ten women in the business and arts community who periodically advise us on legal, economic or artistic matters.

Diversity, access and inclusiveness are basic tenets of Women's Circus philosophy. Any woman can join the circus if she puts her name on the list and waits. As part of this policy of inclusiveness, the circus has chosen to give priority to a number of groups that are either disadvantaged, stereotyped or ignored by society.

At its inception the Women's Circus invited survivors of sexual abuse to join before opening the doors to the general population. Since then, survivors have remained a priority group on the circus waiting list.

Over the years there has been a great deal of discussion in the circus about whether to use the term "victim" in conjunction with the term "survivor" to describe women who have experienced sexual abuse. Though some women, including circus member Jen Jordan, generally referred to themselves as survivors, they also argued it was important to use "victim" in conjunction with "survivor" because this clearly identified that the person had undergone a trauma and illustrated the fact that a crime had be perpetrated against that person. They believed that only using the term "survivor" might, in some situations, play down or detract from the trauma and crime involved in sexual abuse, particularly if the person concerned did not yet identify with being a survivor.

Taking these issues into consideration, the circus has generally chosen to use "survivor" rather than "victim" in literature, media situations and when talking to other organisations, because it is a strong word that creates room for hope. It is a positive way of describing those women who are striving to move from a state of disempowerment to a state of self-determination and pride. At any one time, up to half of the women in the circus would describe themselves as survivors.

In 1993, with an average of fifty to sixty women waiting to join, circus members decided to give priority to other groups so the organisation more accurately reflected society in general and the suburb of Footscray in particular. The two groups nominated were women over forty and immigrant women. Over the next few years, the circus had mixed success in attracting and retaining women from non-English-speaking backgrounds, while slowly increasing the number of older women involved.

Towards the end of 1995, the circus also decided to give priority to Australian Aboriginal women. Many in the circus had expressed a desire to build links with the Aboriginal women's community, but the first tentative steps were not taken until circus members began researching the story of an Aboriginal woman to include in a performance in Beijing as part of the 1995 United Nations Conference and Forum on the Status of Women. The story, developed in consultation with Aboriginal communities in Melbourne and South Australia, became a pivotal and poignant part of both the Beijing show and the 1995 end-of-year show, Leaping the Wire. As this book went to press, circus members had begun to discuss ideas for cultural exchange with Aboriginal women's communities around Australia.

At the Information Day in February 1996, members made another exciting addition to the Women's Circus priority list: big women. It was felt big women were under-represented and under-supported within the circus as they were in the wider community. Rather than specify any cut-off size, the group (known as the "Mangoes") was left open to women of larger build who felt they fitted the description. By training together under the direction of another big woman, Kylie Whyte, and later under Annie Fayzdaughter, the Mangoes hoped to identify and deal with the emotional, physical and cultural issues faced by larger women in society.

While many women in the circus do not belong to any priority group, the circus will continue to try to give disadvantaged or marginalised groups a fair go. As with anything in the circus, these priority groups are not set in cement. They will change in importance and nature according to the demands and needs of each year. What is important is the trying, the hope and the intention. This section outlines the struggles and strengths of some of the women in some of the groups the circus has chosen to champion.

Women's Circus Members – Job Description

Your job is to:

- have fun
- allow yourself time to develop
- challenge yourself
- work with other women in a feminist way, i.e. to recognise all women are different
- support and encourage other women
- treat other women with respect
- come to training on the day when you're tired/too depressed/have a better offer
- work to break down the hierarchical notion that the "most able" is the best
- recognise that there will be conflict while getting this circus together and that it is natural and healthy
- talk to other women you have conflict with "one to one" and to try to resolve it. If that doesn't work, to get another woman you both feel OK about to help facilitate the process
- to arrive at workshops/rehearsals on time
- to be prepared to "take direction" as the show is moving from workshopping to rehearsal
- to support the Women's Circus in ways other than performing
- to recognise that all theatre work is of equal importance, i.e. administration, cleaning up, technical areas, performance, training, rehearsal
- to talk to the trainer, director, other women if you have a problem
- to work safely as an individual and with other women

SURVIVORS SPEAK

The Journey Towards Healing

Jen Jordan

The Women's Circus has a special meaning and significance for women who are victims/survivors of sexual assault and incest.

Jen Jordan

The establishment of a community arts project that specifically invited, welcomed and sought to address the particular needs and aspirations of survivors of incest and other forms of sexual assault was itself a powerful political statement. The feminist philosophy of the Women's Circus not only publicly validated women's personal testimony of sexual assault, but also acknowledged the strengths, spirit and achievements of women survivors.

For survivors such as myself, who attended the inaugural meeting in 1991 alone and with considerable trepidation, the circus offered a unique environment for personal validation, affirmation and transformation. In my experience, and that of many other survivors, it is very difficult to emerge from denial, to be believed and to find genuine and consistent support amongst family, friends, colleagues and professionals.

A climate of denial of sexual assault and its effects persists in Australian society despite current research that indicates forty per cent of females are *victims*. There is increasing evidence that many males are also *victims* of sexual violence. Overwhelmingly, these assaults are perpetrated by males, though a small percentage of females are offenders.

From its inception, the Women's Circus strove to break through the social and cultural walls of silence and denial that continue to isolate and limit the lives of many thousands of victims of sexual assault in Australia. The circus has been an oasis of acceptance for women survivors in a patriarchal society where prevailing social attitudes shame, blame or discredit victims, rather than holding perpetrators accountable for their behaviour.

The philosophy and structure of the Women's Circus brought together a large number of women committed to healing the effects of sexual assault. It has been this genuine commitment to healing and to sharing experiences and collective wisdom that has provided the catalyst and fuel for effective change in survivors' lives.

Since its establishment, the circus has proved to be a liberating force unleashed by and for survivors on many different levels, from the publicly political to the politics of everyday life, and the inner healing journeys of many individual members.

In contrast to the general tendency of social services, professionals and mental health and legal institutions to "pathologise" the victims of sexual assault, the Women's Circus provided opportunities for survivors to honour each others' strength and spirit of endurance, to speak the unspeakable without fear of denial, rejection or withdrawal, and thus to reframe their experiences in an atmosphere of mutual acceptance, respect and understanding.

The effectiveness and benefits of bringing together survivors of trauma in self-help groups has been well documented. The sharing, compassion and support between those who have suffered the same or similar traumas has been shown to strengthen and enhance individual recovery from post-traumatic stress disorders.

Sexual assault can adversely affect many areas of women's lives, leading to difficulties with trust and intimacy in relationships, notably those involving families, sexual contact or physical affection. Sexual assault can also lead to difficulty in trusting, nurturing or valuing the body and the self, low self-esteem and confidence, emotional, mental and physical dis-eases (particularly reproductive dis-eases), drug, work or sex addictions, and eating disorders.

The holistic training philosophy and practices developed and described by Sally Forth were especially valuable in addressing the damage while restoring and enhancing the physical, emotional, mental and spiritual wellbeing of sexual assault survivors. The circus training program provided a safe and enjoyable space for many survivors to learn to respect, protect, value and nurture their bodies, to work on reclaiming, reconnecting and integrating the different parts of the self (including spirituality), to rebuild trusting and reciprocal relations with others, and to rejoice in their own and other women's unique qualities, strengths and successes.

Seemingly simple activities such as stretching, massage, balances in pairs and groups, group relaxation, trust exercises and regular small support group discussions contributed significantly to individual healing and group solidarity. Along with the learning of circus skills, they also challenged many survivors to risk confronting their fears both personally and socially in a safe environment – an essential part of the healing process.

The training programmes in musical and technical skills offered access to learning new skills with group validation and encouragement to survivors who preferred not to perform physically. Survivors within all areas of the circus have worked hard to overcome their fears and to resolve the interpersonal misunderstandings and conflicts that inevitably accompany the journey towards healing.

The processes of healing the effects of sexual trauma are complex, difficult and lengthy. Survivors require a wide range of support mechanisms for both their individual needs and for different stages of their healing journey. The Women's Circus has sometimes been an overwhelming experience for survivors, and it has not always been appropriate for all survivors nor for all stages of the healing process.

The issues associated with the destruction of trust in relationships are complex, especially when sexual assault occurs within families. Women's capacity to trust mothers and siblings may be shaken profoundly in incestuous families. Very frequently, as in my own story, mothers or other females are themselves perpetrators, which further complicates issues of safety and trust within and outside the circus.

The commitment to recover from the effects of sexual assault and incest can sometimes be intensely painful and costly, as well as immensely rewarding. The Women's Circus is unable to wave a magic wand over the world women inhabit outside the circus. Many survivors of sexual assault are still being silenced by families, professionals, colleagues and institutions. Few of us have the resources to ensure perpetrators are brought to justice or the ability to speak out publicly about the crimes. There is a

Nicole Hunter

Bluebird

growing willingness to discredit survivors who do speak out, the False Memory Syndrome Association is a recent obvious example.

Within the circus, the ongoing resolve of many survivors and other members to build relations of trust, honesty, intimacy and reciprocity with each other continues to inform the integrity of face-to-face relationships and the sense of belonging women feel to a community that has mutual interests and concerns. This is a potent source of the warmth, vitality and solidarity that women feel about the circus and that audiences perceive whenever the circus performs.

The role of the Women's Circus in both focusing upon and championing the rights and needs of survivors at political and personal levels continues to be vitally important. The circus has maintained a political role in raising public consciousness about sexual assault and breaking down stereotypes of victims/survivors. In 1995, the Women's Circus again broke new ground when for the first time performances in Beijing and in Australia told the inspiring story of Linda Wilson, a woman in the circus who is a survivor of incest.

Fragment 1: Map 42

Nadia Angelini

It haunts me, self doubt
        still creeps
          it infests itself,
a virus of despair and decay
     it's amnesic in effect
      diffusing into the "selves"
the body – my body
          I'm still punishing myself body
         blaming it
         shameful of it
         loathing with intensity
it terrorises and torments me.

A Survivor Within the Circus

Linda Wilson

I joined the Women's Circus in 1991 as one of the original members. When I joined I had not been long into actively healing from the effects of childhood sexual abuse. During my four years in the circus, amidst the juggling and tumbling, I have been through many changes in my life, both inside and outside.

I've watched my children grow from being toddlers to little people and I've moved house five times. I separated from my husband and I questioned (and answered) sexuality issues. I've given up tranquillisers and I've made new friends. I've trained, and now work, as a masseur and reflexologist.

On a healing level, I have worked with four counsellors, three incest support groups and attended many personal growth gatherings. I've read numerous books, articles and pamphlets. I have spoken about my experience at universities and participated in a television documentary called "Abuse". I have confronted my father regarding his sexually violent acts and I've reported the incest to the police. I've gone through two Crimes Compensation cases. I've self-mutilated, been depressed, considered suicide, had nightmares (both awake and asleep) and have been told I'm crazy or a liar or both.

The counselling and support groups have provided me with strategies and ideas of how to deal with emotions that rise up, and how to delve into and change the deeply buried messages from childhood.

The Women's Circus has enabled me to work physically with my body in a safe environment where I have discovered issues of trust, intimacy and fun. It has been part of the process of my healing.

When I first performed to an audience I was terrified. So much of my childhood had been spent trying to fade into the background. It had seemed vital that I not be noticed for I did not want others to see my shame. So when I was required to stand up in front of a large group of people and perform I learnt that being noticed does not automatically mean being abused or being judged. In fact, along with other women, I was applauded! I have noticed that now when I perform I feel joy more than I

Going solo: Linda Wilson
on unicycle

Naomi Herzog

feel fear and I feel proud rather than shameful.

Trusting others and allowing others to trust me is an important part of training and performing within the circus. Trusting that someone will not drop you when you are balancing on them, trusting that you have the ability to have someone balance on you. Now I work almost exclusively as a "base" (someone who lets others climb all over them). I have trust in my body's capabilities and in its strength. I am learning to trust myself.

Authority figures have always appeared threatening to me. My father (the perpetrator) was in the air force and was quite authoritarian. In the circus it is necessary to take direction when rehearsing for the show. What I have recently learnt is that taking direction from someone does not include taking on their stress and their mood swings. Once I would have taken on board any comments that someone in a position of authority chose to make. Now I understand it is not an all-or-nothing thing. I can take the good advice and choose to not react to any negative comments. What I once would have taken personally, I now understand is not about me. It is more often than not about the stress and tiredness of another.

What I love about the circus is the women and the fun they can bring into all they do. Even after hours of rehearsing, feeling weary, we can often share a joke and a smile. The circus is a place where I usually become quite close to the women I am training and working with. As we are often physically connected to each other when doing balances, an intimacy develops. That intimacy extends beyond the physical as we begin to share parts of our lives with each other. There always seems to be someone who will give me a hug or talk to me if I'm feeling down or disheartened. I have found the support of the Women's Circus wonderful, and the women very accepting and non-judgemental. It is, to me, a safe and friendly environment where I can be myself, meet new friends, enhance established friendships and continue to heal and grow on many levels.

Nicole Hunter

Counterbalance

Fragment 2: Map 42

Nadia Angelini

Finding pure love in true self expression
      expressing mind/body/soul/spirit
      a fusing into unification
      energized/powerful force
      it enters the dark psyche
      where those footsteps are heard and
      still come to haunt –
            the more light that filters through
      the greater the expanse of darkness
      the greater the exploration of my being
      to enter and walk through it
      rather than to hang around my
      neck, like some noose
swinging with the grasp on reality.

Support Group: Tower of Strength

Helen North

As an incest survivor, I found the physical aspect of the circus very challenging – it made me aware of how disconnected I felt from my body at times. I was interested in meeting with other survivors, with the aim of learning from our shared experiences. So I organised a support group.

The group met for the first time on 4 September 1991. The evening's discussion covered a diverse range of topics relating to women's experience of the circus – fears, dealing with fear, performance anxiety, physical issues, changes in levels of personal confidence, commitment, trust, feelings of isolation at workshops, and so on. We shared what we had gained or hoped to gain from our participation in the circus and discussed what hindered us from achieving what we wanted, and ways of overcoming these blocks. The meeting provided me with an opportunity to share with other women our common and diverse experiences, and for us to be supported and strengthened by each other.

Equally important, we developed strategies for building this support into all aspects of the circus: workshops, rehearsals, the performance. One outcome has been the formation of support groups of four or so women within training workshops. These groups became a framework for providing and receiving support within the circus and a means of breaking down individual women's isolation.

Speaking Out:
The Support Group 1993–94

Linda Wilson

Nicole Hunter

Novel support

I organised the Women's Circus support group for two years after Helen North left. We met once a month during the year while training and more often when we were rehearsing and performing.

Women were invited to come along and talk about any issues or problems that they may have concerning the circus, or about their personal life. The issues that came up varied according to the women attending but some common themes were sexual abuse, body image, feeling supported/unsupported, injuries/safety, fun, skill levels, future projects, sexuality, fitting in, anxiety about performing and the stresses of preparing for a show.

The support group worked within a very loosely structured framework. We began by allowing each woman up to five minutes to speak, uninterrupted, about why she had come along to the group. When each of us had spoken we discussed the issues raised.

Often I took notes and without naming names took these notes to the circus director. In this way, many issues were addressed in a confidential manner. There were many things that some people felt too awkward to approach the director with themselves. The support group offered a forum where women could be heard and taken seriously and from there begin to take action. Any information that derived from within the support group was treated in a confidential manner and not discussed outside the group unless the woman's agreement was given.

The group was a place to celebrate personal achievements, big or small, and to give ourselves credit for learning new skills and for growth on an internal level. It was a place to acknowledge the joys of being part of the Women's Circus and to feel the warmth and support of the women involved.

Vivienne Méhes

Referees on a roll: Women and Sport Show, 1993

Fragment 3: Map 42

Nadia Angelini

an energy field of women come together
to reclaim themselves – enriching life by
leaping off the edge
not just for oneself, not just a marker for
one's own understanding. It is also a map
for those who follow after us – sisters and
supporters.
shedding/peeling away at those fears.
magnetic women drawing energy through
physical/performance work
circus skills providing me with the opportunity
to reclaim my body and spirit.

In Memory of Jen Jordan

13 February 1955—8 February 1996

Linda Wilson

On 8 February 1996 Jen Jordan died in tragic circumstances. She was forty years old.

The contributions that Jen made to this book are spread throughout many words and chapters. Her most heartfelt chapter is in the "Survivors Speak" section of the book. Jen was a survivor of childhood sexual abuse and violence and as an adult she was active on many levels in healing from long-term effects of her incest. She was an amazingly strong and compassionate woman. While dealing with her own pain of recovering incest memories and feelings, she was always available and supportive to other women. Jen was also constantly politically active in attempting to break the silence and the myths that surround incest and its emotional impact.

Jen was a vital and vibrant force in the organising and compiling of this book. When reading Jen's contributions we are aware of her energy, her commitment and her sound feminist views. This book was important to her, and she tackled its challenges with her usual 100 per cent enthusiasm. Allen (Jen's partner) recalls many late nights and many cups of tea as Jen wrote, rewrote and rewrote again her allocated sections of the book until she was completely satisfied.

Jen was adamant in relation to women retaining their original voices. She made it extremely clear to the book team, the editors and the publishers that none of her wording or phrasing was to be changed. Everything that Jen has written came straight from her heart and mind and has not been rearranged in any way. Jen stood strong and kept her original voice.

She was a very dear friend of mine, as well as a fellow circus member and we also attended incest support groups together. I was privileged to know this exceptional woman on many levels.

Although Jen is no longer with us, her compassion and beauty will remain in the hearts and memories of all who knew her. Through this book some of her writings live on, and others will continue to be supported and encouraged by this very special person. Jen died before this book reached the final stages of publishing. She would have been proud to see the end result of her many, many hours of work.

We will all miss her. She was a much loved friend and an inspiring member of the Women's Circus.

For Jen, the pain is over and it's her time to rest.

The Web

(for Jen Jordan)

Patricia Sykes

Don't laugh you said
you took your training seriously
using your hands and feet as grapples
to pull your body out of a private hole
even the smallest gig made you intense
each one a chance to climb
one step higher out of the mire
of childhood violence and incest
that sucked at you like a bog
but you gave its mouth no spare flesh
to cling to   you refined
yourself to muscle sinew bone
until you become a flyer
a conqueror of ropes trapeze air

even then the old pain
tried to ride your shoulders
so you turned it on its head
sent it spinning as you spun
upside down on the web
hanging on by one looped foot
back on the ground you linked hands
with sister survivors   helped write
their stories   carried their voices
to the top of women's circus pyramids

year after year you came back
for another season   your body
ready to open itself a little further
to allow itself the pleasure of another skill
sometimes you would have to soothe
your frightened ghosts   trust me
you would say this won't hurt
don't laugh don't laugh

A QUESTION OF CULTURAL DIVERSITY

Immigrant Women

Vig Geddes

Vivienne Méhes

Speaking out: Vig Geddes playing the role of Linda Wilson, an incest survivor and member of the Women's Circus in the 1995 Beijing Show

From the beginning, the Women's Circus encouraged particular groups of women to join. When the circus was established in 1991, priority was given to survivors of sexual assault. Since then they have continued to be given priority on the circus waiting list. Circus training offers women the opportunity to build self-esteem and increase confidence in using their bodies. Women over forty years of age have also been given priority for circus membership. This is an attempt to work against stereotypes about the lack of physical ability of older women while also ensuring a diversity of women in the circus.

In late 1993, circus women were asked their views about which groups should be offered priority in joining the circus. The issue of priority had become increasingly significant, with the number of women on the waiting list maintaining an average of fifty to sixty since the end of 1991. In discussions about priority, circus members affirmed their commitment to survivors of sexual assault and to women over forty. They also added a third group: women from non-English-speaking backgrounds.

While the circus is a diverse group in terms of age, class, occupation and interests, it is predominantly Anglo-Saxon. Clearly the cultural background of the group does not reflect the cultural diversity of the general population and in particular the local population of the Footscray area, with its high concentration of Indo-Chinese, Vietnamese and Latin Americans.

Women in the circus expressed their desire to offer membership to a group that had less opportunity than the rest of the population while at the same time building a circus that was more representative of the community as a whole and would provide a greater breadth of experience and culture from which to draw creative inspiration.

A small sub-group was formed to discuss how we could attract immigrant women to the circus. We discussed whether we should focus on particular immigrant communities, how to reach various groups, whether or not fluency in English was important for circus membership and training, translation of circus leaflets, the use of ethnic radio and press, and whether or not the circus should give priority to requests for performances from immigrant women's groups.

As a result of these discussions, small performances were arranged for immigrant women's groups and contact was made with relevant workers in the area. Some translations of circus material were completed and material was broadcast on ethnic radio.

The major focus of attention then shifted to the Immigrant Women's Conference which was held in March 1994. A large number of women were expected to attend. The circus offered to perform and to provide a circus skills workshop. The performance took place at lunchtime. Most of the conference participants watched and it was well received. The workshop was attended by about ten women and again the response was enthusiastic. The women at both the conference and workshop were encouraged to join the circus and some women subsequently applied. They were automatically accepted and joined just as the new Women's Circus group began training for 1994. The rest of the circus training workshops were already underway. Women who had put aside time to plan and rehearse the performance for the Immigrant Women's Conference went back to training and resumed their regular life routines.

At this point, discussions about attracting immigrant women to the circus ceased, although some women continued to make contact with immigrant women's groups. Circus members made positive comments about the inclusion of this new group but there was no process or support structure set in place to cater for them. Some of the immigrant women from the conference and from the waiting list stayed, some left. There was no follow-up to find out about their experience with the circus, or why some left. The focus was more on getting particular women to join and less on building a circus that could better accommodate the needs of these women.

With this in mind, it is useful to reflect on the first year of the circus when survivors of sexual assault were invited to join. The training sessions were structured to provide a supportive environment. Workshops began and finished with women sitting in a circle and participants were encouraged to give feedback and share their experiences of the training. Trust exercises were incorporated into training, women were encouraged to progress at their own pace, and there was an expectation that women would assist each other. There were also frequent reminders that everyone should be sensitive to the effects that the experience of sexual assault could have on women's experience of physical training. Women were encouraged to contact others who had missed training sessions to check how they were and to offer assistance and encouragement if appropriate. A support group was set up for circus members to share their experiences of physical training and to provide mutual support. Many of the survivors who attended training in the first year described the workshops as a positive environment where women could take on new challenges at their own pace while at the same time having a lot of fun.

Since the first year the structure of training has gradually changed. In most workshops, there is less emphasis on the creation of a supportive environment and more on the physical training and the development of skills. However, workshops for new women have continued the style of the first year. The 1995 and 1996 workshops for new women seem to have been particularly successful in creating a positive environment, judging by the high retention rate and the enthusiastic comments of the new women themselves.

Many women have left the circus, some for reasons unrelated to the circus, some through disappointment or dissatisfaction. Some survivors of sexual abuse have left the circus unhappy with the level of support for survivors and with the lack of discussion of issues related to sexual assault. Women from non-English-speaking backgrounds have also left. Whatever the reasons, it would be useful to know in order to create a structure that will best accommodate the needs of the particular groups we seek to attract. We need to hear from those women who were not so satisfied. There has been no formal follow-up of women who have left, so it is difficult to know in what ways the circus could change to better satisfy women's needs.

At end-of-year evaluation sessions, new women and others have made comments which suggest some changes might be needed. If we are to continue to encourage particular groups of women to join the circus we should also develop a means of getting feedback from those women about their experience of the circus. We can then make changes to our structure and process to ensure that giving priority to a certain group means more than giving them priority on the waiting list. Ideally, priority should extend to the way things work in the circus. This could help ensure the best environment for everyone.

The Women's Circus has provided wonderful opportunities, challenges and joy to hundreds of women. If we reflect on the disappointments of some of those who have left we could build an even stronger organisation that could satisfy a greater diversity of women.

Crossing Cultural Barriers

An interview with Celena Catipovski

Louise Radcliffe-Smith

Celena Catipovski was born in Poland in 1958. Her parents were Macedonians from the former Republic of Yugoslavia. She migrated to Melbourne with her mother and brother in 1979, working first in factories and later in schools as a bilingual teacher's aid. In the 1990s she became a part-time interpreter and full-time mother.

I heard about the Women's Circus on ABC television in 1993 and joined in April 1994. I thought the circus would be a good opportunity to get fit and to learn new, interesting skills as well. I had never done circus skills before and I'd never thought of doing anything of that kind, so it was a completely new challenge for me. Everyone was very welcoming and the long term members were very encouraging and helpful. After I joined the circus I kept coming regularly each week, although

Nicole Hunter

Pike on trapeze

sometimes I would be really exhausted and could hardly get up in the mornings because of a sleepless night with the baby. I would come here and I would be literally energised.

Due to a neck injury that happened before I joined the circus, I decided to concentrate on the tightrope, because it involved the lower part of the body. I didn't have much competition because there weren't many women learning tightrope. So I had plenty of opportunity to practise as much as I wanted, which was good because it's difficult to practise it at home. It's not like jugging balls. I couldn't wait to come to the warehouse and raise the rope just that much higher and see whether I could walk the distance that time. I got to about one and a half metres. Sometimes when I got dreamy I imagined myself walking four metres above the admiring audience.

I was very lucky that I came from a non-English-speaking background and belonged to one of the priority groups, because it enabled me to skip some of the waiting list. But once I was in the circus I didn't feel any more advantaged or disadvantaged than any other person. I'm really excited that we've got a task-force to target women from non-English-speaking backgrounds because I feel physical touch is a wonderful way to overcome the cultural and language barriers. You don't have to talk a lot in circus. You just go to the training and no one is pushing you to do any more than that. Then if you want to get involved in the running of the circus you can do that. Now that there are so many women from different cultural backgrounds in the circus, I would like to see more input and more use of the skills from the cultures of those women. Perhaps they should get together and talk about the issues and put those issues to the director. That way we could incorporate more of the knowledge and skills of these women in the performance.

I'm so glad I made the effort to join the circus. Unfortunately, in 1994, I could not do the things I wanted to do because of a neck injury. My goal was to get involved in a trapeze team or to get on top of a body pyramid. But because of my neck I had to choose another goal for myself. It's fantastic that the circus enabled me to do exactly what it suited my body to do at the time. Now I feel like the lower part of my body is much stronger. I can feel my legs now. It never bothered me before. I feel stronger and more confident that these legs of mine can hold me in a balanced position for quite a long time, or longer than they could before.

If the circus had not offered child care I don't know how I could have managed. It was fantastic to have child care there right next to the warehouse, so I could take five minutes off and go and feed Nicholas. For me it was crucial, otherwise I couldn't have found the time, especially since I had to travel the distance from Brighton. Child care has enabled a lot of breast-feeding mothers to join the circus.

When I mentioned to people that I was in the circus, the response from migrants and from the true Aussie circle was very similar. It ranged from amusement to lack of interest. I think some people were very challenged by the idea of [me being] a circus performer. When I told my mother-in-law, who is a true Aussie, she couldn't have been more surprised than if I told her I was expecting triplets. "A circus?" she said. "A circus?!"

My husband was very proud of me. On those Saturday afternoons when I had to come to the circus he would take our son on a walk to the nearby park and meet the neighbours. He'd tell them Celena was in the circus and the next day they would want to know more about this phenomenon.

I was really scared about the end-of-year performance. Thinking about whether to take part or not take part in the performance was one of the scariest things. I was a bit mystified about what was going to happen. But seeing the newest members who joined in July 1994 really inspired me. I came to the warehouse and saw this group of new women. I had a chat to them and some of them were breast-feeding mothers like me who were prepared to take part in the performance. So I made the decision to do it as well.

I took part in the main show and I concentrated on developing double balance skills. It was fantastic! When I saw people doing these skills before, I thought it would take me a long time to learn, but it was great how short a time it took me.

It was the unexpected things that I didn't plan to learn that will really stay in my mind for a long time. One or two days before the performance started, Donna assigned me the role of crowd controller. I felt a bit quakey, because that wasn't my plan. But, looking back, it was one of the best parts of the show for me. Every performance night at eight o'clock I would slip into the crowd and get an appreciation of the anticipation and enjoyment of the audience. Another member of the crowd control scene said she enjoyed the fact that the crowd felt obliged to move just because she waved her hand. I thought I could be as cheeky as I wanted. I felt really strong and in control.

Before each performance there was so much support from the other women that I wasn't really anxious. More excited, really. I felt a bit of anxiety sometimes, but in a nice way. Like when I expected my nieces to come. One is eight years old and one five years old and I thought: "I hope my legs look straight on those stilts when I walked forward." Sometimes when I was performing I could see them in the audience not recognising me. The next day when I talked to them they told me they wanted to be circus women too. Those are the times I like to think about. They make me feel a bit warm.

What was happening behind the scenes, getting the whole thing together, the way 120 women with creative ideas could get together, gave me a sense of awe and really inspired me. It was wonderful. I think the way things were built together could be a model for other community and business groups: how to co-operate when speaking amongst each other and how to get people involved, how to make sure everyone has the opportunity to have a say if they want to. No one is pushing you in the Women's Circus. I've never experienced that before, certainly not in the workplace where women are encouraged to compete with other women and you never have the chance to learn to co-operate.

I would like to see children of the women in the circus getting involved, because my son enjoyed the colour and movement of the circus and was attracted to the magic of it. One thing I'm very glad of is that he saw me using my body, the physical strength of my body, and using it in a creative way as well. So I'm not only a mum that takes him from one place to another, but I'm a very strong woman who is not ashamed to show her strength. I feel great about that.

The Same Chance

Franca Stadler

Franca Stadler is a photographer and mountain climber who was born in Switzerland in 1959. She joined the Women's Circus at the beginning of 1995.

I grew up in the middle of the mountains of Switzerland in a small village called Altdorf. I was living some of my life there and some in neighbouring villages. I was a self-employed photographer and I made a few exhibitions in my area. But I could not survive just from that. My parents had a restaurant, so I would just jump into other clothes and serve.

My sister Nella was in Sisterweb Circus in Lismore and she came home and told us about it. She said she had fun and got stronger. She also told us about the Women's Circus and I really wanted to be in it.

My partner, Zen, and I came to Australia in March 1995. It was a decision to immigrate here. Zen had been living in Australia for ten years and could not get citizenship in Switzerland. I had travelled in Australia three times before, twice to visit my sister Nella, who lived here for thirteen years, and once to the Lesbian Festival in Perth, where I met Zen.

I chose this country to live because everyone here has the same chance to grow up and be educated. I would feel really guilty and not comfortable to go to somewhere like India and live there. Here I can just be me. I also wanted to have more things to choose from than in a small village.

When Zen and I came over to Australia, the Women's Circus Information Day was in three weeks and we knew there was a big waiting list, but we wanted to try. I went to the Info Day and was very impressed. I didn't know anyone in Melbourne and it was good to meet people.

The circus is not just physical work. There is also some art involved. It's really different. With photography, I am always working by myself but with the circus I made a decision to work in a big group. Before, I made things how I

Photos: Vivienne Mehes

Making it look easy:
Franca Stadler and
Rebecca Jones in the 1995
Leaping the Wire Show

wanted because I was by myself. With the circus, we all have ideas and we take the best. It's very exciting.

For myself, I found it was quite easy to fit in because I was for twenty years mountain climbing, biking and jogging. I also skied all my life. I think pyramids (large human balances) are really exciting. I have never done them before. It's really a thing of trusting. The flier (the one who climbs) does not just go up like an elephant. You have to trust the base (who stands on the ground) and work with the women.

Trapeze

Susan Hawthorne

Susan Hawthorne

There is a trapeze
       at the centre of the
universe swinging in
       time to the beat of a
subatomic clock

       Electrons hurled
through nannotime,
       arcing across the void,
curling, stretching
       swinging back

A circus whirling into
       the spiral beyond
centrifugal weight, a
       lightness of being
grasping the bar, solid

       A moment of steadiness
before flying out again
       like consciousness
sparking at the edge of
       an infinite circle

CROSSING AGE BARRIERS: WOMEN OVER FORTY

Life After Youth

Patricia Sykes

Timing is everything. The Women's Circus was a year old when I heard about it from two women at work: "You'd love it, Trish, you'd love it!" Their enthusiasm convinced me to put my name on the waiting list. Within a few weeks I was sitting in a circle of fifty or more women at the circus on sign-up day 1992. I remember thinking with a touch of panic: "What am I doing here? I haven't got time for this!'"

So why was I there? In the absence of a community of women elders, I was looking for a substitute, a kind of women's country, to help me make the transition into the second half of my life. I was fifty years old, I had left a 25-year-old marriage a couple of years before, I needed new skills to help me move forward, and I wanted to acquire them in a safe but challenging and exciting environment – one that offered drama and performance, and the opportunity to shake my body up and discover what was buried in there.

I soon discovered, painfully, that I had an underground problem about my age. It surprised me when I got a place in the circus ahead of younger women, and even after I realised that this was due to the circus policy of involving women of all ages and backgrounds. I would apologise when I couldn't do things. To compensate, I tried to be perfect in the skills I was good at. It was Sally Forth, the then circus trainer and herself over forty, who showed me that breathing, focus and connection would allow me to do a great many things I was convincing myself could only be done by a younger body. As Sally has since pointed out, these concentration skills are usually more highly developed in older women, who have had longer to grow into

Vivienne Méhes

Branching out: Trish Sykes at the 1993 Williamstown Summer Festival them and so learn more quickly. Gradually, I stopped apologising and being grateful for my place, and by the end of the year, when I was able to walk the tightrope with a degree of skill, I had gained a new confidence.

Where did my feeling that age was something to be ashamed of and limited by come from? It wasn't that I lacked family models. My maternal grandmother was a strong and vital woman well into her old age, and a great inspiration: she went on a pilgrimage overseas when she was seventy-six, even tried camel riding in Egypt, and no side-saddle for her! I think the problem owes much to western culture, for to be an older woman in our society – with its obsessive focus on youth: young, beautiful, sexually desirable youth – is to be tolerated and humoured. At worst it is to be invisible, and you become more so the older you get, especially if you are a widow, celibate, a single heterosexual woman, or a lesbian. Our culture separates us from each other. There is no women's community, no sacred women's business. Each of us must make the age journey mostly in isolation and every generation of women faces the same problem. To create value and meaning in your life as an ageing woman therefore is not simple, even with the help of feminism, which has helped western women particularly to revision and reclaim themselves. You need courage, you need to network, you need support, and you need a viable community.

I found mine at the circus where the word itself (in its sense of a "scene of lively action") has been given new life and where women over forty are not only welcome but invited. It's not a utopia and bridging age differences is not a simple matter, for we've been conditioned by a culture that separates age groups and values them differently, but we're always working at it. In the process we are creating the story of a different kind of women's community and we cannot afford to lose it as so much of women's story has been buried in the past, ignored by the pens that transcribed culture. We are choosing therefore to be our own scribes.

Contrary Mary Joins the Women's Circus

Patricia Sykes

On join-up day
Mary's voices play
cartwheel   the first says fun
the second says too tough
the loudest says you've grown
too old which is mostly why
she stays and joins

Mary waters her fifty years
until they send up
muscles for hand stands
balance for head stands
momentum for forward rolls
a passion for the tight rope
a repellent for the bugs of fear

outside the walls Old
Man History hoots and boos
for Mary is not young
Mary is not beautiful
Mary is no sexy sylph
in sequins and g-string
so he sends in his dogs
to yap at the heels of her stilts
and bite the rude flesh on her bones

Mary dances her bruises away
and waves her red flag
it flames like a torch
Old History burns at the gate
the circus women gather the ashes
Mary turns them into compost
and feeds it to her garden

SPIN-OFFS

The Women's Circus has been the catalyst for many women to "leap off the edge" into other realms of work, performance and place. Some women, as a direct result of their involvement with the circus, are now working full or part-time as lighting technicians, builders, directors, performers, musicians and art administrators. Others (photographers, artists, writers) have drawn on the circus to enrich their professions or studies. This section features some of those women whose lives have been changed and enriched by contact with the circus.

Poems From The Body

Patricia Sykes

I joined the circus a few weeks after my fiftieth birthday. I wanted the challenge, the fun, and the opportunity to work physically in a way I never had before. I wanted the opportunity to go over the top. And I wanted to work with a large group of diverse women who were likewise in tune with the philosophy and aims of the circus.

There were also the buts, the inherited voices: it would be too hard; my age was against me; I had no acrobatic or gymnastic background. Besides, I was overloaded already and, I lived too far away.

The negatives needled me on and off as I learned to stand on my head, my hands, other women's bodies, and as I wrestled with the tightrope – my chosen, special project. This last bequeathed me the bruise of my life on the final night of my first major performance. I was forced to play invalid while women raged and celebrated around me!

I expected the constant pinpricking from the negatives but I didn't expect that so many old emotions and issues would start leaking out as my body loosened and opened up. But there they were, a rather shocking and noisy pile of them. They started talking to me in poems, purple prose and all. I wrote them down, of course – a linguistic opportunist never allows words to slip by.

It wasn't until after a few months had gone by that I realised I was accumulating a lot of poems. I began to take them seriously, recognising they were important aspects of my circus story and my writing life.

The poems are increasing in number, gradually becoming a collection. Several have appeared in the *Women's Circus Newsletter*, one in *Oz Juggle*, some I've read on radio and at the International Feminist Book Fair held in Melbourne in 1994. For me, the most exciting and rewarding performances of the poems were the two Beijing fund-raising concerts at the Merlyn Theatre, the Malthouse, in 1995. As I performed the poems, three pairs of women went through double balance routines in silhouette behind me. Behind all of us was a huge white screen on which flashed a sequence of slides, showing women in action from all the major shows since the circus began in 1991. It was a case of the poems coming back home.

Walking the rope

Nicole Hunter

The Performing Older Women's Circus (POW)

Jean Taylor

The Performing Older Women's Circus (perhaps better known as POW Circus) started out as a six-week series of workshops, beginning in January 1995, to provide lesbians and heterosexual women over forty years of age with the opportunity to learn basic circus and musical skills within a supportive feminist environment. The subsequent hour-long performances for International Women's Day to showcase the not inconsiderable skills these thirty older women had gained over that time were a resounding success. These women were not only hanging from ropes, swinging on the trapeze, walking on stilts, achieving double and group balances and doing clown routine (among other skills), they had also formed a band to provide music for the entire show as well as managing the technical side of things, such as

Act your age: Jean Taylor, POW Director and Women's Circus member

Susan Hawthorne

Still revolting: POW Circus
members in full regalia for
the March 1996 performance

hanging all the lights and working the sound and lighting boards.

As the director, POW Circus has proved to be one of the most exhilarating projects I've ever been involved with and has far exceeded my expectations, as well as challenged a great many ageist assumptions about the physical capabilities of older women. We gratefully acknowledge the invaluable support of the Women's Circus as far as space and equipment are concerned.

POW Circus continues to have fun and work safely at our weekly workshops for both physical and musical training and has already performed smaller gigs for a variety of events as well as shows in March and November 1996.

Masks

Susan Hawthorne

Masks
of white and black
cover your desire
to hide
the extrovert

Act/Don't Act Your Age

Patricia Sykes

(for POW, the over 40 performing circus women)

For consider the old truth
that there's no fool like an old fool

For consider the older woman
is unwise to juggle objects not in focus

For consider that her balance is like thin ice
beneath an ageing tightrope

For consider that her body might forget itself
and aspire to trapeze or stilt

For consider that the crash mat
must be thicker to save her bones

For consider that somersaults and cartwheels
are smooth and easy convolutions for the young

For consider that an acrobatic crone
may not know when to stop

For consider her as tumbler
overturning where she wills

For consider once she's trained
she will suffer no restraint

For consider her as inspiration
how she'll lead her sisters on

For consider now her kitchen
how her pots and pans build pyramids just to win her notice

For consider her as clown
a trickster with a funny face and wildness in her heart

For consider her as mother sister lover friend
and consider how you speak of her

For she can leap upon your tongue

Beating the Negative Self-Talk

Andrea Ousley

Lunar swing: Andrea Ousley on the cloud swing, Moomba River Pageant, 1995

I taught the Footscray Fliers (a kids' circus group based at Footscray Community Arts Centre) in 1995 and really enjoyed developing that side of my training. What I find disturbing is how negative the children already are about themselves. They are so frightened of failure they won't take the initial risk. Their self-talk is already "I can't, I shouldn't, I couldn't". These children are between six and fourteen years old and already they have developed a sense of "I'm no good". The children come into the circus workshops with a well-ingrained sense of competitiveness: it's like "I'm no good unless I beat you". We work towards developing a good sense of self esteem, setting realistic goals, and allowing the children time out. For instance, it's okay to sit out of something if you can't focus/concentrate but it's not okay to stop someone else from having their go.

In the Women's Circus space they learn about having a go, about taking a chance. They love it. I'm very glad that I can take a philosophy of training/teaching that has helped me develop both physical and life skills to a wider community, and if you ever see the kids leaving the space after a workshop, laughing and smiling and talking about how much fun they had you'll see why I love it so much.

> The circus is my university
> Physically
> Emotionally
> I've learnt the science of a hand spring
> I'm learning the art of being with a huge group of people
> I'm learning that the woman sitting next to me has a
>   thousand things to teach me
> I'm learning to learn
> I've learnt to stick at it
> To try
> To believe in me
> To trust other people
> To stand on my head
> To move as myself

I've learnt that the pain will eventually stop
But most of all
To have fun
Self education
Women's Circus
Way to go

big show LITTLE SHOW clowning BRUISES sweat RESIN tiggey AERIALS handspring TUMBLING directing TRAINING set design MUSIC voice CLEANING WHEN IT FLOODS rigging MEETINGS . . . these are a few of my favourite things

Taking New Directions

Loreen Visser

After spending three years performing in the Women's Circus and being a star in my own head, I realised that that was exactly where I was leaving all this knowledge, skill, "show-offness" and energy. Initially I began directing a group of women that included circus and non-circus women and in 1993 a group of fourteen women and one man came together and formed an acrobatic troupe called the Juggonauts.

The troupe had stacks of energy and ambition but was looking for direction. I was asked to direct this handful of feisty, excitable and eager women and one man. I was very proud to have been asked, as these performers were my peers in the circus. They recognised qualities in me before I saw them myself.

When I began to direct the group I realised I had no idea what I had taken on. Everybody had an idea that they wanted included in their planned fifteen-minute show! But we got on with it. The troupe rehearsed and worked extremely hard and within six weeks had put together a very skilful performance. The show opened to a small audience in the Women's Circus warehouse at Footscray Community Arts Centre. Everybody loved it and plenty of feedback was given.

The show then toured the Adelaide Fringe Festival and was a

Vivienne Mehes

All fired up: Loreen Visser twirls a double-ended fire stick in the Work Show, 1992

huge success. I dressed up, lipstick and all, to inform the festival organisers that they had made a very bad error in forgetting to put the world-renowned Juggonauts on a stage. The Fringe organisers went out of their way and organised special times for this group to perform. The tour ended up being successful for festival organisers and performers alike. Juggonauts went on to win the most professional act in the Moomba Parade in 1994, and to perform on television.

This was becoming too much for me, so I was very excited when Donna Jackson announced that directors' workshops would be running during the 1994 circus year. I learned how to do budgets, how to get funding, what colours don't work in theatre, what works outdoors, how to handle conflict in a group, how to deal with media, how to organise the group, and many other skills. The workshops gave a new dimension to my understanding of theatre performance.

The major benefit I now see is that my imagination is limitless and, if I wish, I can create anything with the magic and illusion of theatre. But I will always remember it is simple hard work that creates a show. I believe a director needs to create the vision and follow it through to the end, having patience, understanding, courage, passion, commitment and a determined belief that the show will work. Ultimately, I believe a director needs a high level of humility, which can only be attained by the example of other directors and their work.

The Juggonauts: Relentless Energy, Passion and No Shame

Lynette Mackenzie

Juggernauts – n. anything to which a person blindly devotes herself or is cruelly sacrificed, any large, relentless, destructive force

The Juggonauts began rehearsals in 1993 in preparation for the Adelaide Fringe Festival. We made a motley crew of fifteen. Most of us had worked together in the Women's Circus. A fifteen minute street show was devised, featuring our fabulously

Naomi Herzog

Lynette Mackenzie

exotic circus skills accompanied by live music.

We were out to entertain and have a good time. The itinerary: a taster at the Midsumma Carnival; entree for a women's music night on arrival in Adelaide; main course at the Fringe Festival grounds and dessert down at the City Mall. The crowds were enthusiastic. It was a labour of love with just enough money made to keep us optimistic. The familiar Women's Circus "hutt!" was a feature – we're perfecting variations.

Since that beginning we have performed the Love and Jealousy show at a community centre in North Fitzroy to a crowded house, and have continued our availability for other gigs. Gigs have included performances at Equilibrium benefits, Scienceworks, CD launches, the opening of the Queer Film and Video Festival, a television appearance for last year's Royal Children's Hospital Good Friday Appeal. The list goes on.

Recently we have been hiring specialist trainers to increase our variety of skills. Shows are devised by workshopping different ideas. Roles are exchanged depending on our availability and interests. Each person chooses in a performance either to direct, play music, undertake technical activities, perform acrobatics or fire juggle or partake in any other activity required for the show. We finance our own shows and make our own costumes and sets.

You may find a Juggonaut on a stage in the evening, in a cinema foyer in the afternoon, at a school on a week day or in a shocking display in the small hours. The Juggonauts have relentless energy, a passion for the stage and no shame. At worst we've been shot at, nearly set off a cultural riot, and been credited as the Johnny Young Talent school's "special friends". At best: obscene amounts of money, fine food and drink, and lashings of lovely applause and attention. A Juggonaut may be found high in the air, stilting or trapezing, at eye level on fire and teasing or on ground level and downright sleazing. As the Juggonauts approach two years of age we trundle bravely into a new show, ready for the Melbourne Festival.

Get ready to be consumed by that large relentless force – the Juggonauts!

Images of Strength

Naomi Herzog

Naomi Herzog

At the beginning of 1993 I was just finishing my photographic studies when I joined the circus. For me, photography had been an art form explored through my mind. Circus was an expression through the body, an entirely new concept for me. As I grew stronger with the physical training and my co-ordination developed, as did my skills in working with other people, a change began to occur. My view of myself shifted and transformed. I felt stronger and more capable . . . more rounded.

Yet photography still remained a separate entity. A camera has a way of making you an observer rather than a participant, but then that too changed. At the end of our Sport show, a few of the women asked me to take some shots of them on the special trapeze rig that had been erected for the show. We did the shoot at dawn, with the women nude, using red lights against the backdrop of the dawn sky and the results were an amazing expression of strength and beauty. The camera reflected these women as sculptures of line and form. It was an intimate collaboration and the final images are an expression of that.

Some time after that, Donna asked me to take photos of the circus women as a record of the 1994 year. It seemed simple enough, but then the actual task of photographing 120 women became a documentary in itself. We are all uncomfortable in front of a camera, women especially so in our society of stereo-types. I wanted to show the integrity and elements of the circus as these were reflected in the depth, strength and individual beauty of each woman's face.

With a limited budget, I could only allow four or five frames per person. Each shot was set up in exactly the same way, lighting etc, so that the individual elements of each woman could emerge. The final project was exhibited at Death: The Musical our major show for that year, and the feedback was fantastic.

The project was an enormous challenge and gave me a chance to integrate my art with my circus work. After partici-pating in the director's workshops offered by Donna in 1994, we were offered the chance to direct a performance in the 1995 show Leaping the Wire and to work alongside Donna and

Meme McDonald. I have learned to visualise images through performance, to understand the importance of having a project overview, to develop a concept and take it to completion and perhaps most importantly to work in collaboration with humour and integrity.

Circus Art

Nicole Hunter

Once I felt surrounded by closed doors. There was a world out there, but I was in here. I stumbled across the circus almost accidentally and within months this shy person who had avoided physical exertion of all kinds found herself performing balances and bicycle tricks in front of 600 people. What was happening?

Naomi Herzog

Nicole Hunter

I realised that this was no accident. The workshops, though enormously challenging, were also playful and highly supportive. I wouldn't be letting the team down if I dropped the ball, and it didn't matter how many tries I had! Within the supportive and inspirational circus environment, I began to build strength, stamina and courage. I started to see that practice makes . . . well, better; that there wasn't a fixed gap between me and those who can. As my fears dissipated, I realised that the key to hitherto unimaginable horizons lay in strength, courage and effort. Perhaps most importantly, I began to see possibilities as infinite. Those doors had only been closed because I'd been too scared to open them!

More doors soon started to open for me. One day, I found my anonymous doodles published in the *Women's Circus Newsletter*. These were my first published drawings and I saw that they weren't that bad! I submitted more drawings and after much positive feedback, gained the confidence to draw for my local co-operative and the Wilderness Society. I was approached by the women working on this book to be the graphic artist. Work has been flowing in as fast as I can doodle it out.

I no longer perform with the circus, but I'm drawing every day and I remain physically active. My time there has changed my life. It taught me to step into my dreams. Whenever fear threatens to return, I remind myself that I'm safe, I'm strong and I can leap off that edge if I want to.

We all can!

We all can!

Nicole Hunter '95.

Making Music

Kylie Whyte

Naomi Herzog

Kylie Whyte

One of the major things the circus has done for me is to expand my ability and confidence in performing. When I joined the circus in May 1992, I signed up for both physical and music training workshops, and did both during the Women and Work show, our major performance for that year. I'd sprint from the stunt fighting scene over to the band, running underneath the audience on the tiered seating, trying to get my vinyl costume off without getting too much make-up on it! I realised I loved performing and I began to think my music could be central to my life rather than being just a hobby.

That year was the first time I had ever picked up a bass guitar, and it is now my main instrument. I also had the opportunity, as did everyone in the music group, to help compose the music for the show, and that opened up a lot of worlds for me. I began to see that composing was not as difficult as I had previously thought.

In 1993 I did the special voice and percussion workshops offered as part of the circus training programme, and in 1994 I began studying full time for the Advanced Certificate in Music Performance at Northern Metropolitan College of TAFE, Collingwood. My major study is bass guitar. My electives include singing, percussion, arranging, composition, improvisation, and big band. Currently, I'm a member of Swish Big Band, an eighteen-piece women's band. I also perform with other muso friends when the opportunity is there, and when there is time!

Next year, after my course is completed, I hope to apprentice myself to Marianne Permezel, the circus' musical trainer, and get some hands-on experience. I want to learn how she does what she does, how she is able to combine teaching, creating, and directing in such a skilled way. I've wanted to get into community music work for a while, combining my Bachelor of Social Work degree with my love of music and performance. As well as this work, I want to keep on playing and exploring music, wherever it takes me!

From Techie to Production Manager

Dori Dragon, freelance lighting technician and production manager

Nicole Hunter

When I left school I wanted to study drama at Rusden College but my parents said there was no money in it so I studied science instead. I loved acting but I wasn't very good at it and actually preferred being backstage and behind the scenes. I spent a lot of my time at university involved in the various amateur theatre groups on campus. Life in a laboratory didn't inspire me, however, so after leaving the university and doing several trashy jobs I ended up working in a women's refuge, which is where I first met Donna Jackson, who was one of my co-workers.

I was still working in a refuge when the Women's Circus was born. Donna suggested that I go along to a tech workshop, so I did. I spent the afternoon learning how to roll cables – not as simple as you may think! I must have enjoyed myself because I came back, and before I knew it I was operating a follow-spot in the first ever Women's Circus season. It was cold and wet and the techies all had to wear bright orange overalls. We had to set up all the lights and cables every afternoon and bring them all in again at night after the show. It was hard work but fun and the techies

Techie technique

worked together to become a supportive, efficient and competent crew. We all learned lots about lighting and each other.

Most of us came back for more the second year, along with many new women. It was much easier being inside a warehouse. I was one of three lighting board operators this time. My skills and interest in things technical was increasing and by the end of the season I had decided that I wanted to know more. I'd met several professional women theatre technicians through the circus; I expressed my interest and consequently got occasional work on shows with them. It was usually hard, tiring and dirty work, but I loved every minute. I enjoyed using my body, and physical exhaustion was a welcome relief to the emotional drain of my day job.

It was around this time that I woke up one morning and "saw the light!" After seven years as a refuge worker I needed a change so I quit my job and embarked upon a career as a freelance lighting technician. I set aside twelve months of being poor in order to learn as much as I could about the technical side of theatre and get my name known around Melbourne. I worked anywhere I could – paid or unpaid – and did several short courses in lighting and sound.

When the circus season came around again I was there, this time as sound crew co-ordinator, and also responsible for calling the light cues. From this point on – twelve months down the track as planned – my work really started to kick off. People seemed to like my work and I felt appreciated and respected as a technician. I started to be offered more regular and longer term work outside the circus.

I was the lighting designer for the fourth Women's Circus season. This was a challenge and quite stressful. It was also a paid position, which I found strange, given that I was working along-side many of the people I had started off with when I didn't even know how to rewire a plug! But the show looked great and I was happy with the result.

Since then, work opportunities continue to grow outside of the Women's Circus and I now work freelance in a wide variety of companies and venues. It's a challenging and rewarding career with an ever-changing array of people, places and equipment. It's hard work but I love doing it.

I owe much to the Women's Circus for being where I am today. Without the opportunities, support, training and encouragement it has provided me I would probably not be a technician/ production manager now. The circus has my eternal respect and support, and I hope it continues to grow, change and develop for many years to come.

Meeting Deadlines: From Performer to Arts Administrator

Mandy Grinblat

In 1991, I attended the first inspirational season of the Women's Circus. Like many other women I immediately rushed off to add my name to the waiting list to join the training workshops. It hardly seemed believable that I, too, could learn to roll and tumble and be a part of this remarkable group of women.

Mandy Grinblat

I spent the next few years juggling, balancing, tumbling, waving flags and building human pyramids. I performed in disused warehouses and on river barges. I was challenged and excited. The circus became an important part of my life. Through physical training I acquired greater confidence, more willingness to rise to challenges, and a stronger desire to achieve personal goals and dreams.

For a long time I had been interested in working in the arts industry. However, the opportunity never arose and I lacked the know-how and the confidence to make it happen. One of the remarkable things about the Women's Circus is that it provides opportunities for women to learn skills and to do things that they may not have had the chance to do before. So here, maybe, was my chance!

The circus ran on minimal administrative staff so when I offered to help out in the office on a voluntary basis my assistance was gratefully accepted. I'm not sure I fully appreciated the amount of work and energy that is expended in the administrative side of an arts organisation. It's hard work: unrelenting, stressful and not always very glamorous or exciting!

However, it is challenging and rewarding and my desire to

build a career in the arts is stronger than ever. I feel as though I have embarked on a long journey. The learning curve is sometimes very steep, the demands high and the deadlines always looming. But the circus is a wonderful place to extend fledgling wings. Support and encouragement are never far away. Every working day the circus presents a new challenge, some new task to tackle and also a sense of achievement that makes the hard work worth while.

I guess running away to join the circus to become an administrator disappoints many people's romantic notions of that myth. (I know! I can see it in their eyes when I tell them!) Somehow flying through the air on a trapeze or juggling fire seems much more exciting.

But for me administration is about facilitating the creative process and about helping administratively to do what it takes to realise the creative visions of the women in the circus. And when I watch these women perform I feel the same pride and joy that they feel in their performance, knowing that in my own way I have helped make it happen.

The Sky's The Limit

An interview with Cathy Johnstone

Louise Radcliffe-Smith

Cathy Johnstone, forty, was born in Sydney and studied social work at New South Wales University. After completing her studies, she spent sixteen months touring Europe, the Middle East and Greenland before returning to take up various social work positions in Sydney. Between drama and professional writing courses, she moved to Victoria and lived in a co-operative in Woodend, had a tractor accident, founded a small theatre group and had some poems and prose published in literary magazines and anthologies. She attended the John Bolton Theatre School in Melbourne in 1991, was assistant director for the Women's Circus in 1992 and simultaneously worked as a community arts worker with Coll-Link, an organisation in Collingwood. Between 1993 and 1995, Cathy studied film at Open Channel and Footscray TAFE. In 1994 she wrote and directed a short film called Migisook, a poetic montage based on the life of a woman she met in Greenland. The documentary was one of two Australian films selected for the Hawai'ian International Film Festival in November 1995, and was nominated for an Atom Award in 1996, for best tertiary student production in Australia. In 1996 she completed a graduate diploma in Film and Television at Victoria College of the Arts.

When I joined the Women's Circus I had no prior circus skills, but I had been interested in theatre for a long time. I can't remember not being confident or saying "I can't do it", but I probably did. I know that when we started, because we were the first group, the circus was very supportive, very encouraging. We were all in the same boat. I can remember being so excited about learning a new skill – to three-ball juggle or get up on the trapeze. Even though what I did in the first show was basic, there was a real sense of achievement. It is so hard to remember how you were back then, but then I look at the new women and wonder why they aren't confident and it makes me realise how far I've come.

Before I joined I didn't realise that I felt bad about my body. I think I used to be pretty unaware of how I felt physically. Imitating other people has made me more observant about my own body and the way it behaves. Being in the circus made me feel strong and proud of my body.

I also feel I don't have to do everything or be good at everything. I just choose what I want to do. I'm much more realistic now. I feel much easier about sitting out of workshops, saying to myself: "I don't want to do backflips, I'll just have a rest." Because my main interest is film and I'm not interested in being a circus performer, it's not all-important for me to learn everything. So I enjoy circus as a means of exercise and as a community experience.

I think circus has been good for me. It has taken me all this time to realise how to work to my limits, to challenge myself just enough that it's interesting and exciting and I'm learning something different, but not to challenge myself so much that it's impossible and I just

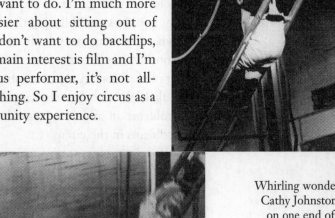

Vivienne Méhes

Whirling wonder: Cathy Johnstone on one end of a spinning ladder designed by Sally Forth and Rosie Finn for the Work Show, 1992

can't reach it. I think that learning has translated into other aspects of my life. The last film I made, I stretched myself enough so that it was still hard but it wasn't beyond me.

I think the thing about the circus that helped me get into film was seeing a lot of women doing physical stuff and being confident. I also felt empowered physically doing trapeze. And I think I felt I could take on something technical, whereas, when I was younger, I wouldn't have felt confident enough. I'm basically interested in writing and directing film, but to do that you really have to know a lot about the technical aspects of camera and lighting. You have to be confident about the technical aspects of film to direct well. So the circus made me see that, as a woman, I did not have to feel intimidated by men in the field. It just opened up potential. I had a sense that other women would support me.

I think the circus encourages women to make their own decisions in their career choices and to be independent. Also to make choices they may not have made before, whether artistic or technical or health orientated. I've seen a lot of people make changes.

I think the circus has a lot of potential to help anyone develop almost anything because it's such a big structure. There are so many areas the circus offers that you can learn from (like publicity, administration and so on). It was good for me to have the opportunity to learn more about assistant directing in 1992, to learn about the skills required to direct theatre, how Donna got her ideas and followed them through. That really went hand in hand with my community arts work, because I would get ideas from the way Donna worked and be able to implement them in a practical way in my own job as a community arts worker with Coll-Link, a community organisation in Collingwood. If I had problems in my job I could see how Donna solved similar problems in the circus.

I found assistant directing really hard, mainly because there was a lot to do and I was performing in the show as well. So I got a bit stressed out. And because it was really Donna's show, in the sense that she was directing, I didn't have the same control or the same leeway to make mistakes as you would if you were directing your own project. In your own project, if you make mistakes or something goes wrong, you take it on yourself. You don't worry about what someone else thinks, and it's easier. I guess I used to worry a lot about things instead of letting them go. It was good to have the opportunity to be the assistant director, but it was also good to do things for myself and make my own mistakes.

The circus is definitely changing. There's a different atmosphere. I know I felt very supported in the first year, even though it was very hard. Maybe that was because we had more support groups. Now, with Sally having gone and different trainers running different workshops, I don't get the same sense of continuity in the circus or the same awareness of the philosophical and political values from the new trainers. I don't feel the trainers have the same sense of commitment to the circus.

But I think it's good that people are now taking more responsibility, like Dori taking up production managment and Margo doing rigging. A lot of people have potential and are interested in learning skills for a career. FCAC does support the circus in a big way and being connected to a wider structure gives us a safety net. But I'm sure the circus has the potential to be independent. I'd be interested to see if things kept going as they are if Donna left, because she's been such a big influence.

The Women's Circus has become very well known in the Melbourne arts community. I saw an article recently about the Rock 'n' Roll Circus (a Brisbane-based group) and it mentioned Circus Oz in the same breath as the Women's Circus. Because we've been around for a few years and a lot of people have come to see the show and respect the quality of the circus performances, the changes in public perception have been quite significant. I've been to see other shows which seem to have been influenced by the Women's Circus, even if they haven't acknowledged it. I see a lot of the performers from Circus Oz and other circuses coming to our shows and I think they take a lot back with them. I also think the Women's Circus has learnt and taken a lot from them.

Our skill level has also increased. People in Melbourne are aware of that and I think they are impressed. I hear so many positive comments about the visual elements of the show, especially having so many women together in the same space so obviously enjoying themselves. I think there are probably some people who think of it as a community event and so downgrade it a bit. Maybe it's a kind of snobbishness that makes people who think of themselves as more mainstream look down on something like the Women's Circus.

Nicole Hunter

Taking a dive

I heard a friend of mine comment after the last show that she liked the freshness and openness of people from the community being up-front and enjoying themselves. And she said there didn't seem to be as much of that in the 1994 show, Death: The Musical, that it seemed to have too much of a professional edge and people were getting too much into acting. She thought that the big tableau worked better. But then, I heard many more comments from people who liked the theatrical elements within the last show and who thought they added greater depth.

I have a friend who was really moved by that show. She had tears in her eyes as she spoke to me about seeing all these women of various shapes and sizes looking as though they were so empowered by what they had done and shown and achieved. Even though she does not want to join the circus, she is able to participate as an audience member and gain a sense of empowerment herself.

I think the circus is political because it empowers women in a practical way. It helps women be stronger in themselves and more in control of themselves, to feel like they can do more with their bodies and can be strong and can achieve goals that initially they thought were really hard. I see women in the new group who say: "I can't do it, I can't do it", without even trying. And you see how many women and young girls in society also have that attitude.

The themes of the circus are often political, too, and I like the way the messages are put across in a subtle rather than a didactic way. The circus isn't trying to be moralistic and say this is the way you ought to think. We try to be sound in our message and ideals and make a general political point in a way that is entertaining. I know Donna used to say she wanted the circus to play to her Aunty Joyce, so she was always aiming for a universal audience. I think the circus is accessible to a lot of people of all ages, both men and women. People are attracted to a theme, as well as to what they are seeing.

Spiral stares: Karen Martin (top) and Georgie Stewart entertain audience members as they wander through the pre-performance industrial alleyways of the 1992 Women and Work Show.

Photo: Vivienne Méhes

Just hanging around: Women and Work Show, 1992.

Making up: Jan Crowe and Judy Crowe don the signature white facepaint and bathing cap in the 1991 Women and Institutions Show.

Photo: *Vivienne Méhes*

The mirror has many faces: Sharee Grinter shows her taste for razor blades.

Photo: Vivienne Méhes

Light as air: Christina Branton in the 1992 Women and Work Show.

Picture of concentration: Thirteen-year-old Melissa Lewis carries the flag for the 1992 Women and Work Show.

Photo: Vivienne Méhes

Having a ball: 1993 Women and Sport Show.

Photo: Vivienne Méhes

Can they see us from the moon? Women from the 1995 Leaping the Wire Show
check out the Great Wall of China.

Photo: Vivienne Méhes

III
The Women's Circus at Work

ROPES 2

upside down you're
a circus gypsy   a wanderer
on a rope who swings
and sings to herself knowing
that an upturned world
makes the proper sense

– Patricia Sykes

Relentless referees: Getting in character for the 1993 Sport Show

THE WHOLE WOMAN: TRAINING

Learning to Leap Off the Edge

Jen Jordan

The extraordinary range of activities, productions and projects undertaken by the Women's Circus between 1991 and 1995 grew out of the philosophy, organisation and training practices established by Donna Jackson and Sally Forth. Part of this philosophy was (and still is) to address the obstacles that prevent victims/survivors of sexual assault and domestic violence from being seen and heard. The original project was ground-breaking in enabling victims/survivors of sexual assault and domestic violence to have a presence and a voice in the community.

In the context of the climate of social denial surrounding widespread physical and sexual assault, oppression and harassment, the founding philosophy, practices and wisdom of the Women's Circus have significance for women more generally. The effects of negative and exploitative attitudes towards the female body and female power are not confined to survivors of domestic violence.

The initial training program combined an empowering and holistic approach to health, fitness and wellbeing, together with numerous opportunities to learn a myriad exciting and enjoyable new skills in a co-operative and safe social and physical environment.

The circus training programme worked to restore the interconnectedness of body, mind, heart and spirit, and thus the integrity and agency of the self. Moreover, it created opportunities to restore broken connections and build relationships between women and their community.

Throughout the life of the Women's Circus, the physical performance, musical, technical, administrative and other training programmes have expanded, diversified and specialised in

Vivienne Méhes

Risky business: Jen Jordan,
Work Show, 1992

response to the changing needs of its members. These programmes have transcended barriers of ability, age, class, ethnicity, sexual orientation and other difference.

Today, the founding philosophy and practices of the circus continue to be reflected in the many ways circus women work together and support each other in a huge variety of learning situations.

Nuts and Bolts

Training sessions last two hours and cover a broad range of skills. Most years there are general, acrobatic, beginners aerials, advanced aerials, manipulation, music and technical workshops. From time to time the circus holds one-off or short intensive courses in areas such as dance, fire or clowning. There are day-time, weekend and evening sessions to cater for all women. Most members attend one or two workshops a week. Some attend up to six. Fees vary according to women's ability to pay and the number of workshops they attend.

Introducing Sally Forth

Naomi Herzog

Sally Forth

The Women's Circus was extremely fortunate to have Sally Forth as its first and longest serving trainer. Sally's extensive and eclectic knowledge, skills and professional experience have significantly contributed to the success of the circus.

For the first three years she acted as trainer extraordinaire, taking workshops in everything from aerials and acrobatics to stick manipulation, juggling, health and yoga.

Her work as a performer with the Australian Dance Theatre and Circus Oz and as trainer and director of Brisbane's Rock 'n' Roll Circus equipped her to train women in a wide variety of circus activities to advanced levels of skill.

Her training programmes promoted physical excellence without compromising physical wellbeing and were an invaluable foundation for the Women's Circus. Informed by her considerable knowledge and understanding of Chinese healing traditions, Sally's holistic approach to mental, emotional and spiritual, as well as physical health, has been an ongoing source of inspiration, strength and energy for many circus women. Her life-enriching ideas and creative training practices have proved to be a valuable legacy.

Relaxation by massage

Mind, Body and Spirit

Sally Forth

In 1991, I started off with the idea that I was training serious circus artists towards performance of specialist acts. I wanted to challenge the general assumption that women who have never done any physical training have no potential to achieve in the physical arena and are only there "for fun". More or less all the women involved came with a serious desire to achieve their dream in their chosen field and their enthusiasm, dedication and application reinforced my original approach.

I was also under no illusion that people miraculously become trapeze artists, especially ones who had no previous physical experience, and I knew certain modifications would have to be made to encompass different ages and physical abilities. Along-side this solo act consideration was the general fitness/health aspect of the whole group, which is the other side of circus training. This was developed in group situations where the emphasis was upon raising aerobic ability, strengthening the physical structure and improving flexibility.

I had been interested for years in developing high-level and/or extreme physicality without compromising or injuring the body through overuse or other stresses (as seems to be acceptable or even expected when people approach physical excellence and adeptness in any area). Disciplines such as yoga and karate instil high physical expectations (without physical breakdown) at all ages. For instance, backbends and headstands are performed not for presentation but because it is good for the circulation when you're seventy. I was happy to incorporate this idea into my life as I wanted to maintain a high level of physical fitness upon retiring from professional performance. I was glad to find more in a backbend than I had realised.

Through these experiences and understandings I developed a training method which was demanding for all ages and expected a high standard of physical commitment. This challenge was eagerly accepted by the women and, although many details have changed within the training, the basic premise remains to fulfil the dream – to become a circus artist, to improve health and vitality, to develop a group identity and strength to empower all women, to broaden understanding and tolerance among people.

The workshops always started with a group warm-up which included stretching, strengthening and orientation. These warm-ups drew on classical ballet exercises, yoga poses, Chinese acrobat basic training, modern dance technique, gymnastic philosophy, corrective exercise and partner and group work.

At all times, the major emphasis with any of these warm-ups was the concentration on the self and the involvement of the mind and the spirit in the exercise. This was usually achieved through concentration on the breath, which helped the individual gain fundamental control of the self. It was important for me to train the mind, body and spirit to work as a whole. The separation of, say, the body, ignoring any emotional involvement, leads to abuse of the body through a lack of knowing what the body is feeling – is it in pain, for instance? An extreme of this separation and lack of feeling can be seen in the eating disorders of ballerinas or sporting stress fractures and injuries. I always emphasised the feelings and pressures expected with each exercise and encouraged people to listen within themselves for indications of overuse or over-stretch.

I wanted to teach the women to incorporate health into their training, to encourage them to be aware of the effects of the exercises on the body and mind. The exercise might be chin-ups, but they knew it was going to strengthen the fundamental centre of their spirit. When people put their heart into their work, they bring more dedication and creativity to the exercise and achieve greater potential and satisfaction. Progress is swift and easy.

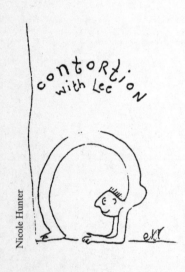

contortion with lee

Nicole Hunter

Training also involved working in pairs to help with stretching or balancing. This meant becoming sensitive to other people, to their balance, support and trust; to lifting and supporting or balancing and being supported. Many people found this close physical contact confronting and I learnt many things from the difficulties that arose. At first I was frustrated by women's reactions to physical exercises. I had to learn to respect women's feelings, realising they were not lazy but were dealing with a lifetime of negative experiences. It reinforced my belief that emotional reactions to physical exercises reveal the close connection between the spirit, mind and body. I am grateful for the perseverance of the women who overcame difficulties and who found new strength and confidence and playfulness. The double balance work is one of the strengths of all the circus performances and friendships have developed while mastering a difficult balance.

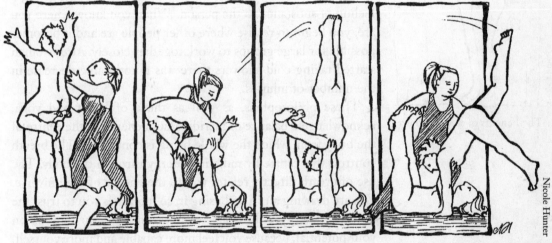

Nicole Hunter

Double balances: Sitting on feet, bending back to candlestick and over

While double balances might reflect one-to-one relationships, the group balances reflect a broader cross-section of society for me. Groups of eight to ten or more are needed to create a whole and we all have found it frustrating and satisfying to go through the many links and relationships within a large pyramid. We love them because they reflect for us the political philosophy of the circus: that together we can do more than on our own. Supporting, balancing and harmonising. No competition, no judgement, and strong backs, arms and thighs. Commitment to something beyond the "me".

It was very important to maintain a feeling of personal safety for everyone within the workshops. Circus can be dangerous. Once, in the early stages of the circus, we were trying a particularly hard balance and a lot of people either got jumped on or hurt in minor ways. This showed the difficulty of close work and the lack of understanding of personal space. So I introduced cold showers for all participants!

Cold showers bring up the idea of auras, meridian energy and chakras. In Chinese philosophy, the meridians are major lines of energy running through the body. When the meridians are in balance, the body can do anything. Chakras (as the energy centres are called in yogic philosophy) are comparable to the meridians of Chinese philosophy. When I train women in circus skills I am training them in the use of their sources of energy, as well as in the use of their muscles. Spiritual body and physical body working in harmony create a healthy aura. Cold showers strengthen the aura and therefore the internal energy, giving a feeling of substance to the person. When you know where you are, you begin to realise where other people are and it becomes possible for large groups to work together closely. After women started taking cold showers there was a noticeable decrease in the number of injuries.

These philosophies, as well as those of ballet and yoga, acknowledge a balance of meridian/aura energy in the centre of the body from which the whole being is controlled. The breath controls this centre by radiating energy through the body. The use of breath directly relates you to the energy of the universe. You are drawing air in and using it, so it teaches you to trust the universal energy. It broadens your vision and your outlook on your potential, because you feel more capable and more yourself. This is very important when you are training physically because you can lose yourself in the body. Integrating spiritual and mental elements into training the body deepens women's understanding of their own bodies and selves. And, in the long run, it leads to great stamina, strength and control.

The two areas of aura and breath control differentiated early Women's Circus training from other more specific programmes and were the main reasons the participants achieved high degrees of skill in many areas in relatively short periods of time. Also included in the training programme was advice on diet to strengthen the bones/muscles, improve flexibility and general

Nicole Hunter

The benefits of a cold shower

stamina. I advised women to eliminate sugar as much as possible and substitute rice malt or barley malt – sugar destroys the minerals in the body, thereby weakening the blood, muscles and bones. This was a further intrusion into the women's lives (cold showers were just the start!) and I was hesitant at first to suggest things. But the minute I suggested one dietary thing I was enlisted to take a series of lectures on food/balance and training. Saturday breakfasts became a big hit. Gruel was popular and this developed further to crews cooking food before the end-of-year performance so no one had to rush to eat before the show – everyone arrived and was fed. Food for work. This established a nice atmosphere before the performance.

By 1994, I had trained a number of assistants who could follow up my theories. I realised the need for specialist trainers and organised myself to be redundant. I am now pursuing further Shiatsu/Zen philosophies to reassess my direction and notating a cookbook for use by the Women's Circus and the world. To maintain a link with the circus, I now run weekend workshops, retreats and put in creative ideas. I find it satisfying to see improvised or devised acts which have evolved from the training enable women to express lots of different ideas and give a great deal of satisfaction to the women participating as well as the audiences.

Game of Balance

Patricia Sykes

The game does not come
in a box   it has no instructions
each woman has to make
her own rules for the tight rope
we play with it   decide
that falling is the first victory
we do it well   but our feet
are not the trip wires
it's our eyes   they can't believe
the point of balance is magnetic

so we rehearse our first crossing
upside down   our backs on the ground
it's the best position for laughing
which is what we do   laugh
like clowns   a mad and hungry laughter
that hides a third eye
out to prove that the ends
are tied in a game of balance

Four Seasons Recipes

Sally Forth

The way food is prepared and eaten is as important as the food
itself. It is good to wash all food before preparation. This
removes poisons and dirt. Thinking good thoughts is another
good way to provide nourishment. The food is fulfilling your
needs and therefore providing a service. Waste is unnecessary
and shows a lack of respect. You should cut food downwards and
away from the body. Hacking or other treatment creates
conflict. Each food has its own energy and input. Wash the knife
and board between each food item to prevent an amalgamation
of energy and taste before further preparation.

Gas is the best fuel for cooking, followed by electricity.
Microwaves oscillate the molecules at 800 000 units per second,
which changes the life force in the food dramatically and leads
to a dissipation and a lack of solidity. Lightly cooked foods and
salads are more appropriate for summer, baking is better in
winter. Avoid using aluminium saucepans because aluminium
leaches into the food as it is cooked. Stainless steel, clay and
enamel are preferable.

You should sit down to eat and allow enough time. Cramming
food while trying to make a point in conversation is not a good
idea. Chew each mouthful at least thirty-two times. Chewing
slows down eating and conversation but leads to a quieter mind.
You should want to eat the food because it is supporting your
life. Don't use food to punish yourself. Feeling bad eating cake is
worse than feeling good eating cake. If you want it, enjoy it.

Try to look at food from a broad perspective – where it is from, who grew it, what it is. Try to eat more locally produced whole, unsprayed, unprocessed food. Avoid additives, flavourings and processing because they lead to anaemia and malnutrition. Eating whole foods eliminates the need to count calories or use vitamin or mineral supplements. Look at your food intake and gain control over your body by reading labels on packaging and buying organic wherever possible.

Health exists if you:

- are never tired
- have a good appetite
- sleep well
- have a good memory
- are never angry
- are joyous and alive
- have endless appreciation of life.

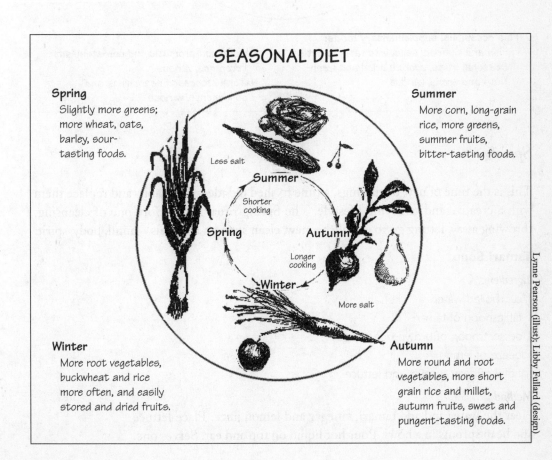

SEASONAL DIET

Spring
Slightly more greens; more wheat, oats, barley, sour-tasting foods.

Summer
More corn, long-grain rice, more greens, summer fruits, bitter-tasting foods.

Less salt

Summer

Shorter cooking

Spring

Autumn

Longer cooking

Winter

More salt

Winter
More root vegetables, buckwheat and rice more often, and easily stored and dried fruits.

Autumn
More round and root vegetables, more short grain rice and millet, autumn fruits, sweet and pungent-tasting foods.

Lynne Pearson (illust); Libby Fullard (design)

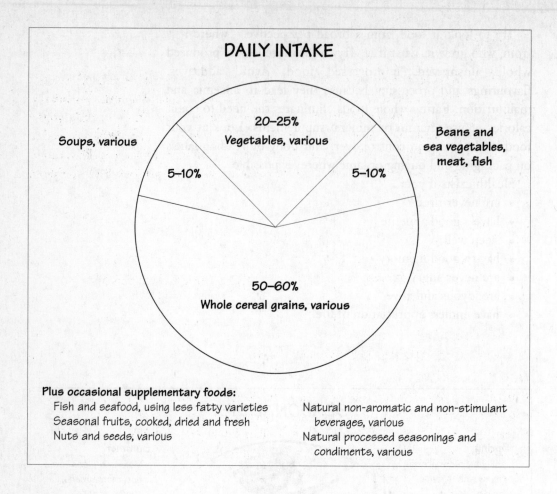

DAILY INTAKE

Soups, various

20–25%
Vegetables, various

Beans and
sea vegetables,
meat, fish

5–10%

5–10%

50–60%
Whole cereal grains, various

Plus occasional supplementary foods:
Fish and seafood, using less fatty varieties
Seasonal fruits, cooked, dried and fresh
Nuts and seeds, various

Natural non-aromatic and non-stimulant
beverages, various
Natural processed seasonings and
condiments, various

Spring

This is the time of new beginnings, a time to shed old ideas and habits and replace them with a creative and satisfying lifestyle. The Spring ritual is therefore one of cleansing, throwing away, letting go to establish a new, clean state on all levels – mind, body, spirit.

Tamari Soup

Ingredients
1 cup boiled water
1 tablespoon of tamari
1 dessertspoon of brown rice vinegar
squeeze of lemon
handful of bean sprouts and lettuce

Method
Heat the water and add tamari, vinegar and lemon juice. Place lettuce
and bean sprouts in a bowl. Pour hot liquid on top and eat. Serves one.

Summer

Summer is the time to feel energy rising. Favour bitter foods to feed the heart (bok choi, watercress, spinach, miso, long grain rice). All green leafy vegetables have this quality. Seasonal summer salad greens (like endive) are excellent and very bitter – a little goes a long way. For a seasonally balanced summer diet, you could also include dandelion coffee (as a good summer tonic), roasted nuts and seeds, and fruit (bitter and sweet). Bitter food eases bitterness and softens the heart centre to enable real emotions to settle and develop.

Pumpkin Pie

Ingredients
Pastry
2 cups wholemeal flour
(Flour that is toxic or old tastes bitter. Buy freshly ground flour wherever possible)
Pinch sea salt
½ cup sesame seeds
1 cup hot bancha tea or water
2 tablespoons cold pressed oil (safflower or sunflower).

Method
Combine 1½ cups of flour, salt and sesame seeds in bowl. Add oil and rub into mixture. Slowly add bancha until pastry becomes smooth. Knead to a roll shape, adding remaining ½ cup flour. Roll into tin. Cook pastry for 15 minutes at 180°C before adding filling.

Filling
2 cups cooked pumpkin
1 cup tofu cut into cubes
1 cup sliced onion
oil for stir-frying (preferably cold pressed safflower)
pinch sea salt
tamari to taste.

Method
Heat pan, add oil and saute onion with salt until transparent. Add tofu and pumpkin and continue to stir-fry. Add tamari to taste. Salt should be added with onions to prevent them from burning and bring out their sweetness.

Fill pastry with mixture, put layer of pastry on top and bake at 160°C for 40–60 minutes or until pastry becomes golden brown.

Autumn

Autumn is all about letting go. When autumn arrives, it's time to release the expansive summer energies in preparation for the contractive energies of winter. Fighting the change in seasons can lead to sadness from trying to maintain over-control, while going with the flow can be highly fulfilling. Strong essences – ginger, garlic, rosemary, pickles – are needed to build blood towards winter.

Risotto
Some people say risotto can only be made with Italian arborio rice – a white, round, absorbent variety. Round brown rice does work, although I do sometimes revert to Italian rice for authenticity. This is a useful and different way of serving grain.

Ingredients
2 cups raw rice
1 small glass oil
1 onion
2 cloves garlic
200 grams mushrooms
1 cup fresh peas or green beans (optional)
4 cups hot vegetable stock
fresh parsley or oregano

Method
Fry onion until transparent and add garlic and mushrooms. Stir until wilted. Add rice and fry in oil – the rice will begin to absorb the oil and this gives a wonderful flavour. Add a pinch of salt. Gradually add half the vegetable stock. Stir and allow liquid to evaporate for 10 minutes. Stir a little but do not break up grains. Add peas or beans if using. Continue adding stock until rice is cooked. Grains should remain separate. Stir in a handful of fresh parsley or oregano and serve immediately. The risotto should be creamy and homogenous but not reduced to porridge. Any combination of vegetables can be used. The oil is what adds an interesting difference and richness. Fresh oregano adds to the Italian flavour.

Winter

Winter is a time of storage and nurturing, a time to go inside oneself and take stock. In winter, eat warm, long-cooked, nutritional foods which replenish, restore and build up the body's energy in time for spring. Minerals maintain the spine and nervous system. Use sea salt, miso, tamari, vegetables and grains.

Rice with steamed vegetables

Using the last 5–10 minutes of rice cooking time, place sliced vegetables on top of grain and steam until grain is ready. Root vegetables take about 10 minutes if sliced thinly: zucchini, broccoli and cauliflower about 8 minutes, and most greens need 5 minutes at most. This is an excellent way to avoid many pots and utilise available energy. Vegetables can be lifted off grain to be served separately.

All Year Round

Miso Soup

This soup provides a balanced supply of all minerals. It aids digestion and is good before or after a hard day's work. Miso can be used as an instant soup stock instead of stock cubes which contain additives and colouring. Always buy unpasteurised miso, preferably from a bulk container. Do not buy miso in plastic bags and don't store it in the fridge. Miso is a live culture and refrigeration kills it.

Ingredients
brown rice miso, 1 tablespoon per person
water (1 cup per person)
pinch of salt
Root vegetable (i.e. carrot)
Green leafy vegetable
Bean sprouts or other garnish
Arame seaweed, washed not soaked, 1 tablespoon per person (optional)

Method
In a pot of water place cut vegetables, salt and seaweed. Cook for 15 minutes. Dissolve the miso in a small amount of stock, add it to the soup and simmer for 2 minutes. Serve with sprouts as garnish. Can be served with pre-cooked grains. Simply put some cooked grains (barley, rice) in a bowl and add soup to heat.

This soup can be eaten all year round with seasonal vegetables. Barley is a good winter grain to use with this recipe and depending on the amount of water used this can become a stew with the grains cooked in it.

Sesame Salt Gomasio

This is a blood strengthener and tonic, ideal for alleviating stress and lack of energy, and for promoting vitality and general well-being.

Ingredients

14 teaspoons unhulled organic sesame seeds
(This means they are not sprayed by DDT or bleached with chlorine)
1 teaspoon good quality sea salt from health food shop (light grey and slightly damp)

Method

Wash seeds in a fine sieve, place them into a frying pan and heat. Slowly turn seeds until they are brown all over and begin to pop. Transfer to mortar and pestle. Put salt in frying pan and heat quickly until salt is golden and dry. Add to sesame seeds. Grind until four-fifths of the seeds are crushed. Use as garnish on anything: toast, noodles, vegetables (as a parmesan substitute), or eat by the teaspoonful when tired. Chew 100 times! Store in a sealed jar out of refrigerator. Keeps for one week only. Discard if unused, as the oil in the seeds becomes rancid and is very bad for you.

Ginger Compress

Ginger warms the body and disperses energy. A ginger compress improves circulation, eases muscular soreness, stiffness and strain, and reduces inflammation.

Method

Grate 100–150 grams of ginger root, tie it in fine fabric, and simmer (not boil) in a pot of water until water turns yellow (about 30 seconds to 1 minute). Soak a flannel in the ginger water, wring out and place on sore area. Cover with a dry towel to hold in the heat. Make the compress as hot as you can bear and change when cool. Repeat 5–6 times. Don't apply to the head and neck, or to cuts or broken bones. Avoid using on small babies and people over seventy.

Four Seasons Exercises

Sally Forth

These exercises are auric exercises rather than physical, and all of them are good for any age.

Autumn

Stand with toes turned in, feet wider than hip width apart. Interlock fingers behind and hold palms together when bending over. Move hands to floor over head. Take five deep breaths. Return to standing.

Sit with one leg bent and other straight ahead. Keep your back straight. Inhale and stretch forward trying to reach toes. Hold breath for as long as possible. Exhale and return to sitting.

Winter

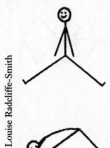

Sit in straddle. Reach both hands from foot to foot. Exhale and stretch to foot. Inhale and return to centre. Keep back straight. Repeat ten times.

Place legs together and flex muscles. Exhale and reach towards toes, keeping back straight and chin tucked in. Inhale and return to start. Repeat five times.

Louise Radcliffe-Smith

Nicole Hunter

Spring

Sit in straddle. Exhale and stretch forward with straight back. Elbows back. Repeat five times.

Lie on back, exhale and cross leg over body. Place closest hand on knee to pull knee to floor. Keep shoulders on the floor. Look in opposite direction with other arm stretching along floor. Inhale and return to start. Repeat five times for each side.

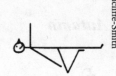

Summer

Sit on ground. Clench thumbs into fists and place in armpits. Pull elbows back. Inhale. Exhale and lean over keeping back straight. Inhale and return to start. Repeat five times.

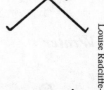

Lie down on back. Place palms of hands on belly button. Only sit up if it is easy. If you feel any pain in your back do not try to sit up; just raise head and shoulders off floor. Repeat five times.

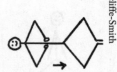

General exercises, all year

If you can, do a backbend. Exhale. Push up. Five deep breaths in position. Inhale and return to start. Repeat five times.

OR

Lie on back with knees bent and feet hip width apart. Stretch arms beside ears on floor. Exhale and lift hips. Inhale and hold. Exhale and close knees. Inhale and open knees. Repeat five times while maintaining the lift through the hips.

Kneel on ground and lower your bottom down between your feet while rolling calves out with your hands.

   Lie back slowly, keeping hips to floor. Try to place lower back on the ground. Hold and take five breaths.

OR

If this is too difficult, lean back on arms and hold knees together while tucking buttocks under.

PASSING ON KNOWLEDGE: THE TRAINERS

The training programmes of the circus have grown each year to meet the needs and aspirations of women of different abilities, ages and backgrounds. Many teachers have built upon the solid foundations of the first year's training programs set in place by director Donna Jackson, trainer Sally Forth, musical director Sue Speer and technical directors Liz Pain and Georgine Clarsen.

While the greatest proportion of circus women are involved in the physical performing skills programme, equally vital to the circus are the musical, technical and administrative training programmes.

Over the years, many talented and committed trainers have generously shared their particular creative skills and professional knowledge with the circus. Their enthusiasm and expertise has enhanced both the enjoyment of learning, and the achievement of the high aims and standards of the circus.

Letting the Individual Shine

Lee Mohtaji, circus trainer

Naomi Herzog

Lee Mohtaji

I have been either working with or teaching circus since I was ten years old. I joined Nanjing Acrobatic Troupe in 1970. For the next five years I learnt various circus skills including acrobatics, juggling, sticks, diablo, tightrope, balances, bike, plate spinning and devil sticks.

Every day my training used to start at 6.00 a.m. and continued right through to the evening. This went on for five years. During this period I only saw my family once a fortnight. In China, the employer has to feed and provide living quarters for its employees. I lived and worked at the Nanjing Acrobatic Troupe from 1970 until the end of 1992 when I came to Australia.

I went through a very restrictive and hard training programme. I could not stop training when I felt like it. For example, for plate spinning I had many practice sessions per day where every session was at least half an hour without stopping, with as many as three plates in each hand, and my arms stretched right out. No matter how painful it was, I could not stop. If I stopped to rest, I was forced to start another half an hour. Often we used thick, heavy steel plates and after a few practice sessions there were holes in the plates because of spinning. This way of training was normal practice for almost every skill. I remember days when I had to stand for hours or I was hung by the back of my neck. One such time the rope around my neck slipped and I passed out and required hospitalisation for almost two weeks. In fact, I was lucky because if one of my colleagues had not seen me when he did I would not be here to write this.

Teaching in the Women's Circus is very different to teaching in China. In China it was my profession and part of my everyday life. Sometimes I used to start at dawn and work right through to the evening. This was every day of the week for a year. This was particularly the case when my students were going for competitions.

In the Women's Circus it is more like a hobby. Students come when they can make it, and only for a couple of hours a week. Here the age group is mixed, where in China my students were very young. In terms of skills taught, in China each student concentrates on one or two particular skills until she or he masters that skill. They learn other skills as well, but there will be one or two that each student will be very good at.

I have been involved in teaching western circus schools for quite some time. When I was in China we used to get students from all over the world, especially Australia. Therefore I am aware of different customs and approaches to teaching circus skills. Since I came to live in Australia I have been teaching in a number of different schools with students coming from various backgrounds. I have been able to adjust my teaching skills to suit the particular individual student. For example, with the Women's Circus, I treat every student individually, and usually I let them choose the skill and the pace they like to work with. I try to push them just that little bit extra by support and encouragement but I don't push them as hard as I was pushing my students in China.

I have to keep reminding myself that this is not China. This is not their life, their profession, so I don't push too hard. I have

Sometimes I need only a little reassurance, a little "well done" quietly but sincerely delivered.

– Michele Bottroff 1993

learnt to adjust my expectations of the time spent by students on each skill. The other issue which makes my job difficult is lack of time. I understand the circus is a hobby for many women but I am used to trying every skill for hours and hours until I am very good at it. However, if a student shows some potential and I feel with a little push she can do better and more, I try to encourage and push her gently. But I let her decide when she wants to stop or try harder. Basically, I try to work together with each student rather than having a teacher-student relationship.

I enjoy being involved in and teaching circus skills, particularly with the Women's Circus. I have found the atmosphere easy, friendly and relaxed where all participants get an equal chance to learn, enjoy and grow. The group is very helpful and supportive of each other. There is no forced expectation to perform or compete and you are allowed to feel good about yourself. I enjoy seeing all this and being part of it.

Juggling with Rhythm and Soul

Kymberlyn Olsen (aka Kim Kaos), *manipulation specialist*

Naomi Herzog

No chaos: Kim Kaos lassos herself

It is difficult to believe that I have been juggling for over twenty-one years now. I learned from a friend to juggle three balls, which at the time was a very exciting accomplishment. As a child I had been very shy, "bookish" and hopeless at sport so this new-found ability was very liberating and challenged my perception of myself as being clumsy.

Keen to share this excitement, I taught juggling to anyone who was interested. It was while teaching informally as part of Colourscape in London that I was approached by RADA to teach drama students. That was the springboard for other formal teaching positions and fired my own research into juggling-related variety and manipulation skills. I began working with clubs, lasso, diablo, devil sticks, hats, fans, cigar boxes and parasols.

About this time Covent Garden in London began to be a viable street-performing venue – well, at least one where you could perform without being arrested! I was asked to do something for an International Women's Day event. Even though I didn't have a "show" as such, I took the plunge and took to the streets. Street performing was good to me and, surprisingly, it was quite a good employment option for a single mum.

From there I was asked to join Circus Burlesque, a no-animal circus with which I toured England. I developed a new character in the circus, "Kim Kaos", and when the tour finished I took my new character and show on tour around Europe and the USA.

My first trip to Australia was based on an impulsive need to escape yet another northern winter. By chance I was asked to perform at Le Joke. From there I went to teach juggling, clowning and tightwire at The Flying Fruit Fly Circus. Performing called me back and soon I was combining skills with stand-up in the Melbourne, Sydney and Brisbane comedy circuits.

About this time I first met Donna. When Donna mentioned the idea of a women's circus I was very excited and hoped to get involved when I returned from a six-week trip to Europe. But six weeks turned into eighteen months when I won "Most Original Act" at the Greenwich Festival and did a tour of Germany.

But I did get back and I did get involved. It was incredible to see just how much had been accomplished in terms of skills, performance and group dynamic. Teaching at the Women's Circus has been one of the most rewarding teaching experiences of my life. Having mostly worked solo and occasionally in small groups (Bizircus, The Late Developers, Fshhh) it was very exciting to be putting together routines with large groups of women. It is also great to see how everyone helps each other to learn new moves and routines.

Manipulation skills can be quite difficult in that a lot of work has to be put in before a skill is ready for performance and even then there is always a chance that something might drop. It was quite challenging to design and choreograph pieces that could incorporate everyone's skill level, and to structure a dynamic piece. Ultimately I believe that the success of these pieces came about as a result of the trust the women placed in my vision and their willingness to attempt the unknown.

One spin-off from my work with the Women's Circus has become a current obsession. Putting together manipulation routines with a large group presented problems of notation. After researching a number of dance notation programs I have found one that can be modified to include objects (only swinging torches and staff so far). I hope that this will help both the development of routines and teaching the individual parts.

Not only the members of the circus but a trainer as well can experience growth and change in unexpected ways through working with this fantastic group.

Juggle Art

Patricia Sykes

Juggle art does not name
it   cannot contain all
the meanings of your hands
flashing from ball to ball
air in between moving
the dance of hands dancing
and the balls like lovers
trusting your palms   coming
back each time saying yes
I will yes though you never held
like this before never held
so light so warm so tough held
so that they had to come
back   had to   up down
again again impossible times
and it's you you only   not afraid
to drop one two three
five even balls rolling at
your feet   waiting to be
picked up thrown high   laughing
laughing all the way down
because it's you up there   you
and the balls dancing   you
tossed held   in your own hands

How to Make Juggling Balls

Louise Radcliffe-Smith

Buy or find:
- A packet of 10 balloons, various colours
- Dry millet, rice, barley or dirt
- A plastic funnel or a piece of stiff paper or cardboard

Instructions
- Place the end of the funnel in the neck of the first balloon.
- Pour millet (or other material) through the funnel into the balloon until the balloon is larger than a golf ball but smaller than a tennis ball and fits comfortably in your hand.

- Twist the end of the balloon so the millet doesn't come out.

- Get another balloon and cut the neck off.
- Stretch open the neck of the truncated balloon and slip it over the balloon full of millet.

- Repeat the process with a third balloon.
- Start again and make another two juggling balls of different colours.

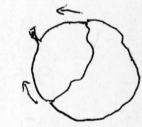

- For extra Brownie points, cut differently sized holes in a fourth balloon and then slip it over the juggling ball, creating a patchwork effect.

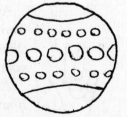

How to Juggle

Kymberlyn Olsen and Louise Radcliffe-Smith

Juggling Three Balls (The Cascade)

One ball

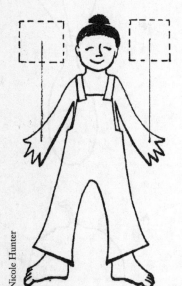

Start with one ball and throw it from your right hand into an imaginary 30 cm square above your left shoulder.

Catch the ball with your left hand and bring it in towards the mid-line of your body before throwing it up towards the imaginary square above your right shoulder.

Catch and throw with upward-facing palms. The balls should trace a figure of eight (or infinity sign) in the air.

Remember to keep your hands below the level of your chest when you catch and throw.

Two balls

Pick up a ball in each hand.

Throw the ball in your right hand up to your left shoulder. When Ball One reaches the peak of its flight, throw Ball Two from your left hand to your right side. Practise starting with both left and right hands.

Three balls

Pick up two balls in your dominant hand and one ball in your subordinate hand. Throw Ball One from your dominant hand, saying "one" aloud.

At the peak of Ball One's flight, throw Ball Two from your subordinate hand, saying "two" aloud, then catch the downcoming Ball One in your subordinate hand.

As Ball Two reaches its peak, throw Ball Three from your dominant hand, saying "three" aloud, then catch the down-coming Ball Two.

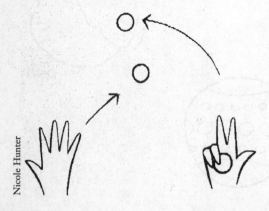

Nicole Hunter

When Ball Three peaks, throw Ball Four from your subordinate hand. And so on. Try to build up a rhythm.

Each time you throw a ball count to yourself. Always throw the ball that is next in line, even if you know it's going to drop.

Handy tips

1. Dropping is half of juggling. It is not failure. Never be afraid to drop. The most important thing is to get technique right.

2. Stand loosely with feet planted solidly under your hips and knees slightly bent. Keep your elbows at 45 degrees to your body. Your elbows stay still and your forearms rotate as your hands catch and throw the balls smoothly. Keep your shoulders loose and remember to breathe.

3. The centre of balance in your body lies within your belly, not in your head.

Naomi Herzog

Club juggle: Penni Clarke and Danielle Edwards passing clubs

Stick Manipulation

Melissa Iddles, circus specialist trainer

Vivienne Mêhes

Struggle and strife:
Stick-fighting women in
the underworld, Death:
The Musical, 1994

Note about Warm-ups

To avoid injury and to allow maximum
flexibility it is important to stretch and warm-
up the following muscles and joints:

- spine (flex and stretch in *both* directions)
- neck
- shoulders
- elbows
- wrists
- fingers and hands

before practising or rehearsing stick work. Also warm up hips,
knees, ankles and feet for any lunging or movement to go with
the stick work.

The Moves

Nicole Hunter

Butterfly

- Hands remain fixed in same position on stick but are always
flexible, allowing the fingers and wrists to manipulate the
directions and angles of the stick.
- The stick circles on a horizontal plane, remaining within
that plane the whole time (i.e. not travelling on any angles,
therefore looking graceful and controlled).
- Swing stick to the right, tucking under the right shoulder
- Then swing stick around in the other direction, over the
head, to tuck under the left shoulder
- Maintain flexibility in bent elbows, keeping stick low over
head and as much within its plane as possible

Variation: Stepping within the direction of the stick (i.e.
circling from left to right). Perform as many circles in each
direction as you like while holding the stick overhead. When
going right, step on the right foot first and vice versa – RLR
change LRL change RLR, etc.

Rowboat

Note: Palms to the sky – the front end of the stick is called A and the other end is called B.

Nicole Hunter

The plane is vertical; the stick stays within this plane and as close to the body sides as possible. In this version the stick looks as if it is turning faster and a lot more than it is. It's really only doing half a rotation either side of the body. It always looks more complicated than it is.

- Starting with the stick on right side of body, the right hand takes the stick, bringing B over and forward to scoop down on the left side of the body.
- B scoops down on the left side of the body and then over and forward. B is now pointing forward and A to the back. Right palm of hand to the sky.
- At this point, bring in the left hand, palm to the sky and take the stick in left hand.
- Left hand brings A over and forward to scoop down on the right side of the body. A continues over and forward. Left palm now pointed to the sky. Bring in the right hand, palm to the sky, and take the stick, bringing B up and over, etc.

Variation: Allow the stick to do an extra half turn either side of the body, therefore the point of exchange between hands is not when the palm is to the sky, but when the wrist can twist no further. Then the other hand must take the stick, coming in with palm to the sky.

Club Swinger

Kathryn Niesche, aerial trainer

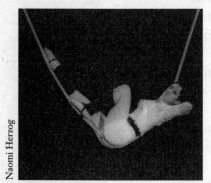

Kathryn Niesche

I grew up in Adelaide where I studied dance and drama at Flinders University. Since 1982 I've worked with lots of companies, ranging from dance theatre, community theatre, variety, theatre for young people, women's theatre and circus theatre. I started dabbling in circus in 1983, then became seriously hooked when working with Legs On The Wall in Sydney, a company which presents traditional vaudeville and circus arts in a contemporary theatrical style. In 1990, with the aid of a professional development grant from the Australia Council, I pursued my dream of studying aerial skills and New Circus overseas. I studied "motivity" (contact improvisation and trapeze dance) with Terry Sendgraff in San Francisco, flying and fixed trapeze at the Ecole de Trapeze Volant Jean Palacy in Paris, as well as seeing many of the great European circuses. In 1994–95 I joined with three others to form a women's aerial performance company called Club Swing. Our first show, Appetite, directed by Gail Kelly and Robin Laurie has been seen in Melbourne, Adelaide, Perth, Sydney and Edinburgh, and in 1996 I toured Auckland, Manchester, Glasgow, Brighton, London and Munich.

When I first saw aerialists Sue Broadway and Jane Mullett performing during the early days of Circus Oz, I was completely amazed by their physical strength and also by their "big" presence on stage. Being a performer of similarly slight stature I was immediately inspired, started training, and soon became addicted to being airborne.

The pain factor with aerial skills is high – rope, metal bars and gravity are all very unforgiving on soft skin and muscles. However, the first time you feel you can lift your own body weight; the first sense of being in control of what you are doing – these moments make all the bruises and rope-burns pay off.

Though I love the trapeze, I have become particularly inspired by the cloudswing – a difficult apparatus despite its deceptively simple appearance (a seven-metre-long rope hung from a swivel at each end, which means it rolls and turns on itself). I particularly like its simplicity and the fact that it doesn't look like a piece of equipment, as does a trapeze. I think everyone can relate back to their childhood joy of swinging on a piece of rope.

I would certainly encourage any woman to take up aerial training – even those afraid of heights (as I am!) Developing upper body strength is a great feeling, and despite the fact that you may find yourself de-railing sliding doors through brute force, the confidence you gain is invaluable.

Singing with the Body

Helen Sharp,
theatre director and body voice teacher

I work with the cast in relation to body and voice. I'm interested in body and voice as a personal sort of healing and a journey through self. It's a way in which, by tracking your body's voice, you can also track your own story at a psychological level and unravel it. The experiences of the past are remembered in the body and also in the voice. And some of them need remembering so you can reconcile yourself with them.

Gender and voice are culturally constructed. Women have been denied a voice in this culture, both through written and spoken words. Women and children are meant to be "seen and not heard" and their access to the vocal possibilities of the body has been limited to the higher tones. Women in this society are not meant to be connected to the body or the gut tone of the voice. One problem I've noticed is that women are locked into the notion that they must speak in a "nice" voice. But access to the whole range of voice and body is essential to your emotional health and allows you to experience the expressive possibilities of being human.

When I saw the 1992 Women's Circus show, I couldn't help but project my own ideas. It was tremendous to see so many women working together, but as an audience member I would have derived more satisfaction if at moments in the show women had a voice. So I approached Donna with the notion of breaking the silence. (For the first three years, Women's Circus performances did not involve voice.)

In the workshops I put a lot of emphasis on feeling the voice, rather than thinking about it. We started by establishing a tactile relationship with the voice, not judging the quality of the sound, but working for your own pleasure and noticing where it felt good. This might mean humming, chanting, seeing blue sparkles coming out of one's mouth or standing in a circle panting while trying to imagine that the person opposite was a bowl of dog food. I tried to connect people with the qualities of energy in the body and to help them feel the emotional expressiveness of the voice. I tried to help them see the voice as the body, to establish the connection between movement and vocalisation, and to prove that everyone can sing. There is absolutely no doubt in my mind that everyone can sing, and that in itself is an incredibly personal and political issue. I also love the joy of doing voice work with people; the sound of a voice or voices travelling through space. There's a sense of sharing as voices merge and collide.

A lot of the women in my body voice workshops had been with the circus since the beginning and took things on readily and solidly. Being in the circus had instilled trust in themselves and within the group. But still, I felt as if women in the group took very strong personal risks with their voices. Being heard is pretty confronting, and being looked at while you make sound is enough to bring on a massive anxiety bout. But I tried to create an environment where it was quite acceptable to feel anxious, terrified, even ashamed. I made it clear that the work could bring up intense laughter or crying and whatever it brought up was alright. I really admired their sheer guts. I wanted to create a context in which women could use voice and anything was acceptable. For me, that was the starting point.

Sports Acrobat

Dorota Scally

Naomi Herzog

Dorota Scally

Dorota is twenty-seven years old and of Polish origin. A sports acrobat for fifteen years, Dorota was a world champion – she was fourth in the world ratings from 1988 to 1989. She has now been in Australia for two years. In this time she has combined working for the Little Big Tops and Circus Oz with the Women's Circus. Teaching acrobatics is a major love for Dorota and she especially enjoys her involvement with the Women's Circus. It is our commitment, our dedication and our will to work, she says, that makes the difference.

In 1995, Dorota took the keenest circus members for intensive early morning training, starting at 7.00 a.m. on Tuesdays and Thursdays and 10.00 a.m. on Saturdays. The intensives aimed to build strength and flexibility over a short period of time. Dorota was enthusiastic about the intensives, having seen a marked improvement and development as a direct consequence of specialist training. She said she hoped to make Women's Circus members better acrobats – to work together to enable us to do everything.

The Trainers

Physical Trainers

Sally Forth (general)
Lee Mohtaji (general)
Dorota Scally (acrobatics)
Kymberlyn Olsen (manipulation)
Jane Mullett (aerials)
Yosaino Worth (general and aerials)
Annie Fayzdaughter (beginners)
Kathryn Niesche (aerials)
Kylie Whyte (beginners & mangoes)
Karen Martin (beginners)
Louise Radcliffe-Smith (beginners)
Amanda Owen (acrobalance)
Theresa Blake (acrobatics)
Margaret Kirby (aerials)
Christina Branton (aerials)
Jules de Cinque (beginners)

Musical Trainers

Sue Speer
Radha Claridge
Marianne Permezel
Helen Sharp
Paula Dowse

Technical Trainers

Jane Mullett
Georgine Clarsen
Liz Pain
Michele Bottroff
Ursula Dutkiewicz
Alan Robertson
Dori Dragon
Margo Storm
Gail Davidson
Maureen O'Connor
Nicki Clarke
Carmel Duffy

THE STRENGTH IS IN THE DOING: THE TRAINEES

It is also important to acknowledge the contributions of members of the circus who have voluntarily shared their personal skills and knowledge, formally and informally, with each other, in fields as diverse as health, the arts, media and administration.

Women have taken responsibility for their own training in numerous ways apart from the Labour Exchange – organising extra practise sessions among themselves, or choosing to pursue more unusual and personally challenging skills.

Through all the avenues of training within the Women's Circus, women have learned to take risks, to own success and handle setbacks; to work together in conflict and in harmony; and to enjoy living fully in the present.

The Circus as a Metaphor

Adrienne Liebmann

Vivienne Méhes

Defiance: Adrienne Liebmann playing Dr Ma Thida of Burma in Leaping the Wire, 1995

The Women's Circus came into my life at a time when I was looking for something that would enable me to express my feminist politics and beliefs. But I didn't realise immediately what the circus had to offer me. During training I noticed that my vocabulary began to include words such as "focus", "challenge", "decisiveness", "strength", "goal setting", "risk taking", "courage". I began to realise that these concepts were as valid within the circus space as they were in that other world beyond the warehouse.

Physical strength became an issue for me, too. I had never sought strength, but that all changed when I joined the Women's Circus. It confronted me. I recognise now the need for women to be physically strong, as well as mentally, emotionally and spiritually strong, because having physical strength influences other aspects of our lives and unconsciously affects our personal view of ourselves as women in this world.

As one of the smaller women in the circus I have found a need to prove to myself and others that smaller women can develop great physical strength and can be trusted to base (hold other people up) in many circumstances. I realise now how easy it is to fall into the trap of allowing others to do things for you because of your size, and this can be so disempowering.

I see the skills we learn in the circus as a metaphor for something in our lives. Juggling, diablo and devil sticks are manipulation skills, and this is what we do as women, manipulate and juggle the many parts of our lives. To be a "base" in a balance act is to provide support for the woman who "flies", and to fly well you need to feel light as well as have a positive mental attitude. The cartwheel is like the wheel of life as it turns around and around, and the stilts are a metaphor for feeling taller than we really are and doing grand things in our lives. The aerials enable us to reach for the sky, swing through the air and reach out to whatever we want. A handstand is like doing the impossible upside down; fire sticks represent the passion and desires that we have within ourselves. And then there's the rope.

After two years in the circus, I finally discovered an activity which I enjoyed and wanted to pursue: the rope. I couldn't understand this interest in something that didn't seem to have a metaphor in my life, but gradually the realisation came. Most of my life has been defined by others and I have struggled for a very long time to find out who I am without others imposing their perceptions on me. Now I feel that I am beginning to discover me, I am casting off the many layers that have cloaked me for so long, and am defining "me" for myself. I cling as tightly and fiercely to the rope as I do to my new-found identity and I'm not letting anyone take that away from me.

"In many ways I am nothing like the woman I was and far more like the one I always yearned to be."

– Art gallery postcard.

Cleaning up the Playground

Patricia Sykes

It's not the first time
she's tried the upside
down position   she remembers
that view from school
the bite of stones and eyes
as she stood on her hands
to be in to prove she could
gritting her teeth
on the victorious agony of it
fat girls couldn't of course
and some didn't want to
and most boys gathered
only for the knickers
which is all her grandmother's
elastic would let them see

now she's at it again
though she's not really
supposed to at her age   what's more
she's a fat girl in knickers
an unseemly unsightly unbeauty
who's helping shift history
with her cartwheels and rolls
and when her friends say
ooh and aah she says
it's all part of the act
of cleaning up the playground

Whip-carrying Women

Fi Bowie

Whip-carrying women – characterising what? Aggression? Dominance? Why not sensuality . . . sensitivity? Ease, control, timing, fluidity? The art of whip-cracking relies on these qualities and not those of strength or physique.

The whip itself has a solid handle which gives way to a plaited eight-, six- or four-foot tail. Added to this are "fall" (a short piece of single leather) and a "cracker" (a six-inch plaited plastic cord) which, as indicated by the name, gives off the ear-breaking sound.

To crack the whip one must send the "cracker" at the speed of sound into and out of a bend or fold. The body of the whip allows us to produce this necessary speed. Swing the whip around the head then change its direction by pulling it back and down; the whip should extend out in front of the body as it makes its noise.

Hats are a wise addition to your clothing during the early stages of learning!

Perfecting one's skill and transferring the whip from the dominant to the weaker hand requires a relaxed, smooth and concentrated mind and action. The whip flies through the air in a beautiful arc. Enhance this with timing and style, add speed and grunt when the action is perfectly fluid, not before. My experience in learning to crack a whip is characterised by my increased awareness of timing and my left hand co-ordination.

The art doesn't have to be about power, dominance or aggression; it is about sensitivity, style and timing. Enjoy it!

Vivienne Mêhes

Stepping out: Fi Bowie abseils down a factory wall in the Work Show, 1992

Nicole Hunter

Whip-cracking

Skate Away

Jean Taylor

When I mooted the idea to Donna that I might like to learn to roller-skate as one of my circus skills (an idea which she encouraged, I might say), I had only a vague sense of the time and effort it would require to gain even a modicum of expertise on the damned things. Still less that it would prompt others, much more practised than I, to skate with seemingly consummate ease around the warehouse every week.

Nevertheless, and small though the gains may be, I have improved since that first day when, even to the least jaundiced eye, it was quite obvious I was a mere beginner and a fearfully inexperienced one at that. So, apart from the day when I fell and jarred my neck and wrists quite badly, I've enjoyed myself.

When I'm tentatively wheeling my way around that concrete space and someone else thunders up behind me to pass, I get nervous, insecure on my wheels as I still very much am. However, as I did in 1991 on the stilts, I'm determined to persevere. And, I hope, get to that stage where I too can wheel and turn with the grace that I have, as yet, only done in my dreams.

First published in the *Women's Circus Newsletter*, September 1992

SPECIALIST TRAINING WORKSHOPS

For a number of years the circus has invited members to participate in specialist workshops. These have ranged from clowning intensives to ten-week directors' workshops. The policy of in-house education enables the circus to employ its own members to train or direct other members, rather than always relying on outside workers. Specialist workshops also spread skills across a broad cross-section of the circus community, so expertise does not reside only in the hands of a few women. Some women have used the specialist training programmes as stepping stones towards full or part-time employment as trainers or directors.

How to be A Stupid:*
Angela De Castro's Workshop

Patricia Sykes

Part of being a Women's Circus performer is learning how to trust each other with our bodies. For five days in 1994, for a lucky group of women, this was extended to an emotional trust. Under the observant, caring eye of clowner extraordinaire, Angela De Castro, the women revealed their deep selves. Through the tears, the laughter, the sweaty palms, and the anger, these women shared a common vulnerability in their pursuit of the clown that is within us all. What they gained as a result was greater self-knowledge, technique, a sense of achievement, and a daring and readiness to explore further what it means to be a stupid: a clown.

Largely as a result of Angela's workshops, clowning has taken up residence at the circus and promises never to go away. Its spirit energised the sideshow acts in Death: The Musical, the major show for 1994, and surfaced again in the 1995 show, Leaping the Wire. It also appeared strongly in the first performance by POW, the over-forty women's performing group, and continues to be part of their drive and energy, a clear indication that clowning is one of the older woman's most powerful allies.

During 1995, women who undertook Angela's clowning intensive continued meeting to help keep the spirit of clown alive, to help integrate clowning into circus performances, and to keep training so that they would be able to fulfil their objective of one day running their own clowning workshops. For all these women, clowning not only meant satisfying personal growth, it gave them an opportunity, as Bridget Roberts put it, to "connect deeply and powerfully with audiences, to be complicit with them, to invite them to play, commiserate and empathise".

* Written with reference to an article by Karen Martin
in *Women's Circus Newsletter*, September 1994

Training the Trainer

Louise Radcliffe-Smith

I've always been good at organising, explaining and communicating. In 1995, I decided to fulfil a long-term ambition to train other women and direct them in performance. My main concern as a trainer was to maintain the holistic mind-body-spirit focus that had been introduced to me by Sally Forth. So I enrolled in the Train the Trainer weekend offered by Sally early in 1995, knowing that only a week later I would start to put into practice what I'd learned.

Sally taught us how to plan a workshop and how important it was to be clear about our goals and reasons for running a class. We covered three different ways of approaching training: dance and movement, Oki-do yoga and Iyengar yoga. We looked at how important it was to involve the mind and the soul as well as the body in training programs and to incorporate the principles of focus and energy through breathing and relaxation. We learned the principles of physical movement and how to detect signs of stress and strain. We also looked at how to correct posture and how to help women extend their range of movement, flexibility and strength. I came away from the weekend feeling more confident and perceptive, as if I had learnt a lot very quickly.

The following week I started training the 1995 new women's group with Karen Martin. We had twenty new women to train. None of them had any circus experience. A few were familiar with dance or yoga, but most hadn't touched physical skills since school. Given that a fundraiser to send women to Beijing was due to be held at the Malthouse Theatre in June, we only had nine weeks to teach the group basic skills and coach them towards a performance.

The first few workshops concentrated on strength, flexibility, respect and safety (both mental and physical), then extended into counterbalances and small pyramids. This allowed the women to find their own place within the group. Their ten-minute performance at the Malthouse became a physical representation of every circus woman's journey: from individuality to community.

For the remainder of 1995, Karen and I built up the women's skills, strength and flexibility, introducing club-swinging, stick manipulation, tightrope, fire, acrobatics, and so on. We maintained the ritual of support groups, encouraging women to meet in small groups at the end of the workshop and debrief one another about anything they found challenging or rewarding. This helped bring women together and provided an avenue for airing problems or worries.

In October 1995 I undertook the directors' workshops with Meme McDonald and directed the new women's group in a section of the Leaping the Wire show. The group told the story of Agatha Uwilingiyimana, the first woman Prime Minister of Rwanda, who was killed when war broke out in Rwanda in 1994.

Directing was much more challenging than I expected. At the start I felt completely lost and isolated, both from the other directors (who had more experience than me) and from the group itself. I found it difficult to settle on a storyline and then to find a way of physicalising what I wanted to say. Once this was sorted out, the rest followed. I realised that, as usual, I was taking myself far too seriously and there were better things to worry about. Ironically I also realised that while training and directing were skills I could master, they were not skills I wanted to pursue any further, at least for the time being.

Specialist Trainers

1991	Natalie Dyball	Acrobatics
	Kathryn Niesche	Aerials
	Nicki Wilkes	Acrobatics
1992	Emily Lindsay	Tightrope
	Amanda Owen & Nicky Fearn	Acrobalance
	Anna Shelper	Acrobatics/aerials
	Clair Teison	Comedy character
1993	Rinske Ginsberg	Contact dance
1994	Teresa Celis & Sonia Ganza Grunvald	Spanish acrobat duo
	Angela De Castro	Clowning
	Melissa Iddles	Stick manipulation
	Donna Jackson	Directing
1995	Niki Fletcher	Dance
	Sally Forth	Training the trainer
1996	Sarah Cathcart	Theatre skills
	Robyn Archer	Theatre skills
	Andrea Lemon	Theatre skills
	Jenny Kemp	Theatre skills
	Amanda Owen	Mask, Theatre games

Music Training

Jean Taylor and members of the Music Group

Music has been an integral part of the Women's Circus from the beginning. The first music workshop was held on Monday evening, May 13th 1991, and continued every week throughout the year, under the capable direction of Sue Speer, who had this to say:

> *I enjoyed my involvement with the circus and learnt much from the women in the group. I worked on this show for the involvement of the music group in the production and also for the opportunity to work with other women in music and produce a worthwhile piece of theatre both artistically and politically.* (WCN, February 1992)

Carrying a tune: Ria (centre) and the music group in the Institutions Show, 1991

Ria, one of the women who regularly attended the weekly music training sessions during that first year, wrote about her experiences in the music group:

> *As a woman with a physical disability, I thought acrobatics training would be totally beyond my capabilities and thus chose to concentrate solely on music-making (a decision I've since regretted). I'm an experienced muso from way back but I've certainly never worked on a project like this before! I might be a classically trained "opera singer" but that doesn't mean I have to perform "art music" all the time; circus gives me the opportunity to break free from the shackles of that expectation (yippee!!) I can work on percussion, or keyboards or brass, or play my clarinet or recorder. I can improvise the things I want rather than having to rigidly follow a pre-written score (you just don't get to jam around in choirs and orchestras!) Best of all, the music workshops to date have emphasised exploration and*

enjoyment at least as much as they have technical perfection. I really needed the freedom from pressure.

I would've liked to have broken out even more (found the early workshops really basic and could've done more interesting things with my time) but generally wouldn't have missed circus for the world.

In some of my darker moments, while desperately wondering how I'll get through the day/week, I realise how much the circus and the women in it have come to mean to me – I often decide I can hold out until the workshop without falling to bits, and when I get there I feel better.

Can't wait till the show starts! (*WCN*, October 1991)

Into the second year and the music workshops continued as before on a weekly basis with Radha Claridge hired to be the music trainer. Or as she put it:

I have seen myself as the workshop person, trying to impart skills to people playing together and helping them become more confident to make up their own ideas and see how all the parts fit together to make songs. I'm not the musical director. I'm waiting for the musical director to take over. My role was to prepare the people, to get them to the skill level where they felt comfortable working with each other, where they felt more confident about the ideas they had and could see how these ideas were valid and could be turned into a musical piece.

(*WCN*, September 1992)

This is how Janet Patterson, one of the members of the music group wrote about her experiences of working with Radha:

We started off with about twenty women and now fluctuate at ten to fifteen. For a few weeks we played with sounds and rhythms and now we're exploring musical styles – rap, blues, reggae and chaos. Radha explains the theory behind the style, we listen to examples and then get into it! We're a challenge to Radha with our skill levels all over the place. We're discovering lots of hidden talents – writers and singers, nimble guitar players and enthusiastic percussionists. The music group provides a friendly and supportive environment and people seem to feel free to take risks and experiment with music without feeling any pressure. The sense of achievement is fantastic! I've no idea how it will all work in the long run, but we have faith in the process!

(*WCN*, June 1992)

Even though the Women's Circus gets invited to do the occasional gig throughout the year, taped music is used to highlight the action more often than not. However, there was the occasional event that did bring the performers and a few of the musicians together. One such small show was devised for the Williamstown Summer Festival in January 1993. Kylie Whyte had this to say about the musicians' involvement under the direction of Marianne Permezel:

> The music was developed especially for the show, following the mood of what the physical performers were trying to achieve. A lot of percussion was used to mark and highlight different acrobatic feats. Because the show was outdoors and people wandered everywhere, the music was important to focus people's attention and to keep the mood going so the acrobats had time to get in the trees before the audience came through the gates.
>
> The funniest thing was the day a car blocked the entrance from the gardens to the forest, so when we ran to the podium to start our percussion piece there were no drums. What Donna said kept running through my mind: "It's not a crime to make a mistake, it's a crime to let the audience know there has been a mistake."

> (WCN, May 1993)

And again later in the year, as Sue Speer, the musical director, wrote about the introduction of different skills into the music group:

Nicole Hunter

> This year's music group has concentrated on learning body voice work with Helen Sharp and percussion skills with Paula Dowse. They have already developed one fantastic percussion piece, which was used in the Fringe Parade down Brunswick Street, and are now working up a number of other pieces for the November show. The band has gradually moved away from a "band in the middle, performers in the centre" concept to a more integrated concept, with music women participating in workshops and helping teach various forms of stomping, chanting and percussing to others within the circus. As in the first November show, we are developing a mixture of performed pieces and taped soundtracks, but this time musicians will have the opportunity to perform as well as play.

> (WCN, October 1993)

As Kylie Whyte, who attended Helen Sharp's often quite challenging workshops, put it:

> It gradually dawned on me that what we were doing – humming and chanting through sit ups, headstands, frog-leaps and so on – was learning how to connect our bodies and minds with our voices. We were learning how to express ourselves vocally and how to "take up space" in new ways. For someone who has always been fairly quiet – afraid of

opening my mouth in case I might impose on someone else – it was great to learn I can be a real loudmouth, and make some interesting sounds in the process. The music workshops have also been a great way to learn to really listen to each other and work as a group. I found the voice workshops a challenge and enjoyed them a great deal. I've certainly been left with a lot to work with. (*WCN*, September 1993)

At the beginning of 1994, Marianne Permezel returned as the musical director. Trish Sykes reported:

Marianne's aim for the Women's Circus is to have live band music for our 1994 performance season although there may be some linking between live music and taped keyboard music to be provided by the group. She says the music group is a fantastic team and very supportive of each other.

The group is learning to read music as an added skill and are about to begin composing music for the show under Marianne's guidance.

(*WCN*, September 1994)

Some members of the music group had this to add: "We've turned into a terrific musical band incredibly quickly thanks to Marianne" (Alice). "High energy rock and roll" (Barb). "Innovative! Inspirational! Original! Very interesting!" (Lorraine). "Alright!" (Kath).

Throughout 1995, and again under the capable direction of Marianne, the music group was called upon to provide the musical backing for a few of the Women's Circus performances including the fundraiser for Amnesty International's birthday celebrations at Budinski's in May, the Leaping into Action Concerts at the Malthouse in June–July and the Arts Vic performances outside the Vic Arts Centre on 30 July. Without the band to provide the drumming and percussion these high profile performances would not have been nearly as successful as they undoubtedly were.

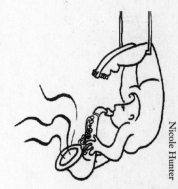

Nicole Hunter

I'll Count You In

Members of the Music Group

The Women's Circus Band began in May 1994 with eleven members who had little or no experience playing music or performing with a group of people. Thursday evening workshops opened the door to developing music skills in a safe place where (in the words of one band member) "community, creativity, co-operation, capability, confidence, culture and commitment" could flourish.

The women involved in the group came from diverse backgrounds, experience, age and politics, but with a common purpose – an interest in music. Conflicts that have arisen – especially during the stresses of performance – have been handled amicably and maturely, with an honest desire to work together and support each other in the context of the group. The strength of this support came through most when the demands of performance during Death: the Musical were the greatest.

In particular, what has led to the birth of "The Women's Circus Band", from a group of women getting together to learn music, has been hard work, practice and commitment from each woman, through the musical direction and leadership of Marianne Permezel.

Marianne's wide musical experience and brilliance as well as a gift for teaching, has helped individual women, and the band as a whole, to develop the skills and confidence to adapt to change, and the discipline to meet the challenges of performance.

Her personal qualities have also contributed to the band working successfully as a musical unit, flexible enough to complement the role of the physical performers. Her modesty and tolerant attitude to others has given band members the reassurance needed to work together – by listening to each other as well as the director – learning how each party fits into the whole piece.

Her teaching style has catered for different learning styles and paces of learning. The discipline required to master musical skills has also kept us on our toes. We are expected to work at things till they're right and incorporate changes to suit the mood, rhythm and themes of the performance piece. We have improved our skills, stamina and quality of sound.

So, while being part of the band is enjoyable, it is the enjoyment of achievement rather than "fun". What we have done in our workshops over the past year or so is:

- build on a beginning of simple rhythms
- try out instruments we've never played before
- improvised rhythms for input into the themes of performance and musical pieces composed by Marianne
- taught each other rhythms, particularly those who joined the group later
- spent hours of hard practice working on each piece and drawing them together with attention to detail, cues and timing
- for each show we have collectively played a wide range of percussion instruments, including keyboards, guitar, bass, saxophone, flute, recorder, clarinet, melodica, trumpet, ocarina, drum kit, mandolin
- read and write music
- use vocalisation.

One of the most important skills developed by each of us has been to listen:

- listening to other women and adding a rhythm to hers
- training our ears, with a greater awareness of how the rhythms and instruments work in different musical pieces
- counting in your head $(1+2+3+4+)$
- awareness of the importance of timing
- listening to each other as we play and getting into synch
- listening to and watching for cues from the director
- listening critically to our own performance

Vivienne Mêhes

Musical beginnings: Sue Speer (right) takes a workshop in 1991

We are more confident about expanding our musical horizons and working more independently. As a dynamic entity, we have learned flexibility and adaptability to meet the needs of the Women's Circus.

We see ourselves as playing an integral role in the whole circus, particularly during performance. Even though we train separately, when we come together with the physical performers, we become part of a powerful expression of something innovative and meaningful. This requires effective communication between the circus director and the musical director.

As most circus themes are non-vocalised, the music helps set the mood for the show. This two-way process gives meaning to the performance and the music. Many physical performers have said they feel inspired when the music is incorporated into the message they are trying to express, which helps give their characters more meaning.

Women in the band have also gained a lot from being involved in different aspects of performance. For instance, creating our own masks and costumes, being part of the story creation, playing roles in certain sections of the show.

But performances are also stressful times – dealing with individual emotions or when one person is out of rhythm creates difficulties working together. But the highs of the audience applause and appreciation of the music "working" in the show has helped us to identify ourselves as the "Women's Circus Band".

During the 1994 show people were asking us for a recording of the music. We also wanted a souvenir of our collective achievement – so it was produced live. This year we plan to make a studio recording of the pieces we have performed from 1994–95, using a wide repertoire and range of instruments and rhythms. With money raised from the sale of this recording we plan to buy instruments for the band which will enrich the music for the 1995 show.

A year ago we wouldn't have realised the significance of Marianne saying, "I'll count you in". But that was a year ago.

Labour Exchange

Elizabeth Grady & Judith Shapland

The purpose of labour exchange is to enable women of limited financial means to take part in physical and music workshops. Women exchange work in return for participation in training. The Women's Circus is then able to get jobs done that it could not otherwise afford to employ women to do.

Vivienne Méhes

Waterworks: Judith Shapland holding the water hose on the 1996 Moomba River Pageant barge

Completing an hour of labour exchange allows the worker to attend a two-hour training workshop free of charge. Since 1995 workers have received one coloured token for every hour of labour exchange, which they present at workshops in lieu of money. Each member of the exchange negotiates their contract with the circus workshop co-ordinator.

Labour exchange has helped circus women extend their skills in areas other than music or performance. Some women enjoy becoming computer literate by updating the members' mailing list. Others have become adept at checking trapeze and rope rigging, in addition to taking care of circus equipment. The circus *Newsletter* is folded and posted, documentation made accessible and filed, and the essential "cuppa" is always available at training thanks to labour exchange. The warehouse training space is kept tidy and vacuumed, the first aid kit replenished and social activities organised. It's a variety of tasks we undertake!

Because of the work done by labour exchange, the Women's Circus manages to survive with a small budget. The exchange is an integral, essential function of the Women's Circus, enabling women to become fitter, stronger and more confident in acquiring new skills as they contribute to the structure and organisation of the overall group.

CREWS:
ALL IN A DAY'S WORK

The Women's Circus survives through the energy, co-operation and commitment of all women involved. What the audience sees at the end-of-year show and at small gigs throughout the year is not just a performance, but an event that is only possible through women's dedication and belief in the circus. The Women's Circus is a community project. Aside from a few paid professionals, it is up to the women of the circus to provide the energy and inspiration to get things done. Much of the work done within the organisation is handled by "crews", a notion which began to develop in 1991 and was formalised in 1992. Each crew has a "Top Dog", the Women's Circus equivalent of a co-ordinator, who liaises with the circus director and with the women of her crew.

Newsletter Crew

Deb Lewis

Deb Lewis

The *Women's Circus Newsletter* is the information link between the circus and its 500 sisters and supporters. The three or four members of the crew write, illustrate, chase up material, advertise, edit, layout, fold, stuff and post the newsletter four times a year. Sometimes women bring their own skills to the job. Other times, producing a newsletter is a major learning curve for the participants.

I joined the circus Newsletter Crew in 1993 to develop my desktop publishing skills. Prior to joining, I had none. Now I have worked on four different publishing packages in both Macintosh and IBM environments (one of the perils of not owning my own computer). I also produce a newsletter at my day job which goes out all over the country, and I am very proud of my work and my constantly developing level of skill.

I had the privilege of working with a delightful group of hard-working souls from 1992 to 1996. The team consisted of Karen Martin, the editor and copy writer; Louise Radcliffe-Smith, copy writer; Nicole Hunter, graphic artist and Patricia Sykes, poet and copy writer. I mainly worked on the layout and submitted a few articles when I had a burning desire! Karen and I could often be found reading and laying out contributions over numerous cups of tea and occasionally a couple of children as we aimed to achieve a better publication each time. We worked to an often self-imposed deadline and managed, with mutual respect and ever-developing skills, to come out laughing and congratulating each other at the end of a long session. Many a night I sat up (as I am this very evening) until the small hours of the morning working on my material. Sometimes I had the support and good humour of my daughter, Min, or my long-suffering friend Liz, both of whom are now very efficient proof readers. Our heart-felt motto was "it's not good enough until it's as good as we can get it".

Working on the newsletter crew was often an adventure, as fellow crew member Rad has noted:

> *The most memorable part of these newsletters has been the variety of spaces we occupy in any one meeting. Some days we were evicted from the*

boardroom, then the music room and ended up on the floor in Donna's office. Another time we snatched half an hour on the empty stage of the Carlton Courthouse before one of the crew members had to get dressed and perform! Once, when typing and editing a newsletter at a local university campus, we spent two hours waiting for security guards to let us in – the next time we sneaked in through the boys' toilets.

For me the circus is where I can put in as much or as little as I want to depending on my need to contribute and the amount of time I have to spare. It is also a place where I can build and foster friendships, develop all sorts of skills both physical and practical and grow emotionally as a result.

Child-care Crew

Jules De Cinque

Mothers are traditionally an isolated group within our society, expected to fulfil the majority of parental duties within the domestic sphere. This has often meant that the physical health and self-esteem of mothers has suffered. The circus aims to address issues of wellbeing through physical activity, so it seems appropriate that mothers are supported to be active members of the circus.

The Women's Circus is committed to the fundamental feminist principle of access. For mothers, this has been translated into providing funds for child care to support those who wish to participate in the activities of the circus.

Nicole Hunter

Windmills in the creche

A further positive outcome of the involvement of mothers in the circus lies in the future. Children who have watched their mothers be physically active, politically involved and courageous are more likely to perceive women as strong and creative. These children, throughout their lives, will have a model with which to challenge the sexist view that women are powerless and less able than men.

Over the years, the number of circus mothers requiring

child-care facilities has increased dramatically, from two to about fifteen. A structure has been devised that aims to provide equal access to quality child care for all mothers during the year. Mothers participating in daytime workshops drop their children off at a creche before the session and pick them up afterwards. The circus is billed for this at the end of every school term. Women doing night workshops can pick up a set amount of money from FCAC and arrange for a babysitter to come to their home. This way they do not have to pay up-front.

From the Journal

Circus Mother

Naomi Herzog

Janine Edwards and Jess

My first post-natal workshop! Bizarre, bizarre to be away from Finn for such a long time, but GREAT to be "home" to this circus space. Three months after first being thrust into the realm of motherhood and I feel both relieved to be back here and somewhat incredulous that these three hours have passed so easily. It seems as though I never left here. And Finn absorbs it all so easily. Never out of my sight before, barely out of my arms, and he sleeps peacefully now in a stranger's. Warmth is warmth.

After one and a half months in bed and the sensation, when I did begin to walk again, that I would always carry with me this sense of restriction, the need to protect myself, to be slow – I'm pleased to be back and feel encouraged that my pace is respected. My strength of course has dissipated, or rather been redirected!, but feel completely supported here to honour my maternal body . . . and take it easy!

– Sharee Grinter, 1994

SMALL GIGS

For a Variety of Causes

Jean Taylor

At the end of each year the Women's Circus puts on a highly publicised and successful season of performances. What is not so well known is that the circus also performs many smaller gigs throughout the year for a variety of causes. These are not usually as spectacular as the main show and range in size from half a dozen participants up to about twenty or so, depending on what's required and the number of women who are interested, have the time to do the rehearsals beforehand and are available on the night.

These gigs could roughly be divided into perhaps two main categories. The smaller gigs of around fifteen minutes duration usually consists of a few double and group balances and maybe a skill or two such as stilts or flags. These performances are for when we're asked to perform for special one-off occasions such as the launch of the resource book for survivors of sexual assault, *Sharing the Journey*, or to provide entertainment for the Women's Balls. The other category is those events that are more like shows in themselves: for example, the three afternoon performances we did for the Williamstown Summer Festival, the captivating show we put on for the Rural Woman of the Year Award at the National Gallery and all of the stunning acts we've done on the barges being towed down the Yarra River for Moomba.

So, what is it that prompts us on top of everything else we're doing with the circus, the training workshops, labour exchange, the newsletter and research for the shows (among other things too numerous to mention) to take on extra gigs? When, let's face it, they involve quite a bit of time and effort to rehearse as well as perform and they're over so quickly you hardly have time to appreciate them properly.

The performance at the Maribyrnong Community Centre was a nerve-wracking time for some and others were totally confident, which helped us nervous ones enormously. Donna was great, she said: "Relax and have fun." (Easier said than done.) Then we were on! We went through the performance without any hitches; everyone was great. It was a terrific experience. After the show many of the audience commented on how much they enjoyed it.

– Jan, *Newsletter*, October 1991

The post-performance break seemed brief before we took over the Williamstown Botanic Gardens, for a few days in January 1993. This mobile performance culminated with women hanging out of trees against the blue sea/sky back-drop and the final percussion scene which proved that nearly all of us has some sort of sense of rhythm. I have never been so hot in my life and one could hardly describe the experience as physically pleasant, but, I wouldn't have missed it for the world and proudly drag out my photos for anyone who will sit still.

– Deb Lewis, *Newsletter*, October 1993

The performance worked with images of harvest and fertility and the role of woman as nurturer and provider. It explored images of women's journey through life; from maiden to mother to crone – knowledgeable, powerful and wise. The performance incorporated a range of circus skills: aerials in the turrets high above the Great Hall, balances, poses, Chinese ribbons, stilts, fire manipulation and stick twirling.

– Mandy Grinblat,
Newsletter, September 1994

Naomi Herzog

Veiled resistance: Women telling the story of Katia Bengana, an Algerian woman who was shot for refusing to wear the veil (this show took place outside the Victorian Arts Centre in 1995)

Well, sometimes we get paid and the money goes towards keeping the circus alive and functioning. They're usually for a good cause and we want to support other women's groups with what they're doing in the community. They're good experience in terms of performing before a supportive audience for the first time and can help lessen the pre-performance nerves for the larger show at the end of the year. For the most part though, I suspect, because they're fun things to do.

One of the largest small gigs the circus has ever done was almost a whole show in itself over the Invasion Day weekend in 1993 where some twenty women did three shows for the Williamstown Summer Festival in near 100°F heat.

Another of the larger gigs was a mini-show for the Australian Rural Woman of the Year Award where the performers started in the foyer of the National Gallery – with double balances and individual skills, changed costume and moved into the second part of the show to an enthusiastic audience of six hundred at a sit-down dinner in the Great Hall and changed again for the finale outside in the courtyard for a dazzling fire display.

Unfortunately, during the rehearsals for one of the very first gigs the circus ever did – at the Malthouse for Writers' Week – a women fell and was seriously injured emphasising the need for correct safety features and being careful to monitor our own level of health and fitness. Despite that, the four shows of eight minutes duration went well.

After four years there were some highly talented and competent performers in the circus. We often utilise part of acts we've done before, not to mention costumes, music and all the rest of it, to cut down costs and to spread the effort round a bit. It would be difficult coming up with something innovative and totally different every time.

However, it's the performances on the barges for Moomba that have perhaps mobilised the most enthusiasm and excitement. Rehearsing outside in usually balmy weather at dusk and then performing at night under the stars before an audience of thousands while being towed slowly down the Yarra River has been most gratifying.

In 1994, with Donna directing the entire fleet of barges, there were not one or two barges but several, where the Women's Circus featured in one way or another. Women abseiling across the side of one of the barges as they painted designs on the corrugated wall, Loreen doing an opera singer impersonating the prow of a boat as she hung suspended by a harness at the front of another barge. The nightmare barge: "Imagine it! Five long-legged, multi-coloured, vinyl-covered creatures, with torch-like eyes, moving menacingly through the smoke to the awesome sounds of drums beating and dogs howling. The Bitches from Hell ride again," wrote Jean Taylor in the Winter 1994 *Newsletter*.

There were more gigs in 1995 than ever before. During May there were no less than four small gigs which were directed by different directors and culminated in the celebration for Amnesty International's thirty-fourth birthday at Budinski's Theatre of Exile. For this brief performance the stories of the women who were going to be portrayed in Beijing were featured for the first time. The coalition with Amnesty International brought a whole new dimension to the circus' style of political performance.

Following on from the Amnesty performance, we went straight into rehearsals for the major fund-raising concerts at the Malthouse on 30 June and 1 July. The somewhat amazing line-up included Joan Kirner, a former state premier, singing with The Sharons whose lead singer is Donna Jackson, as well as several entertainers who gave their time and energy in support of the circus. However, it was the circus acts that seemed to gain the most applause on the night.

We continued this theme "Leaping the Wire" for two performances outside the Arts Centre on Sunday 23 July where once again the audience was moved to tears by the stories of these women whose courage in the face of extreme adversity is an example to us all.

As can be seen there is a diversity of style and a great deal of commitment needed from the costume designers, the techs, the musicians, the administrators, the directors and the trainers as well as the performers, to put on these gigs. It's a demanding as well as a creative process and certainly gives all of us the opportunity to show off our skills between the major shows as well as gain some performance experience in company with women we might not otherwise have got to know. And after all, isn't that what the Women's Circus is all about?

> The performance was of absurdist style. To enhance this style we wore our hair up under bathing caps, donned . . . black sunnies and wore our circus T-shirts with black pants. I came away feeling inspired and very much looking forward to the show in November.
>
> – Kayt, *Newsletter*, October 1991

Susan Hawthorne

Hero girls: Women performing outside the Victorian Arts Centre in 1995

Moomba Madness

Louise Radcliffe-Smith

Vivienne Méhes

Clocking on: The Moomba River Pageant barge, 1993, celebrating the 8-hour day

Why do we do it? That's what I want to know. It's madness. It's exhausting. It's compelling and uncomfortable and sometimes dangerous. It's not my idea of a relaxing summer on the banks of the Yarra at all! So why do I bother? Why do I wander into the pre-Moomba pep talk every year saying: "Ooh, I'll just sit in to see if anything interesting's going on," when two hours later I know I'll volunteer for bloody nearly everything – barge, dance workshops, sideshows in the city square for "Family Day". It's the Saturn Return. That's what it is. I've been having one for years.

Seriously, folks and folkettes. We stepped back in history this year and enveigled (or envaudevilled) our way into the sightlines of unsuspecting Melbourne families. Eight sideshow acts and sixteen performer-musicians. Not a bad effort for the summer break, really. I chose my usual retiring sort of act – twirling fire clubs on a six foot ladder in the rain while my partner walked on razor-sharp glass. The kind of thing I do before breakfast on an ordinary sort of day. Some of the other acts we lifted out of last year's show (Swords in the Box, Flamenco Dancers Swallowing Razor-blades, the Jelly Botty Brothers and Madame Espiritus the Psychic) while others were put together especially for the occasion, like the Snake Women Acrobats.

We performed four times during the afternoon, kicking off each run-through with a musical march around the city square. Drums, percussion, loud squeaky instruments, funny walks. That sort of thing. This not only served to gain audience attention but successfully trashed any other acts foolish enough to compete with the big, bold, brash Women's Circus. This was my first involvement in percussion work and I loved every minute of it. Marianne Permezel was a delight to work with, as were the other women.

Performing with a smaller group is one of the main attractions of Moomba. The process is not as unwieldy as the end-of-year performance, the group dynamic much closer. Not to mention the buzz of performing on barges and in mainstream public venues before a 100 000-strong audience. Perhaps that's why I do it. Perhaps I'm just an ego-maniac. Or perhaps I just don't want to miss out on the fun.

Barges

Bridget Roberts

Standing on the barge in my grey skirt and red bellboy jacket, my eyes on the bankside crowds, the night air on my face, I rested and waited for the cue to begin the dance.

In the first year it had been the 8-hour day, women's work, rest and play, then three barges – graffitists abseiling on the prima donna's dress, nightmare dogs on stilts and helmeted workers doing acrobatics under and on a giant hammer. This time we had a barge for the aerial sprite scene from the Death show, and a post-modern (or so they tell me) creation of classical columns, futuristic costumes, pagan dance, acrobatics and fire. The process of being in the River Pageant is familiar now, but no less exciting.

The barge moves off. Gently, and clear of the other barges and the bridge. None of the clashing of lighting towers that marred the dress rehearsal. Ahead of us the aerialists are already swinging to the music that is so evocative of the last big show.

Standing near me, Maureen pushes the smoke button and I laugh as I'm unexpectedly in a dense cloud. The beat of our drummers sends us spinning, then throwing high kicks towards the audience. I love the exuberance of the dance, the way we say, "Look, Melbourne, this is us and we're taking over". It's our own powerhouse of International Women's Day celebration. I imagine I'm kicking away everything that hinders us and I send my smile and my pride to the women and children.

Altogether I found it a very humbling and moving experience to work on ritualising aspects of the lives of women who have dared to challenge the world-wide patriarchal brutality and madness. It made me realise why we need to make these more personal connections on a global basis with other women who are oppressed in ways we can only just begin to comprehend, living as we do such privileged lives, for the most part.

– Jean Taylor, *Newsletter*, Spring 1995

Night life over Melbourne: Aerialists on the Moomba River Pageant barge, 1995

Vivienne Mehes

The act – affectionately known as "The Skirts" – performed in part on the Moomba Barges this year; "The T-Shirts" – a comedy routine performed by six Circus women creatively enticing you to buy the fabulous Women's Circus Beijing T-shirt; and our much loved and very hard-working Women's Circus Band, who just get better and better, delighted the audience on both nights. Our new women, who had only been with the Women's Circus for seven weeks debuted (at the Malthouse Theatre if you don't mind!) with a very tight display of choreographed warm-up and balances.

Despite this fantastic line up, my favourite part of the night was the beginnings of the Amnesty Show which we are working on to take to China. Simple in its poignancy – even in the rehearsal period, this brought goose bumps to my back and neck and tears to my eyes.

– Deb Lewis, *Newsletter*, Spring 1995

We move from dance into pyramids, more dance, a ritual with fluorescent light sticks, and back to begin again. Repetition makes the action sharper and the transitions cleaner. Drummers and dancers work more closely.

We have to judge when to break out the fire clubs so that they are under way when we are passing the bulk of the audience and the sponsors. In my eagerness not to miss them, I give the cue too early and a few lucky people on Swan Street Bridge get the full glory.

Back at the quayside, we have swung back into the dance and pyramid routine and I don't want to stop, ever. But we're moored with our backs to the shore and the nearest crowds. I suppose we had to stop sometime. There's nowhere to exit to – the stage suddenly reverts to a dressing room and we just have to pretend no one's watching us as we bump out.

For about two weeks afterwards, I wake up nearly every night in the middle of some routine or other, sometimes actually out of bed and getting dressed for it! I realise how over-committed I was, with the POW performances and Moomba, and in the evaluation of Moomba we all acknowledge that the whole circus was very stretched. We also, though, welcome the knowledge that we had so much stamina and creativity.

Nicole Hunter

Circus Barge

Patricia Sykes

Women on the edge
we talk to the river
a dirty heart thick with silt
like ours   just like ours   bearing our
lives to the sea   jugglers
acrobats who won't stay clean
who fight the old roles
of sweetness cuteness meekness
no deals no playing dumb

we built the barge
mother river   it's ours it's ours
take our white painted faces
and we'll brave the equator
fight fire with fire
execute our stories
with rage with pride
circus skills we can take
to the grave   can bequeath
to our old ghosts
travelling behind

IV
In the Spotlight

**If you stuff up, look arrogant
and pretend it's part
of the routine.**

– Donna Jackson

Naomi Herzog

Censored: Paper representing the torn-up remains of Dr Ma Thida's writings fall upon the actors below in the Leaping the Wire Show, 1995

PRE-PERFORMANCE

Research:
Developing the Storyline

Louise Radcliffe-Smith

Research is an integral part of the circus year and the beginnings of the end-of-year show. All members are involved in researching the topic. This process allows women to contribute to the development of the storyline and thus to create a show that is representative of the circus. It also means women have a sense of involvement, belonging and ownership, which in turn gives greater depth, meaning and quality to their performance.

Research is usually carried out over a six-week period and presented at an information day in August. Women report back physically, verbally, on paper, in posters, cartoons, videos, cassettes, poems or pictorial booklets. Some concerns are raised time and again. These often make up the heart of the show.

Once feedback is given, the director's task is to integrate women's research into the storyline, matching physical actions with themes and scenarios, devising ways to use circus skills to tell a story and make theatre. For the first four years, Donna Jackson was the only director and the main scriptwriter for the circus. In 1995, eight circus members worked with individual groups to research and develop eight scenes for the show, overseen by guest director Meme McDonald. This took the process of community ownership one step further.

Whether controlled by one director or many, research for the end-of-year show involves a long process of consultation, the aim of which is to give every woman a strong sense of how she came to hold views on the performance topic. It gives women the chance to share experiences and knowledge, to explore commonality and difference.

Rehearsal:
Cancel Your Social Life!

Louise Radcliffe-Smith

Once the research period is over and final funding submissions posted, the Women's Circus goes into overdrive. It is September. The show is in November. We look up from our comfortable training routine and panic! There is so much to do!

It is both our strength and our weakness that things don't just happen in the circus; we make them happen. Women are both the machine and its components. We achieve only what we put in. We hammer the nails, raise the money, find the site, paste the posters, organise security, child care and food. At home the cycle continues: we feed the kids, earn money for rent or mortgage, learn life's lessons for better or worse, and return to the warehouse for a little sanity.

At this moment in the circus calendar, the list of "things to do" seems insurmountable. It is a period of chaotic not-knowing. The performance site has not yet been secured. The budget is tenuous, since we are still waiting for submissions to be answered. None of the costumes or props have been thought about, much less designed, and scenes are still on paper awaiting rehearsal. Technicians haven't even started hunting around for lighting, sound and props equipment to borrow. We are working in the dark. But, of course, we are used to leaping off edges into unknown futures. We do it every year. Donna's advice to everyone at this point is "cancel your social life", which most new members think is a joke until they try to fit one in between work, rehearsal and home life.

SCENE	PHYSICAL	WHO	FUNCTION	TONE/COLOUR
1	CONTACT DANCE	BUILD SLOWLY	INTRODUCE FERAL	PAGAN
	DOUBLE TRIPLE BALANCES	TO ALL	WOMEN, LIKEABLE	BROWN/WHITE
	SMALL AMOUNT FIRE IN BINS		FREE – LARRIKINS	BLACK/GREY
	BUILD PYRAMIDS			
	WOMEN PERFORM PHYSICALLY			
	TO ENTERTAIN EACH OTHER			
	SOME HARD/OTHERS WHIMSICAL			
	FUNNY PERFORMANCES			

About six weeks before the show, the director presents the group with a storyline based on earlier research. The women talk through the storyline and make suggestions. At this stage, many of the scenes are conceptual. The women talk about the meaning, the narrative and the message of the show. They also discuss the function, physicalisation, music, mood and colour of each scene. For instance, the function of an outside scene along the Maribyrnong River in 1991 was to lure the audience to the performance space by surprising and enchanting them. Performers did this by rolling, balancing, pretending to sell objects, hanging from trees, and teasing the audience. Musicians surrounded people as they walked, then disappeared. The mood was surprising, magical, earthy; the performers wore red and purple and took on individual characters (pickpockets, sellers, mad or wild women).

From the moment the storyline is set, training workshops turn into rehearsals. Each training group works on a particular scene or scenes. Some scenes that draw on people from all workshops, such as juggling or fire and stick twirling, are rehearsed separately. The workshop director gives the women a concept and the women translate that concept into physical form. For instance, the director might say: "You have fifteen minutes to come up with a low, middle and high balance representing birth, growth and death." Workshop members draw on their creativity and skill to develop a piece, then show the group as a whole. What works stays. What doesn't is adapted or ditched. In this way, rehearsals continue the process of collaboration. Everyone has the chance to develop her own character or skills, but ultimate artistic control remains the director's prerogative.

Directorial control is most evident during the two or three pre-show rehearsal weekends, when all hands are on deck ten

LIGHTS	MUSIC	AREA	AUDIENCE FEEL
LOWISH	WOMEN BUILD FROM LOW LEVEL PERCUSSION TO BIGGER AS SCENE DEVELOPS	SPREAD ACROSS LAWNS SOME GROUPS ON BRIDGE, ROSE GARDEN DOWN CENTRE SPREAD	CHARMED ENJOY ACTS CLAP

hours a day to block (construct), walk through and practise the sum total of our labours. This is the point at which all the scenes from individual workshops and rehearsals are slotted together like an enormous theatrical jigsaw. It is painstaking work. It can mean blocking a scene in the morning and hanging around for two hours until next needed. Or it can mean standing on stage taking orders for hour upon hour upon hour. Tempers fray. Voices are lost. Time alternately drags and flies.

On the last rehearsal Sunday there is a technical walk-through to co-ordinate lighting, music and performance cues. This is often the first time musicians see the show, or performers hear the music. Even though the show is to open in two days, everything is still in pieces. We stop, start, experiment with lighting states, change scenes or cut them completely. The reality of showtime still seems a million miles distant. For those who have sacrificed up to twenty-five hours a week over the rehearsal period, putting on a performance at this point feels more a matter of following orders and remembering storylines than creating art.

If everything runs according to schedule, which it usually doesn't, the technical walk-through is followed by a full technical rehearsal on Sunday night, a dress rehearsal on Monday night and a preview showing on Tuesday. By the end of the preview, tiredness is a way of life. Bodies ache. Minds bend. There is little room for nervousness. Bed and bath are on every woman's mind. And that magic monosyllable: "sleep".

Be bold, brassy and brazen.

– Donna Jackson

Musical Chairs

Louise Radcliffe-Smith

The music group enters rehearsal about the same time as the performers. Having played together and developed pieces during the year, the musicians (coached and encouraged by the musical director) create sounds to suit each scene – revolution, death or joyful celebration. Whatever the concept or the tone, the musicians give it form. And often they do so in isolation from the performance group. Musicians and performers rarely see or hear each other's creations before the final rehearsal weekend. Until that moment, performers juggle or dance to invisible beats while musicians take their cues from imaginary actions.

Tech Talk

Louise Radcliffe-Smith

The circus is not all playtime and face paint. Behind the scenes there is a group of diligent technicians who not only turn pipe-dreams into reality, but hold that reality together for the duration of the show. Each year, while performers rehearse, fifteen to twenty-five techies wire, gaffer, mend, hammer, shift, borrow, barter, scrounge and build a space for performers to bounce, balance and swing from the rafters.

Venues: Claiming the Space

Louise Radcliffe-Smith

Performance sites are often secured only weeks before the show. The venues change each year. Finding them is always a problem. Cheap, large performance spaces are nearly impossible to come by and usually difficult to modify. Performing inside means we have to adapt the space to suit the show; building, fixing and negotiating the addition of hygienic necessities such as toilets and change-rooms. Performing outside brings with it a different set of difficulties. The space may be muddy, uneven or full of holes, making it tricky to install seats, lights, aerial rigs and a front of house area. To add to the chores, all lighting and performance gear has to be disassembled and stored after every show, in case of rain, a real trial for the terminally tired.

The first show in 1991 was performed outside in a partially completed amphitheatre 500 metres from the Footscray Community Arts Centre on the banks of the Maribyrnong River.

Vivienne Méhes

In full voice: Kathrin Ward speaks to the multitudes 100 feet below from one of the kiln towers at the Brunswick Brickworks, 1995

The space was rectangular, backed by a 10-metre high brick wall and secured on one side by an elevated square section which became the band stage. Before the space could be used, circus members levelled the ground, removed truckloads of weeds, filled in drainage holes and mended railings.

In 1992, Donna managed to secure a warehouse 500 metres in the other direction along the Maribyrnong River. This huge space had to be swept and cleaned, doors secured, dressing-room built, toilet fixed and aerial rigging attached to the ceiling. In 1993, for lack of an alternative, the circus performed outside on the lawns at Footscray Community Arts Centre. Two 10-metre aerial rigs and an enormous lighting tower were installed on the rounded edges of a 45 degree slope.

The following year, 1994, we cleaned up a filthy abandoned warehouse in North Melbourne. Loreen, a founding member of the circus, had managed to secure the site from a massage client for $1 nominal rent plus $600 administration fee. Once again, techies accomplished the impossible and turned a dump into a spectacular performance space.

In 1995, the circus was offered the use of the 100-year-old brickworks in Brunswick. The factory site had closed in 1993 and was awaiting redevelopment. Though the towering kilns and ancient brick archways were visually spectacular, mud traps, crumbling walls and large quantities of rusty machinery meant parts of the site were difficult to work in safely.

Historical backdrop: Women rehearsing at the Brunswick Brickworks in 1995

Naomi Herzog

Costume and Design

Deb Lewis & Louise Radcliffe-Smith

Once rehearsals are underway, the directors liaise with the costume designer (Wiggy Brennan in first year and Wendy Black the following years) to create the "look" of the show. This is more difficult than it sounds. The trick, of course, is to clothe seventy women in non-stereotyped costumes for almost no money in a ten-day time frame. The Women's Circus look started with white bathing caps and sharp lines, overalls and skirts. Later it moved into vinyl, recycled tyre tubes and thermal underwear. More recently it has gone boldly technicolour – red, yellow, green and purple.

Most of the material is begged, scavenged or purchased cheap. The women take 20 kilograms of reject-quality tyre tubing, cut it up, staple it together and wear it. Worn-out tablecloths are turned into brilliant swirling skirts. Vinyl off-cuts look great in red and yellow! Performers follow Wendy's lead and become opportunity shop queens. The bathing cap retailers love us. In 1994, Donna wanted twenty-five bizarre and colourful animal hats. No problems – we all sat down one afternoon with newspaper, masking tape, glue and primary paints. Hey presto!

From the Journal

It is a Sunday afternoon of black rubber costumes and wind tearing at the tin roof. Women are grating away at old tyres to rough them up so they'll stick and metamorphose into skirt shapes, bra shapes, pant shapes, even tabards. It's like watching the emergence of a new species of black butterfly, bred for toughness and endurance. How will we look on the first night as we dance through the rose garden, play with fire, swing on the ropes, the trapeze, and trounce the queen? Almost I wish I could be in the audience and watch this new breed transform the garden and lawn area. It will never be the same and no one will ever guess that it all began to take shape during a seemingly innocuous sewing circle in an old butter factory.

– Patricia Sykes,
24 October 1993

Naomi Herzog

Headline: International
Women's Day, 1996

Naturally, given the cast size, not everything gets done on time. It's not unusual for women to staple their dresses because they haven't time to sew, or to stand in the wings waiting for their first scene having their clothes sewn together.

The costume-making workshops with Wendy Black have not only proved a great time and money saver, they have also become part of the tradition that brings performers together. Women talk and snip and sew and paint, debrief, compare notes and have a good chuckle. Who needs money when imagination serves as well? Makes you wonder what opera companies do with their budgets.

Pre-performance Crews

Louise Radcliffe-Smith

A few weeks before the show women divide into crews. These crews cover everything from publicity and food to programme design and props. Some crews swing into action prior to the show; most are maintained over the performance period. By having crews the circus aims to distribute workloads according to ability. Each circus member nominates the crew/s to which she wants to belong – a crew which suits her skills, time and interests. Women with small children may not be able to stay overnight to secure the space, but they can volunteer for other jobs. Some women work full-time and can only help out on performance nights; others are unemployed and spend weeks doing administrative jobs around Footscray Community Arts Centre or the performance space. Either way, the jobs get done.

Paste-up crew

The paste-up crew identifies shopping centres and likely venues for potential audience members. The aim is to have posters and fliers in as many shops, businesses and other public places as possible. This is a co-ordinated effort needing a large number of women. It must happen quickly in the weeks leading up to the performance and occur in concert with the activities of the publicity crew in order to reach as many people as possible.

Costume Crew

Our costume designer of four years, Wendy Black, must be a bit of a masochist. She works with a tiny budget on an extremely tight time frame and manages to make everyone look gorgeous! The costume crew offers Wendy assistance with measuring, fitting and sewing costumes for the seventy-strong cast, as well as helping clean and care for costumes during the performance period.

Programme Crew

The programme is one of the ways in which the political content of the Women's Circus can be conveyed to the public. The programme crew researches, writes and co-ordinates the production of the programme. For instance, for the 1994 production, Death: The Musical, women collected wills, interviewed funeral company directors and investigated the treatment of the dead in other cultures. The document they produced offered many options for dealing with the death of a loved one.

Rigging Crew

In 1991, the Women's Circus employed Alan Robertson to hang trapezes in our performance space – he was the only man on site. From 1991 to 1993 Alan designed and built aerial rigs and specialist gear for the circus, including a rotating ladder. By 1994, women were building their own trapezes, and cloud swings, ropes and other aerial equipment were hung by women.

Performance Crews

Deb Lewis

Cleaning Crew

All members are asked to help with the initial clean-up which, given the circus' choice of performance sites, is often a huge and dirty task. Performers, techies and musicians combine to sweep, scrub, cart rubbish, pull weeds, fill holes and carry out many of the other inglorious tasks involved in the early stages of a putting on a performance. The cleaning crew is a smaller group of women who tidy the site on a daily basis over the performance period, emptying bins, vacuuming the stage prior to performance and keeping the toilet area clean.

Dressing Room Crew

Sometimes known as the nurturing crew, this group of women set up the dressing room with mirrors, make-up and the creature comforts needed by performers and musicians. Sometimes, depending on the crew's membership, they provide massage, aromatherapy oils and general "healing" to the rest of the group.

Child-care Crew

The child-care crew makes sure quality care is available for the children of all circus members during training, rehearsal and performance time. Over the years, the number of circus members with young children has increased from one or two in 1991 to fifteen in 1995.

Documentation Crew

Documentation is an important part of circus herstory. It is part of not allowing the circus to fade into history unrecorded. The small but dedicated documentation crew have the task of gathering copies of material written about the circus. They also record radio and television interviews, shows and collect articles for archives.

Circus women have appeared on numerous community and mainstream radio shows, including 3CR, 3RPH, 3LO and Radio National; on television programs such as "Good Morning Australia", "Healthy, Wealthy and Wise"; on Victorian

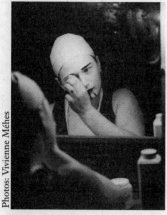

Photos: Vivienne Méhes

Kiss and make-up: (top to bottom) Liz Cooper, Kathryn Edwards and Josie Kristensen

television news; in several magazines including *Woman's Day*, the *Age Good Weekend*, *Women's Weekly* and *New Idea*; and in local and major newspapers.

Support Groups

Another Women's Circus tradition is that of support groups. These run throughout the year within some training sessions, and also meet one evening a month. They are designed to enable circus members to discuss issues that arise during training and how those issues relate to their lives. During rehearsals and the performance season, time is set aside for support groups, thereby ensuring that friction between circus members is kept to a minimum. There is a recognition that with such a large number of very different and quite stressed individuals who become progressively more tired as the performance season continues, the provision of such support is essential.

First Aid Crew

Over the rehearsal and performance period, a number of qualified circus members nominate themselves for the first aid crew. These women monitor the health of other members and make sure there is a stocked first aid kit on site. However, given circus women can't administer first aid while a performance is in full swing, two or three friends of members (trained first aiders or nurses) volunteer to sit in on all the shows in case disaster strikes performers, technicians or audience members.

From the Journal

The standard of safety is excellent and the women were well trained and very conscious of avoiding injury. Pre-performance warm-ups were obviously a very important factor. Part of the privilege of being First Aid person for the circus was getting to see nearly every performance! The great thing about this opportunity is seeing dress rehearsal, preview, opening night, the middle performances and closing night. It is exciting watching the show change, the performers finding their places within the show and feeling the energy of a different audience each night. Many audience members say there is so much to see and watching all the performances, I still didn't get to see everything! I love being able to be of service to the circus; it is good to able to give freely of a skill I have to the women's community.

– Liz Cooper, first aider 1992–94

From the Journal

Christina, Karen, Janine and I decided to form a support group of our own prior to performance time rather than end up with a more random group. This proved invaluable for me as I tried to cope with the demands of being a full-time worker, single mother/homemaker and mum to another circus performer. These women were always there for a hug or a few words when I needed them.

– Deb Lewis, 1994

Food/Wellbeing Crew

The food crew takes on one of the most vital and demanding jobs over the performance period: feeding the masses. The attitude of Sally Forth, the circus' original trainer, to health and nutrition continues to pervade the preparation of food for the whole circus community. The food crew prepares healthy, simple soups from organic ingredients. Much of the food preparation occurs at the homes of the crew members and, at the beginning of each performance night, huge pots of hearty soup are heated on the stove at the performance site. This means women, especially workers and mothers, are guaranteed a sustaining meal without having to make extra time to cook. The sharing of food is also a way of bringing women together at the beginning of each performance evening. Between 6.00 p.m and 6.30 p.m., women fill their bowls, grab a piece of bread and sit down to chat. It is the transition time of the day when members throw off their daily concerns and take on the role of circus woman. It is a fantastic way to begin each evening.

Food for thought: Preparing a feast for the 1993 Sport Show

From The Journal

Decision to take on most of the cooking/preparing ourselves. Or at least have the one person cooking a whole meal – in one place, rather than having it spread over three homes. The gas (at the performance space) can then be used to heat, and only the finishing touches need be added "on site". Hopefully this will reduce some stress.

Basically: a grain, a pulse, a vegie or two plus miso/garnish.

Mostly soups as they are one-pot meals. Maybe bread, though my feeling is that this – sourdough/organic – will eat into quite a large percentage of our allotted money. Bread, or, for that matter, meat can easily be brought individually if people feel that the meals need supplementing.

A consensus that organic food should be a priority. I believe that we should be able to shop well and come in under budget while still giving our utmost respect to the food that we use and the industry in general.

– Sharee Grinter, 1994

Publicity Crew: Media Mania

Publicity has become one of the major performance and pre-performance tasks. The circus has received an enormous amount of attention since its inception, some of which is due to the employment of publicists to spread word of circus exploits around Melbourne and interstate. Circus women have featured in almost every Melbourne suburban newspaper and regularly star in the *Herald-Sun* and the *Age*. They have also appeared in news bulletins on every TV channel and claimed space in the "7.30 Report", "Good Morning Australia", "Sunday", and "Healthy, Wealthy and Wise".

The publicist is one of the few paid workers employed prior to performance. She is of vital importance, as all our hard work in pre-performance and performance time would be wasted if it weren't for the audience. The publicity crew and the publicist work hand in hand. The publicist helps produce a poster and flier. The publicity crew organises circus women to conduct a massive paste-up of all the major streets of Melbourne two weeks before the show. The publicist organises media calls. Publicity crew members turn up and pose for the camera or chat on the radio.

But contrary to the views of star-struck television addicts, publicity is not all it's cracked up to be. Over-exposure has generated a certain amount of media-wiseness among circus members, who may or may not have had positive experiences at the hands of journalists and photographers. Occasionally performers put on costumes and white face and the photographer never arrives. Sometimes tired women are asked to repeat the same balance with the same smile and the same twirl of the fire club just once too often. Other times the questions are a little too personal or simply repetitive. And after all the politeness and posing, there is no guarantee the photos or words will appear as expected.

What Will We Wear?

Kylie Whyte

I really didn't think, when I wrote my name down as one of the many interested interviewees, that I would end up accompanying director Donna Jackson onto the Bert Newton-hosted "Good Morning Australia" program. "What will we wear?" we joked to each other, as we make plans for our debut on national TV. The fateful day came and we set off for Channel 10, armed with borrowed clothes, fire sticks and a double balance routine. I've never laughed so much in my whole life. As we were ushered in to get our make-up on, the make-up artist looked at me and said: "So, what are you wearing?" "What I've got on," I replied. "Oh," she said non-committally. "Oh, well, that'll work. Yes, that's nice."

After we asked her for "the natural look" in make-up she began plastering on layer upon layer of foundation in a vain attempt to cover up the bags under my eyes. When we walked into the waiting room our chaperone-type person asked us again what we were going to wear on TV. Ho hum.

I'm spending so much time on the lead-up because it was far more exciting for me that the two minutes with Bert on TV. I must say, though, that Donna was fantastic and while I didn't say much, I was there in spirit. At one stage Donna went into her fire-eating act, posed, looked at the camera people and said: "For the benefit of viewers at home, this morning I'm eating kerosene, but shellite tastes better." I could just imagine all those kiddies at home torching themselves in their back sheds! Bert was impressive, too. It took a lot of skill to find the time to ask whether either of us were "victims of incest" and to insult the older members of the circus by calling them "Granny Davises". All in a two-minute interview. Oh well, the perils of mainstream media.

Women's Circus Newsletter, Summer, 1994.

PERFORMANCE

Performance

Patricia Sykes

The costume waits limp
on the floor   lethargic
with absence   the body
redefines with make-up

      so do it now
      be proud
      be joyful
      celebrate
      you
      are a woman working

      move your body
      show
      what women
      ordinary
      can do
      we will show
      them all how
      give it
      move it
      in this space

it's more than a ritual
the pep talk is a coda
that runs through the blood
like adrenalin   it's a song
the circle sings face to face
before the door opens
and our legs find their bones

then the heat rush
to the heart and the entry
to our hands on the drums
behind the lights   behind
the controls the tickets
the drinks   circus women
in freefall   "Leaping off the Edge"
working our story home

Big Gigs

Deb Lewis

Physical training would not be complete without the end-of-year, large-scale performance. It gives structure and direction to our year. During training we concentrate our energies on developing the skills of our choice (juggling, balances, tight rope) and on our level of fitness – some women train up to six sessions per week. Come the end-of-year show, we can show off a little of what we have learned and achieved.

At this point, the scenes of the show have been strung together like fairy lights on a barge, the performers have their costumes made and ready to wear, the site is clean and awaiting the audience. We have entered the performance phase.

Like all performance groups that work together for a number of years, the Women's Circus has developed rituals and traditions that allow its members to work together as co-operatively as possible. A performance night goes something like this: everyone arrives at 6.00 p.m. for a meal prepared by the food crew. While eating, women catch up on gossip, verbally re-block (re-organise) scenes and cues, or meet in support groups. At 6.30 p.m., performers warm up physically – all musicians, techs and front of house women are welcome to join in. At 7.00 p.m., Donna re-blocks or rehearses any scenes that weren't up to scratch the night before, while musicians tune their instruments and technicians check lights, rigging and sound equipment. Women at the front of house sell tickets, organise drinks and popcorn for the audience, set up displays and generally maintain crowd control. In the half an hour before the show is due to start, performers and musicians put on costumes and white face paint. Technicians are asked to wear all black. Five minutes before the show starts, Donna comes into the dressing room and gives her famous pep-talk.

Once outside the dressing room, performers and musicians are asked to be "in character". This means not talking to the audience, not letting facial expressions give you away when something unexpected goes wrong in a scene. And if anyone falls "out of character", Donna is sure to see the *faux pas* and bring it up in "notes", the list of suggestions and instructions to performers and musicians she usually delivers straight after the show. Once "notes" are over, women pick up and store props before joining the audience for a drink and a chat.

Feeling Well During the Performance Season

Sally Forth, circus trainer

Meeting the physical demands of the show
- Take some holidays from work/take it easy at work if possible.
- Don't rage a lot.
- See friends who you know will be supportive, rather than those who might not understand the demands you're under.
- Try to eat well and get adequate sleep.
- Have hot baths after performance.
- Remember you might feel stiff after shows but you will recover by the next week if you do some light stretching.
- If you know you have a physical weak spot, structure something in during the performance period to help, a massage for example.
- Know your manageable level of alcohol/drugs after performance, taking these at this time could be unhealthy and debilitating.

Building the foundations: Sally Forth, Women's Circus trainer, 1991–93

Vivienne Méhes

Other life demands

- Have your car serviced and tuned.
- Work out your priorities and deal with them; do your tax, for instance.
- Identify what pressures you put yourself under (if you write lists of "things I must do", then throw them out the window).
- Let your friends know you are busy until the end of the show so you don't have to make excuses for not returning phone calls or socialising.

Remembering sequences

- Use some visualisation and "stretch the reality" – see yourselves doing your routine perfectly! This can be done when you are physically tired.
- Remember how much you *do* know.
- All sixty women will not forget sequences, so you will be able to follow other women's cues if you forget it yourself.

Doing it well

- Remember if you are not doing the show to the best of your ability, you are not doing it well. You can achieve satisfaction through strong expression.
- Practise and give yourself time. You may not feel it comes together until the third week. Expect development and improvement.
- The show is about enjoying and expressing ourselves, not about trying to be like someone else.

Performance environment

- Don't take risks, ensure your safety.
- Be focused, don't be distracted by the sounds or lights.
- Spend some time in the performance space before the show and check it out.
- Be involved when the equipment you will be using in the show is assembled – aerial rigs, fire, and so on.
- Be open to modifications if safety becomes an issue.

Injury prevention

- Take responsibility for your own space, especially when flags or sticks are around. Look to see where props are set and avoid sharp objects, such as spinning sticks and fire clubs, at eye level.
- Group cohesiveness – being aware of where you are in relation to other prevents impact injury.

- Pace yourself and know your own limits to avoid heart attack and high blood pressure
- Modify your routine if you have a muscle weakness or injury, and communicate this to others. Tired muscles strain easily.
- Don't push yourself to learn new things during performance time. This creates unnecessary stress.

Physical arena

- Hold one foot with both hands and press the sole of your foot in the middle near the instep (below the base of the first and second toes) with thumb. This builds willpower and whole body strength.
- Taking cold showers and scrubbing your skin with a loofah or rough flannel releases pressure and stops nerves becoming jangled. It will also help you feel where your body begins and ends.
- For insomnia; avoid strong teas like valerian and drink mild ones such as chamomile or lemon balm.

Negotiating with 120 women

- Make an effort to meet and talk with women you have not yet met.
- Use support groups to talk of fears and other issues.
- Put out positive energy to others; it is often returned.
- Remember to say "no" if that's how you feel.
- Pair with different women in warm-ups before performances.

Food

- Eat well, don't eat take-aways.
- Plain food is better than hot, spicy food.
- Cut down on sugars as they are bad for your adrenal system and menstrual cycle. If you are craving sugar, substitute rice or barley malt for honey and eat sweet root vegetables (pumpkin, carrot, sweet potato).
- Eat lots of grains, wholemeal breads, miso, malt, rice.
- Eat small meals more often rather that skip meals.

Intuition

- Examine your mind-set about the show: Thinking "It's going to be hard, scary, painful – how am I going to do it!" means we create self-doubt in our minds. "It's going to be hard, challenging, exciting, I'm going to enjoy it!" means we create self-belief and confidence.

Security: Locked Up Tight

Deb Lewis

One of the greatest traditions of the Women's Circus is security. As show time draws closer and equipment arrives at the site, the security crew asks performers, techies, musicians and front of house women to sign up for at least one day or night of security – three women at night and one or two during the day. Officially, this means guarding the large amount of equipment mostly begged and borrowed from other more affluent institutions from the final rehearsal weekend until the season closes. In reality, security often affords an extended tea break over cards and chocolate in what is generally known as "the girl's dorm". The security xrew usually manages to borrow

Van guard: The overnight security caravan, 1993

enough to make the duty pleasurable – a caravan, a television and video, beds, chairs, books . . . it's almost like home. While on security, women often spend hours poring over or confiding in the circus journal and many a funny story has gone down in writing. Like the time Maureen O'Connor surprised a burglar sneaking through a broken window at two o'clock in the morning and rose from her bed, demanding in an enormous voice: "What the fuck do you think *you're* doing here?!" The terrified bloke fled and was picked up by the police half an hour later.

From the Journal

Sitting on the banks of the Maribyrnong at midnight on security, watching a freight train crossing the bridge to the city, seeing the lights reflect off the water and the skyline, finding the scene almost pretty. The sound of the trucks in the foreground, the monotonous movement of freight, the activity concealing another life around Westgate. A lull in the industrial landscape leaves space for something profound: the songs of a nightbird, and possums, and crickets singing a "round".

– MGB, 1993

BEHIND THE SCENES

The Technical Crew

Georgine Clarsen, production manager

The fascination and challenge of the Women's Circus is to combine seemingly incompatible elements: non-professional community theatre with performances that strive to be theatrically innovative and satisfying; feminist politics with a show that aims to appeal to a broad audience; work which challenges and stretches the individual members of the tech crew without introducing an air of competition; artistic decisions placed in the hands of individual tech crew members while still maintaining high production values; fun times with a safe and disciplined working environment.

Vivienne Méhes

Bike act: Tech co-ordinator Georgine Clarsen dinking director Donna Jackson around the Brickworks site, 1995

There is now a solid core of the tech crew who have worked on most of the major seasons of the Women's Circus. These women, a few of them now beginning to earn a living as theatre technicians, are essential to the success of the technical work. They take on an area of work – such as staging, or lighting design, or follow-spot lighting – and get a crew of less experienced women to work with them. They then teach these women, assemble the equipment, design the work, get it happening, develop cue schedules, run the shows and, with the performers' help, dismantle it all at the end of the season.

Each year, up to half of the tech crew are first-time members. These women prevent the tech crew from becoming a closed, static group. They bring a freshness and enthusiasm to the work, as well as new skills, which helps remind us what's good about the project. There always seems to be a good balance of new and old members. There is enough experience to make sure

This has been my first year with the Women's Circus. I've been in the tech crew and had a lot of mixed emotions about it, from the time I got involved through two friends and came to my first tech workshop feeling overwhelmed and shy at the number of women there, many of whom knew each other from previous performances. While I felt awkward, I also sensed a great deal of support and joy and hoped that I would be able to overcome my shyness and tendency to keep to myself. And I have to a certain extent. By the time we were in production week I was talking and laughing and sharing with other women in the crew, learning heaps of new things, using my initiative, being constantly amazed by the generosity and stamina of the other women.

– Nicki, 1993

that the work can proceed, but a sense of openness remains.

My role as tech crew co-ordinator is to teach the skills needed to get the shows up, to make sure that all areas of the work are covered and that the designs are as good as they can be within the budgets, to set up each area as safely as possible for each crew and to make sure that everything conforms to the laws covering public performances. During the shows, I mainly do general maintenance and trouble-shooting, and try to leave each part of the tech crew to work directly with the artistic director in establishing the "look" and "feel" of the show. I try to intrude as little as possible into final decisions.

The work for the tech crew generally begins about six weeks before a season, with workshops covering a wide range of technical skills as well as introducing new women to the aims and working methods of the circus. The skills I teach are determined by the needs of the participants in any one year, but they are intended to give general life competencies as well as specific theatre skills. Some of the most popular topics covered are: knot-tying (the three knots essential to life – clove hitch, bowline and truckie's knot); basic electrics (such as wiring plugs, fuses and circuit breakers); use of tools (which includes the safe use of ladders and power tools as well as how to select a basic tool kit); an introduction to the lighting and sound equipment the crew are likely to use during the season; and the principles of lighting design.

The workshops are an important time in establishing the "working ethic" of the tech crew. It is a time when new members get to know people and develop some confidence about their new knowledge and their ability to find a meaningful place in the whole process. For experienced members of the tech crew, the workshops are a time for refreshing and consolidating their skills by teaching others, for bringing together ideas about the shows that have been fermenting for the past year and to start thinking about what areas of technical work they would like to tackle. Inevitably, a lot of the planning is done in a vacuum, given that the form of the show is still only known in broad outline, that the venue is probably still not finalised and the equipment available to us (much of which is borrowed) is also unknown!

The production week prior to performance is highly stressful for everyone, the hours demanded are long and the activities are driven by the need to be ready for tech rehearsal night, rather than the needs of the group to continue learning about the equipment and how it can be used. It is an abrupt change from the easy pace and sociable fun of the workshops. At this time the tech crew co-ordinator relies totally on the experienced members of the tech crew to get together a small group of their own and take over a particular area, be it outdoors lighting, follow-spots, fire extinguishers, stage managing or general show lighting.

The co-ordinator's role is to set up each of the smaller groups with what they need to get their area happening and then move on to help get the next group organised. This time can be a little confusing and disillusioning for some of the crew, since the co-ordinator is spread too thin and can't provide all the direction and encouragement that is needed. If the circus could expand the technical budget its first priority would be to hire other theatre professionals to work with each crew in the pre-performance week.

However, each year the abilities of individual women expand to fill the roles available. At very short notice, they assess what needs to be done, divide the work among themselves, design how they are going to do it and then, somehow, get it done safely, in time and within budget. And all done with a generosity of spirit and air of mutual support.

What represents a challenge and achievement or the high point for each woman varies widely. What women get out of their involvement is often quite unexpected. For some it's designing a lighting rig, for others it's climbing a ladder or driving through the city to collect equipment. One year a woman told me that the highlight for her was to work out for herself how to change a fluorescent light tube. Such skills and increased confidence stay long after the work of circus is over.

The technical work of the circus is, however, not without its downside. The major problem, I believe, is ironically related to the history of success of the technical work. The job is getting so big. Each year it seems more is expected of the tech crew, as well as the performers. Higher standards. Less room for error. Less room for experimentation. Less time for fun. More hard work and stress. There must be a limit to such expansion. This issue needs to be addressed.

Another problem that concerns me is that of making meaningful the ideology that all women in the circus are equally important, and technicians are not there as lesser "servants" to the performing group. The ideology of breaking down the barriers between performers and technicians tends to remain only that – an ideology – because even though many performers express a genuine interest in the technical work, the reality is that during the set ups and the shows they are far too absorbed in their performing work to give it any thought. It's just not practical to think that it would be otherwise.

The only way around this impasse is to take a long-term approach. The chance for performers to develop more understanding and awareness of the technical work comes at the end of each season, when the demands of performing have passed. After the final show, before the cast party, all performers, technicians, musicians and front of house women help "bump out" or dismantle the set. Bump out involves cleaning the site, returning circus equipment, mats and props to the training warehouse, pulling down the seating banks, taking down lights and rigging, and a myriad other things. This gives performers an opportunity to learn about the technical work, and get a sense of what goes on around their performances. The knowledge they acquire during the previous year's pull down is then brought with them to the next season. Gradually, in this way, there can be a lessening of the distinctions between technical and performing work and a greater understanding between the two groups.

Nicole Hunter

Breaking Down the Mystery

An interview with Rosie Finn

Louise Radcliffe-Smith

Rosie Finn hails from Brisbane originally but has called Melbourne home for most of the last twenty years. A woman of diverse interests and hidden talents, Rosie has worked in women's and welfare services, refuges, rape crisis centres and community development organisations. She made her first sally into theatre with Donna Jackson in the early 1980s, helping stage a play about domestic violence called No Myth. This was followed by another performance called Seven Minutes in Seven Women's Lives and a number of jobs stage-managing small productions at Footscray Community Arts Centre. Since joining the circus as a technician in 1991, Rosie has gone on to work on Moomba, the Melbourne Fringe, the Next Wave Festival, Midsumma and Melbourne International Festival.

When I joined the circus I was still at a learning stage with my skills. I'm not actually that skilful, but I'm extremely practical and I really like the challenge of finding out how to do things or where to get things. I find working on a small budget quite challenging, and it fits in with my personal philosophy about recycling. If I can re-use something for another purpose it makes me happy. For me, being in the tech crew is a lot about recycling, getting things for free, trade-offs.

Naomi Herzog

Rosie Finn

The techie workshops prior to the show opened up women's vision. I've seen a fear of electricity transformed into a healthy respect for electricity in the workshops. Women realise it's a good thing to use and not a mysterious thing you have to get someone else in to take care of. Women were taught to put power plugs on leads, what was negative and positive and what was the earth wire. And now they know these things they realise they are not restricted as to where they put the fridge or the stereo in their own homes. They can run a cord around to wire things up. We also did a sound course, understanding how electricity led to sound and how sound worked as well as lighting.

In the tech crew, women learn that most things are quite logical. Each person in the tech crew was asked to get a shifter and then we realised that with a shifter we could just about undo anything. For instance, there were group bikes in the show and I showed one woman how to take off a back tyre, to lay it out in a row and put it back in reverse order. And she said later it was a great moment for her when she was able to fix her kids' bikes. Her kids said: "Oh, the bike's broken, we'll have to wait till dad comes home from six months at sea." And she said: "No, I can do it." So then the kids didn't see her as just someone who cooked and cleaned; their view of their mum changed. And she didn't feel so helpless in the world.

As women we are very much taught to be helpless, and I think the circus transforms that, whether you do the hands-on things yourself or just see other women doing it. You learn anyone can do it. And I think a lot of the kids like to see their mums do things. We're not just changing us, we're changing other generations as well.

In 1991, my first show, Donna asked me: "Could you get a boat?" So I looked everywhere for someone who would give us a boat that could have fire all around it and possibly on it, which is quite a proposition to put to someone. I quickly worked out that a wooden boat was not a good idea.

On that first show women did all the hard physical work. The site was a Community Employment Program work project that was never finished, so it had open drain holes on the performance areas. We had to build covers to put over the holes and they had to be quite strong because we didn't want people jumping off a trapeze down a 9-foot hole and coming out in the Maribyrnong River sometime later. It was really good to see women reclaiming the site and doing things they had never done before.

In the second year, 1992, Donna asked: "Could you get a train?" The idea was to move the audience from Footscray Community Arts Centre down to the warehouse space. At first I used to be stunned at Donna's requests but now I'm not surprised. I just know that it will fit in somewhere. I really try because I just know it will be worth it. So I said, "Oh, well there's a train track down the bottom of the centre there, it's not such a silly request." It's amazing when you go off asking, the things that can happen. So I actually went off to the state railway system chasing a train. And I found out there are a few women train drivers around. But it turned out to be a really expensive thing to do because you didn't just have to have the train and the driver, you had to have guards. It wasn't practical, so I had to let it go. But it would have looked fantastic.

For the 1992 show in the warehouse, Women and Work, I worked with Alan Robertson in the Circus Oz workshop and we did a lot of welding. I learnt lots from him about rigging and safety and the use of pulleys, how to get stuff up high. I worked with him before the show building things. We made the cart and a few of the props that had to be quite sturdy. That was a huge change for me, working with big heavy bits of steel, getting them up to the ceiling. We had problematic things like welding bars to steel rafters and working out how to get the welder up there. We also built a rotating ladder. Sally and I had seen a rotating ladder in an old vaudeville movie once and decided we wanted to see if we could make one. It was actually just the two bodies on either end and how far they moved from

Vivienne Méhes

Lighting up: Techie, Carole Neal rigging lights, 1993

each other that made the ladder spin. The centre had a giant pin through it. It didn't have any mechanical device. It was really good to make something that looked like it was incredibly complicated but actually was very simple.

For me, the Women and Work show was physically hard work and quite challenging. And it was also a bit isolating because to start with I was removed from the tech crew and the performers. It was a good lesson for me to realise how daunting it is for people to come into such a huge group of women who have already bonded in different ways. It's a bit dinosaurish. It's still friendly and quite embracing, but still daunting. So I've particularly gone out of my way to talk to new people since then and I hadn't really before. I think it's important that we remain friendly and supportive and don't let the circus become such a big thing that people are isolated.

But then I came on board during the performance, brought in my tools, and became the general fix-up props person. I mended cable barrels, designed the tightrope, built security and change-rooms for the cast, checked the rigging each night, taught the "police" to march, and so on. And that helped the transition from feeling a bit separate to becoming part of things. In one of the scenes, we had to stage an industrial accident, so I got to let off a big bang which made me happy. One night I had to move a 2-inch deep, 8-foot by 4-foot puddle with a paper cup. It took two and a half hours. Another time a performer mentioned her hem was coming down. I don't sew. I only rig and gaffer. So I stapled up her dress.

In 1993, the Women and Sport show, I liaised with outside groups and the State Emergency Service. I talked the SES into erecting the front-of-house marquee as a training operation. It was great bridging the gap between groups. The SES crew all came to the show, and some will now advocate for the Women's Circus all over the western suburbs.

In 1994, I built and acquired props. We had magic tricks in the sideshow scene and to set the atmosphere we had some props from the Victorian State Opera. Usually there's quite a fee, but I did some negotiations and we saved a lot of money. That year I did a lot of moving props and equipment from FCAC and various places. We hired, borrowed, acquired (which is a fancy word for steal) from lots of community groups. Circus Oz have been really supportive; we use lots of their equipment, and

Vivienne Méhes

Fine focus: Techie Jan Howard setting up lights for the 1992 Work show sometimes we pay for that in labour and sometimes with money.

We also needed to create ten little stages for the sideshow acts, so once again I called on my mates at the SES and we put up big tarps behind each roller door. I also built a coffin and that was pretty interesting. We were in a big space in 1994 and had a big rehearsal area. At 11.00 p.m. at one rehearsal, Donna decided we did not have enough carpet to cover the stage and asked the tech crew to get the rest carpeted by rehearsal the next day. That night, when I was asked, I thought it was impossible, but somehow we managed to do it with the help of the rest of the tech crew.

The tech crew becomes a family, really. Part of it is necessity. We have to work well together and trust each other. Being 20 or 30 feet up a ladder you have to trust that the person will not let it slip or go off and have a cup of tea. It's teamwork.

Also, no-one is precious about knowledge or skills and people feel free enough to say; "Oh I don't know how to do that." Production week gets pretty hectic, but people are still free enough to say: "I don't feel confident enough to do that yet, could you do it with me?" A lot of that comes from the fact that many of the tech crew have been there for years. But it also comes from the co-ordinator, Georgine, who is very open with her knowledge. She always asks: "Do you know how to do this?" Or "Do you feel all right doing this by yourself?" And if not she'll stay and give you the knowledge and expertise.

Vivienne Méhes

Technical detail: Tech crew hard at work, 1992

The circus tech crew is different from other work crews. I think it's different because it's women and women are used to having to make households and families work. There's more preciousness in other organisations. People have the attitude that "I'm the carpenter and I do the woodwork and I only talk to the plumber if I have to." In the circus it's more about multi-skilling and co-operation. We're all here to make the whole circus work. I think our skills of co-operation and working together are ones that can be used in the boardroom or on the building site.

The level of personal commitment from women to the whole thing has amazed me. We can be so physically exhausted that we're in tears but we're asked to run it again and we just get in there. Production week is taxing physically and emotionally. It's hard work and a lot of hours. I've learnt that some people work okay for six hours and then they lose the plot and that's how they are. Whereas I'll stay there until it's finished.

I was around in the 1970s when it was: " Oh God, we're so hard done by, you [the men] have been doing it wrong for centuries." The Women's Movement spent twenty years writing books and saying: "This is why we're not mechanics, lawyers, doctors, politicians." Now, there are women politicians, and there are lots of women technicians. I really like this transition the circus has gone through. We've stopped identifying the problem. We're saying: "Look, let's just get in there and do it." Women are strong physically. They can swing from a trapeze and lift up other women. We're clever, we can rig a complicated lighting set. If you see a strong woman with two other women standing on her shoulders, there's no way you can't believe it. You have to change what you think. We're strong, we're capable. That's what I believe and it's really important to me. I really feel proud and inspired to be part of it.

Lights, Cables, Action

Maureen O'Connor

Maureen is a hard-core techie from way back. Since joining the tech crew for the first performance in 1991, she has put her heart and soul into the circus and its women.

There's sound, there's lights, there's cables running everywhere, not to mention a buzz of activity around the techie desk. All through the seating banks and from just about every rafter, ladder, nook and cranny, women yelling out across the space, calling out numbers, calling out instructions, concentrating, heads in the air, lifting and lugging lights of every shape, size and description. The space is converted from nothing to a performance area and you might wonder how the hell this all happened. You are not alone. The conversion of an empty warehouse or open area is a time-consuming and labour

Susan Hawthorne

Leading light: Techie
Maureen O'Connor

intensive task; the skills required to convert a space and to make a show happen are countless.

Leads, cords, lights and lighting boards – this is my involvement in the Women's Circus. Five years ago Donna Jackson had a dream to start a women's circus. I, for one, was not interested in performing as such but I was very interested in the technical side of the affair (affair is what it has become for me). So there I was, one of the techies for the first show. That show was one of the best times of my life. I had a lump in my throat the size of a warehouse. The first night was wet. As I was making my way to the venue I was sure that it would be cancelled. When I arrived I sank up the top of my shoes in mud; but the Women's Circus did perform that night and for the whole season.

Since that time I have been a techie on all the shows including the Moomba River Parade. You may ask why? The Women's Circus to me is what feminism is all about, women working together to create an environment that is as close to perfect as possible. Women in the Women's Circus are survivors of lives that are less than perfect. "But whose life is perfect?" "No one's," is my answer, but some have had it better than others. The circus offers women the chance to prove to themselves that they can do almost anything. My advice to all women who come into the technical side of the circus is to try everything once. I believe that by working on the circus tech team you learn you can tackle anything and succeed. We can take a disused warehouse and make it into a performance space within fourteen days. Macaulay Road, North Melbourne, the sheriff's office – we made that derelict building into a magic place for four weeks in 1994. The magic of the Women's Circus is something to behold. The first day I saw the space was when it was an inch thick in dust, had fences everyway, desks and weeds. Anyone who has not worked with the Women's Circus would not have believed that we could transform it into a theatre!

The Women's Circus has given me some of the best times of my life. The women I have met have enriched my life, and helped me feel good about myself. When I see the women come out and perform I am so proud to be connected with the wondrous and fulfilling Women's Circus. I often question what I did before the circus. I have recently become involved in the Performing Older Women's Circus, POW, and have, after five years of being Maureen ("I don't do warm-ups") O'Connor, become a performer and I am loving it. I now understand the thrill that goes with performing. The fun and hard work that I have found with both circus areas that I am involved in is the essence of what I believe the Women's and POW Circus is all about.

The women of the tech crew are very special women. There have been some who have joined the tech crew and have now gone on to performing. Then there are others that have just stayed with teching. Each year the women who join the tech crew learn new skills and these are both practical and impractical. There are some women who come to the tech crew who have never handled power tools, are afraid of ladders, have never made up power cords and were afraid of electricity. The tech crew offers a chance in a protective environment to try all the above and then some. The tech crew is a place where you can admit you have never done this or that before and not be made to feel useless just because you have these fears. Thank you, Women's Circus, for all you have given me.

An Eye for Safety

Ursula Dutkiewicz

I am a technician in the Women's Circus and have been since the first show. I have mainly concentrated on lighting but a circus technician is called upon for many tasks. With a keen eye and tools in hand I wander the performance space in search of the jobs that need doing that no one sees. A small inconspicuous bolt protruding from the cement floor unnoticed by all who pass by. You may say, "So what?" but a good techie knows the damage it can cause. Out comes the angle grinder, on go the goggles and the accident that might have happened never will. An electrical cord needs fastening. It's hanging in the path of the stilt walkers who come through in the dark. I move a 30-foot extension ladder against a crossbeam. Someone foots the ladder and up I go rung by rung balanced precariously. I fasten the offending cord and am contented as

Illuminated: Ursula Dutkiewicz sets lights, as she has for almost every Women's Circus show

the job is done. Not bad for a woman who four years ago was terrified of heights. I love that about circus – there are always new challenges no matter how small or big.

A Designer's View

Wendy Black

Vivienne Méhes

Shoestring budget: Costume designer Wendy Black (left) paints overalls with a roller and housepaint

In my working life particular theatre companies, productions or people have moved me on in my experience. The Women's Circus is one of these. Previous to working in the circus I had been in theatre for twenty years, designing and constructing for over sixty productions, in England, Hong Kong and Australia. In Australia I have worked with all sorts of companies – fringe, mainstream, opera, dance and circus. Theatre is demanding and being a workaholic I ground myself down to a burnout. Very few projects grabbed my imagination and enthusiasm and I reached an impasse. I gave up the profession that I had always been passionate about in order to re-evaluate.

Wendy Black: Working drawings "A referee"

Years later, an actor friend gave my name to Donna Jackson, and I went along to talk to her out of curiosity more than anything else. I was impressed with the unusual nature of the project, structure and way of working. Although I had almost divorced theatre – I got sucked in.

The decision to work for the circus has rewarded me in many ways since. It has given me new confidence, engaged me in different ways of working, enlightened me and given me contacts that have opened many doors. Footscray Community Arts Centre asked me to teach an evening class. Teaching had never appealed to me before, but I took on the challenge and enjoyed it. Through that experience I am now teaching full-time at Swinburne University in the costume department. Access to the costume department has benefited both the circus and the costume students. Students are involved (where appropriate) in making circus costumes, gaining valuable external experience.

My main objective, when I started to design for the circus, was to preserve the individual nature of each performer – not to stifle this with a design concept. The design had to be an integral part of the process and reflect the performers' philosophy. We wanted to find strong, fresh images of women. The individual nature of the costumes has been preserved by involving the women in making parts of their costumes. Costume workshops allow hidden creative urges to be revealed and many hands to make light work.

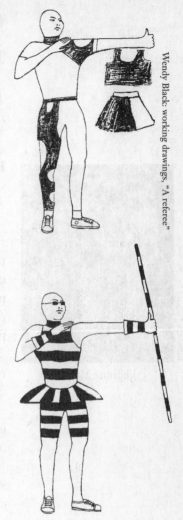

Wendy Black: working drawings, "A referee"

Capturing the Raw Energy:
Photo-documentation

Vivienne Méhes talking with Alison Richards

Elizabeth Gilliam

Vivienne Méhes

I am a professional documentary photographer and have worked since 1981 in a community arts context on projects about migration, work, cultural and domestic life.

My contact with the circus began in 1991 when I was photographer in residence at Footscray Community Arts Centre. As this was the year the Women's Circus began, I was able to work closely with the women who joined at its inception. I photographed the workshop and skills development process. At the end of my residency I came back to document the first performance season.

These photographs formed the beginning of what is now a record of every aspect of the circus' work. I have since built an archive with images of every major performance. These images extend far beyond the usual staged PR shots – they include images of women in rehearsal backstage and in performance and tell the story of the intimate moments as well as the highlights.

That first season affected us all with its raw energy and the sheer willpower it took to get it together with such a large number of women. I was overawed by the experience and shot every performance! My theatre photography exploded into wild red images of strong women doing extraordinary things. I was passionately committed to the Women's Circus from that point. I focused on non-stereotypical images of women – women who have determined every aspect of how they see themselves, and how they want to be seen.

A lot of the new women don't necessarily know me. I work closely with Donna to draw out that moment in the show to make the pre-performance publicity shot. Since that first season I haven't been around for workshops so I only turn up just before the performers go on and the exhibitions suddenly materialise in the foyer. My sense of continuity with the circus is in a different time frame from the one the performers are working with.

After the performance is over, it's the images that remain. At the time, I'm invisible, dressed in black in the shadows with the techies. People are just getting on with what they're doing and the best shots are when they're not aware I'm there. So while I have to know each show intimately, and even take on the same energy as the performers so I can get into position, find the best angle for that particular part of the action, in a way I'm always working alone. It's only afterwards that people see the photographs and their eyes light up. The performance lives again in the way the images are used.

I travelled to the NGO Forum in Beijing with the Women's Circus group. It was a demanding but exhilarating time for us all. I was able to feel part of that experience, and it was exciting for me, and important for the archive to be able to record the circus' presence on the world stage of women.

As well as my paid work for each performance, I have, on my own initiative, produced colour and black and white posters for sale. I wanted to make the images available at an affordable price. A3 photographs are incredibly expensive, so this way circus members and supporters can take home their favourite image. It's also been interesting to me that each year I've been able to select a series of images that live in different ways. They emerge as a documentation of the whole history, as well as a solid view through each show. Because I've done an exhibition for most seasons, my relationship to that stock of images is much more intimate. It's become a living documentation, not just a stack of publicity shots.

The archive that has accumulated is a unique resource in community theatre. The images are in demand throughout the year – they reflect the investment of time, and the mutual exchange between a visual artist and the circus as it continues to develop.

Hitting the High Notes: Music in Performance

Jean Taylor and members of the Music Group

Vivienne Méhes

Hats off to the music group:
Leaping the Wire, 1995

The Music Group has always played an integral role in the whole circus, particularly during performance. Even though musicians train separately, when they come together with the physical performers they become part of a powerful expression of something innovative and meaningful. This requires effective communication between the circus director and the musical director.

As most circus themes are non-vocalised, the music helps set the mood for the show. This two-way process gives meaning to the performance and the music. Many physical performers have said they feel inspired when the music is incorporated into the message they are trying to express, which helps give their characters more meaning.

Women in the band have also gained a lot from being involved in different aspects of performance; for instance, creating their own masks and costumes, being part of the story creation, playing "roles" in certain sections of the show.

Performances are stressful times – dealing with individual emotions or coping when one person is out of rhythm. But the highs of the audience applause and appreciation of the music "working" in the show has, over the years, helped the Music Group identify itself as the "Women's Circus Band".

For some women, the end-of-year show is the highlight of their time in the circus. It not only makes sense of all the hard work and training, it pulls everyone together from diverse workshops into a cohesive whole for the first time. The performance gives musicians and performers the opportunity to see the results of months of training.

I'd like to draw attention to the commitment of the musicians in the show for their incredible enthusiasm and tenacity, for lugging all the equipment across and back for every performance, for coming in early afternoons on the day of the shows to rehearse and for writing new music for inclusion in the performances and even after the show had opened. The support for each other was fantastic and by the end of the show we'd all realised just how much had been achieved. I worked on this show for the involvement of the music group in production and also for the opportunity to work with other women in music and produce a worthwhile piece of theatre both artistically and politically.

– Sue Speer (1991 Music Director), *Newsletter*, February 1992

Radha Claridge was the music workshop co-ordinator throughout 1992. She developed an innovative style of musical percussion, commonly referred to as "industrial grunge", to fit in with the "Women and Work" show at the end of the year. Towards the end of that year Marianne Permezel came in to bring the music group to performance stage.

After seeing the show Radha was most impressed with the music group's performance.

After seeing the preview and then going again later, I thought they were doing a fantastic job, especially knowing they had only two run throughs of the show (before it started). They were a lot more prepared than they thought they were. It's just the nature of theatre. I think everyone was just incredibly proud. They have got a lot of positive feedback (from audience and cast). And I think they have established strong bonds with each other. Some people want to get a band happening outside the workshops.

– Radha Claridge, *Newsletter*, December 1992

Kylie Whyte was not only a member of the music group, playing bass, electric guitar and industrial junk metal, she also nipped on and off stage as a performer. She wrote:

It was quite anxiety provoking, the build-up to the show, because we did not get to move the instruments in till just before the show and we did not work with the physical performers. So there was quite a lot of anxiety about whether the music would fit in. But it was also really exciting and really built a solidarity within the group because we were working together composing music at the last minute. The most amazing thing was the transformation that happened. All of a sudden when we were rehearsing for the show we came together and began working as a group. The first time we played on stage we got off afterwards and marvelled.

One time we played the celebration scene while people were warming up and they all stopped and cheered. It was such a buzz!

For me the last night was the best because we were all so excited and that really brought the feeling of the music up. And in the final scene (it was great) being able to smile and be with them all.

– Newsletter, December 1992

Sue Speer came in at the last minute and taped music for the Women and Sport show in 1993. This was the least involved the music group had been in the annual end-of-year show, with members reduced to drumming in the bushes for one of the scenes. In all other shows, the music group played an integral part in the overall performance. Nevertheless, Sue's taped music did provide an interesting, innovative and relevant score for the performance as a whole.

In direct contrast to the experience of 1993, the involvement of the band in the 1994 Death: The Musical show was so successful the music group went on to produce a live recording of the performances. Individual musicians also took part in the sideshow acts at the beginning of the show, dressed in colourful, innovative outfits.

Marianne continued to train the music group in 1995, but resigned as musical director around the time rehearsals were about to begin for the 1995 show, Leaping the Wire. This created a large degree of insecurity and prompted several of the music group to also pull out, leaving only four women who had trained throughout the year. However, there were a number of women on the waiting list who were interested in joining the music group and ended up contributing to the show at this last minute.

Fortunately too, Paula Dowse who had worked with the music group in 1993, agreed to take on the monumental task of pulling this disparate group of women into a cohesive and workable music group in the four week lead-up to the show. That she succeeded is a credit to her skills as a musician and the dedication and perseverance of the musicians themselves.

Musical Notes

Zen Atkinson

Wow! What a year! Shows, shows and more (fill in the blank) shows. I managed to secure a place amongst these feisty, drumstick-wielding, bass-slapping, wind-blowing, string-bending women known as the Women's Circus Music Group in May 1995. Under the directorship and tutoring of Marianne Permezel I eagerly absorbed all the practical and theoretical musicianship that we crammed into the weekly three-hour sessions. Then came the show rehearsals and the shows themselves. I tend to go through a range of emotions during this time, starting with excitement, then experimentation, intense concentration, information absorption and memory programming (starting with stress) then when you think you've got it and you're starting to feel comfortable with in, it gets changed or new bits are added and there's less than a week until show time (now I'm really stressed) and then it's showtime, and I'm not stressing, I refuse to, this is it and I am going to enjoy every second of it. And so, as a group we were directed through the Amnesty International abuse of women's rights shows, with lessons in between by Marianne, supportively and successfully working openly, determinedly and with commitment with a small group of people such as the music group.

Sounds of Sydney: The Music Group perform on the streets for the Sydney Festival, 1996

Towards the end of October, Marianne announced that she needed a break due to exhaustion and that she would hopefully return in 1996 refreshed and raring to go. For some old and new members, the uncertainty in the directorship time period and the short amount of time until the end-of-year shows was too stressful and so we lost a few people along the way.

With only three weeks until the end-of-year shows, incoming director Paula Dowse and twelve new members who were bubbling with enthusiasm managed to pull together a solid group. We steamrollered through lessons and gruelling rehearsals, sweating pearls of inspiration and determination, with wicked senses of humour and moments of madness to release the pressure valves.

Immediately after the end-of-year show it was time for the Women's Circus Sydney Festival Tour rehearsals. Luckily, my application was accepted and excitedly I got to experience another area of this wondrous thing we know as the Women's Circus. Sydney was like the dream tour from heaven (almost – we have to get the Goddess to bump up the *per diems*). Accommodated comfortably, working functionally even on days when the schedule was tight, you couldn't go wrong really. In all areas of our performance presentation we did quite brilliantly, attracting and holding good-sized audiences and generating positive press publicity. Paula directed the music group during this time as well, clearly, educationally, annotatively and inspirationally.

Now it's 1997 and in a few weeks another Women's Circus Music Group year will commence. See ya there!

One Octave at a Time

An interview with Marianne Permezel

Louise Radcliffe-Smith

Vivienne Mêhes

High powered: Musical director Marianne Permezel and director Donna Jackson, 1992

Born in Adelaide, Marianne Permezel, thirty-two, studied flute at Adelaide University before becoming interested in writing music for theatre and video production. She played in "Sticky Beat" and "Sweethearts of Swing", then moved to Melbourne in 1990 with a band called "Basso Continuo". Since the big move she has worked with Arena Theatre and "Rapunzel Gets Down" and spent a year with Circus Oz as musical director. She is now lead singer with heavy-metal band "Arcane". Although Marianne joined the Women's Circus late in 1992, inspiring a gutsy junk percussion sound for our Women and Work show, she did not take on the role of full-time musical director until 1994.

In 1992 the circus was very different to what I thought it would be. I was surprised by the scale of the shows and the venues. I didn't expect them to look so spectacular. The show was a lot harder and the commitment from the members was a lot stronger than I expected. In other community theatres I've been involved in, people have not been so committed. They don't turn up to rehearsals. Whereas people in the circus turn up all the time. There are different demands in this job, too. You are required to make sure that everyone gets something out of the workshops, whereas, in other jobs, you just do your own thing.

I have noticed a change in confidence and the group's fear of making a lot of noise as a group. Their skills as a team helped. On opening night for Death: The Musical in 1994, when everyone else was so nervous, they were just a powerhouse. They were so confident they blew me out. The band wants to go on this year and learn new things, now they have had a taste. There is a willingness to change around and try lots of different instruments, not just stick to what they know.

Before I joined the circus I was becoming quite narrow in my musical taste and I feel like I am opening out a lot more, diversifying. It is good for me to get interested in other kinds of music, because I have been playing in bands for so long. With Moomba I had to go into the recording studio and record the sprite scene again. I have always had other people pressing the buttons for me before, so I had to teach myself [how to make a recording]. I also feel like my confidence level has gone up heaps. The feedback from people in the circus has been a large part of that. Just the fact that there was a live band through a lot of the show changed everything for me. The music sounded so good.

It's very difficult because not everyone is being paid to work. So you cannot expect a lot from people. Sometimes you have got to hang back and say to yourself: "Don't push too hard, these people are doing this because they like it." Also, [it's hard because] there is a great diversity of skill level. But a lot of the people who have higher skills really help out the others. The people in the group are so supportive, and you don't often get that from every member in a group.

For me, it's good to remember why people are in the circus. Sometimes it's hard to be aware there are other reasons for being in the circus than doing the show. Most people have fairly strong politics and I have to be aware not to step on people's toes. I have learnt a lot, even though [before the circus] I thought I was not doing too badly.

Circus Anthem 1.

Keeping the Beat

An interview with Sharon Follett

Louise Radcliffe-Smith

Sharon Follett was born in the western Sydney suburb of Parramatta in 1959. She lived the larger portion of her twenties in London before moving to Melbourne. In 1988, after fifteen years of office work and computer operating, a friend challenged her to extend what had long been a hobby and "get on the other side of the massage table". Eight years later, she practises massage and aromatherapy with the Spotswood Health Group while studying Chinese medicine and acupuncture

When I found out what the circus was all about I had to come and play. I just loved it: the political statement, the physicality, the creativity and the community. These were all things that I wanted in my life and appealed to me greatly. At first I joined both physical and music workshops, then I wasn't very well and I found the group physical work too challenging. I'd go home crying every week and it was just too much for me. So, after five or six weeks, I dropped the physical and stayed with the music for 1992.

I had only done very informal drumming before. I'd never studied music, didn't read music and never considered myself musical. It had only been a few years before that I'd started to relax with social music, singing with friends and so on. I wouldn't call myself a musician now, but I'd call myself musical.

The music group's sense of self has really changed over the past four years. In 1992, we spent a lot of time looking at different styles of music; using the same range of instruments, but learning what makes latin latin, what makes blues blues, and so on. It was all very new to me. When we got out there and actually made the music happen in performance it was a real surprise that we were so capable. We developed a real attitude of being "the band"; we started to call ourselves that. In that year there was a core group of women only doing music, and there were women participating in the physical performance as

Heavy metal: Playing
junk percussion, 1992

Vivienne Méhes

well as in the music, so we had to work out how to support them.

In 1993, in an attempt to open up the barriers between music and physical performance, Helen Sharp started doing voice body work with the music group. Women who did physical workshops joined the music group and a few of us from the music group also joined physical training. But as we were no longer a specialised skills group we lost our rapport. I never had any sense of there being a "band" in 1993. Sue Speer pre-recorded music for the end-of-year show and the circus attempted to "find its voice" with the entire cast singing an anthem. Live music and the role of musicians were not such important components. We lost our support for ourselves.

As a physical performer, you can find the connection with your main training group dissipates once you hit rehearsal time. But with the music group it gets tighter. In 1994, Gael would bring a picnic for all of us and we created our own physical territory, as a result we felt confident about being in the performance space.

Follow the leader: Marianne Permezel (right foreground, with whistle) directs performers in a musical tour of the City Square, Moomba 1995

Whenever we performed, I had such pride in what we did. It's very similar to the physical side of circus. You never get the overall view when you're out there being part of a pyramid. But it's your responsibility to do your bit to the best of your ability and to work in harmony with those around you. Every beat is part of a balance.

In 1994, I was the only woman in the music group also doing the physical workshops and myself and Karen and Barb were the only women who had been in the circus before. Everyone else was new. It was really interesting. Some women had experience with instruments and they got together separately. Others were completely new to the whole thing. So, there was a complete range of experience, or lack thereof. But that didn't seem to be a problem at all. Marianne Permezel had the teaching skills to incorporate everyone and there was plenty of space to offer creative input. I never felt like contributing was a problem. Even if your ideas were never used, there was an opportunity to voice it and to play with ideas. There was a choice about level of participation.

In 1995, I had the year off. Marianne Permezel trained the music group most of the year, but then pulled out towards the end because of other commitments. There was some uncertainty within the group and many women dropped out before the show. Percussionist Paula Dowse then stepped in and brought together the three remaining experienced women and ten new women in time to perform brilliantly for the end-of-year show. Paula also worked with myself and three other women to develop music for the Human Rights: Women's Right show in the Sydney Festival in January 1996, my first experience of touring.

When I think about my first performance in 1992, I remember I was very scared about mixing with the larger group. I found it very daunting. I was absolutely convinced everybody knew everybody else and I was the only one who didn't know people. And women were so confident about being in the warehouse space for the performance. I was thinking, "Oh, this is all I'm doing, just a bit of drumming, and they're doing all that specky stuff." It was a bit overwhelming and quite frightening sometimes. And yet I also felt a bit in awe, saying: "Wow, is this what I'm a part of?" I can remember getting the talk from Donna about make-up and why we wear it. The whole process of creating the show was fascinating.

I guess I found that year very stressful because it was my first experience of performing. Sometimes it felt like music had no priority and we had to fit our rehearsals in where we could, quite often being told not to make so much noise, which was hard when the next moment we're told to be out there and be bold. A lot of the music in 1992 was devised at the last minute so we had notes all over the place, some of them quite complex. Marianne wasn't on stage, so we were cueing each other: "Well, when her elbow goes up that's the cue to get ready for the next stage and when Sue Slammer's toe reaches there I'll cue you." It was on the edge some nights!

For me the most exciting moment [of 1992] happened during rehearsals. We were up on that wonderful high stage and it was the first time we had a full run-through of the celebration piece with the PA system. Part way through the piece we suddenly realised the women in the rest of the circus were out there dancing to it and we thought: "They're dancing to us! We're making this sound!" It was so exciting. If someone does something specky I'll give them a big cheer, but it was wonderful to have that reciprocated for the first time ever. And getting it from our peers was more exciting than getting it from the audience, who are in some ways anonymous. It gave me a lot of faith in the whole group dynamic, knowing that as a group we could do it. And it made me realise how important each specialised skill is.

1994 brought greater recognition of the music and the need for the band to be a band. It's not about being elitist, it's about recognising our need to work together as a group. For the Death: The Musical show Donna said, "You lot will be in costume and you will maintain the carnival characters throughout the performance." As a result, we had more of a sense of our place theatrically. I value having a sense of being part of the larger circus community, not feeling like I'm stuck in the music group and can't reach out.

In 1994, being one of the few who had been in performance before, I found myself passing on little bits of information that I didn't even know I had. I know a lot of women in the circus now and I feel comfortable with the women I don't know. I still feel a bit daunted when I get in the space and everybody's there. I still have moments where it terrifies me. But in general I know how to survive that scene better. I feel comfortable walking around talking to people. And I noticed the women from the music group who were new to it all getting closer to each other and talking a lot to each other about their anxieties, being supportive.

The music group is now sure of its survival. We've had five years to see what works and what doesn't work and we've had enough continuity to see the place of the music group evolve within circus and understand the part our music plays in performances.

FRONT OF HOUSE

Up Front

Louise Radcliffe-Smith

Front of house is a disparate group of circus fans and past performers who sell tickets, food, drink, T-shirts, programs and other merchandise. Front of house women show people to their seats, guard the gate against show-crashers, count box-office takings and keep the visible machinery of circus performance oiled and running smoothly. Front of housers provide audience members with their first and last contact with the circus, answering innumerable questions with good grace and humour. They act as a buffer zone between the audience and the circus generally.

Vivienne Méhes

Keeping on track: Front of House holds a meeting on the only available space, the train tracks, 1992 Work Show

About twenty women participate in front of house every year. They usually meet a few weeks before opening night to organise tasks such as ushering, ordering food, cleaning, serving and decor. Because women can volunteer to work as many or as few nights as they wish, front of house is a good alternative for those who don't want to train physically or technically and only have limited time to devote to the circus.

Although there is always good camaraderie among the front of house crew itself, the enormity of the circus and the separate work carried out by performers, tech crew and musicians have sometimes left the front of housers feeling undervalued and under supported. This feeling of "belonging" changes from year to year according to the friendliness of the site and the make-up of the group. Gradually, as front of housers go on to become performers and performers "retire" to work on front of house, the group has become an integrated and celebrated part of the overall production team.

Merchandising

Louise Radcliffe-Smith

Joining the circus is like joining a community. It is a community with minimal hierarchy, a broad power base, an ever-changing network of friendships and partnerships and a strong sense of group identity. Though women join the circus for a variety of personal and political reasons, underlying all these is the recognition of the strength, vitality and diversity of women. To help engender group identity and support positive feminism within the broader community, the circus produces and promotes strong visual imagery which is representative of the group and its culture. This started with the initial Women's Circus emblem produced by Lin Tobias, a striking purple and red female figure "leaping off the edge" into an unknown future. In 1994, artist Amanda Neville reinterpreted the image as a curvy, colourful, playful figure, juggling stars and moons in the same way that circus members juggle the different aspects of their lives. Both incarnations have graced thousands of T-shirts, badges and stickers, and are still going strong.

Most circus merchandise is sold by front of house members during the end-of-year performance season. More is distributed to women when they join the circus and receive a membership package. Non-circus people can also choose to become sisters and supporters by buying a $25 or $35 membership package. These packages include a T-shirt, sticker, badge, poster, balloon and yearly subscription to the circus newsletter.

The circus has tried other forms of merchandising, producing showbags for Death: The Musical in 1994. The showbags (which contained plastic skeletons, balloons, information on death and dying, stickers, and other paraphernalia) were not a huge success, but proved an interesting learning experience for all those involved in its production.

The Beijing T-shirts were a highlight of circus merchandising. About 200 long-sleeved grey, purple and black T-shirts were printed to raise money to send circus women to the United Nations conference on women, held in Beijing in August-September 1995. A small group of women worked out a comedy routine for the Malthouse Theatre fundraiser in which they modelled the Beijing T-shirt as lingerie, climbing gear, sleepwear, wedding veil and cocktail outfit. The T-shirts sold out immediately and another 200 were printed.

Over the years, the Women's Circus symbol has taken on a life of its own. It crops up on cars, bikes and T-shirts at women's dances, rallies or pubs. It has become a sign of familiarity, safety and belonging. It is a way for members to recognise each other and for non-members to proudly support women's strength and achievement.

She Has the Answer

An interview with Marg Dobson

Louise Radcliffe-Smith

Front of house co-ordinator, Marg Dobson, thirty-five, is a gregarious girl from Reservoir who has clocked up more than fifteen years of theatre involvement. In 1991 she co-wrote and performed "The Whole Shebang", a one-woman show about Madonna and school bullies performed with a watch, a piece of chalk and a black leotard. She has worked with The Women's Season as part of Melbourne's Fringe festival and spent two and a half years with Vox Bandicoot introducing wombats and lizards to school kids. She is often to be found dancing through street festivals with cymbal, snare drum and distinctive hat as part of the inimitable music performance group, the Tea Bags.

Front of House Co-ordinator
Marg Dobson

In the first year we had a skeleton staff and skeleton arrangement. The bookings were all made over the phone through the Footscray Community Arts Centre, which was a nightmare from hell. It was all right the first week because not a lot of people came, but by the third week people were desperate to get in. They played the most amazing emotional trips on me, like: "My mother's dying and if I don't see this show she's sure to die." It was total emotional blackmail and I wasn't prepared for it at all. I just kept apologising. It was all I could do. I don't think anyone was prepared for how many people turned up or how desperate people would be (in the first performance season). And that desperation has continued for the last four years.

There was a fantastic incident in 1994 with one woman who said she had left her ticket at home and locked her keys in the car at the venue. So she couldn't get into her car and she couldn't get into her home. And I had to take her on trust. I just decided it was such a bizarre story she couldn't have made it up. If she was good enough to fool me with that one she deserved to get in.

There was another woman in 1994 who was getting really aggressive with the box office people. I wasn't around at the time but Donna just happened to be walking past. So the front of house people said, "I think you need to talk to this person." Of course, the woman was a lunatic from hell. She was the one who was going to take the circus to the Equal Opportunity Board because there weren't any tickets at the door and it was discriminating against people because you could only buy your tickets at Bass. Luckily I missed out on her. We usually have a couple of drunks step over our tape – security's incredible! – and I play the big bully and help them step back over again.

My strategy with aggressive people is to let them talk. I ask them a lot of questions, so they get to say a lot. The hardest thing is having friends turn up expecting me to let them through the door and I can't. You can't do that, especially when it's so important for the circus to make money. So there were a few uncomfortable moments when people would look at me as if to say, "How much am I your friend?"

It's pretty busy before the show. It's not as though we stand around doing nothing, because when a lot of people want popcorn you have to make it pretty quickly. And sometimes the T-shirts would sell like crazy and you had to be so careful someone didn't walk off with them. Once the show starts people have a break and relax. Box office people have to go and count the money and balance it, which isn't as easy as it sounds. Then the concession people stock up for the post-performance sales and catch up with each other. Every night I asked who wanted to see the show, because I thought it was important. Everyone saw the show at least twice, and some more.

I think the most popular questions from the audience are "How long does the show go for? Do you know my friend . . . Susie? She's in the show." And I wouldn't lie. I'd just say,: "Oh, I'm sure I'd recognise her." Often people ask: "Where is the show?" One woman in 1994 said: "I don't think I'm getting it. What does it mean?" about the sideshows. And I said: "Look,

Be very afraid: Referees carry out the Queen's orders in the Women and Sport Show, 1993.

Photo: Vivienne Méhes

Royal performance: The Queen's Rig, designed by Sally Forth for the Women and Sport Show, 1993.

Photo: Vivienne Méhes

Flagship: The Women and Work Moomba barge, 1993.   Photo: Vivienne Méhes

Screws on stilts: The 1991 Women and Institutions Show.

Photo: Vivienne Méhes

River sports: An aerialist swings over Melbourne's Yarra River, Moomba barge, 1995.

Photo: Vivienne Méhes

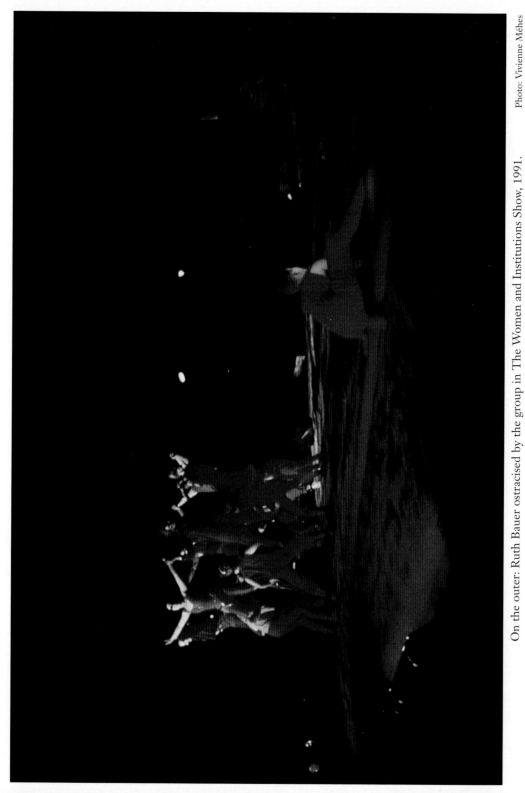

On the outer: Ruth Bauer ostracised by the group in The Women and Institutions Show, 1991.

Photo: Vivienne Méhes

Living dangerously: Graffiti artists abseil precariously from a barge in the 1994 Moomba river parade. Photo: Vivienne Méhes

Cerberus at the Circus: Stilt walkers as the hounds of death in Death: The Musical, 1994.

Photo: Vivienne Méhes

it's like life, you get this one, you miss that one."

People always had surprise questions, the most bizarre things. Even setting up was hilarious. People would wander up and ask: "Where's the (blah)?" and I'd say: "I don't know." Because there's such chaos about building the whole thing, the chaos of creation, and people wander off with your string and your tape and your scissors and they always came back. I think people expected me to know everything. I was very happy when I realised one day I could say: "It's not my department, mate."

In terms of building and maintaining, I did occasionally get to breaking point. But I knew I could always ask for help. At the end of the 1994 season I had to move this huge fridge back to FCAC and I was wandering round in a daze, mumbling: "fridge, fridge." But as soon as I opened the problem up to someone and said: "Hey, look, I've got a fridge to move", they said, "I've got a trailer, you don't need to come, I'll move it." It was those little things that lifted my spirits, because no one can do all that stuff on their own. It's just a matter of finding a way to communicate to people what you need.

For me, it was wonderful to see the circle of circus "mums" who were able to make sure that the larger circle happened. Georgine (production manager), Rosie (techie) and Donna (director) are this most amazing network of older experienced

Time out: Trainer Sally Forth and Director Donna Jackson, Sport Show 1993

"mothers" who can keep tabs on everything that goes on. To me these women were like the "mums" in the caravans, wondering what the girls were going to do, looking after the girls. They know when they need to be at a particular place at a particular time, which always made me feel secure. Georgine was always at the gate in case anyone got heavy, especially in the last week when people started to get really desperate. I'm sure that happened in other years as well, but because of the sideshows in 1994 it felt even more like a circus.

The thing that attracted me to front of house work and the thing I like about the job is dealing with so many audience members. That part of it is as easy as pie to me. If I needed to I could get them all into seats by myself or ask them to walk single file out of one door. I can do that. I can command that. The biggest part of my personal journey has been looking after,

From the Journal

In late 1994, I was approached to be involved in front of house. There were several things that stand out. Having recently completed a large-scale event I was delighted to be told what to do. Stuff the show bags. Lay out the T-shirts. Pour coffee. Sell show bags. Move the furniture. Climb the ladder. The variety of tasks and the sheer joy of being responsible only for my own little area was wonderful.

The other part was seeing the show over and over. I carried the images of the show in my head and wrote a poem based on the show before seeing it. I then saw the dress rehearsal. Nothing could have prepared me for the leap that occurred – performance-wise, technically and in every other way – from the dress rehearsal and the preview to the first full performance. Each week I turned up on my night and watched in awe as the show transformed before my eyes. It made me absolutely determined to join the circus.

– Susan Hawthorne, 1995

managing and co-ordinating the front of house members towards a common goal, to try and make them feel as comfortable as possible, to help them feel that they are valued and to show them how much I appreciate their hard work. For me, dealing with that personal responsibility has been the hardest thing.

In 1994 I had a problem making sure that front of house women came back, because the conditions were quite difficult at Macaulay Road. It was hard to give people a sense of where they could hang out because all we had was the small tent. People would say they would come but then they would never turn up. So I felt I was always in a position of having to maintain a group feeling. The biggest thing I could do for the people who came was make them feel appreciated. Which I found hard because I haven't worked a lot with volunteers. I think they are so wonderful to be a part of it. And I know the people who turned up had the best time.

Someone I met recently from front of house said a really good thing to me about a night her friends came to see the show. She told them to book if they wanted to be sure of getting in. Of course, they turned up and hadn't booked and it was one of the nights when we were totally sold out and I couldn't give them a ticket. This woman was mortified and panicking about the fact that her friends couldn't get in. She felt responsible. And she told me later: "Oh, you said the best thing, Margaret. You said 'Look, they've got to be able to deal with their own lives, don't you take it on'." I really appreciated her telling me, because in the heat of dealing with this, that and the other it's good to know I could hit the nail on the head. It's a real challenge to deal with people in the middle of everything going on; people vomiting, people in wheelchairs who arrive, helping drunks back over the security tape, and 650 people wanting to see the show. It's fantastic!

There is a lot of support stuff that happens in front of house. There were a few past performers, and there were also people whom I could see the circus helped to motivate over time. While the performance was on we would often talk about what people were up to, and the changes people made over the three weeks (of performance) were just incredible. One woman said in the first week that she was thinking about starting up her own business and we all said "go for it". By the last week she was designing her business cards.

It is sometimes difficult for front of house people to find their own place within the circus and find an opportunity to be with other groups. We have a couple of meetings before the season starts to give people a chance to familiarise themselves with the site and the sort of things they will be doing. In 1993 we had a tech and front of house meeting where everyone was in the same room for five minutes. Having that time meant front of house people felt more of a part of the overall show. That meeting didn't happen in 1994. The only time we were in the same space at the same time was the final bow in the final last show. And that was an incredible moment for me, to see the support staff and realise there are just as many techs and front of house as performers.

Also, for me, the finale is always the tech and front of house show during the bump out party on closing night. It's such a relief and so much fun to put together a piece that sends up the performers. The whole thing about doing a pyramid is we have to practise it and go through all these health and safety issues to deal with it. I just laugh hysterically from the moment we start rehearsing. And it's such a relief for us to poke some fun.

The Cents Behind the Circus

Mandy Grinblat

The survival of any arts organisation depends not only on its ability to produce innovative, high-quality work, but also on its ability to raise sufficient revenue to fund its activities. From the outset the Women's Circus has drawn financial support from a wide range of community, government, corporate and philanthropic organisations, as well as individual supporters.

Nicole Hunter

Financial management and fund-raising are often areas fraught with difficulties for political organisations such as the Women's Circus. The circus has developed policies which enable it to make clear decisions about the activities which we undertake for political reasons, and need to ensure are affordable to everybody (such as workshops), and other activities which are fund-raisers, and as such, serve a purely revenue-earning purpose.

Much of the circus' initial support came from other women's organisations and individual women involved in the areas of health, sexual assault and domestic violence. The circus has sustained relationships with many of these organisations and continues to receive support from them. Philanthropic trusts with an interest in women's issues and community development have also played a significant role in the financial survival of the circus in its early days.

Support from these organisations enabled the circus to establish a recognisable artistic style, organisational structure and philosophy and to develop skills within the community to continue to grow as an arts company and to further explore the form of circus/physical theatre.

The circus has also been assisted by government at various levels. The Commonwealth Government, through the Australia Council for the Arts, its funding and advisory body, has been a consistent supporter of the circus through its Community Cultural Development and Performing Arts Board. The Victorian Government, through Arts Victoria, a division of the Department of Arts, Sport and Tourism, has also been an important source of ongoing financial support. Particularly significant has been the funding by the Community Cultural Development Board and Arts Victoria of the wages for a co-ordinator. This kind of infrastructure support has been, and still is, vital to the operation of the circus. At local government level, the Women's Circus has been assisted by the City of Maribyrnong.

However, it is important to point out that the circus has never been completely dependent on grant revenue. Considerable revenue is generated through workshop programs, membership and box office. In 1995, a very successful fund-raising campaign was run to enable the circus' first international tour to Beijing to go ahead. The success of this campaign revealed the extent, and depth, of support which exists in the wider community for the circus. It is the financial support and goodwill of women from all around Australia that is the greatest asset the circus has.

Merchandising, such as T-shirts, badges and stickers, also plays an important role in the financial life of the circus. Good-quality products at a reasonable cost are not only a regular source of income, but also play a significant part in marketing the circus to the wider community.

Corporate sponsorship has also been forthcoming, and while

much of this support has been in-kind rather than financial, it is an area of increasing importance to the Women's Circus and its future activities.

It is impossible to talk about the financial background of the circus without acknowledging the ongoing support offered by Footscray Community Arts Centre. Because the Women's Circus was established within an existing organisation, it has always had access to all important infrastructure facilities, such as photo-copiers and telephones! FCAC's financial skills and services ensure that the circus is in a position of relative financial security and that the funds that are raised are managed effectively. A complementary style of working and philosophy has enabled the circus and the Arts Centre to develop a mutually beneficial relationship.

Regardless of how well managed our financial resources are, there is never enough money to embark upon the full range of projects we'd like to, and inevitably, we survive because of the volunteer work done by women, and goods and services which are provided to the circus for free!

Think lateral: when there's no budget

Georgine Clarsen

It was a perfect site for the Work show – a wonderful building – but not enough power to run the lighting. The usual solutions were out of the question . . . Generator hire would consume the whole budget . . . To bring in three phase from the nearest street would take out next year's allocation as well.

But there is plenty of power so nearby! We can feel it humming away on the other side of the wall! So we compose beautiful letters on official-looking letterhead, and dress our best to meet with the manager of the factory next door. We've thought of everything – a meter, a deposit, repairs to the wall before we leave, free tickets, generating community goodwill . . . Did he ever send us that bill?

THE SHOWS

1991, Women and Institutions

Deb Lewis and Louise Radcliffe-Smith

River of fire: Louise Radcliffe-Smith and Loreen Visser on the Maribyrnong River in the 1991 Institutions Show

The first large-scale performance of the Women's Circus took place up the Maribyrnong River a little way from the Footscray Community Arts Centre, the home of the circus. The performance combined a controversial and thought-provoking theme, original live music and the circus' mass physical acts. The amphitheatre provided a natural stage and the outdoor setting – stars above and river behind – gave the audience a very different kind of performance. In what has become one of the signatures of the Women's Circus, the performance was in two sections.

The first involved the audience walking from the Arts Centre along the railway track by the river as performers stood on posts, rowed along the river, knitted on unicycles and swung out of trees. Once the audience had circumnavigated this magical moving spectacle, they sat in an enormous open air seating bank and waited for the performance to begin. As the notes in the 1991 programme showed, the theme was simple:

> They lived along
> THE RIVER
> Strange Women who did not fit in.
>
> So, they were locked
> away in
> THE INSTITUTION
> Rules, games, tricks
> for food!
> THE BETRAYAL
>
> DIVIDE AND RULE
> The technique used to
> keep women divided.
> She stepped out of line.
> We punished her.

The show told the story of women in an imaginary institution. These women wore red and purple and were forced by the "screws" (stilt walkers dressed in black suits carrying umbrellas, or women carrying whips) to perform tricks for food. The screws tried to divide the women so they would remain oppressed. One woman stole bread because she was hungry. She was hung by the other inmates. Her death shocked the women into action and prompted a rebellion in which the screws were banished. This was followed by a celebration.

From the Journal

What is it about the circus that draws us? The camaraderie is extraordinary – so little tension, so much patience, commitment and understanding. It's as if a magic ribbon is wrapped around all of us. Despite the work and the long rehearsals it's still hard to comprehend the scope of the amazing moving heart that is the Women's Circus. Together we are unafraid of physical restrictions, unafraid of eyes watching intently just metres away. And we take this strength, this newness, and wander away from here into the "outside" world where it helps change our lives.

– Louise Radcliffe-Smith, 1991

1992, Women and Work

Deb Lewis & Louise Radcliffe-Smith

Vivienne Mêhes

Roll out the barrel: Nicole Hunter (left) and Deb Lewis in the 1992 Work Show

Inspired in part by the climate of economic recession and by the explosion on 21 August 1991 at the chemical storage facility at Coode Island – 200 metres down the Maribyrnong River from the warehouse training space – the theme of the 1992 show was brazenly and unapologetically political. At the time of the explosion and resulting fire about twenty-five women were at the warehouse training for the 1991 performance. The area had to be evacuated and was pronounced "safe" three days later. Director Donna Jackson has always had an interest in safety in the workplace and has noted that in Australia more people are injured and killed while at work than on our roads, a fact that is hard to come to terms with.

The Women and Work performance combined new circus and elements of theatre. It reflected our research into work and the changing nature of the workplace. Circus traditionally is a place where people come to escape the pressures of daily life. Audiences watch performers taking physical risks and thrill at the danger of the performers' work. However, Donna believes that the audience is not just there to be entertained. It is also important to take a message from each performance. This performance aimed to show that amidst economic doom and gloom, there were still some islands of inspiration where the impossible is made possible and happy endings are mandatory.

A huge warehouse and alleyway between several other buildings was chosen as the site for the second offering of the Women's Circus. On their way to the seating bank, the audience meandered through an industrial alleyway where women dressed in black and white overalls imitated mechanical actions. Another group of women in swirling skirts helped entice the audience along by posing, then moving to another site. As the audience waited for the show to begin, they watched three women folding, carrying and hanging sheets on a tightrope. The story showed a dangerous work environment where the "Boss" ordered the women to work harder and faster. The harder they worked, the more dehumanised they became. The Boss travelled on a cart pulled by servants. His minions displayed large signs emblazoned with words like "contracts" and "enterprise bargaining". Two thirds of the way through the show there was an industrial accident (represented by a loud explosion), after which the workers rose up, overthrew the Boss, swept the workplace clean and took over their own destiny.

From the Journal

It's the little things in circus that provide the buzz. Checking out the audience whilst upside down. Massage during warm-ups. Finding some cream in the Ponds jar (for taking off make-up). Catching glimpses of the show while waiting to go on. Discovering that your body has stopped bruising, hurting, screaming. The biggest buzz of all is being with ninety women night after night and wowing the audience.

– Anon,
31 October 1992

Trust

Mavis Thorpe Clark, AM,
a Sister whose grand-daughter and
great-grand-daughter are circus women

My reaction to my first attendance at the Women's Circus was purely from the angle of theatre. I knew little of the company's background; in fact, only that the performers were all women. From the moment I turned in at the gate of the warehouse, I was stimulated – by the director's original offering – to expect something different. Those acrobatic acts being performed along the route into the theatre area, and especially the mask-like countenances held by the acrobats, made me want, at once, to see behind those masks.

And that's exactly what happened. It happened because from start to finish, the show involved *me*. The artistry, the enthusiasm, the confidence, the trust in each other, all became mine. I'm not young, but I was one with the execution of every act. My foot kept time to the compelling beat of the music, and my body to the rhythm of it. I identified with the actual performance, as though I was part of the group; as though I was one of those demonstrating body control in balance and movement. And carrying that control into life.

The storyline of women in work, with all the ups and downs of the workforce, was told in body actions and body control that were right on target, and superbly portrayed. No need for dialogue in this production. Actions were indeed more impressive than words. To so involve an audience without dialogue is surely true theatre.

I'm glad I attended that first performance with so little knowledge of the group's "unprofessional" background, because my reaction was solely due to the quality of theatre. And I found the second attendance, with knowledge, no less stimulating, involving, exciting and enjoyable.

I have great admiration for those women in their perfecting of balancing and acrobatic skills, and their sensitive understanding of the movements that revealed the story. I'm grateful, too, for the joyousness of the finale. The triumph in their eyes, the confident smiles, the happiness, as the cast bowed goodnight, was something so good to take home.

Work

Rachel

head down, bum up
chained to the wheel
the daily grind
put your back into it
put your mind into it
nose to the grindstone
workaholic
bureaucrat – eurocrat – femocrat
working up a sweat
put your bestfoot forward
working around the clock
put a little elbow grease into it
working my fingers to the bone
working my butt off
all work and no play makes a dull boy
to train without pain
is to train without gain
work yourself into a corner
work around it
work it to the bone
many hands make light work
work your way up
work your way in
across
through

Nicole Hunter

Work

Cathy Johnstone

I believe in sweat
my sweat
our sweat
we're building up a sweat
we're sweating up a building
I'm building on your hands
my feet have left the ground
I'm upside down
turned around
on your hands
you're holding me
your hands hold me straight
you hold my weight
(thanks,
I forgot to tell you that)
you hold me and I don't fall
you hold me in my sweat
you hold me tall
now I walk straight
I'm sweating for my life
for your life
for women's lives
for our lives
we're alive
I'm building up a sweat

1993, Women and Sport

Deb Lewis & Louise Radcliffe-Smith

Vivienne Méhes

In black and white: Referee group balance in the 1993 Sport Show

Defying the predictions of inclement weather, the third major November performance took place in another outdoor setting – this time on the hilly slope between the Footscray Community Arts Centre and the Maribyrnong River. Two towering 10-metre aerial rigs were erected, one astride a beautiful garden of yellow roses. On one show night it did rain – tiny droplets not much bigger than mist – and the audience was so impressed the performers went ahead that no one left. The performers were so impressed at the willingness of the audience to endure less than perfect conditions that they gave their very best performance. And from a performer's perspective, the rain in the lights against a starry sky added magic to the spectacle.

The theme for this show started off being Women and Sport, but as women conducted research they realised that sport, like

I have never been so fit in my life, and my relationship with my body is greater that it has ever been. After that first week of rehearsals I thought I was going to die of exhaustion and I was absolutely amazed at what my body endured.

– Liz Cooper, 1993

Wendy Black

Design sketch of
Queen's costume

many other forms of human interaction, revolves around power and competition, around who can be best, fastest, cleverest. It also reminded us of the fact that the circus works deliberately against abusive hierarchical structures that create difference rather than acceptance. We wanted to show that the circus model of co-operation works much better than the traditional patriarchal structures based on competition. The idea grew into a scenario where two teams dressed in red or yellow competed for the attention of the Queen, a larger-than-life figure wearing a tall yellow and black vinyl hat and matching gown.

The Queen ordered the two teams to participate in ridiculous competitions (allowing the circus to show off women's skill in double balance, hoops and trapeze). The tension built up as two women (representing each of the sides) hung from their ankles and spun on a rope, encouraged furiously by the others barracking below. Naturally, one of the characters died. She was mourned in a surreal scene that came to be known as "the legs of grief", where women did headstands on the gravel in the rose garden, twisting their legs into anguished positions. Then all characters rose up and vanquished the Queen. Since the republican issue was receiving a great deal of media attention at the time, many audience members interpreted the show as a statement about Australia's relationship to the monarchy.

Nicole Hunter

The Queen's rig

1994, Death: The Musical

Deb Lewis & Louise Radcliffe-Smith

Vivienne Méhes

Jelly Botties trebled:
Death Show, 1994

The fourth performance took place in a huge, dirty warehouse in North Melbourne which had served as the local council lock-up for seized goods. We established a makeshift dining room in the sheriff's office, hung aerials from the rafters and arranged the mats and carpets with care. The style of performance changed this year, with circus members directing small sideshow acts for a colourful vaudevillian prelude to the indoor performance. Ten roller doors were raised to reveal "death-defying" knife jugglers, razorblade swallowers, levitators and three-headed monsters, dressed in orange, green, yellow or purple. For the first time, circus women spoke in performance. Spruikers encouraged audience members to "roll up, roll up", adding to the carnival atmosphere.

At the end of the sideshow acts, a performer posing as an audience member pretended to die. The cry went up: "She's dead!" Other performers dressed in black robes picked up the "dead" woman and carried her into the warehouse, led by a priest figure towering over the audience on stilts. As the audience followed this procession they were handed white-painted branches or pieces of rosemary (for remembrance). These they lay down under the coffin as they were shown to their seats. The show was based loosely on the Greek myth of Persephone's journey into the underworld. We reinterpreted this as a daughter searching for her dead mother. The daughter faced various tests, making her way through the cheeky sprites (aerialists swinging *en masse* from the ceiling), escaping the monstrous dogs (women dressed in vinyl on stilts), fighting against stick-carrying women, until finally she found her mother in the company of Death, whom we personified as a white and silver ten-armed creature pulling a cart covered with fairy lights. Of course, reality prevailed and mother and daughter were forced to separate, the mother to remain with Death while the daughter returned to the overworld.

One of the aims of this show was to provide audience members with straightforward and useful information about death and dying. As the programme stated:

> *This performance is the result of a great deal of research by women involved in the circus. As we have discovered, you cannot control death but you can control your funeral arrangements. Many people are alienated by western society's approach to death. This system sees a series of experts (doctors, clergy and funeral directors) take control of the funeral process and remove the dead person from close friends and relatives soon after death. Often, the mystique surrounding funeral arrangements and the stress caused by the notion of "funeral etiquette" tend to discourage bereaved people becoming involved in planning funerals.*

Nicole Hunter

CIRCUS WOMENS NiGHT OUt

For me, the Women's Circus is about ordinary people working damn hard to produce an extraordinary thing. It's about co-operation, determination and people power and reveals a side of human nature that is way too rare. The fact that this is done by women, and particularly by women who have been disempowered in some form or another in their lives is inspiring.

– Feedback from audience member, Meredith, 1994

The Dead

Susan Hawthorne

I found freedom in the underworld, where circus
jesters, acrobats and long-limbed stilt walkers play

Russian roulette with their souls. When I saw her
I hardly recognised her. Is that you? Is that really you?

I ask, repeating the question over and over. Fire
breathing women walk by, each question punctuated

by a flaring of the mouth. Her soul retreats again
and I reach out to grab her hand. Death is wheeled by

on a cart such as Athena once invented. The underworld
is not technologically literate, but a primitive world

full of primitive passions. Death casts her eye over me
and passes on. Not yet. Not for me, at least. There she

is again. Mum, I call. She turns, her eyes owl-grey,
where once they shone blue. A beach ball flies

between us and spirited sprites rush after. I hold her
cold hand and press it to my hairline. Her gaze passes

over my left shoulder and I wonder who she sees.
I want to talk, but no speech can creep between my lips.

When her mouth opens, I see neon words fly like birds
but no sound . . . I strain to hear. There are only the

faint strains of an accordion, like a circus passing by
on a distant road. She makes the leap as Death passes

by us again and takes her place on the horse-drawn
cart. No backward glance, no regret, simply passing on.

As I turn to leave the overcrowded world of the dead
my eyes catch another face I know. No warning

and the dead throttle past me in their rush for eternity.
A pomegranate rudely torn open tempts me, a glass

of red wine is proffered. Souls bustle into the seats nearby,
the storytellers take their place around the table and begin . . .

"She's dead!" they cried

Melissa Lewis

Melissa (Min) was the youngest circus performer in 1994. At the age of fifteen and a veteran of three years, she found herself protecting the "dead" woman from well-meaning audience members who, reacting with speed and skill, began checking for signs of breathing!

I found that being part of the sideshows was the most challenging part of the Women's Circus in 1994. The sideshows were made up of different scenes full of many women, and it gave me energy and strength because there was so much for the audience to see. Mingling with patrons while the sideshows happened, constantly passing by Donna's note pad and voicing that infamous cry of "She's dead!" when the sideshows ended, all left me quaking before every performance. I enjoyed the fact that many in the crowd felt obliged to move just because I waved my hand and I felt great satisfaction because I knew what act was coming next and where. It was great to follow Robyn and watch her "die" before a somewhat startled crowd. Their reactions were always amusing and unpredictable.

Opening Night Nerves

Linda Wilson

Energy pulsated through my tired body. It was a bizarre feeling. After two weeks of intensive rehearsal I was physically and mentally weary, yet I also buzzed with the excitement of opening night.

The roller door in front of us opened and there we were – "The Rising Roses". So began the levitation act. I could not see the audience in front of me as a hot yellow light glared straight into my eyes. I felt my skin start to perspire under the face make-up. My head felt tight from the bathing cap and mask/hat we were all required to wear for this opening scene.

With a smile fixed on my face I walked to the table and lay down. I was the one who would levitate. I heard my Rose sisters around me. The cue was given and I began to rise in the air. I wasn't smiling any more. This was hard work. Levitating is not as easy as it appears. I heard a few gasps from the audience. I stared up as I got closer and closer to the ceiling. I stopped and swayed up there for a few seconds. I heard applause. I tried to gently lower myself down but I went too fast and landed with a bump. We presented ourselves to the audience for applause, all smiles again. The roller door then shut.

We scrambled in all directions taking our props with us. I ran to get partially changed for the next scene. I snuck in a cigarette while I waited. I wasn't tired any more but my nerves were raw.

There are three of us, pulling up another roller door. Two balances then a pose. We watch the "dead" body as it is brought to the coffin. Slowly, in character, I move back to get fully changed for my plate-spinning act. I need to go to the toilet, but I don't think I've got time.

I put on a new mask/hat, a long shirt and a white top. I change my shoes. I grab my stick and my plate. I look for the others in this scene. We walk to where we need to be, spinning plates all the way. We arrive way too early but at least we won't miss our cue. We hear the audience inside the warehouse, we hear the music from the band, we keep practising our spinning. We support each other, we talk through our routine. We are standing on cement steps waiting for, yet again, another roller door to rise. It does. We step in, spinning, spinning, spinning. I've been told to look straight ahead. I'm too nervous so I look up at my plate. Slowly we walk toward the coffin. It is difficult to spin a plate and walk slowly. The lights are blue. It feels eerie. We get to the coffin and two of us kneel. It's easier to spin the plate now, but still I won't take my eyes off it. My leg hurts. I want to change position. I wish the cue to leave would hurry up. Finally we can stand and slowly walk out. Down the steps and the roller door closes behind us. Relief, my arm is aching terribly. Hurray, I didn't drop my plate.

Jean and I are running. She is in the next scene and needs to change quickly. I help her put on her stilts and change her costume. In a hurry she strides off to the stick/stunt fighting act of the show.

I have got a little bit of time, but still I quickly prepare for the

The only certainty is change.

– Donna Jackson

"Dogs from Hell" part of the show. The costume is big and heavy. A vinyl dog mask with glowing eyes, dog body and big dog arms. Dog legs go over stilts. I'm ready. Must remember to look down so the audience sees the dog face and not my face. I need assistance to get with the other dogs. I'm scared on stilts, sacred that I will fall. I feel unsteady and the dog mask is tied too tight under my chin, but it's too late to adjust it.

The music changes and four huge dogs prowl menacingly onto the stage. I love the music for this scene. Suddenly I forget I'm scared and then I'm not unsteady. I look at the carpet and follow the dog legs in front of me. In this scene we chase two women who play the mother and daughter. I really feel the part and try to trap them. They escape but we soon lead them into the ropes, exactly where they're supposed to be. The dogs stomp off stage.

Karen is suddenly next to me. I remember again that stilts scare me and I take her outstretched hand gratefully. Once I'm sitting down we both work frantically to get the dog costume off. I'm in the next scene. I don't have time to put my shoes on. Karen and I run and we are just in time to be part of the huge balance that represents a wall. Karen does three balances on me. We are particularly proud of the first one. It took a lot of weeks of practise to be able to do it.

We hear the cue to come down from the balance (a loud "hutt" shouted by one of the performers) and run off stage. I run, run, run for I've got to change completely for the next scene. It is the last scene of the show – the Celebration. I change back into my "Rising Roses" costume and take a swig of water. My throat is still parched, despite the drink.

Nadia, my balance partner for this scene, grabs my hand and we quickly jog to the stage edge, ready to go on. I see the cue and Nadia and I are the first ones on stage. For one awful second I wonder if I misread the cue. Relief. Others are now swarming around us. Nadia and I do a double balance routine that we have rehearsed for months. The music is upbeat and lively. We have big smiles on our faces. We are supposed to smile in this scene, but behind our grins we are tired. It has been a long night and it is not quite over.

Then everyone is in a semi-circle, waving to the audience. The performers arrange themselves in a line and we do the traditional taking off of bathing caps one after another. The audience applaud. We run off stage then straight back on and jump into a final, mass thigh-stand balance. For some reason we do a second bow, even though we were told not to. Then off we go, out of the warehouse, with the clapping and cheering ringing in our ears.

I feel good and happy as I walk back to the change rooms. The show went well and I know I've earned my sleep tonight.

The Nightly Performance Ritual

Deb Lewis

My first step each night was to leave behind the role of full-time worker in a rather stressful job and move into my evening role as performer. Prior to the Women's Circus, I had not been on stage since my compulsory appearance in a school play at age twelve. Each evening I'd walk in my front door, put down my work basket, shower (with the obligatory cold blast at the end – thanks Sally!) and dress in clothes that would get me to circus that evening and also be suitable for the post-performance wander around the space and the chat to friends.

Next came the packing of the costume box. In previous years I had managed to arrive without some vital piece of clothing or prop. Out to the clothes line to redeem the singlet and shorts that were washed after each performance. Then to the list which was sticky-taped to the wall above my daughter's list. I'd read each item as I repacked it, not trusting my memory: yellow pants, green socks, orange vest, bottled water, face washer . . . Meanwhile Min would do the same and we'd try to eat something – but who is hungry at five in the afternoon?

The trip to the warehouse in North Melbourne was always an adventure, especially the Alexandra Parade section where we saw the local pool closed, blockaded and finally reopened, then the plantation trees painted with crosses, marked for removal, smaller trees planted by protesters, and finally the bulldozers move in to widen the road. We never knew exactly how long it would take to make our way up this piece of road, but at least we had only to travel as far as North Melbourne which somehow seemed much closer to Balwyn than Footscray. Sometimes we'd listen to music or sit in the silence of our separate worlds. Sometimes we'd have a mock screaming match and shout every rude word and expression we could think of. I'm glad I had someone to laughingly travel with.

The site always seemed dusty, dirty, uninviting and always too hot. Min would start to whinge that she was too tired and didn't want to perform and I'd wonder why we put ourselves through this each night. Then I'd see Ursula working on the rigging and we'd hug and exchange a few words and it wouldn't seem quite so bad.

I'd quell my feelings of isolation in the group each night by hanging around the outskirts and by taking a walk to set my props – my mask and stick in the box I'd placed under the seating bank. I'd take a ride around the bike track to see how the carpet, mats and seats were potentially interfering with my safety. People generally left me alone which was good because this was the time when I claimed the space, claimed my part in the performance and focused my energy inside myself prior to making contact with others.

The ability of the circus to cope with individual differences was demonstrated for me when the soup crew took on my inability to tolerate garlic and cooked a special garlic-free pot of soup with me in mind. Not being used to such kindness and consideration, I was very surprised and grateful.

During soup each night I'd connect with one or more of my support group. It was Christina's idea to nominate a small group with whom we felt safe and she negotiated with these women when we were still in the training phase of the year. Karen, Janine and Christina were incredibly important to me during the performance. They were women I could trust for a hug or a few words when I needed them. Our network grew during the official support group time – Naomi and Louise also provided invaluable support.

Warm-up was the time when I took responsibility for preparing my body and mind for the performance. I especially concentrated on the muscles that were most at risk during performance; my thigh muscles were put to the test during cartwheels, and my back when lifting Denise and lowering the

Nicole Hunter

coffin. If there was time before the pre-performance mini-rehearsal I'd grab Karen and we'd do a couple of laps on the bike so I'd feel safe, strong and comfortable with that final part of my performance.

Practising the mourning and the stunt fighting was a major drag each night and I was always very glad when the lantern carriers had to rehearse because I got a break. If I hadn't caught up with the lovely Maureen by make-up time, she'd always find me, wish me all the best and give me her special hug.

Most nights I was late getting my make-up on and sometimes had to put it on in the dark, then I'd meet the rest of the Escape from Chains DeVola sisters – Nola, Lola, Zola and Mola – usually with my arms and neck paint still wet. Escaping from chains made me extremely nervous each night, especially when we were told to tie the chains tighter. I am still trying to work out if there is a trick to the escape, but I did finally work out that my first job inside that bag was to remove my blindfold so at least I wasn't working in total darkness! I was probably more surprised than the audience that I re-emerged unharmed each night and we'd congratulate ourselves on yet another successful escape.

I'd leave the excitement, noise and colour of the sideshow to walk across the backstage space in the dark and place my fabulous orange sequinned waistcoat (which Min found the fabric for and I constructed) on my bike in preparation for my part in the finale.

My costume change was a time to relax briefly and cool down before meeting the Black Theatre group backstage and moving into position while the Jelly Botty Brothers performed their knife-juggling scene. Sarah and I opened and closed the roller door and assisted with costume changes.

Stepping up four feet onto the stage with Denise, the dead mother, on my back was a challenge I could only rise to with Sarah pushing from behind and Naomi pulling from in front. After placing Denise in the coffin, I had to attract Janine's attention, whilst avoiding being hit in the teeth by the frankincense she vigorously swung. Janine played the priest and towered over the audience on 5-foot stilts. When the wind came up, her long black and white costume behaved like a sail and threatened to carry her off like Mary Poppins or the Flying Nun. Helen and I held her down and I swung the frankincense while we slowly led the procession of mourning performers and intrigued audience members to their seats.

Once inside, I positioned myself beside the coffin and held one plank of wood while the coffin was moved into place on top of a 4-foot stand, then joined Christina for the grieving scene.

Lowering the coffin each night was one of my major challenges, especially given the accident we had during rehearsal weekend when we dropped her to the ground head first. Afterwards, I was happy to take a breather and allow my heart rate to return to normal as I huddled with a small group on stage before Joanne (who played the daughter) vaulted at us and we held her high in the air. I checked the carpet for twigs as Denise was carried off in the coffin.

Walking back behind the seating bank was a chance for me to collect myself before tying on a belt made of pieces of hose stuck through vinyl and selecting a stick for the stunt fight. Min was my partner in this scene: mock anger and aggression directed at my real-life daughter!

We replaced the hose costumes with the mother and daughter mask and the mood changed from anger and aggression to softness and fluffiness in the mother and daughter double-balance reunion scene, again with Min.

Moving off stage, I returned my mask to the dressing room and waited by the fridge for Janine so I could help her take off her dog costume and stilts. It takes a while to put on the suit but about 30 seconds for a team to remove it! Together Janine and I would run to our position in the double-balance wall that stretched right across stage and wait for Cathy and Margot to join. Then I gave my one cue for the evening when the mother and daughter separated – the indication for the wall to collapse.

Backstage, I'd gather up two sets of fire clubs and pass the second set to Margot on the way to the fire scene. Some of the hotter nights I felt like I was standing in the middle of a bushfire with my brow sweating and my make-up melting. Techies would mysteriously appear to put out our fire clubs and vanish as quickly.

I'd have a minute to compose myself for the final hot spot in the performance – two laps on the bike, the first with Helen and the flag and the second with Karen on the front as well. This was a tricky part because carpet and mats had often moved during the performance and excited performers would forget that we were coming and race out onto the bike track in their enthusiasm!

Final bows, hats off and we were real people again – laughing and congratulating each other!

Last night I dreamt I was flying. I flew right over the heads of my captors to freedom. Thank you a million times everyone who has been involved. It has been a fantastic experience and a huge step forward for the world.

– Katy Brown, 1991

Each Night A Journey

Karen Martin

The circle of painted faces breaks up. There are smiles, clasps of hands, small touches and brief nods. We are off . . . beginning a journey that takes only about an hour. A journey shared between sixty women and reaching out to about four hundred people.

Waiting in the darkness, glimpses of light and noise break the hushed silences. Applause. We're ready, props set, door slightly raised. The banging of the door comes with an introduction from the spruikers, then the roller door is raised. It's heavy, it's stiffness becoming part of the dialogue of our scene. A sea of faces, pink light in my eyes, "Well hello . . . ". Applause. Close the door. Feelings of jubilation, a natural high of adrenalin and that indescribable something that makes me want to perform forever.

Dim lights waiting to shine for a capacity crowd. Techies silently finishing those odd jobs. Ladders still on stage, ropes being rigged. There are smiles but no talk. We have things to do. The show has begun and we are now within a sphere that exists only momentarily. Each moment precious and cherished.

Back stage. A bit of time to relax, to prepare. Jokes abound. Women come up frantically putting on last touches of make-up, costume changes. Cues. We're on again. The audience attentive and excited. They follow the funeral procession enticed by music and bodies into the main arena. Seating takes forever. I cross the stage, my flowing cape makes me feel regal. I feel naughty. I want to play. I look at the line of women. I sneak a smile. I take my place behind the band waiting for my next cue. This group grows. There are quiet jibes. We are relaxed and feeling united in something big. Our cue. We sing. The band takes over and the mass of bodies flee the scene into other directions.

My journey is shared at different points with different women. This pattern is not broken and it is comforting and fun establishing a routine that becomes as important as the performance itself. I add to my costume, I set other props and then run into the night to return at another entrance. I stand in the wings behind massive scaffolding and hundreds of entranced spectators. The music is uplifting and the scene captivating. Night after night this does not change. We're on. My status as an individual off stage transforms into a group consciousness on stage. Lights in my eyes. Movements and choreography flow through our bodies, our minds free to add the intent, the motivation of the scene. I am on for a few scenes before running off to prepare for another. Mask on. Greetings backstage reassuring that all is well. On again. Off again. Grab a techie and haul over a large table, waiting for my partner of the next scene. She is on stilts. Her costume change has to be quick. She grabs me when she comes off stage. Others help. She sits on the table and systematically we strip her of her dog suit. Ready. We hold hands, pause momentarily for our cue and on we run. The pace is fast, hearts beating. We run to our position.

Breathe, concentrate, balance, hold. Eye contact. Smiling eyes shining with the sensation of achievement. Rolling off. Preparations for the final scene. I dress quickly. Time is short and precious. Quickly and quietly I make my way to the next entrance. The group gathers. We are in unity, waiting. On again. Joyous. This is the last scene. It has been good.

The music builds. We come together as a group. Hats off. Here I am. Applause. Stomping. We are off, trying not to trip up on each other, then on again.

It is nice to finish the night in a final balance working with special friends. Sometimes this may be the only connection in the evening. More applause. The audience are smiling. We are smiling. We run off. Off to the dressing room. The sounds of cheering reverberate through the building. Through our soul. It has been good. Some run and give themselves a hoot. Others clasp hands, arms, bodies, lots of hugs. Lots of laughter. Make-up off, faces washed, bodies dressed. Time to wind down blending audience, performers, technicians, musicians in after show chats. Lots of eye contact, lots of laughter, continuing into the night.

> Dear Donna,
> How old do I have to at least be to help with your excellent circus?
> Would you please give mum the answer
> From the girl who likes your circus most Catherine
> P.S I play tenorhorn
> I do drama and I go to Guides
>
> I Love Womens Circus

Catherine's mother is a circus musician

Coffin

Denise Johnstone

Naomi Herzog

Denise Johnstone

OK, give me the most dangerous, highest, most physically exhausting, frenetically active role in the Circus. No! Be still! Still for twenty minutes, maybe fifty minutes. Very still.

I watch the coffin being built and try to quell misgivings. It'll be simple, right? I work with the mask. It's overwhelming and scary. I am supported.

Trust other women to lower you in the coffin. Trust without moving, without communicating. Trust after they drop the coffin with you inside it.

"It must be so peaceful lying in the coffin." It's hot. A really humid, heavy night and the incense overwhelms me. I try to focus. Will I focus when I get up? Or fall, from dizziness? Will my mask be on? (Am I the mask?) Will I be able to see? Focus!

Where am I? Where is everyone? Now I'm in pain, I'm angry – where is everyone? Don't move if you're in pain. People are watching. If you move they'll know. Everything is not OK!

I get up out of the coffin – too early. My pain matters. I don't endure it for five, fifty or five hundred others, any more.

I spent about eight hours in the coffin during performance time. I learnt, I am learning and I will learn. Now, how do I thank everyone in the Women's Circus?

Not Just Entertainment

Mavis Thorpe Clark, AM

When told the name, Death: The Musical, for this 1994 offering by the Women's Circus, I was a little uneasy. How could such a theme be a vehicle for successful entertainment? Isn't the commitment of a circus, more than any other of the performing arts, to entertain?

My concern was needless. The subject was handled with delicacy, skill and understanding. It not only entertained – there was place and room for the laughter and joy that are part of living – it promoted a certain philosophy; this was to widen the scope of the perimeters of life, revealing that scope to be more than the boxed in space between the drawing of the first breath and emitting the last, offering a sense of coming from and going to. A sense of continuity.

There are many people today searching the yellowing records for clues to their ancestral identity. These people are struggling to gain some sense of a continuity of life. But when coming to the search for something beyond death their desire isn't as easily satisfied. Nevertheless, deep down in consciousness, most of us would be able to tell of some happening, experience, feeling, that hinted at the unexplainable.

In Death: The Musical, the separation lines or walls between this life and death are allowed to merge, to sway together. It was easy to accept that wafting back and forth over the borderline. There was a rhythm to it, a joyousness, in the graceful symmetry of the performers. While some of the thundery acts spoke of the problems humans face in this stretch of living, the gentle coming and going of those already off the edge had a hopeful reality about them.

The humour in the interflow detracted in no way from the subject matter, but rather gave both "beyonds" a contagious buoyancy.

The whole was an astonishing achievement in great spectacle and performance by this Women's Circus. A piece of theatre that should be seen by all.

No Blood!

Nicole, Emily and Joanna van der Nagel

Potential circus performers, sisters Nicole (7), Emily (6) and Joanna (3), discuss the carnival scene.

Nicole: The three-headed monster – that was my favourite – the middle one had no arms so it couldn't do anything. She put her head down in the coat she was wearing and juggled with her mouth! Dad's favourite part was the person who was doing exams – he thought that was funny. All the way home Emily said, "The Jelly Botty Sisters . . . hmm hmm hmm . . . I mean Brothers!"

Emily: I said that 154 times on the way home in the car because they were really girls! And they had funny moustaches!

Joanna: And they had big bottoms.

Emily: And they had big muscles – about as big as the whole world. I got a fright because I didn't want to test the glass [for the glass walker] – I said, "I'm not going to test that!"

Joanna: But she didn't . . . she didn't get blood!

Emily: She didn't cut her feet!

Joanna: There were no blood – nothing!

Emily: Maybe she had invisible shoes . . . ?

1995, Leaping The Wire

Deb Lewis & Louise Radcliffe-Smith

Vivienne Mêhes

Swirling dervishes:
1995 Finale

In 1995 the Women's Circus started to look at feminism internationally. The end-of-year performance grew out of a production toured by the circus to the United Nations Fourth World Conference and Forum on Women. The Beijing production was based on a world-wide Amnesty International Campaign, "Human Rights – Women's Rights", and told the stories of twelve women from around the world.

The end-of-year show told six of these stories – from Algeria, Rwanda, Burma, Tibet, Romania and Brazil – and two others closer to home. One of the stories we added celebrated a member of the circus, Linda Wilson, whose journey as a survivor of sexual abuse represented many women both within the circus and the general community. The second was the story of an Aboriginal activist who struggled to initiate a Royal Commission into Black Deaths in Custody after her son died in a white jail.

These eight stories were true. Each depicted a form of human rights abuse and represented the struggle, to death or victory, of millions of women around the world.

This show was performed at an abandoned brickworks in Brunswick, with towering kilns and 100-year-old archways as a backdrop. Many things were different about this show. For one, it had a narrative spoken by the eight main characters or their representatives. This was the first time the Women's Circus had used spoken word in performance. For another, the eight stories were developed and directed by eight members of the circus, overseen by Donna Jackson and guest director Meme McDonald. The collaboration between ten directors gave greater depth to the show and took the circus policy of community ownership one step further.

Circus Beasts

Patricia Sykes

There's no place for them here
the whips the chains
the only animals in sight
are the feral women
who refuse to be tamed

they bend and stretch
at first light   run full pelt
into the winter sea
for softness is too much
a luxury on their road

and when they feed
their jaws have the power
of bears fresh from hibernation
they know this is their time
these circus years to train
their wildness so that their eyes
never die their teeth never blunt
so that the sticks they twirl
never turn into cages

Discovering the Place Within Myself

Elizabeth Connolly

I first experienced a Women's Circus show in November 1994, as part of the audience, a gift from a dear friend. Well, what a gift it was! The circus was, for me, like taking a deep breath. I remember walking through the gates after the show and standing on the street outside feeling so empowered. I can't remember another time when I felt so "there" in my body and enjoying it. And I was an audience member! What would it be like to be any one of those excellent and vibrant women? I decided to run away with the circus the very next day. When I was notified of a place in April 1995, my children said: "Cool, mum." So there I was, part of the troop, a mother of four in my thirty-eighth year.

Warm-ups: Elizabeth Connolly (front), 1995 Leaping the Wire

The circus has been for me an extraordinary process, a source of growth and more fun than I could ever have imagined. It is very physical and focused, and because of this I have discovered a place within myself which I have remembered only flickeringly. This place has no particular story. When I am there I feel grounded, entire and in control, and this spills out into my whole life. I love it. Being with the circus is a very special passion of mine. I have spent a third of my lifetime being the odd kid out at the sidelines of the playground. Now I am actually "coming out to play", and it's powerful!

It is a great experience being involved in an all-women production. I was taught very little in the way of "women's business" as a child and adolescent. I have floundered along ever since, managing through bits and pieces of information picked up along the way from friends, books and magazine articles. Often I would go into an experience boots and all, learning by trial and error. This is how it has been for me, and this missing knowledge has become all the more potent since I have had three daughters of my own. Working with the circus is helping me fill these vast gaps. There are women here from all corners of life, such a banquet of knowledge and wisdom.

From the Journal

There is space here. When I couldn't perform physically, there was room, when I was pregnant, there was room. This to me is testament that the model is working. It's inclusive. In 1994 I was breast feeding and there was just no questioning it. The circus has the capacity to absorb it all. I still performed rigorously, but safely, because the choice is ultimately mine. And my son Finn couldn't have a better "family". And through it all, the strength and capacity of women is evident.

– Sharee Grinter, 1995

Nicole Hunter

I was involved in two gigs in 1995, the Malthouse fund-raiser for Beijing and Leaping the Wire at the Brunswick Brickworks. Both times I went through an extraordinary process. When I am out there in the bright lights, I always make a point of involving the audience in all that is happening on stage. It may be a look, a smile or quick hip flick. I glance into all those wonderful faces individually and pass on to them what I got when I saw my first Women's Circus show.

We are all connected – those who come to see us, those who support us, those who work so hard and professionally behind the scenes, the gorgeous performers and brilliant musicians. It is this connection that I cherish, and all this together creates the special magic they call the Women's Circus.

Circus of Joy and Politics

Helen Thomson

The Women's Circus makes a powerful statement in support of human rights.

This is the fifth Women's Circus and I think the best to date. There are several reasons for this apart from the accruing of skills over time. One is the superb site this community arts group has found this year. The other is the focus, the new ideas and enthusiasm that participation in the Beijing United Nations Conference and Forum on Women brought about.

The Urban Land Authority brought the Nubrik Brickworks site to the attention of the circus, and it constitutes a set that an avant garde opera director would kill for. The last three Hoffman kilns in existence are there, two of them more than 100 years old. Huge chimneys stand above tunnels and openings that have been beautifully lit, and the audience is taken inside on their way to the performance space.

The scale of the human figures against the enormous industrial structures perfectly represents the show's theme, human rights violations against women, also the main focus of Amnesty International's 1995 campaign. Eight women's stories are told and each one reveals a woman large in moral courage and stature, but dwarfed by the military and political power controlled by men.

So the dozens of female figures we see streaming out of the many apertures in the huge, looming kilns, sometimes carrying flaming torches or flags, keep reminding us of women's persistence and energy. The fact that they all wear self-devised costumes made from tyre inner-tubes, a truly bizarre collection of body decorations, not only deconstructs the industrial in an unlikely recycling exercise, it is also intentionally funny.

This show is not simply an expression of victim feminism. The sheer joy of performance, of each individual woman being her personal best at a variety of circus skills, underpins the celebration of women who are defeated by force, but morally triumphant. And the message is not only directed to women, nor about them. Two of the stories centre on the loss of sons, one in Argentina, the other an Australian Aborigine who dies in custody. The victims of brutality are as likely to be men as women, but it is the inevitable woman who mourns them on whom we focus here.

Every one of the eight women fights against the violation of human rights. Two of them, the Prime Minister of Rwanda, killed when fighting broke out between the Tutsi and Hutu, and Aung San Suu Kyi, Burma's leader of the oppression, were and are themselves powerful figures representing far more than their own sex. The tight-wire act was entirely appropriate as an expression of Rwandan tribal tensions.

The most effective and moving stories were those of the Algerian girls, one killed for not wearing the veil, the other shot in retaliation because she did wear it, and the Aboriginal death in custody. A genuine theatricality has developed in the use of group movements, individual acting ability, and excellent use of music. The musicians performed splendidly all evening, providing a powerful commentary of rhythm, melody and sound effects. There are no individual stars, however, in this most communal of theatre projects. The best effects come from the sheer number of performers, with a huge range of abilities, and the combination of group discipline with individual, sometimes idiosyncratic, performance styles adds up to a spectacle where there is always something to engage the audience.

The harnessing of this circus to distinctly political aims raises it from a simple affirmation of female self-empowerment to a much more focused project.

The skills of tumbling, trapeze, balancing etc have become tools rather than just ends in themselves.

There are serious ideas and aims that have pushed both directors and performers into more creative uses of their skills.

Perhaps the most powerful statement made by the Women's Circus is its totally democratic form, and the sheer joy of working together that comes across from its performers. It is this that makes the deliberate sexual differentiation so important. This show's international emphasis, its assertion along with Amnesty International, that human rights are women's right, broadens and deepens the moral authority of its own feminist rationale.

Age, 27 November 1995

INTERNATIONAL TOURING: LEAPING THE WIRE

Getting to Beijing

Jean Taylor

Vivienne Mêhes

Photo opportunity: Doing the Elephant balance in Beijing, 1995

It was back in June 1993 that Donna first mentioned that the Women's Circus was considering attending the United Nations Fourth World Women's Conference and Non-government Organisations Forum in Beijing in September 1995. This exciting prospect was then raised at subsequent information meetings where the idea of going was discussed at great length. The main worry was whether or not it would divide the circus because realistically the circus could not afford to send everyone who might want to go. Despite doubts about introducing a project that could be a divisive rather than a positive experience we began to plan tentatively towards the proposed tour in case we could successfully resolve all the inherent difficulties and somehow raise sufficient funds to get to Beijing after all.

The plan was powerful. So much so, that the "World Conference Information Kit on Women" put out by the Office of the Status of Women in 1993 mentioned that "The Women's Circus in Victoria wants to run circus skills workshops at Forum 95 and with Asian women's groups en route." It seemed that the word had got around already almost before we'd properly had a chance to come to grips with it ourselves or to work out what influence it might have on the circus community as a whole.

"We are also trying to organise sponsorship for a trip to Beijing in 1995 for the United Nations World Women's

Conference," Donna wrote for the *Newsletter* at the beginning of 1994. By the middle of that year policy and planning meetings were being held on Saturday afternoons to work out a business plan for the next three years, and to draw up policy guidelines as well as to discuss the potential of participating at the Forum. As Donna went on to say in her report in the Winter 1994 *Newsletter*: "The number of women able to perform at such an event would depend on the amount of funding we are able to generate for airfares and accommodation." That this was the first time that the circus had ever had to consider restricting the number of women who could participate in a show made it that much more difficult to contemplate.

Nevertheless, the circus was still very much committed to the concept. "To help test the feasibility of this objective the Director of the FCAC, Elizabeth Walsh flew to New York to attend the UN's NGO Forum 94", Patricia Sykes wrote, "Elizabeth's report to her sponsor emphasises that Forum 95 is an opportunity to present the Circus' innovative Australian contemporary performance style to a world audience, a style she believes would communicate very effectively across cultural and language barriers . . . something unique and inspirational – community art at a global level." Then again, as Patricia went on to point out, it wasn't going to be all that easy, "the timeline is very short, there is no guarantee of funding, and Beijing is only one aspect of the circus' current three-year plan." Unfortunately not long after this, Liz Walsh, who not only had been very supportive of the circus going to Beijing but had considerable experience of overseas tours for circus groups, resigned her position as the director of FCAC which left a considerable gap in terms of support and expertise for the project overall.

As a result Heather Tetu, an experienced circus performer with touring and Mandarin language skills, was hired to co-ordinate the project and lobby on behalf of the circus for support and funding. "Creating the 'Beijing Brochure' was one of my first tasks," Heather wrote for the *Newsletter* in September 1994. "A fund raising committee was formed out of the information meeting, and this group is starting to put fund raising ideas into action. A target of $15,000 has been set for the Women's Circus to raise."

Following on from this and leading into the show at the end of the year FCAC launched a major fund-raising campaign to assist the circus in its plans to go to Beijing. The amount of funding being sought at this stage was in the region of $350 000. This was to cover the costs of approximately thirty women as well as aerial rigging in the form of a freestanding triangle which would be erected once we got there as well as other equipment, an extremely ambitious project.

None of our doubts were satisfactorily resolved one way or the other during the two years of lead-up. That is, we were no nearer working out a process whereby we might choose who was going partly because we were too busy just keeping the circus going as well as rehearsing and performing in the various gigs and the main shows. And we didn't want to have to deal with the hard task of excluding anyone, given that there were probably twice as many women who wanted to go as we could realistically afford to send.

At the beginning of 1995 Rosemary Hinse was employed to co-ordinate our registrations, and Wendy Lasica was hired to seek corporate sponsorship and to help us work out some ideas for fund-raisers. We were asked to make a selection, out of a comprehensive list of corporate sponsors, of those businesses we felt wouldn't compromise the feminist principles of the circus if we accepted money from them: that is, ones we considered to be ideologically sound (not many, in the final analysis). The fund-raising ideas being considered included a concert at the Concert Hall, selling Beijing Tour T-shirts and an auction. We had also approached the international touring section of the Arts Council with an submission for $80 000 as well as lobbying Arts Victoria for an additional $40 000.

However, it wasn't until March 1995 that members of the circus were asked to put in an application stating our reasons for wanting to go, what skills we had to contribute and why we felt we ought to be chosen. Several scenarios were still being considered with an optimum number of twenty women going plus equipment, down to scenario F with Donna plus three workshop leaders.

In the meantime, most of us had been running ourselves ragged trying to raise money. There were no less than four gigs during May, two full-on evenings at the Malthouse and a gig at the Footscray oval planned for the weekend of 30 May/1 June, and the auction and the Vic Arts performance coming up in July, with all the attendant lengthy rehearsals and time-consuming

I loved it, I hated it. By the time I began enjoying it, it was over.
And it still amazes me how well women work together.

– Maria

organisation these events entailed. Most women, including Donna, were stretched to the limit. Even so, and despite the misgivings along the way, the commitment and energy towards getting to Beijing was still quite enormous considering the strain the women both on and off the lists were under and with no real idea of who and how many would eventually go.

On 28 June there was a much clearer financial report and at this stage it seemed we would be able to raise enough money from our combined efforts and projected estimations for Donna and four women to go. On Friday 30 June we heard that $20 000 had been confirmed from Arts Victoria and Donna announced at the concert at the Malthouse the following night that two paid workers and nine performers would be on the plane to Beijing. We did eventually raise enough money to send eleven performers altogether.

As processes go, this one of deciding how we were going to manage it and who was going to Beijing obviously left a lot to be desired. In hindsight perhaps we were too ambitious to begin with. (Or not ambitious enough – who knows?) But the original budget estimate of committing ourselves to raising over a quarter of a million dollars was perhaps too daunting and, in the event, an ultimately unachievable financial objective for our first attempt at touring overseas. The overall budget we ended up with (total expenditure $92 000) is obviously a lot more realistic for a women's community group in terms of fund-raising ourselves as well as attracting the necessary government money.

As far as our decision-making processes are concerned it seems that we need to be a lot clearer about how we choose who is going to be included in overseas and interstate tours because the upsets this one caused were painful in the extreme.

Beijing: Hail the Convocation of Women

Bridget Roberts

Vivienne Méhes

Capping it: Bridget Roberts

On 29 August 1995, fourteen of us went to Beijing for two weeks. This trip was the biggest challenge the circus had faced since the first performance. To meet the challenge we had not only to do what we were good at, but also to break some risky new ground. We acquired bruises on the way, but ultimately we believe we made it.

We aimed to show the women of the world at the largest ever global gathering – the fourth UN World Women's Conference, that feminist community circus could empower individuals and be a liberating force for those who were suffering. We went to show other women our way of using physical theatre to reclaim our bodies and celebrate our strength as women. We hoped we might inspire others to begin similar projects in their own communities. We also went to learn from the women we would meet there; to hear about their struggles and to share skills with other women who used theatre, music, dance or circus. If there was a main purpose it lay in the content of our performance, which told the stories of twelve women from around the world whose human rights had been abused.

In the months before the tour our attention to news reports sharpened. We tuned in to the debates about the agenda for the conference, the difficult negotiations between the Organising Committee and the United Nations in New York, and the latest events in the countries of the women whose stories we were telling. We felt an expanding awareness of the global context of our efforts to speak out for women's rights.

The pervading sense was one of uncertainty. Would the Chinese government provide a satisfactory venue for the government conference and the non-government forum? Would they ensure safety and freedom of speech therein? Would they issue visas to exiled Tibetans and activist lesbians and anyone else who overtly challenged their ideology? There were also threats unconnected to China, as some fundamentalist Islamic governments united with the Vatican to get the conference to backpedal on sexuality and women's right to choose what to do with their bodies.

Closer to home, we faced a succession of uncertainties about such things as how many women the circus could afford to send, who they would be and whether they would be issued visas. Logistical planning was hampered by having very little information about what to expect in China. Yet somehow we were well prepared to handle uncertainty. Our experience of putting on a variety of shows in different and often bizarre places had given us skills that we could use and develop to meet this next challenge.

In the preparatory stage, two main tasks were new to us as a community: we had to select the women who would travel and we had to raise large amounts of money ourselves. The whole process tested our sense of cohesion and our ability to deal well with different needs and feelings.

Vivienne Méhes

Balancing act: Vig Geddes and Bridget Roberts in a double balance in Beijing, 1995

HUMAN RIGHTS ARE WOMEN'S RIGHT

The Women's Stories

Phuntsog Nyidron – A Tibetan nun imprisoned for staging a peaceful demonstration in support of Tibet's independence from China

Dr Ma Thida – A writer and doctor from Burma who is in prison for campaigning for democratic leader Aung San Suu Kyi

Agathe Uwilingiyimana – The first woman prime minister of Rwanda, killed for supporting a coalition government between Hutus and Tutsis

Katia Bengana – A 16-year-old Algerian woman who was killed for refusing to wear the veil

Linda Wilson – A member of the Women's Circus and an incest survivor

An Australian Aboriginal woman whose son died in a white jail. She was instrumental in initiating a royal commission into black deaths in custody. (We have not used her name at the request of her family.)

Maria Moldovan – A gypsy from Romania who was harassed, fined and imprisoned for protecting her rights

Edmeia da Silva Euzebio – A Brazilian woman who helped found the "Mothers of Acari" and who was shot and killed for testifying about the police involvement in the disappearance of her son

Faye Copeland – An American placed on death row for crimes her husband committed

Hamda As'ad Yunis – A teacher imprisoned for continuing to accept a salary as a public servant during the Iraqi occupation of Kuwait

Eren Keskin – A Turkish lawyer who was imprisoned (and later released) for writing articles the government did not like

Mirjana – A Bosnian woman who was gang raped by her neighbours

Selection

We began thinking about the selection process very early in the project. We even considered whether Beijing was worth the probable pain involved in forming a select group. What would be the effect on the rest of the circus who could not or did not want to go? What about our philosophy of including every woman in a performance regardless of what she could do or how long she had been a member?

At regular policy and planning meetings attended by anyone who was interested, we decided on selection criteria and invited women to write down why they wanted to go to Beijing. Initially a questionnaire provoked much thought and discussion. Later twenty-eight of us wrote letters of application. A small group of non-applicants then joined Donna Jackson in choosing twelve physical performers, three musicians and a technician, forming a troupe which we thought gave us a realistic fund-raising target and the ability to perform effectively.

All of us had to face the prospect of being disappointed and to commit ourselves to living with whatever was decided. The selection group found the experience painful and difficult: no one who had applied could be judged inadequate to the task – all were skilled and responsible women. But the choices had to be made and everyone, whether chosen or not, responded as best she could. As if this was not enough, the composition of the touring group changed three more times as the fortunes of the fund-raising efforts fell, fell again and finally rose. With only a few weeks to go we realised that we could fund a director, a tour manager and eleven performers, including two financed by performers' personal donations which were later reimbursed.

Each of these changes carried its own drama. One factor is

Vivienne Méhes

Uncensored: The Tibetan temple balance in Beijing, 1995

notable as an illustration of the way we were constantly trying to do things better: we moved to selection by a secret ballot within the group of twelve concerned rather than make the decision through a panel of non-applicants. This made the choices less painful but also less transparent and accountable, and those disappointed had no way of getting an explanation as they had when there was a selection panel to turn to. We realised that selection needed much more discussion and experimentation, and that we would continue to work it out in our own way without resorting to traditional auditions and hierarchical structures.

Fund-raising

The fund-raising exercise showed us where the heart of our support still lay. The women's community donated whatever they could to an auction – bikes, massages, banquets, child care, haircuts, legal services – then turned up on the night with their cheque books; they performed at and attended a benefit extravaganza at the Malthouse (incidentally our first mainstream venue), came in droves to our film and pub nights, and bought T-shirts and raffle tickets. Circus members put in hours of planning, organisation, rehearsal and performance.

Over a hundred businesses were approached for corporate sponsorship. The list might have been longer had we not cared about the ethics of our sponsors, asking ourselves "would we wear their name on our T-shirts?" We attracted nothing in this way from the wealthy private sector. Aussie Jigsaw Mats were notable as a small family-owned enterprise who donated two portable circular performance mats, one painted with the Women's Circus logo.

Federal arts funding helped to get the whole project started, giving us the help of two fund-raisers and a publicist. The State Government joined in at the last minute with a grant which greatly increased the numbers of women who could get on the plane.

Tour manager Georgine Clarsen considered the ways in which the support we had from other women was significant:

In the first place it was significant for the circus because each one of the hundred or so women who could have gone, and each one who supported the fund-raising, was in other ways very much there in Beijing with us. Many followed the events through the press, read our emails,

This year the circus has been in an almost constant state of high activity, much of this directed towards fund-raising to get as many women as possible to Beijing for our first international tour to the fourth Non-Government Organisations Forum and the United Nations World Women's Conference.

– Deb Lewis, *Newsletter*, Spring 1995

discussed the happenings in Beijing with each other and with other friends and were hanging out to hear our stories when we got back. They brought Beijing to our own backyard.

Secondly, the collective effort was very important for the small group of us who travelled. We were very aware that we were there because so many others had made it possible and that any one of them would gladly change places with us. That thought often got us out of bed at 6.00 a.m. to board the early bus when we did not really want to and strengthened our determination to use every minute of our time in the best way possible.

Finally, our community support was very significant for the larger group of Australian women who went to Beijing. It helped to broaden the composition and range of skills in the delegation. Our relatively rough, knockabout quality, our "attitude", our use of visual performance rather than talk, gave us a presence in the Forum that went beyond language and cultural barriers. We gave Australian women an added profile by speaking in a different and highly visible register.

Preparation

In the weeks and months before the tour, the main tasks beyond fund-raising were to develop and rehearse a show, to work in crews to cover all the supporting functions from freight to photographs, to build ourselves as a team and to organise our personal lives to preserve relationships, jobs, homes and energy levels.

Nicole Hunter

One-armed handstand

We worked with the Amnesty stories for three other shows before settling into the Beijing version three weeks before departure. In these earlier versions of the show, different women portrayed the key characters, each bringing something of herself to the role. We played in a small nightclub setting, a traditional theatre and outdoors at the Victorian Arts Centre. We experimented with ways of telling the stories physically and symbolically, emphasising, under Donna's inspired direction, the spirit of the women rather than the realistic detail of their situations. In researching and representing real women we had to find new levels of skill, testing our voices and our hearts as much as our acrobatic muscles. Audiences were impressed and moved. It became more and more clear that we could carry our message strongly to Beijing.

Once the final group was established, rehearsals became even more fascinating and intense. We used some material from the earlier shows and refined it, but much was new, notably the Aboriginal scene about black deaths in custody. The story had emerged from consultations with Aboriginal people in the Native Title Unit. Permission to use it was granted and representatives came to a rehearsal to see what we were doing and give us further advice. The story of Linda Wilson, the Women's Circus member, grew in the rehearsals and in consultation with Linda into the scene which would be the emotional, celebratory climax of the performance.

Each of the eleven performers played a key character at some point in the show (one of us played two) and each developed a very personal relationship with her story. We watched relevant videos, read through the Amnesty International files and where possible made contact with exiles living in Melbourne. In particular some of us got to know Kelsang Wangmo, a quietly spoken Tibetan woman who was hoping to go to Beijing with funding from local support groups. All this research enriched the show. Hours of musical direction from Marianne Permezel gave us an extra dimension for expressing our message. Costume making with Wendy Black, using tyre inner tubes, resulted in a distinctive and powerful black-on-white look. Donna Jackson kept us working so that we could perform with a clarity and a passion which would cross language barriers. Guest community theatre director Meme McDonald came in with new ideas and much support which heralded her later work with the broader circus community on the end-of-year show.

The tasks involved in actually taking this production to China, having a good time and coming home safely were potentially overwhelming. We were very glad to have a tour manager, Georgine Clarsen, whom we knew and trusted from her work on the production side of the annual performances, and to have a sizeable group in which tasks could be shared.

In five short planning meetings at each other's houses in the weeks before we left we slowly built up a shared picture of what we might expect in China and how we could best work together. And we practised quick and effective decision-making so that we would have a familiar process to draw on when everything else was strange and uncertain.

We set up working crews with detailed job descriptions to cover health and first aid, media liaison, networking, freight, daily living, food and documentation. Step by step, the venture began to look manageable.

The Organising Committee in China had allocated us time for one workshop and one performance, although we had applied for daily opportunities. Given this limitation and the enormous uncertainty about the readiness of the forum site and about the numbers of women who would get visas and actually arrive over the ten day period to put the 200-page pre-arranged programme into action, we decided to create our own opportunities and to be as self-sufficient as possible. This resolve and advance preparation gave us added strength: we could see what our path might look like even if the surrounding landscape was hidden in mist.

As Georgine said:

All of us worked enormously hard in the weeks before the tour. That this was done successfully was a testament to our experience, commitment and enthusiasm, but it meant that we arrived at the airport extremely tired just when more energy was demanded. The flight was actually welcome mainly for the opportunity it gave us to do nothing for twelve hours. We made mental notes to try and have a weekend's rest before any future tours. We also knew that this problem was built into the nature of community theatre: we would always be working on inadequate budgets to achieve the apparently impossible in too short a time. On the other hand, we would not give up on our basic Women's Circus aim of having a high quality experience with minimum risk of exhaustion, accident or injury.

The tour

On the plane to Beijing, we passed around our tour journal. The opening pages were filled with audience responses to a preview performance we had given for circus members and friends in the Footscray Community Arts Centre amphitheatre: "An incredibly moving experience . . . what wonderful role models . . . a great celebration of courage . . . I feel so proud to be part of this circus of women . . . you can represent me in Beijing."

Networking among the women on the plane gave us a foretaste of the forum. We met a community arts group called the Women of the Barkly, five Aboriginal and five non-Aboriginal women from Tennant Creek; we pinned on Tibetan ribbons handed out by Kelsang Wangmo from Melbourne and Dorji Dolma from Sydney; and collected leaflets from the Australian Women's Party and the Women's International League for Peace and Freedom. To help the Tibetan cause through Chinese customs, one of us took charge of the stock of Tibetan ribbons and another a video about repression in Tibet.

Performer Deb Lewis wrote of a moving encounter: "An older woman reached out and took my arm as I passed on a mission to get a drink of water. She said 'when I was a little girl at school we were asked to write about what we wanted to do when we grew up. I wrote a story about how I wanted to join the circus. The nuns beat me with a cane'."

From the Journal

Fourteen women, over 300 kilos of mats, props, fire sculpture gear, costumes, photographic equipment and the odd small bag of personal necessities are now packed away on the plane. Some emotional goodbyes at the airport. Now it's just us. I feel really well prepared and well supported, that we have already worked well together and will deal proudly with whatever comes. I'm excited!

Georgine's first impressions of the forum

My first impressions were of absolute chaos at Beijing Airport, with many hundreds of women arriving together and being ushered straight past customs checks and onto buses (Kelsang Wangmo being one heart-stopping exception as the official wondered whether she was a Tibetan undesirable who had been given a visa by mistake). We were taken directly to the Workers' Stadium to pick up our registration ID cards and buy Beijing bus passes. It was there that I started to get some sense of what it was going to be like.

Beating the drum: Andrea Ousley and Annie Fayzdaughter celebrating Dr Ma Thida's 29th bithday in Beijing, 1995

I saw so many women, by themselves and in groups. Easy to talk to – where are you from? How many from your country are here? Where will you be staying? As the week went by the questions became different – how are you doing? Have you been sick? Are you finding your workshops? As there became a sense that the Forum was nearly over, questioning turned to urgent and direct shorthand – what are the main issues for women in your country?

On that first day, my strongest visual image is of groups of African women in fantastic coloured headscarves and long dresses made of material designed and printed specially for the Conference. Each African country with a different design and colours. Our Women's Circus T-shirts were great, especially since they were printed in Chinese and English, but not a patch on the Africans for style.

Next day – up early and onto the bus. The first taste of the four hours a day of travel between our Beijing hotel and the Forum in Huairou. Lots of questions – Why are people sweeping the freeway? Are there normally so many coloured flags around? And giant banners proclaiming "Hail to the Great Convocation of Women" or "Be a Worthy Host to the Conference of Women". Why is there a policeman at every intersection? I didn't expect so many trees, somehow – but why are they so small? Where is the rest of the traffic? Are all the houses usually painted a fresh white? Who put the pot plant arrangements on the side of the freeway?

We step out of the bus with all our equipment and are pointed in the direction of a road that seems to go on for ever. As we walk the stream of women becomes a milling mass, with nobody quite knowing what was happening. A main gate with security checks. Alarms flash and beep constantly as women pour through. Finally the checkpoints have to give way and make only a token effort.

The space is huge. Rumour of an opening ceremony some-where. We have too much to carry and even at 10.00 a.m. it is too hot. We have to rest and orient ourselves without these metre-square bags full of performance mats. So I sit on the bags and watch while everyone else goes off to explore the site.

There is a hunger for leaflets and fliers. Women are sticking notices up everywhere. Very soon it is hard to see anything amongst the information that is screaming to be looked at. Every woman comes out of the central tent with an Esprit "Look at the World Through Women's Eyes" calico bag. Is that what unifies us? I see some rather ugly sights. Women shouting at puzzled Chinese student interpreters whose English skills are not really up to the task. A lot of complaining about how hard it is to find anything, maps that are inaccurate, buildings unfinished, portable toilets that you have to squat over and a programme that is pretty much out of date from day one.

Then our women come back excited and with good news. Yes, they had found a corner of a tent to store our gear and they had performed human pyramids at an Amnesty International demonstration outside a plenary session. The world's media had descended on them. This was more like it. This was what we had come for!

Our major task for the first day was to set up our performance and workshop programme. The sites allocated to us were not suitable, as we had suspected before we left Australia, and the one performance and one workshop they allowed us were not quite what we had in mind. We planned a lot more work than that! So we decided to forget about the organising committee and look after ourselves. We set about building ourselves our own venue. Shirley-Mae Springer-Statten, the head of the cultural committee, warns us that if we try to make ourselves a permanent site the security guards will move us on. We decide to try anyway.

It works. We set up our own area, using a new Chinese-made banner, bunting and performance mats. We are in a corner of a large open area which has parasols, tables and chairs; a busy place from which we can draw an audience. We catch the interest of the security guards, but they never quite see us moving rows of potted plants to make space for our audience, and they never move in to ask questions. Every day, weather permitting, we do public workshops and performances there.

On the day of our first planned performance, however, torrential rain flooded the forum site and undermined a wall, which collapsed to block a major walkway. We took the opportunity to stretch our muscles, cramped by the journey and the heat, and to rehearse in a function room in our hotel. We performed that night at "Womenspeak", a plush venue for Australian forum and conference delegates to meet and lobby. The organisers had been harassed by the Chinese, who wanted no political meetings outside the Forum. So, out of fear of losing the space, the organisers asked us to censor the Tibetan story, the most overtly contentious feature. We had the choice of compromising our politics or disappointing an extremely large and eager audience. We huddled into one of our hotel rooms to decide. We proposed that we perform the story but that I, as

I celebrate the adventure of my lifetime – one which I will always remember for the diversity of experience, emotion, culture, political women, and toilets.

– Janine Edwards

This has been one of the major projects both politically and personally . . . stunning in the living of it, the performances, the workshops, the other participants, the music, the colour, the politics, the food, the weather and most particularly the company of all fourteen of us.

– Jean Taylor

This trip has given me enormous respect for the members of the Women's Circus in the group: the ability to work together, support each other, be open to the audience and put on fantastic shows under very arduous conditions. And all with good humour and warmth. More broadly, it has given me a sense of a vital and generous global Women's Movement which is beginning to recognise and value the enormous differences between us. The Beijing experience has given the group inspiration and confirmation of the broader relevance of our work. It has opened the group's eyes to the global issues that will face women in the next years. Our networks have moved far beyond Melbourne into the rest of Australia and countries far beyond. And it has given us energy to continue to push the boundaries of the creative form we have chosen.

– Georgine Clarsen

imprisoned nun Phuntsog Nyidron, would keep silent. (If I had known how the Tibetan women in exile were going to demonstrate on the following day, I too would have worn a scarf across my mouth as a symbolic gag.) It worked: women understood and were moved. We didn't like being silenced, but the silence was eloquent in the outspokenness of the whole performance. The standing ovation and some detailed feedback from Aboriginal and non-Aboriginal women from all over Australia sent us on our way with extra layers of pride and confidence.

In the following days we did daily lunchtime physical workshops and performances at 4.00 p.m., sometimes in blinding sun, sometimes in drizzle. Mornings were devoted to tasks which were variously frustrating, hilarious, tedious and rewarding. Some women shopped for shellite fuel for the fire routines, using doubtful interpreters, mime and bits of paper inscribed by helpful Chinese with completely misleading messages. Others chased up media contacts, arranging and giving interviews to the world via Reuters, Japan Cable TV, FIRE (Feminist International Radio Endeavour) and more. Some women sent email reports back to Footscray or worked on publicising our workshops and performances around the Forum.

Sometimes we had a chance to absorb other women's stories. We attended workshops: on Tibet, Bougainville, Tennant Creek, Fiji and lesbian rights. We also just talked to women as we met them: the Papua New Guineans who had sold fish in the market for months to be able to get to Beijing, the Indian village women who had never before been out of their state, the dancer from Laos who had come all by herself to perform on the main stage. We saw women meeting across barriers: the Tibetan women in exile reaching out to those sponsored by the Chinese government; Catholics and Muslims from the Philippines and the Middle East celebrating the Virgin Mary as a symbol who could unify women; Korean women demonstrating with Japanese women against Japanese war crimes.

Glad of having our established corner to return to, several of us conducted or supported the Women's Circus workshops. After briefly talking about the aims and herstory of the Women's Circus we led women into stomping routines, simple balances and a lot of laughter. Numbers were low, partly owing to the difficulty of getting accurate information into the daily forum newspaper.

The performances in our space attracted about two hundred people at a time. Georgine noted "a strong response from the audience. Lots of intent listening and watching. Silence! A rare commodity at the forum. 'Shh!' from the audience to anyone speaking. Strong applause." Many were moved. Brazilian women approached Karen, who was playing Edmeia da Silva Euzebio, a woman who was killed for testifying about the police involvement in the disappearance of her son: "Thank you," they said. "Thank you, you have spoken the truth." Another audience member wrote in our journal: "I am a holocaust survivor from Cambodia. What you've done here is an incredible gift from the heart. It touched me so much that I silently cried in my corner the first time I saw it . . . You remembered and cared for the survivors, the unheard, the unseen. Thank you for the gift." Some Chinese women walked away with their interpreters when the Tibetan message became clear; many stayed to listen.

We made other appearances in other parts of the forum. One day we noisily celebrated Burmese writer Ma Thida's birthday at the Amnesty International stand, drumming alongside some ebullient and skilful Koreans; the next we attended a silent vigil against violence against women. The main stage for evening entertainment was organised by region: on Asia-Pacific night we followed singer-songwriter Judy Small with a hastily abbreviated version of our show. Never before had we re-blocked so efficiently nor been applauded by so many. On the last day we performed in the Asia-Pacific regional tent, adapting to a low roof and small space, and were invited back to the main stage by the young women organisers of the closing celebration to add some drumming and some fire to their dancing and singing.

The latter innocent request led us at our last performance into our only direct confrontation with authority. We had been constantly aware of the presence and scrutiny of security guards, although we had not suffered anything like the harassment inflicted on the Tibetan women in exile. On this final night, however, they announced that we were not allowed to perform. The unspoken reason was our treatment of the Tibetan independence story, which conflicted with the Chinese government view that all was well in an autonomous region which was reaping the benefits of civilisation. While the Forum organisers tried to dissuade them, they stood implacably in our way, even when the compere had announced us and had told the

Today, a few weeks after Beijing I watch women rehearsing the end-of-year show. Echoes of what we did in Beijing resound with the rich new ideas and energy of the larger troupe. The other annual shows have been rewarding, but this one will have to be the closest to our hearts. We are more in touch with the reality of violence against women and how it can be expressed through physical theatre. Our own pain and need for support are becoming better recognised and we are doing more for other women – not only by inspiring them, but by speaking out for those who cannot speak for themselves. I still feel a tiredness born of a long and intense year of circus projects. But it can't erode the immense pride that I feel. I think that overall we avoided the feared burnout and have experienced a tremendous creative explosion.

– Bridget Roberts

audience of thousands that we were being prevented from getting onto the stage. In our costume and make-up, with our drums slung about us and fire clubs held high, obedience to the 7-foot tall security chief was the furthest thing from our minds. As a body we swung away from the blocked entrance in the wings and drummed our way to the front steps of the stage. The throng of media crews there made space for us and the surprised security men could do little as we pushed our way through and firmly but harmlessly squashed them against the crowd. This drama may have taken its toll on the sharpness of our fire routine, and drumsticks slipped from rain-soaked and over-excited fingers, but the atmosphere among audience and performers was triumphant.

Keeping a record: Vig Geddes interviewing one of the workshop participants in Beijing, 1995

What did we achieve?

The whole Beijing project, from its inception to the day we returned to Melbourne, was a huge experience which even at the time of writing, four months later, is still sinking in.

We were certainly part of an historic occasion. Pamela Bone wrote:

> *The Beijing Declaration had all the nations of the world agreeing for the first time that women's rights are human rights. For the first time, there is an international agreement (with reservations by about twenty countries) that women have the right to decide freely on matters of their sexuality and childbearing.*
>
> *The Declaration says the systematic rape of women in war is a war crime and that perpetrators should be treated as war criminals; that domestic violence is a problem in every country and that governments should intervene; that the genital mutilation of girls, attacks on women because their dowries are too small and sexual harassment at work are all violations, not of women's rights but of human rights. Though it does not explicitly give women the right to abortion, it stipulates an end to penalties for abortion in countries where it is illegal. Most of all, it recognises that throughout the world, girls and women are discriminated against in ways boys and men are not.*
>
> *Age*, 20 September 1995

The lesbian rights movement was disappointed that the words "sexual orientation" were dumped from the declaration, but there was pride that at least there had been some debate about the issue, with many countries in support.

We will never know how the Women's Circus contributed to the formal outcome of the Beijing conference. All we can say is that our show was relevant to all the concerns of the Declaration and that it spoke to many people across language and cultural barriers. The outcome was far from predetermined: there had been many gloomy forecasts that the Conference would undo even the progress made ten years before in Nairobi. That enough minds were changed during the Forum and Conference to make new progress must be attributable to all the women who went to Beijing and worked hard and creatively in spite of all the odds.

Leaping the Wire

Kath Davey, Amnesty International

"Leaping the Wire" was the title dreamed up by Jen Nield for the joint project between Amnesty International and the Women's Circus. The wire, of course, is the barbed wire that symbolically encircles the candle in our logo, the leaping being part of the circus' own logo. Significantly in this case, the Amnesty International candle is evocative of the Chinese saying "better to light a candle that curse the darkness". Certainly performances of the Women's Circus in Beijing and Australia were a window of light on a very dark subject.

Amnesty International is a world-wide human rights organisation with over one million members in 150 countries who work to prevent some of the gravest violations by governments of people's most fundamental human rights. We respect all cultures but focus our campaigns on those who torture, imprison people for their beliefs, do not conduct fair trials and who "disappear" or execute. On International Women's Day, 1995, we launched a world-wide campaign to highlight the invisibility of the human rights violations suffered by women throughout the world. The Women's Circus became one of the most important ways in which this message was brought home to the women of the world at Beijing and in Australia. Women suffer human rights violations in many different ways *because they are women*. Sometimes it is because they are mothers, sisters or daughters of men who are a difficulty to governments, sometimes because they are activists in countries where women are supposed to be passive, sometimes because they just happen to be in an area of conflict and are seen as possessions of the enemy to be raped and abused.

In late 1994 I was in Bonn with thirty of my Amnesty International colleagues from around the world, deciding how we would run the women's campaign, and my colleague from Pakistan, Dr Habiba Hassan, said: "How are we going to get our message across to women who can't read or write, who don't have electricity, but who can think and talk?"

We had no real answer but it was a great question that started me thinking. In early 1995 when I was planning for the Amnesty International women's campaign in Australia, I heard that the Women's Circus was going to Beijing. Having just returned from twenty years living and working in regional and rural Australia, I had never actually seen a performance of the Women's Circus, but had read a lot about it and heard it spoken of highly throughout feminist and artistic circles. As a life member of the Board of the Murray River Performing Group (which established the Flying Fruit Fly Circus) I am extremely aware of the power of performance in enabling people to develop their own skills and also in delivering a social and political message. So I rang Donna Jackson, circus co-ordinator, explaining we were planning a campaign that involved Beijing and asked what the circus were planning to do. Donna's reply went something along the following lines: "Well we're not quite sure at the moment. We don't want to come across like a bunch of didactic 1970s feminists going to Beijing and telling women from other cultures what they should do".

Wondering whether I was indeed a "didactic 1970s feminist" and not at all sure what that meant, I suggested I might send her some of our stories of women in various countries who had been subjected to human rights violations. As everyone who has read such stories or seen Leaping the Wire will know, these stories are very powerful and moving. After she had read them Donna rang back and said: "Now we know why we want to go to Beijing."

And Beijing was indeed wonderful. Amnesty is never backward about highlighting to governments the atrocities they commit. The Chinese hosts showed abysmal disregard for the rights of their own citizens, and threw everything in the way of the non-government organisations who attended: logistical hurdles; intimidation; physical threats and the force of blatantly unacceptable local laws. While many governments and foreign observers tiptoed round the issues, Amnesty and the Women's Circus, outmanoeuvred the authorities. The Women's Circus in particular had them puzzled. Many security men with cameras and mobile phones watched for quite some time before they realised that this was in fact a political statement being performed and it included comment on China. The courage and strength of the women performers in the face of continued surveillance and harassment was a privilege to witness. Many times I saw tears before and after a performance as women struggled with the emotion of presenting such harrowing stories as well as handling the pressure of being watched and followed, never sure if their show would be stopped. I also saw many tears from the thousands who saw the performances as they were moved by the presentation of these stories and by the sheer delight of seeing woman use their bodies in wonderfully strong ways to highlight the ways in which women are abused.

Amnesty people from throughout the world were at Beijing and hailed the Australian Women's Circus as one of the most successful parts of the NGO forum and certainly one of the most powerful ways in which we have been able to get our message across.

For me, working with the Women's Circus on this project was the highlight of the campaign and of Beijing. I probably am a didactic 1970s feminist but I was proud to be part of and work with the new face of feminism in the Women's Circus.

Vivienne Mehes

On Death Row: Joanne Donne, Annie Fayzdaughter and Jean Taylor performing a ritual for Faye Copeland of the USA, in Beijing 1995

V
Evaluation

. . . the revolutionary feminist process,
learn new skills, develop the ones
I already have and enjoy being part of
such a large group of dedicated and
skilled circus women. Taking risks,
meeting new challenges, moving our
bodies beyond endurance and leaping
off the edge, indeed.

– Jean Taylor, 1992

Naomi Herzog

Women's Strength: Naretha Williams and Franca Stadler performing the
Aboriginal Deaths in Custody story for Leaping the Wire 1995

CELEBRATION

A Circus Woman:
Five Years in the Making

Jean Taylor

Back in 1979 I remember being particularly inspired by the Wimmin's Circus who were a highly entertaining and politically motivated group of women dedicated to presenting feminist circus in a theatrical way. Years later when I first heard about the possibility of another women's circus from Donna Jackson I was intrigued and enthused by the concept but suspected that I wouldn't be able to join because I was already forty-seven, generally unfit and lacked any kind of circus skills whatsoever.

1991

However, when funding was made available I went along to the information night and launch of the Women's Circus in April and found myself signing up for the Wednesday afternoon training workshops with Sally Forth. I can hardly begin to describe how stunned I was by the rigorous warm-ups we did during those first few sessions nor how sore my body was for days afterwards. Every workshop was two hours of non-stop movement and I could hardly believe that I was doing forward rolls, practising handstands and learning to do thigh stands when I hadn't done anything more agile than pushing a pen or typing my manuscripts for years.

And at the same time I was thoroughly enjoying myself. Here was a group of women, at least half of whom were dykes like myself, and together we were learning new skills and developing something that had never been done in quite this way before.

Besides, I was learning how to juggle. Then I discovered I had an affinity with plates. And I was gradually and slowly becoming a stilt-walker. The whole process of having those

wooden stilts strapped to my legs, so that I was a horrifying few feet off the ground and couldn't move without a very real possibility of falling, terrified the life out of me.

Appropriately enough, in October, my very first performance for the Women's Circus was walking on stilts to lead the Reclaim the Night march in Geelong.

I still regard that first Women and Institutions show as one of our best efforts. That Donna was able to create a dynamic performance out of such a diverse range of skills and abilities from four workshops with up to sixty women on stage at any one time was nothing short of miraculous to those of us who'd not been involved in anything like it before. I also think that the hanging scene was one of the most dramatically moving scenes we've ever done, and community theatre at its best.

Because I had become proficient on the stilts by the end of that show, although it wasn't until our last three performances that I really considered myself a stilt walker, I undertook to help run a stilt-walking workshop for kids over in Deer Park in December with a couple of the other circus women.

As a kind of finale to that first year, I was also one of the performers who performed on stilts before an audience of several hundred women in the gig for the Women's Summer Ball at the San Remo Ballroom in December.

1992

The following year I was encouraged to pass my stilt-walking skills onto a couple of other women in the workshop who were interested. I very quickly became proficient on the medium-high stilts at the same time. Which has become one of my greatest sources of pleasure in the circus and I'm very glad that I managed to overcome my fears sufficiently to feel safe doing it.

I was finding that the regular workshops were extremely beneficial to my general wellbeing and improved level of fitness. At the same time it was also pleasing getting to know, and becoming friends with, the other women involved.

All through that second year I extended my balancing skills, especially once I realised I was a strong reliable base for other women to climb on, learnt how to spin plates on the end of long sticks, kept practising on the stilts till I felt very confident indeed, and bought a pair of secondhand roller skates and was teaching myself how to roller skate.

The Women's Circus was again asked to do a small performance for the Women's Spring Ball in September where once again I stomped through a routine on stilts while waving a flag.

Come rehearsal time for the end-of-year show, I was practising with the other stilt-walkers, working on a cable barrel and sheet routine, perfecting the fight scene, preparing my plate-spinning act, in training with the roller skaters, continuing with the pyramid and other balances and generally looking forward to what was shaping up to be a dynamically political performance around women and work.

Then early in October, two weeks before opening night, I fell off my roller skates and injured my coccyx so badly that by the time I got home from the rehearsal at the warehouse where the show was to take place I could barely walk. Loath as I was to miss the show altogether, I agreed to be one of the lackeys pulling the cart and only ended up spinning three plates on sticks at the same time in the celebration scene with a couple of balances in between. Despite it all the show was a tremendous success. My favourite part was when I held up the "contract" sign and the audience started booing and hissing to reflect the hostility the workers of Victoria were feeling towards the newly elected government.

1993

With my back now healed, I undertook to do the rehearsals for the Williamstown Summer Festival show over the Invasion Day weekend at the end of January. We did three afternoon performances in the Williamstown Botanic Gardens and the nearby park in near 100°F heat. However, the setting by the sea was inspirational and we'd got the three aspects of the show together in less than a month.

Straightaway into rehearsals for the one of the Moomba barges on the Yarra River for Labour Day in March. This was another equally invigorating experience, doing acrobatics, balances, flags, ropes, the ladder and sheet routines on a walkway over a barge as it was being pulled slowly down the river at night, the banks crowded with thousands of people cheering.

By the time workshops began again in April I felt as if I'd already done my performance work for the year. However, it was fun getting back into training all over again and meeting up with the women I hadn't seen for a few months as well as getting to know the new ones. Then one afternoon I happened to pick up the diablo to give it a try, found I liked it and after a bit of basic instruction on how to throw it in the air and catch it as well as a few other tricks, I was well on the way to learning yet another circus skill.

We were so adept at putting on these small performances that the Wednesday workshop group was able to devise a series of routines involving plates, balances, unicycles, acrobatics and whatnot one week and perform them the next to support the launch of *Sharing the Journey*, a book about incest. I also did the show we put on for the Women and Planning Conference where I twirled fire sticks for the first time. My first public appearance with the diablo was at the Lesbian Spring Ball in September before a packed audience of enthusiastic women.

In October I bussed across the Nullarbor Plains of Central Australia to the National Lesbian Conference and Festival in Perth where I facilitated my very first circus skills workshop. This was so successful that I ran a repeat one for the WISE festival down south a week or so later and in such a way that the participants were able to put on a small act for the concert that evening to show off their newly acquired skills.

I was back in time for the rehearsals outside on the lawns at FCAC, the site for the Women and Sport show which was the most disappointing and the least inspiring, as far as I was concerned. I couldn't relate to the politics, I'd never been interested in competitive sport in any way whatsoever. I wasn't impressed with the vinyl (and particularly didn't like having to wear a short vinyl skirt) and as my role had been reduced to virtually nothing more than following the Queen around, I was frustrated at not being able to do any of the balances and other routines I'd been practising for months.

All I was able to do was my plate routine although we did manage to get some of our diablo skills in, albeit so briefly that on some nights they didn't feature at all. I eventually had to settle for the indubitable enjoyment of at least being there every night and being part of it along with everyone else.

1994

At the information day in February, I found myself enthusiastically agreeing to be a dog on stilts for the Nightmare Barge. Donna was the overall director for the entire Moomba parade. A most agreeable experience it was too, being on stilts on a barge moving down the Yarra River.

Not long after we'd begun the weekly training workshops for the year I got involved in rehearsals for the Rural Woman of the Year award being held at the National Art Gallery at the beginning of July.

In between times I went to the National 10/40 Conference in Tasmania and held another circus skills workshop where, because it was a conference for feminists forty years of age and over, all fifteen or so of the participants were naturally over forty and at least half over fifty. Working with so many of my peers while they were learning to do forklifts and three high pyramids was a whole new experience for me.

When I was approached to form a circus for women over forty, at first I was reluctant to take on anything more than my already overcrowded schedule could possibly handle. However, once I'd had a think about it, it did seem feasible to maybe hold a series of workshops, over perhaps a limited period, possibly during the summer months while the Women's Circus was in recess.

But I'm getting ahead of myself. In July of that same year I went to Brisbane for the National Lesbian ConFest and yes, ran yet another circus skills workshop. I arrived back in Melbourne and was straight into the weekly directors' workshops that Donna was running over the following couple of months. At the end of these I did my required production brief on the proposed "circus skills workshops for women over forty project". This pulled together the vague ideas I had into a more coherent and manageable six-week process, tentatively aiming towards a small performance for International Women's Day 1995.

Overlapping this, I enrolled in a week-long series of clowning workshops with Angela de Castro with nineteen other circus women. I'd waited a long time for something like this. Clowns and clowning have not been encouraged at all in the circus and as someone who regards comedy as an essential in life I was pleased to be able to at least begin working on my own clowning potential.

After my rather negative experiences in the previous two end-of-year shows I wasn't going to let that happen again so with

Death: The Musical. I put my name down for every possible scene and then some. I directed one of the sideshow acts and performed in another one called "Sexperts" or "Sex Diablo". In the main part of the show I spun two plates at the same time, walked on stilts, was one of the Dogs, did more diablo and a couple of double balances. I loved every minute of it especially being able to dress up as a clown for the sideshow act which always set the mood for the rest of the show as far as I was concerned.

Afterwards, I put some of my newly acquired director's skills to good use by helping to devise and perform in a small gig for the Matrix Guild before a women-only audience in December.

1995

For me, 1995 can be summed up in one word: Beijing. Or to put it more accurately, the Women's Circus tour to and participation in the NGO World Women's Forum which was an experience I'll never forget.

The year actually started in mid-January with the project I initiated for women over forty which has since become the on-going Performing Older Women's (POW) Circus with myself as the director. At the same time I was rehearsing for yet another one of the circus Moomba barges where we did balance, dance and fire routines. After that, I went to Sydney for the National 10/40 Conference to run a couple of circus skills workshops and, amongst other things, direct a small POW Circus performance for the concert.

Back again, I was immediately busy with the full-on fundraising and the organisational details in the lead-up to Beijing. I performed in all four and directed one of the gigs in May. I was also in a couple of the items for the Malthouse concert, performed as a dog on stilts at the Footscray oval and was in the Arts Victoria show. Then later I helped with the auction, attended the film and pub nights and by this time was also rehearsing and getting everything together for the show we were taking to Beijing.

It was a very emotionally demanding few months. We had to familiarise ourselves with the stories of the women highlighted in the Amnesty International campaign plus the two from Australia as well as going through the process of selection which caused a great deal of distress for everyone concerned.

It was all worth it, as far as I was concerned.

Just being in Beijing and participating in the NGO Forum, running circus skills workshops, performing in our show nearly every day and going to workshops to learn about what was happening to other lesbians around the world was the most exciting and stimulating two weeks I've enjoyed in a long time.

That I was then able to follow this by going to Alice Springs for the National Lesbian ConFest and co-facilitate another circus workshop and direct an item for the concert made it all the more worthwhile, for some reason.

Back in Melbourne I was immediately involved in the directors' workshops with Meme McDonald and in getting a storyline and a script together so that the Wednesday morning workshop could rehearse Dr Ma Thida's life story.

Performing in the Leaping the Wire end-of-year show down at the old brickworks in Brunswick as well as directing was, as always, one of the best highlights of the circus year for me. While it wasn't always an easy process being one of the new directors I learned a lot and it was an invaluable experience.

What more can I say? As a fifty-one-year-old lesbian who is politically active around ageist issues, as a circus performer who is learning the skills of being a trainer, a director and a clown, and as a feminist committed to social change, the Women's Circus, not too surprisingly, is one part of my life that I find to be that much more challenging and rewarding than most.

Nicole Hunter

Workshops

(Selected from "The Womyn's Circus", a poem in two parts)

Emily George

years ago
I saw them
womyn on stilts
eating fire
cracking whips
and being strong
holding each other up
in pyramids of breath-taking effort

> by challenging the stereotypes
> we women were encouraged
> beyond the boundaries
> to be ourselves

> the circus is coming
> the circus is coming
> to take us away
> let's run away
> and join them

stepping tentatively
into the warehouse
during that first week
of workshops
being pushed stretched made to
bend every which way
we left
somewhat alarmed by
the serious intensity of
this womyn's circus business

> I wanted to be a clown
> and found myself
> doing sit-ups from hell
> and soaking aching limbs
> barely able to walk

hup hup hup
one two three four
five six seven eight
arms up, deep breath
hold it and stretch
bend
breathe out
and relax those shoulders

every week
there we'd be
all ninety-odd of us
to begin with

what do you mean?
I have to get up on the
trapeze
do a forward roll
climb that rope
allow a womyn to
stand on my shoulders?

I haven't done a handstand
in years
nor a cartwheel
and I can't remember
the last time
I did a shoulder stand
legs up and over
touching the floor

juggling looks easy

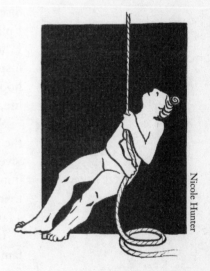

Nicole Hunter

Fantasy

Louise Radcliffe-Smith

I see the circus stretching like a bridge of definition across my life. The tightrope is an act of focus, the physical equivalent of meditation. Juggle clubs loop like pieces of a larger jigsaw before my eyes – work, love, home, learning. Double balance is a symbol of friendship, a delicate moment of support, flight and creation. And sometimes, in moments of phoenix joy, I hold fire and swing and touch the sky, the clubs an extension of my arms, the weight carving arcs of flame from the air about my body.

I measure circus time in skills, friends, workshops, rehearsals and performances. Four years have passed since first I entered the warehouse doors, a tremulous twenty-five-year-old with low self-esteem and limp arms. I walked the tightrope and discovered a tempting point of balance buried deep in my belly. I played trust games and recovered lost moments of childhood. I heard women tell stories of new beginnings and circus-inspired achievements, stories of struggle, recognition and hope. I learnt, as a woman and a feminist and a participant in life, that the strength is in the doing.

So the years went on and I kept coming back. I was here at the beginning, and the end seems a long way distant. Time has given me a strong body and a series of kaleidoscope images hung like pearls on a string of memory. Sometimes I replay them in my mind like a personal potted version of "the show", a fantasy.

In this fantasy, it is usually opening night. The audience is familiar and generous, waiting to see their lovers, friends and family, their "couldabeen" selves up on stage. I feel excited and comfortably hidden under white face and op-shop costume.

In the dressing room, clothes fly on and off, make-up is applied and reapplied, problems are solved in frantic whispers and nervous gigglers hushed by those too nervous to giggle.

Techies are everywhere, busy in black, holding the place together, swapping tools and fags and a handy hint or two. They wait in position for the moment when all their shifting and carrying, their gaffering, wiring and problem-solving comes to electrifying fruition.

Donna (the director) is up in the back row trying to calm her opening-night nerves, pencil ready to capture any *faux pas*. Later, in the dressing room, she will deliver her verdict (known as "notes"): "Stand tall, straighten your arms, don't wear red spotted knickers under white tights, synchronise those movements and for God's sake smile at the audience. Be bold, brash and brazen!"

At last the lights are dimmed and a spotlight picks out Christina's lithe form swinging on a trapeze through the gloom of an abandoned factory, now reclaimed and transformed into a place of play and possibility.

Sharee, five and a half months pregnant, clambers hand over hand to the top of a three-tiered pyramid, smiling from ear to ear in a delighted celebration of herself and those of us whose hearts and hands keep her up.

Deb stands at the centre of another pyramid, like Atlas holding up the mountain, powerful and focused. As the weight becomes almost unbearable she remembers Sally's words, "stand strong, stand proud", and one more woman climbs aboard.

Dressed in multicoloured masks and costumes, the musicians say with melody what we choose not to say with words. They outline the emotional detail of each scene, their flutes putting air beneath the cheeky sprites as they swing and tease on trapeze, turtle horn calling the many-armed death cart and its haunting retinue of moon lanterns.

Suddenly the music changes. Junk percussion turns soft grief to technicolour and heralds the entrance of red-eyed dogs, massive in vinyl and stilts, prowling the stage like hungry warriors.

After them comes Karen (alias the Queen), invading the proceedings like a giant yellow and black spider, her enormous vinyl costume surging about the stage like a vicious wave. She flicks her diablo contemptuously in the air and orders her minions to compete.

Min rushes towards me from the aisle, aims a reluctant fist at my head, then a reluctant foot and kickboxes me to the ground. She is fourteen. I am twenty-eight. We play this game every night.

As the pace builds, Jen and Deb hang from their ankles and spin wildly ten feet above a garden of yellow roses. Their arms are splayed, their bodies tense with exhaustion, whirling on the web of theatre. They are urged on by two teams of frantic, stomping, chanting competitors, dressed in red and yellow. Deb collapses and slides down the rope to waiting arms; Jen marches triumphant. Both pretend from that space inside they call acting.

The lights go down and from an eerie blue stillness come the legs of grief, thirty women doing headstands on gravel in the rose garden. Their various angled limbs speak a strange kind of post-modern anguish. Their hands afterwards complain of gravel rash.

My role varies in this dream performance. Sometimes, I see myself towing fire drums behind a dinghy on the Maribyrnong River at twilight, fighting the tide and pre-performance jitters. At other times I balance precariously on a tightrope, hanging sheets to entertain audience members as they file slowly to their seats. In moments of bravado I steal fire from the queen and balance with hoops shoulder-high on a 45-degree slope. Occasionally I relive the vertiginous sensation of swinging clubs on an invisible railing ten metres above the stage.

As always, I am there when the show explodes in celebration. The oppressor is vanquished, the philosophical conundrum explained and the future opened wide with possibility. There is never, for us, a single message or belief. In those final moments of the performance we speak our diversity in every way we can: with flags and ropes and double balances, with acrobats and fire twirlers, with music and motion. It is our gift to the audience and to ourselves. It is our fantasy come true.

Nicole Hunter

House balance

Lay-off Season

Patricia Sykes

Outside the kookaburras laugh
like a well-timed cliche
as if there's some joke about
the slack rope swinging
like a hammock between the trees

the year's stretch marks
are invisible   there are no notches
to count   things have died
and been born from too deep
a place to masquerade
as symbols or metaphors

we visit each other during
the lay-off to break bread
to recreate each other's faces
to ask about our return
knowing there are more women
than places to be filled

knowing too that each woman's
circus is a journey that each year
requires choice   being on holiday
the season abdicates   the decision
remains a woman's prerogative

those who have come this far
have practised their catching skills
if a leavetaking comes
there is nothing dropped no burial
only another name added
to the circus women's tree

LOOKING BACK

Evaluation

Jean Taylor

Evaluation meetings, that is, a set time to evaluate the major show and the year's work, usually take place about a week after the last performance of the show towards the end of the year. Evaluation can also take place after the smaller gigs, too, albeit in a much simpler format.

The annual evaluation meetings run for at least three hours with a set agenda and facilitators. Once the preliminaries are established the large group breaks up into smaller groups such as the techs, musicians and front of house, while the performers divide into either random groups, support groups, crews or areas of interest. Each group is then given a set amount of time to write down the things they enjoyed and consider were positive aspects about the show and the year's workshops, and what could be improved for future reference. This feedback is then read out loud to the larger group when it reconvenes.

Sometimes the same problems crop up time and again without being properly addressed and occasionally difficulties are aired that ought to have been solved months beforehand to be effective. And there's never really enough time to do justice to everything that needs to be discussed. However, the evaluation is an essential part of the process. Not only because it enables everyone to work out how to improve the organisation of the show for next time but also because it is a necessary means by which we can personally and collectively congratulate ourselves on a job well done after all the hard work.

And besides, it's an excellent opportunity to watch the video, look at the photos and especially to catch up with the rest of this large community of women, most of whom we've got to know really well over the previous intense couple of months of rehearsals and the show itself. It's also a final chance to be with those women we probably won't get to see again till the workshops start up again the following year. When the whole cycle begins again.

Change and Evolution

Jules De Cinque

The Women's Circus is a political theatre group. It is about action. It is about change. For the last five years the circus has clearly demonstrated this commitment to presenting ideas in an art form that not only entertains but challenges an audience to think. It is made up of women from a variety of live experiences. The circus uses its richness of observations, knowledge and understandings to offer a different way of seeing the world and our place in it and a fresh perspective on the way things are and could be. It is theatre of spectacle and beauty that pushes the boundaries of traditional circus and feminist community theatre.

It is the steady progress in the development of an unique style of theatre that best indicates the growth of the Women's Circus over the years. The many changes, highlights, achievements and innovations contribute to the ultimate expression of the circus – the performance. It is with each performance that the Women's Circus celebrates a feminist theatrical process that works. It is because the process is feminist, and thus insists that there is access and that women's voices and stories be heard, that the circus is able to pursue the creation of a theatrical style that is instantly recognisable and very successful.

The increasing public profile and media attention on the Women's Circus is one indication of its success. While the circus has become an integral part of the identity and culture of the western suburbs of Melbourne and is often featured in local papers, it has also enjoyed state-wide and national coverage on television and in magazines and newspapers. In this way the circus was brought to the attention of Amnesty International and these two organisations formed a partnership which

Naomi Herzog

Plastered: Joanne Donne preparing her mask for Death: The Musical, 1994

produced Leaping the Wire. This show was taken to Beijing for the United Nations Women's Conference in August, 1995. The circus was then invited to perform Leaping the Wire at the 1996 Festival of Sydney. Touring to China and Sydney has provided a way for the Women's Circus to expand artistic and political networks through linking with individual women and organisations throughout Australia and internationally. It has also been a special opportunity for members of the circus to perform, share their skills and be politically active in an exciting environment.

Within the circus itself there have been many developments since its inception. Significantly the major changes have opened the way for more women to gain access to training, performing, employment and directing, as well as become part of the decision-making and organisation processes of the circus. The Women's Circus has an ever-increasing and active membership, and a waiting list of women eager to join that has grown longer each year. Up to seven training sessions per week are offered to cater to the swelling group.

Rehearsals are now a weekly concern as the circus is in demand for performances throughout the year. Circus women perform at festivals and special events as well as teach circus skills in schools and community centres. In order to accommodate such a growth in activity and numbers, the structure of the circus has had to be modified. A workshop co-ordinator and an administrator have been appointed to assist the director in overseeing the operation of the circus. An advisory group was established in 1995, the function of which is to make recommendations regarding policy, future directions and day-to-day organisation. This group consists of representatives from the crews, smaller groups which are responsible for each facet of the circus from child care to maintenance of the space, finance to documentation.

As the Women's Circus crews as a whole have developed over the years, so have the individual women that make up the group. Much knowledge and many skills have been amassed since 1991, so much so that women are in a position to take up employment opportunities both within and outside the circus. The paid work now being offered to skilled women includes teaching, running workshops and performing. Women's Circus members are often sought by other organisations and

The show is almost over,
the audience is gone,
our circus touched the hearts
    of many
but most of all our own.

The memories of laughter,
of sweat and tears remain,
strength and hope
    and courage
to face the world again.

Months of building bridges,
of overcoming fear,
our circus is a celebration
of humanity all year.

– Jen Jordan, 1992

community groups to work as teachers, technicians, musicians and performers. Women have also been inspired to make their own theatre. The critically acclaimed Leaping the Wire, as presented at the Brunswick Brickworks in November 1995, involved eight woman from within the circus directing one of each of the stories. Members of the circus are constantly being challenged to go further, take risks and be creative. The circus, because of its expansion and the desire of the group to continue to grow and be dynamic, is now able to offer the opportunities, resources and support for women to be successful.

There are many qualities inherent in the Women's Circus that have guided its progress over the last five years and will, no doubt, continue to inform the operation of the circus.

- *Access* is a key feminist principle and means that any women can join the circus, any women can learn any skill and any woman can be supported to participate in any activity. Access is essential if the circus is to retain its dynamism and credibility and continue to attract public support.

- *Trust* is implicit in every relationship within the circus group. When working with others a performer/musician/technician must trust her partner and peers. The performer-director and teacher-student relationship can only work successfully with trust. All members trust that the circus will be administered honestly and efficiently and the Sisters and Supporters trust that the Women's Circus will continue to be politically and theatrically provocative. Without trust the Women's Circus would not be able to move forward but instead stagnate in safe waters.

- *Questioning* is crucial to feminist debate. The Women's Circus is not a homogenous organisation and therefore has investigated ways to express artistically and politically the variety of perceptions and ideas of the many women in the circus.

- *Communication* is important within such a large group and the challenge is to create efficient processes which facilitate effective communication. Again, communication is an integral part of all relationships within the circus. For example, communication between performers may be essential for safety, teachers need to be clear about technical instructions in order for women to learn and improve, and directors and performers need good communication so as to work together successfully. Access to all parts of the circus' organisation cannot happen without communication. A group of people cannot create something without communication.

- *Support* is often talked about amongst the members of the circus and is the linchpin of the group. It has been provided in many forms over the years. Support groups have met regularly to discuss issues and concerns, a system of labour exchange has been established to support those who are experiencing financial difficulties; support is also provided through informal talks and debriefing and offers of assistance and coaching. Support is necessary in order for women to be able to overcome fears and take risks. Many women come to the circus as survivors of sexual abuse and with poor self-esteem and body image. They see the circus as an opportunity to work with women to improve the quality of their lives and produce worthwhile theatre, and in doing so give and receive support.

- *Empowerment* is another idea that has been pursued over the last five years. The Women's Circus is not about victims, it is not about accepting limitations. The circus strives for artistic excellence and political vision. Individually, each women is able to take responsibility for her participation in all facets of the circus, buoyed by the support of others. She can then enjoy the feeling of empowerment that comes from working as part of a group, from being able to do things and from improving health, fitness, self-esteem and body image.

So these last five years have seen the Women's Circus flourish. This book is testimony of that. The energy and enthusiasm brought to the group by the performers, musicians, technicians, directors, administration workers, trainers, Sisters and Supporters, the Footscray Community Arts Centre and, indeed, the audiences themselves ensures that what is presented is more than just a show. It is a theatrical event that is the culmination of a creative process that has worked toward empowering everyone involved. In this way the Women's Circus has made a huge impact on the lives of many women and within the community. It has entertained, provoked and moved audiences. It has challenged, supported and given a voice to its members. With the knowledge and experience gained by the circus since 1991 it seems certain that audiences will continue to see ordinary women doing extraordinary things.

Reflections on a Journey

Sharon Follett

My sense of place and my sense of self have expanded greatly since I joined the circus. My journey has been one of various kinds of relationships, some of which have become very good friendships and some of which will only ever remain very superficial. For four of my five years in Melbourne I've been in the circus. The connections I've made here are part of my sense of being at home in this city. I knew two people in Melbourne when I arrived, but I feel very at home here now as part of the broader women's community.

The Women's Circus is a community circus, and we do reflect certain aspects of the women's community in Melbourne, but we are also a community unto ourselves. That was what I saw when I first joined the circus; I saw it as a women's community.

I was at a point where I wanted to change how I was with my physicality, and the circus has been a big part of the journey I've been through. It's been about the training from Sally Forth and others, about learning to use my body in ways I hadn't understood before. Sally helped me make connections between my mental and emotional and physical states that just weren't there before, and my presence in my body has changed. I feel like my sense of what I can and can't achieve in life has expanded hugely because of the circus; expanded in terms of being physical, musical, being creative and expressive, and in terms of working with others. It has made me be physically close to others in ways that would have really scared me before.

The biggest thing I've learnt from Sally and from my participation in the circus is that the strength comes through the doing. I have stopped thinking I can't do things. Instead I think I could do that if I pulled my finger out and put the effort in. I may not have the strength to do something now, but if I work on it I'll get it. I tried aerials one day. I went down in the pit. And I actually have reasonable back strength and arm strength, but my abdominals are out to lunch. I had a go on the

Women supporting women: Training workshops in the Warehouse, Footscray Community Arts Centre

Naomi Herzog

trapeze and thought: "no way, that's it". I walked away and said to Sally: "You're never going to get me up on aerials". She gave me one of those dead-set Sally looks and said "the strength comes through the doing. Give yourself ten years and you can do anything you want in life". I believe that now. I could do it if I wanted to. And knowing that has changed me in a big way.

Celebrating other women's growth and achievement is fantastic, hearing them say "I finally did this or that". Women never cease to amaze and astound me. I love our diversity and willingness to have a level of honesty. There's still a lot of front and bullshit going down, but I find myself inspired by other women.

I see the changing role of the circus reflected most in the feedback I get from others. Women feel free to criticise the circus now in ways I didn't hear years ago. They say things like: "I hate those white faces, why do you keep doing them? And I hate the white hats. It's demoralising to women". Rather than feeling like we're precious and they have to support us and can't pull us apart, I hear the women's community offering more critique and personal opinion on the circus. Perhaps it's because they now know we have the strength and can take feedback. And also that we have a future and there's real potential about what we can do with the strength we have. We value ourselves and have become more confident. We are not a youth theatre group and we look towards presenting ourselves in a non-amateur style. I think that gives us a lot of credibility. The broader women's community see us as an asset. A lot of people ask us to their openings and functions. Being an all-women group is such a big political statement.

Within the circus we are taking more risks; the whole thing of new people, trainers, direction. There's a hierarchy forming within the circus by default of who has been around the longest, who has what skills, who puts what effort in, which is inevitable. I see that as a challenge for us to deal with, creating a hierarchy that is not disempowering or oppressive. I feel the circus has stopped being the "Donna and Sally Show" in a way that's double-edged. I miss Sally greatly for what she contributed, but the circus has to move beyond personalities. And while we couldn't have done without Donna, we wouldn't have existed, I really value the way she is delegating more and more. I see us evolving.

Vivienne Méhes

A feel for balance:
Walking the tightrope
in the Warehouse

Why are we the largest successful community circus in Australia? I think it's because we are about action and not theory. I love the theory of feminism, yet you don't have to be a theoretical feminist to be in the circus. There are women who join who probably don't call themselves feminists at all. I actually like the fact that it's not a lesbian circus. It's not about sexuality. I like the fact that there is a certain amount of process and we do take time to talk about what we are doing and put it in a context, and that is political. You get a bunch of women together and that's the beginning of a political statement.

But it's the action that's the important thing, and so much of the action is about our personal achievements. There's space for the personal in the circus. Yet I know that while I'm there taking training and resources, I not only give back to the circus as a closed unit but I have the opportunity to give back to the broader community through actions. I think one of the successful things about the circus is we are not exclusive to the women's community. We take ourselves out there with workshops and performances, we contribute to the whole community. We are not a closed circuit.

Thankyou

Carole

Giving power and strength
without diminishing
what I have.
Understanding at once
the importance of being
able to live as I choose,
to keep being me.
A hug, a smile,
a reaching out in friendship
wonderful to receive and give.
Just ask, you say.
I don't feel helpless,
I feel warm and loved.
I can say too, just ask.

Nicole Hunter

Think, Debate, Decide, Act

Donna Jackson

The circus is a cultural and political organisation. Women involved are being trained to make physical theatre that communicates their interpretation of the world. The circus should not be evaluated by the number of women who can do handsprings, juggle fire and swing through the air on trapezes but by the changes and challenges women have made and undertaken as a result of their experience in the circus.

The circus is a metaphor for the potential women have, physically and politically, when we work together in a diverse team that can aspire towards goals beyond the agendas of individuals.

If we have inspired women who see our shows, or who read this book, to take a risk and make the seemingly impossible happen, then we have succeeded.

Vivienne Méhes

Encore: Sport Show, 1993

The Women's Circus is like a woman: treat her with the same respect you would another woman; allow her to change; allow her to be wrong; and allow her to grow into the woman she needs to be.

– Donna Jackson

Chronology

1991

23 April	Launch of the Women's Circus
April	First edition of the *Women's Circus Newsletter*
7 May	Information night
13 May	First music training workshop with Sue Speer
15 May	First acrobatics training workshop with Sally Forth
July	Women's Circus mural planning meetings with Swee Leng Lim
11–12 September	Gig at the Malthouse for Writers Week
18 September	Gig for the Western Women's Health Service's AGM at the Marie Mill Community Centre
19 October	Mural opening in the Footscray Mall
25 October	Gig for Reclaim the Night at Geelong
5 November	Preview night
7 November	Opening night of the Women and Institutions show
23 November	Closing night, bump out and party
28 November	Evaluation meeting
13 December	Gig for the Women's Ball at San Remo Ballroom

1992

January	Summer training begins every Saturday morning
12 March	First physical training workshop
4 September	Gig for the Women's Spring Ball at Melbourne University
September	Workshops taken by the Russian Circus trainers with the Flying Fruit Fly in Albury
September	Women's Circus *Leaping off the Edge* information booklet
20 October	Preview night
22 October	Opening night of the Women and Work show
6 November	Closing night, bump out and party
21 November	Evaluation meeting
28 November	Summer training begins

1993

29–30–31 January	Performance at the Williamstown Summer Festival
8 March	8 hour day Women and Work Moomba barge on the Yarra
27 March	First physical training workshop
14 May	Gig for the tenth anniversary of the Women's Trust at the YWCA
2 June	Gig for the launch of a resource book for survivors of sexual assault, *Sharing the Journey*, published by WESTCASA and the Survivors Coalition at the Highpoint shopping centre
8 July	Gig for the Women and Planning Conference at the Dallas Brookes Hall
21 August	Health workshops start (with breakfast)
28 August	Women's Circus truck with percussion in the Fringe Parade
September	Gig and workshop for the Daylesford Young Women's Group
10 September	Gig for the Lesbian Spring Ball at Melbourne University
10 November	Preview night
12 November	Opening night of the Women and Sport show
4 December	Closing night, bump out and party
11 December	Evaluation meeting

1994

January	Summer training begins with Sonia and Theresa from Spain
14 March	Nightmare barge, Women and Work barge etc for Moomba
6 April	Start of physical training workshops
22 April	Presentation of the Citizen of the Year to the Women's Circus by the Footscray Council
1 July	Performance for the Rural Woman of the Year at the National Gallery
16 July	Nine weeks of directors' training workshops start with Donna Jackson
August	Mandy Grinblat hired as the adminstrator
5–9 September	Clowning workshops with Angela de Castro
15 November	Preview night
17 November	Opening night of Death: The Musical
3 December	Closing night, bump out and party
10 December	Evaluation meeting
10 December	Gig for the Matrix Guild Victoria Inc fund-raising dinner at the Brunswick Town Hall

1995

7 January	Summer training begins with Dorota Scally
12 March	Sideshow acts in the City Square for Moomba
13 March	Performances on two Moomba barges, aerials and dance, fire and pyramids
26 April	First physical training workshop
1 May	Gig for the launch of the *Violence Against Women* booklet at the Galleria, Bourke Street
15 May	Gig for Body Wise Conference at FCAC
26 May	Gig for intellectually disabled groups at the Spotswood Community Centre
28 May	Gig for Amnesty International's 34th birthday at Budinski's Theatre of Exile
June	Judith Shapland hired as the workshop co-ordinator
30 June–1 July	Performances for the Beijing fund-raising concert at the Malthouse
1 July	Gig for the Footscray Football Club
21 July	Fund-raising auction at the Brunswick Town Hall
30 July	Arts Victoria pre-Beijing performance outside the Victorian Arts Centre
29 August–15 September	Thirteen circus women go to Beijing for the Fourth UN World Women's NGO Forum and Conference
20 November	Preview night
23 November	Opening night of the Leaping the Wire Show
29 November	Rehearsals start for the Sydney Festival tour in January 1996
9 December	Closing night, bump out and party
16 December	Evaluation meeting

1996

5–15 January	Sydney Festival tour
12–19 February	Double balance and improvisation workshops with Amanda Owen
14 February	Jen Jordan's funeral and memorial service
24 February	Information Day and sign up for workshops
26 February–1 March	Mask workshops with Amanda Owen

8 March	Abseiling and performance at the Melbourne Town Hall for International Women's Day
9–10–11 March	Barge for Moomba on the Yarra River
11 March	Physical training and music workshops start
11–17 March	Installation of twelve Amnesty International altars by Ursula Dutkiewicz combined with six afternoon performances for the Celebrating Women 1996 season at the Victorian Arts Centre
13 March	Mangoes, a new group for big women, begins
1 May	Contract for the Women's Circus book signed with Spinifex Press
22 May	Circus Outreach Team formed to improve access for non-English speaking background women
24 July	Gig for the Community Development Society International Conference at the World Congress Centre
27–28 July	First Women's Circus Health Weekend
August	End-of-year show postponed until April
September	Extensive renovations to improve and revitalise the warehouse and circus space begin
11–13 September	Robyn Archer's workshops with the musicians
14–15 September	Second Health Weekend
15 September–17 November	Sarah Cathcart's workshops on Sunday afternoons
18–20 September	Robyn Archer's workshops with musicians and performers
September	Judith Shapland resigned
9–10–11 October	Jenny Kemp's workshops
17 October	Donna Jackson resigned
16–17 November	Third Health Weekend
6–9 November	Andrea Lemon's workshops
20 November	Interviews for a new Artistic Director
8 December	Collective Vision Day to meet the new director and set future directions
14 December	Donna Jackson's farewell party
16 December	Appointment of new circus director, Sarah Cathcart
21 December	Final workshops for the year
31 December	Donna Jackson's resignation effective

Glossary

Aerials. Trapeze, ropes, cloud swing; any aerial act or skills.

Angle grinder. Hand-held power tool with a wheel that cuts through metal.

Arame. Japanese seaweed. Rich in vitamins and minerals.

Aura. Subtle energy emanating from a body and surrounding it as an atmosphere.

Bancha tea. Japanese tea made from twigs. Useful as a cleanser and digestive aid.

Base (basing). The base, primary weight-bearing position in double balances, group balances and pyramids.

Big sisters. Advisory body of women drawn from the arts, legal, business and academic communities.

Bizircus. Based in Western Australia. Mixed gender, non-animal contemporary circus which works around theatrical themes.

Block/blocking. Building and running through sequences and scenes; a directorial procedure used to develop and refine a show.

Bok choi. Green-leafed Chinese vegetable.

Bowen technique. A form of remedial massage that uses subtle pressure on trigger points to balance muscles and stimulate energy flow through tissues. Based on the teaching of the late Thomas Bowen of Victoria.

Bump out. Dismantling a show, cleaning up the performance space and returning equipment to the circus warehouse/training space after the final night of a performance.

Chakras. The energy centres in the body as defined in yogic philosophy.

Chamomile tea. Relaxes nerves, relieves muscular pain and spasms. Also beneficial as a general tonic.

Circus Burlesque. Based in England. Non-animal, mixed gender contemporary circus which operates as a collective.

Circus Oz. An ensemble-style contemporary non-animal circus based in Melbourne which tours nationally and internationally. One of the initiators of contemporary circus.

Cloud swing. Half-circle of rope suspended from a ceiling or from high rigging, used for aerial acts.

Colourscape. Based in London. Multi-coloured inflatable performance and visual arts environment.

Coode Island. Chemical storage depot on the Maribyrnong River opposite the Footscray Community Arts Centre.

Devil stick. A stick around 65 cm long, which may be tapered in the middle or the same thickness along its length. It is tapped backwards and forwards by two smaller sticks so that it appears to be suspended in the air. Devil sticks with cloth ends can be used in fire tricks. Chinese in origin.

Diablo. A spool made from wood, plastic or rubber which is spun, thrown and caught on a string attached to two hand sticks. The origin of this prop is also Chinese.

Doc Martens. Boots.

Double balances. Body balances performed in pairs.

Double-double. Synchronised trapeze routine performed by two pairs of aerialists.

Fag. Colloquialism for a cigarette.

Fall. Short piece of single leather. Part of a whip.

FCAC. Footscray Community Arts Centre.

Fliers. The performers who climb to the top position in double balances, group balances and pyramids.

Flying Fruit Flys. Based in Albury, New South Wales. Originally a one-off project during the International Year of the Child. Now Australia's premier children's (non-animal) circus. Tours nationally and internationally.

FOH. Front of House. Responsible for admission, crowd control, displays, merchandise, food and drink during performance season.

Footscray Fliers. Circus workshops for children run by Footscray Community Art Centre's theatre department.

Fssh. A duo comedy and juggling act who toured England and Germany. See article by Kymberlyn Olsen.

Gaffer/gaffering. Taping electrical leads and lighting cords to the floor with gaffer tape (electrical insulation tape) to minimise risk of injury. Securing other potentially dangerous obstacles such as protruding bolts or metal plates with gaffer tape.

Gig. A performance.

Good Friday Appeal. An annual appeal to raise funds for Melbourne's Royal Children's Hospital.

Group balances. Various body balances involving a number of women on two or more levels.

Gruel. A savoury porridge made from whole rice, barley or other whole grain.

Hutt! Voice signal used to cue beginnings, changes and ends of group balances, pyramids and other acts requiring synchronisation.

Invasion Day. The name given to Australia Day by the Aboriginal people who view 26 January as a day of mourning and the so-called settlement as an invasion of their land for which there has been no official recognition nor recompense.

Iyengar yoga. A strong form of traditional yoga.

Juggonauts. A troupe of women circus performers, most of whom worked together in the Women's Circus.

Labour exchange. A system of exchange enabling low-income members to pay for training through their labour.

Lemon balm. A relaxing herbal tea. Also good for memory and concentration.

Little Big Tops. A non-animal children's performing circus originating in Thornbury, a northern suburb of Melbourne.

Manipulation. Hand-based skills such as juggling, club swinging, diablo, devil sticks, ribbons, hoops, plates.

Meridians. Major lines of energy running through the body as defined in Traditional Chinese Medicine and Japanese Zen Shiatsu.

Miso. Fermented soy beans, whole brown rice or barley.

Moomba. An annual Melbourne festival held in March. An urban myth says that when the organisers were looking for a name they approached some local Aborigines and asked them for a word meaning something like "let's get together and have fun". The Aborigines gave them *Moomba*. It seems this was tongue-in-cheek. Linguistic evidence verifies that the word's meaning is closer to "doing something with your bum" – *up yer bum* seems to be the myth's favourite. Whatever the exact definition, it is clear that the joke was on the organisers!

NGO. Non-government organisation.

NESB. Non-English speaking background.

Oki Do yoga. A blend of strengthening and corrective exercises, meditation, breathing, shiatsu and natural nutrition. Derived from a union of Indian yoga, Chinese Taoism, oriental medicine and Japanese Zen.

Per diems. Literally means "by the day". A daily allowance for living expenses while travelling in connection with one's work.

Police. Characters in the Women and Work show.

POW. Performing Older Women's circus.

Pulses. Peas, beans, lentils, and so on.

RADA. Royal Academy of Dramatic Arts, London.

Reiki. From the Japanese: rei = soul, ki = power (or "Universal Life Energy"). A hands-on healing modality that empowers a person to heal themselves emotionally, physically, spiritually through the agency of a Reiki practitioner.

Rock 'n' Roll Circus. Based in Brisbane, Queensland. A non-animal, mixed gender, contemporary circus company which tours nationally and internationally.

Security. Sleepovers on a site during performance season to protect circus equipment, rigging, costumes and make-up.

Shiatsu. A Japanese word meaning "finger pressure". Practitioners stimulate meridians or acupressure points along those channels to enhance the flow of ki (life force/power). A holistic modality developed from Traditional Chinese Medical theory and traditional forms of physical therapy.

Shifter. Spanner with an adjustable head.

Sisters. Women who support the circus through membership and attendance at performances.

Supporters. Men who support the circus through membership and attendance at performances.

Tamari. A wheat-free soy sauce.

Tarp, Tarpaulin. A heavy sheet or covering of canvas coated with tar or some other kind of waterproof cloth.

Techie. Member of the technical crew, responsible for sound, lighting, rigging, etc.

The Late Developers. All-woman group of street performers who combined circus, music and mime. Emerged out of the Desmond Jones School of Mime, London. See article by Kymberlyn Olsen.

The Web. An aerial act performed on a vertical rope that hangs from a ceiling or rig. The performer weaves a series of shapes and poses at right angles to the rope, making it appear like a vertical floor. The rope hangs loose but can also be spun by an assistant at ground level.

Tofu. Soy bean curd.

Top Dog. Co-ordinator of a crew, who takes responsibility for seeing that the crew's task gets done.

Valerian. A herbal sedative/tea that promotes a healthy nervous system and helps induce sleep. Promotes normal blood pressure, helps relieve tension, headache, stress, muscular twitching and cramps.

WCN. Women's Circus Newsletter.

WISE. Women's International Spring Event.

Biographies

Adrienne Liebmann, a member of the book crew, is forty-four years old and has a seventeen-year-old son. She was a primary school teacher for fourteen years, and then ran away to join the Women's Circus. She also does improvised movement and dance, which she loves, and is currently seeking a new and challenging career.

Alison Richards is a theatre worker and academic who has been involved with Australian feminist experimental and community theatre since the 1970s. She is the Chair of the Committee of Management at the Footscray Community Arts Centre. Alison has also written about the Circus for *Meanjin* and in *Australia for Women: Travel and Culture* (Spinifex Press, 1994).

Andrea Ousley. At thirty-one, a full-time mum, Andrea discovered the circus, so she ran as fast as she could to get there. Now she spends most of her time imbibing this passion, teaching and performing circus, working as a trainer for various circus and performance groups. She also performs wild and wonderful acts on aerial gear whenever she can get a gig.

Bridget Roberts has performed on numerous occasions since 1992 and has developed a variety of skills. She has been a trainer for new members and for the first Performing Older Women's season (qualifying as a forty-six-year-old). She works as an outdoor adventure facilitator with people living with mental illness and was involved for several years with Greenham Common Women's Peace Camp in Britain. Her ambitions are to help develop the Women's Circus as a medium for both serious and frivolous feminist entertainment and to practise hand stands into old age

Cathy Johnstone has produced, written and directed a number of short films including "Migisook", which was nominated for Best Tertiary Production at the 1996 Atom Awards, won an award at the 1995 Melbourne Fringe Festival of Film and Video and screened at the 1995 Hawaii International Film Festival. She is presently employed as short film co-ordinator at the Melbourne International Film Festival.

Deb Lewis tries to squeeze too much into each day. She was one of the lucky women chosen to perform in Buijing. She is a member of the book and newsletter crews, a full-time worker and a full-time single mother. She is currently experimenting with relaxing a little.

Denise Johnstone works part-time as a lecturer at Burnley Horticultural College and lives with her five-year-old son in Melbourne. Denise is a survivor of sexual assault. She continues to train, perform and grow with the women of the Women's Circus.

Donna Jackson grew up in Melbourne. Donna founded and directed the Women's Circus from 1991–1996. She performs with a 70s glam girl band, The Sharons. Donna has written and performed a one-woman show Car Maintenance, Explosives and Love. She is currently writing a circus script and working as Artistic Director of the Maribyrnong Festival.

Dorianna Bicchierai (Dori Dragon) works as a freelance lighting designer and has been involved in production and stage management and some sound work. She has worked with the Flying Fruit Fly Circus, Handspan, Back to Back Theatre, Danceworks and several smaller theatre companies and dance parties. She also runs tech workshops for the Women's Circus. Dorianna recently toured with Circus Oz in the production of Aqua Profunda.

Dorota Scally is twenty-seven and of Polish origin. A sports acrobat for fifteen years, she has now been in Australia for one and a half years. In this time she has combined working for the Little Big Tops and Circus Oz with the Women's Circus. Teaching acrobatics is a major love for Dorota and she especially enjoys her involvement with the Women's Circus. "It is our commitment, our dedication and our will to work," she says, "that makes the difference."

Elizabeth Connolly currently works as a nurse, and has a small natural healing practice. She lives with her partner, Darcy, and four children, Cailtlin, Gemmah, Lyndton and Noella on an acre of natural bushland in the Dandenongs. She believes in all things holistic, simplicity and protecting the indigenous integrity of the bushland and its people. Her feminist philosophy is a strong basis in her life.

Emily George is the pseudonym under which Jean Taylor has written several novels including *Sappho's Wild Lesbians* and *Loose Women*.

Fi Bowie was born, the doctor's only daughter, in 1962, in a smallish town in New Zealand. She and her three brothers grew up cycling to various sporting activities – for Fi it was horse riding. In this way they all kept out of trouble. After studying physical education and teaching, Fi left for Australia, where she teaches in an alternative high school.

Franca Stadler was born in the middle of winter in Switzerland in 1959. Since moving to Australia, Franca has enjoyed the fact that her birthday is now in the middle of summer. As a child she wanted to be a sport trainer but became a photographer with passion. The Women's Circus is her latest passion. Franca says, "It doesn't matter if it's up on a trapeze, a tree, a pyramid, a scaffold or a mountain – I just love heights."

Georgine Clarsen is a qualified social worker and motor mechanic. She has worked with Circus Oz for many years and with the Women's Circus for the past five years. Georgine is currently working towards a PhD in the History/Women's Studies department at the University of Melbourne, researching women and the early days of motoring.

Helen Sharp is Artistic Director of Body Voice Projects. She has also worked as a theatre director and teaches body-voice work. Helen focuses on creating contemporary performance work especially in the area of voice opera linked to physical theatre. The work at the Body Voice Centre in Footscray integrates training, research and performance.

Jean Taylor was born in 1944. She is a lesbian, a writer, a radical feminist activist, a performer and a grandmother. She is one of the original members of the Women's Circus as well as the book crew, and is also the Director of the Performing Older Women's Circus.

Jude Johns was born 17 November 1970 in Melbourne. She has a passion for music, words, images, compost, bush, women and good conversation.

Jules De Cinque is a thirty-something mother of two who works as a teacher in the community. She joined the Women's Circus in 1994 after being inspired by a performance held at the Footscray Community Arts Centre. The circus provides the perfect opportunity for her to combine physical skills and performance with ideas of social justice and feminism.

Karen Martin has worked in theatre for ten years devising, writing, performing and directing. She is a founding member of the Women's Circus and specialises in body balances and diablo.

Kath Davey is Victorian coordinator of Amnesty International Australia and a life-long campaigner against abuse of power and for the rights of women.

Kylie Whyte was born in 1969 in Newcastle and spent most of her first five years in Hong Kong. Her academic achievements include a Bachelor of Social Work and an Advanced Certificate in Music Performance. Kylie currently works part-time with people who have mental health issues and spends the rest of her time composing and playing music and frolicking by the ocean. She is a founding member of the big band "Swish".

Kymberlyn Olsen also known as Kym Kaos, has led a travelling life from her earliest days. Although not born into a circus family, circus skills and street performing have enabled her to travel the world. At nineteen she was taught to juggle by a friend. This gift opened many doors and in the last twenty years she has taught over 8000 people to juggle. As the first solo woman to perform in Covent Garden, Kym helped redefine the concept of "women working the street". One of her goals is to increase the profile of contemporary circus and street theatre in Australia, and to this end she produces *OzJuggle*, a quarterly magazine with subscribers around Australia.

Lee Mohtaji was born in Nanjing, People's Republic of China, in 1960. At ten she joined the Nanjing Acrobatic School and began training in various acrobatic skills. Lee performed with the Nanjing Acrobatic Troupe in America, Australia and Europe and eventually migrated to Australia in 1992 to set up a family of her own. She is currently a trainer with various circus groups.

Louise Radcliffe-Smith (Rad) is a country-born, cat-loving journo turned sub-editor who practises shiatsu and Traditional Chinese Medicine and runs the occasional circus workshop. Rad joined the circus in 1991 after bumping into someone on a plane who introduced her to someone who encouraged her to come along for a look. She did, and never left.

Mandy Grinblat. Born London 1956. Accrued pieces of paper: BA, Dip Ed. Arts and Entertainment Management. Travelled extensively in Europe and Asia. Ran away from school (teaching) in 1992 to join the circus. Appointed as circus administrator in 1995. Lives happily with two beautiful cats – Thursday and Chalky White – and wonders, sometimes, what life would be like without the Women's Circus!

Maralann Damiano has a background in community and pastoral work within the Anglican Church, and continually struggles with its traditional framework. She is a proud mother of two daughters and two grandchildren. Maralann is also a member of POW.

Margaret Dobson was born in Carlton in 1959, just in time for lunch and the Dobson's first TV. The seventh of nine children, she learnt how to work an audience early. Singing, tap dancing, congas and writing keep her heart beating, while snorkling and canoeing are her new physical challenges.

Maureen O'Connor is a fifty-year-old lesbian who is a techie for the Women's Circus. She is also a clown in POW. Both of these involvements, though different, give Maureen much pleasure and pride.

Mavis Thorpe Clarke (AM) is the author of thirty-four books – biography, factual studies, children's books. Biographies include *Pastor Doug*, and *No Mean Destiny*. Her award-winning children's books include: *The Brown Land Was Green*, *The Min-Min* and *Blue Above the Trees*.

Melissa (Min) Lewis joined the circus in 1992 at age twelve and performed that year with a broken arm. After her continued participation in 1993 and 1994, she decided to take two years off to complete her secondary studies, but hopes to return in 1997.

Naomi Herzog. At nineteen I began carousing the globe for six years, wandering nomadically. That particular experience led me to photography and film where I've worked artistically and professionally. That, in turn, led to performance in circus – circus aerials, circus acrobatics, double balances, with a brief side step as a director. I finally landed in the cyber-reality of computer animation. And here I am.

Nicole Hunter was born in Melbourne in 1965. After completing a BA in Graphic Design at RMIT in 1987 she spent two years travelling in Europe and Asia. Since returning to Australia she has worked on art projects for community groups while maintaining her involvement with the Women's Circus as a performer and illustrator. Nicole is currently living in Cairns, managing a guest house and working as a freelance illustrator.

Nicole, Emily and Joanna van der Nagel live in North Box Hill with their parents, cat Dermie, chooks and fish. They go to Mont Albert Primary School. Joanna has always stated her ambition to be a "Circus Woman", just like her special aunt, Deb Lewis and cousin Min.

Patricia Sykes is a poet and story teller specialising in women's stories. As a teenager she was passionate about limbo dancing. She is currently a non-performing member of the Women's Circus and a member of the book group. Trish won the 1996 FAW (Fellowship of Australian Writers) John Shaw Neilson Poetry Award.

Sharee Grinter was born in Footscray in 1969. Grew up in Adelaide and Melbourne's west. Homeless, finished school, bought a house, joined the circus, found her head, had a son with no medical intervention whatsoever, travelled. Doesn't wash her hair.

Sharon Follett was born in the western Sydney suburb of Parramatta in 1959. She lived the larger portion of her twenties in London before moving to Melbourne. In 1988, after fifteen years of office work, a friend challenged her to extend what had long been a hobby and "get on the other side of the massage table". Eight years later, she practises massage and aromatherapy with a group of women in Spotswood while studying Chinese medicine.

Sue Speer is a freelance Melbourne composer. She was Musical Director of the Women's Circus in 1991 and again in 1993. She is a regular performer in jazz bands around Melbourne and has been a commissioned composer for the Melbourne Fringe Festival, the Next Wave Festival and Melbourne's Moomba Pageant.

Susan Hawthorne is a writer, publisher and academic. She was born in Wagga Wagga, NSW, and grew up in the country, where each time a circus passed she dreamed of running away to be an aerialist. At forty-two, she finally joined the Women's Circus and is a founding member of the Performing Older Women's Circus. She imagines a future as an eighty-year-old aerialist. Her books include *The Falling Woman* (1992) and *The Spinifex Quiz Book* (1993). Two anthologies, *Car Maintenance Explosives and Love and other contemporary lesbian writings* and *Cyberfeminism* will be published in 1997.

Ursula Dutkiewicz was born into an artistic family in Adelaide in 1958. Art, music and theatre have always been an important part of her life. She was a founding member and drummer for Adelaide band "Sticky Beat". Her current preoccupation is ceramic art. She has been working in the Women's Circus since the first big performance and says she loves it.

Vig Geddes is a left-handed, left-winged, lesbian Capricorn born in Launceston in the Year of the Rat. She has a tendency to work too hard and play too little and always welcomes advice, suggestions and invitations. Vig says she has seen beautiful places and has wonderful friends. She has been a member of the Women's Circus for 12.5 per cent of her life.

Vivienne Méhes has, since 1981, worked as a freelance photographer specialising in black and white documentary photography working mainly through community arts structures.

Wendy Black trained in London and arrived in Australia in 1981. She has worked with Anthill, VSO, Circus Oz, State Theatre of South Australia, Playbox, Sydney Theatre Co., Australian Dance Theatre and Women's Circus. She is now teaching at Swinburne University in the costume department. She recently designed the set for "Sing Sing" at the Concert Hall for the 1996 Next Wave Festival.

The Book Group: (back row, left to right) Jean Taylor, Deb Lewis, Karen Martin, Adrienne Liebmann; (front row left to right) Patricia Sykes, Louise Radcliffe-Smith, Jen Jordan